I0595432

William Roscoe

Life of Lorenzo de' Medici

Vol. 2

William Roscoe

Life of Lorenzo de' Medici
Vol. 2

ISBN/EAN: 9783337306885

Printed in Europe, USA, Canada, Australia, Japan

Cover: Foto ©Raphael Reischuk / pixelio.de

More available books at **www.hansebooks.com**

THE

LIFE

OF

LORENZO DE' MEDICI,

CALLED

THE MAGNIFICENT.

BY WILLIAM ROSCOE.

VOL. II.

BASIL:

Printed and fold by J. J. TOURNEISEN,

MDCCXCIX.

C H A P. VI.

SOON after the termination of hostilities between Sixtus IV. and the republic of Florence, Lorenzo began to unfold those comprehensive plans for fecuring the peace of Italy on a permanent foundation, which confer the higheft honor on his political life. Of the extenfive authority which he had obtained by his late conduct, every day afforded additional proof; and it appears to have been his intention to employ it for the wifeft and moft falutary purpofes. By whatever motives he was led to this great attempt, he purfued it with deep policy and unceafing affiduity; and finally experienced a degree of fuccefs equal to his warmeft expectations.

The fituation of Italy at this period afforded an ample field for the exercife of political talents. The number of independent ftates of which it was compofed, the inequality of their ftrength. the ambitious views of fome, and the ever active fears of others, kept the whole country in continual agitation and alarm. The vicinity of thefe ftates to each other, and the narrow bounds of their refpective dominions, required a promptitude of decifion in cafes of difagreement, unexampled in any fubfequent period of modern hiftory. Where the event of open war feemed doubtful, private treachery was without fcruple reforted to; and where that failed of fuccefs, an appeal was again made to arms. The pontifical fee had itfelf fet the example of a mode of conduct that burft afunder all the bonds of fociety, and operated as a convincing proof that nothing was thought unlawful which appeared to be expedient. To counterpoife all the jarring interefts of thefe different governments, to reftrain the powerful, to fuccour the weak, and to unite the whole in one firm body, fo as to enable them, on the one hand, fuccefsfully to oppofe the formidable power of the Turks, and, on the other, to repel the incurfions of the French and the Germans, both of whom were objects of terror to the lefs warlike inhabitants of Italy, were the important ends which Lorenzo propofed to accomplifh. The effectual defence of the Florentine dominions againft the encroachments of their more powerful neighbours, though perhaps his chief inducement for engaging in fo extenfive a project, appeared in the execution of it, rather as a neceffary part of his fyftem, than as the principal object which he had in view. In thefe tranfactions we may trace the firft decifive inftance of that political arrangement, which was more fully developed and more widely extended in the fucceeding century, and which has fince been denominated the balance of power. Cafual alliances, arifing from confanguinity, from perfonal attachment, from vicinity, or from intereft, had indeed frequently fubfifted among the Italian ftates; but thefe were only partial and temporary engagements, and rather tended to divide the country into two or more powerful parties, than to counterpoife the interefts of individual governments, fo as to produce in the refult the general tranquillity(*a*).

(*a*) It is commonly underftood that the idea of a fyftematic arrangement, for fecuring to ftates, within the fame fphere of political action, the poffeffion of their refpective territories, and the continuance of exifting rights, is of modern origin, having arifen among the Italian ftates in the fifteenth century. *Robertfon's Hift. of Cha.* V. *v. i. fec.* 2.

But before Lorenzo engaged in thefe momentous undertakings, he had further perfonal dangers to encounter. The moderation of his conduct could neither extinguifh nor allay the infatiable fpirit of

But Mr. Hume has attempted to show that this fyftem, if not theoretically underftood, was at leaft practically adopted by the ancient ftates of Greece and the neighbouring governments. *Effays, v. i. part.* ii. *Effay* 7. In adjufting the extent to which thefe opinions may be adopted, there is no great difficulty. Wherever mankind have formed themfelves into focieties, (and hiftory affords no inftance of their being found in any other ftate,) the conduct of a tribe, or a nation, has been marked by a general will; and ftates, like individuals, have had their antipathies and predilections, their jealoufies, and their fears. The powerful have endeavoured to opprefs the weak, and the weak have fought refuge from the powerful in their mutual union. Notwithftanding the great degree of civilization that obtained among the Grecian ftates, their political conduct feems to have been directed upon no higher principle; conquefts were purfued as opportunity offered, and precautions for fafety were delayed till the hour of danger arrived. The preponderating mafs of the Roman republic attracted into its vortex whatever was oppofed to its influence; and the violent commotions of the middle ages, by which that immenfe body was again broken into new forms, and impelled in vague and eccentric directions, poftponed to a late period the poffibility of regulated action. The tranfactions in Italy, during the fourteenth and fifteenth centuries, bear indeed a ftrong refemblance to thofe which took place among the Grecian ftates; but it was not till nearly the clofe of the latter century, that a fyftem of general fecurity and pacification was clearly developed, and precautions taken for infuring its continuance. Simple as this idea may now appear, yet it muft be confidered, that, before the adoption of it, the minds of men, and confequently the maxims of ftates, muft have undergone an important change: views of aggrandifement were to be repreffed; war was to be profecuted, not for the purpofe of conqueft, but of fecurity; and above all, an eye was to be found that could difcern, and a mind that could comprehend fo extended an object.

revenge that burnt in the breaſt of Girolamo Riario. Defeated in his ambitious projećts by the ſuperior talents of Lorenzo, he once more had recourſe to his treacherous praćtices; and, by an intercourſe with ſome of the Florentine exiles, again found, even in Florence, the inſtruments of his purpoſe. By their inſtigation Battiſta Freſcobaldi, with only two aſſiſtants, undertook to aſſaſſinate Lorenzo in the church of the Carmeli, on the day of Aſcenſion, being the laſt day of may, 1481. This attempt was not condućted with the ſame ſecrecy as that which we have before ralated. The friends of Lorenzo were watchful for his ſafety. Freſcobaldi was ſeized, and having upon his examination diſcloſed his accomplices, was executed with them on the 6th day of the following month (a). The treachery of Freſcobaldi occaſioned at Florence general ſurpriſe, and was almoſt regarded as an inſtance of inſanity. He had been the conſul of the Florentine republic at Pera, and it was at his inſtance that Bandini, the murderer of Giuliano, had been delivered up by Mahomet II. Yet neither the atrociouſneſs of the crime, nor the dread of the example, deterred him from a ſimilar enterpriſe. From this circumſtance Lorenzo perceived the neceſſity of being more diligently on his guard againſt the attempts of his profligate antagoniſts; and whilſt he lamented the depravity of the times, that rendered ſuch a precaution neceſſary, he was generally ſurrounded, when he appeared in public,

(a) The other conſpirators were Filippo Balducci, and Amoretto, the illegitimate ſon of Guido Baldovinetti. *v. Ammir. lib.* 25.

by a number of tried friends and adherents. In this refpect he has not however efcaped cenfure, although from a quarter where it fhould have been filenced by the fenfe of decency, if not by the feelings of gratitude. The kindnefs fhown by him to Raffaello Maffei the brother of Antonio, who, in the confpiracy of the Pazzi, had undertaken to be the immediate inftrument of his deftruction, has before been noticed (*a*). In return for fuch unmerited attention, this hiftorian has availed him-felf of a meafure which was rendered neceffary by repeated inftances of treachery, to reprefent Lo-renzo as a gloomy tyrant, who fupported his authority, and fecured his fafety in Florence, by the aid of a band of ruffians, and who found in mufic alone a folace from his anxiety (*b*). The reputation of Lorenzo is not however likely to fuffer more from the pen of one brother, than his perfon did from the dagger of the other.

On the conclufion of the conteft with the papal fee, the firft object not only of Lorenzo, but of all the Italian potentates, was the expulfion of the Turks from Otranto. For this purpofe a league was concluded, to which the Venetians only refufed to

(*a*) *Vol. i. p. 212.*

(*b*) " Poft hæc Laurentius defunctus periculo, refipifcere paulatim,
" majoreque poftmodum apud fuos cives effe auctoritate, ac Tyranno
" propius agitare; cum ficariis incedere, excubiis ac nunciis diligen-
" tius invigilare. denique amiffas in bello facultates undecunque
" recuperare cœpit. Vir afpectu trifti, ore truculento, fermone
" ingratus, animo factiofus, in curis agitans continuo præter unum
" muficæ folatium." *Raph. Volt. Com. Urb. p.* 153.

accede. Sufpicions had already been entertained that Mahomet II. had been incited to his enterprife by the reprefentations of that ftate; and thefe fufpicions were ftrengthened by the indifference which the Venetians manifefted on fo alarming an occafion. It is however probable, that they kept aloof from the conteft, merely for the purpofe of availing themfelves of any opportunity of aggrandizement, which the exhaufted fituation of the neighbouring ftates might afford. With the powers of Italy, the kings of Aragon, of Portugal and of Hungary united their arms. The city of Otranto was attacked by a formidable army under the command of the duke of Calabria; whilft the united fleets of the king of Naples, the pope, and the Genoefe were ftationed to prevent the arrival of further aid to the befieged. The place was however defended with great courage, and the event yet remained doubtful, when intelligence was received of the death of the emperor Mahomet II. who had eftablifhed the feat of the Turkifh empire at Conftantinople, and been the fcourge of Chriftendom for nearly half a century. Upon his death, a difagreement arofe between his two fons Bajazet and Zizim; in confequence of which, the Turkifh troops deftined to the relief of Otranto were recalled, and the place was left to its fate. A capitulation was concluded on the tenth day of September 1481, by which the Turks ftipulated for a free return to their native country; but the duke of Calabria, on the furrender of the city, found a pretext for eluding the treaty, and retained as prifoners about fifteen hundred Turks, whom he afterwards employed in the different wars in which he was engaged (a).

Whilst the other states of Italy were thus engaged in the common caufe, the Venetians had been devifing means for poffeffing themfelves of the dominions of Ercole d'Efte, duke of Ferrara, and by the affiftance of Girolamo Riario, had prevailed upon the pope to countenance their pretenfions. The duke had married the daughter of Ferdinand, king of Naples; an alliance, which as it contributed to his credit and independence, had given great diffatisfaction to the Venetians. The firft aggreffion was the erection of a fortrefs by thofe haughty republicans, on a part of the territory of Ferrara, which they pretended was within the limits of their own dominions. An embaffy was immediately difpatched by the duke to Venice, to avert, if poffible, the hoftile intentions of the fenate, and to conciliate their good-will by the faireft reprefentations, and the fulleft profeffions of amity. Finding his efforts ineffectual, the duke reforted for fuccour to the pope; but Sixtus was already apprized of the part he had to act, and whilft he heard his folicitations with apparent indifference, was fecretly preparing to join in his ruin. The motives by which Sixtus was actuated are not difficult to be difcovered. If the family of Efte could be deprived of their dominions, many circumftances concurred to juftify the pretenfions of the papal fee to the fovereignty of Ferrara. That city was itfelf ranked among thofe over which the

(a) Murat. Ann. r. ix. p. 537.

pontiffs afferted a fignorial claim, which lay dor-
mant, or was revived, as circumftances required;
and although Sixtus could not fingly contend with
the Venetians in the divifion of the fpoil, yet he
well knew that the reft of Italy would interpofe, to
prevent their poffeffing themfelves of a territory
which would add fo confiderably to their power.
In the conteft therefore which he fuppofed muft
neceffarily take place, Sixtus was not without hopes
of vefting the government of Ferrara in his own
family, in the perfon of Girolamo Riario, who was
indefatigable in preparing for the approaching war.

In this exigency, the duke of Ferrara had two
powerful refources. One of thefe was in the fupport
which he derived from his father-in-law the king
of Naples; and the other in the claims which he
had upon the known juftice of Lorenzo de' Medici.
Neither of thefe difappointed his hopes. By the
interference of Lorenzo, the duke of Milan joined
in the league; and the marquis of Mantua, and
Giovanni Bentivoglio, alfo became auxiliaries in
the caufe. The command of the allied army was
intrufted to Federigo, duke of Urbino; but the
preparation and direction of the war chiefly refted
on Lorenzo de' Medici, on whofe activity and
prudence the allied powers had the moft perfect
reliance (a).

The firft object of the allies was to difcover the

(a) Fabroni has preferved a letter from the duke of Urbino to
Lorenzo de' Medici, which fufficiently shows the confidence that
was repofed in him by the allies, and the active part which he took
in preparing for the conteft. v. App. No. XLIII.

intentions of the pope. No sooner had the Venetians commenced their attack on the territory of Ferrara, than a formal requeſt was made to Sixtus, to permit the duke of Calabria, with a body of Neapolitan troops, to paſs through his dominions. His refuſal ſufficiently diſcovered the motives by which he was actuated. The duke immediately entered in a hoſtile manner the territories of the church, and having poſſeſſed himſelf of Terracina, Trevi, and other places, proceeded without interruption till he arrived within forty miles of Rome. At the ſame time the Florentine troops attacked and captured Caſtello, which was reſtored to Nicolo Vitelli, its former lord. By theſe unexpected and vigorous meaſures, Sixtus, inſtead of joining the Venetians, was compelled to ſolicit their aſſiſtance for his own protection. The duke had approached ſo near to Rome, that his advanced parties daily committed hoſtilities at the very gates of the city. In this emergency, the pope had the good fortune to prevail upon Roberto Malateſta, lord of Rimini, to take upon him the command of his army. This celebrated leader, who was then in the pay of the Venetians, on obtaining their permiſſion to aſſiſt their ally, proceeded to Rome. Having there made the neceſſary arrangements, Roberto led out the papal troops, which were ſufficiently numerous, and were only in need of an able general effectually to oppoſe their enemies. The duke of Calabria, being in daily expectation of a reinforcement under the command of his brother Federigo, would gladly have avoided an engagement, but his adverſary preſſed him ſo vigorouſly, that he was compelled either to riſque the event of a battle, or to incur the ſtill greater danger of a diſorderly retreat. This engagement, we are aſſured by Machiavelli, was the moſt obſtinate and bloody that had occurred in Italy during the ſpace of fifty years (a). After a ſtruggle of ſix hours, the conteſt terminated in the total defeat of the duke, who owed his liberty or his life, to the fidelity and courage of his Turkiſh followers. Having thus delivered the pope from the eminent danger that threatened him, Roberto returned to Rome to enjoy the honors of his victory; but his triumph was of ſhort duration, for a few days after his arrival he ſuddenly died, not without giving riſe to a ſuſpicion, that poiſon had been adminiſtered to him by the intervention of Girolamo Riario (b). This ſuſpicion received confirmation in the public opinion, by the ſubſequent conduct of Sixtus and his kinſman. No ſooner was Roberto dead, than the pope erected an equeſtrian ſtatue to his memory; and Riario proceeded with the army which Roberto had lately led to victory, to diſpoſſeſs his illegitimate

(a) " E fu queſta giornata combattuta con più virtù, che alcun' " altra che fuſſe ſtata fatta in cinquanta anni in Italia; perchè vi morì " tra l'una parte e l'altra più che mille uomini." *Mac. Hiſt. lib.* 8.

(b) Gli ſcrittori dicono che fu foſpetto che egli foſſe morto di veleno, & io nelle notizie private di Malateſti ritrovo, che l'autore di tanta ſceleratezza fu creduto eſſere ſtato il conte Girolamo, nipote del papa, o per invidia, o pure con ſperanza di poter metter le mani a quello ſtato, non laſciando Ruberto figliuoli leggitimi.

Ammir. lib. 25.

fon Pandolfo, to whom he had bequeathed his poſſeſſions, of the city of Rimini (*a*). In this attempt the ecclefiaſtical plunderers would probably have been fuccefsful, had not the vigorous interference of Lorenzo de' Medici, to whom Pandolfo reforted for fuccour, and who fent a body of Florentine troops to his fpeedy relief, fruftrated their profligate purpofe. Riario then turned his arms towards Caftello, which was courageoufly defended by Vitelli, till the Florentines once more gave him effectual, aid. A fimilar attack, and with fimilar fuccefs, was about the fame time made by Sixtus on the city of Pefaro, the dominion of Conftantino Sforza; who having firft engaged in the league againft the Venetians, afterwards deferted his allies, and entered into their fervice, and was fuppofed to have died of grief becaufe they had defrauded him of his ftipulated pay (*b*).

Whilft Sixtus was thus employed in defending his own dominions, or in attempting to feize upon thofe of his neighbours, the duke of Urbino had oppofed himfelf to the Venetian army; but not with fufficient effect to prevent its making an alarming progrefs, and capturing feveral towns in the territory of Ferrara. The death of that general (*c*),

(*a*) *Mac. Hiſt. lib.* 8.

(*b*) " Conftantinus Sforzia Pifauri princeps fidus antea Florentinis, " durante adhuc ſtipendio, defecit ad Venetos. Neque multos poſt " dies, tertiana febri correptus, mœrore ut creditur violatæ fidei, & " a Venetis pacti non foluti ſtipendii V Kal. Sextilis interiit."

Fontius in Annal. ap. Fabr. ii. p. 235.

(*c*) The duke of Urbino and Roberto Malatefta died on the fame day; one at Bologna, the other at Rome; each of them, although at

and the ficknefs of the duke of Ferrara, which
rendered him incapable of attending with vigor
to the defence of his dominions, opened to the
Venetians the fulleft profpect of fuccefs. This
fudden progrefs of the republican arms was not
however agreeable to the pope; who, having given
no aid in the conteft, began to be apprehenfive
that he could claim no fhare in the fpoil, whilft fo
confiderable an acceffion of power to the Venetians
might fcarcely be confiftent with his own fafety.
At the fame time he perceived a ftorm gathering
againft him from another quarter. The emperor
had threatened to call together a general council
of the church; a meafure either originating with
or promoted by Lorenzo de' Medici; and for the
effecting of which he had difpatched Baccio Ugolino
to Bafil (a). Induced by thefe various confiderations,
Sixtus was at length prevailed upon to detach himfelf

the head of adverfe armies, having recommended to the other the
protection of his poffeffions and furviving family: " A di 12 di
" Settembre, 1482, ci fu nuove ch'il Magnifico Roberto de Rimini era
" morto a Roma di fluffo. Stimafi fia ftato avvelenato. El duca
" d'Urbino era morto in Bologna, che era andato al foccorfo di
" Ferrara. Morirono in un di, e ciafcuno di loro mandava a rac-
" comandare all' altro il fuo ftato, e l'uno non feppe la morte dell'
" altro." *Ex Diario Allegretti ap. Fabr. v. ii. p. 245.*

(a) Ugolino tranfmitted to Lorenzo, from time to time, a full
account of his proceedings in feveral letters which are publifhed by
Fabroni, *in vità Laur. v. ii. 227.* From which it appears, that he
was not without hopes of accomplifhing his important object. " Non
" & non domandate," fays he, " come quefti dottori della Univerfità
" leggano con fervore le fcripture che io ho pubblicate qui in Confilio.
" Che più? Il papa è più invifo qui che cofti, & fe l'Imperatore non
" ce la macchia, non fum fine fpe di far qualcofa."

from the Venetians, and to liften to propofitions for a feparate peace. Under the fanction of the imperial ambaffador, a league was concluded at Rome for five years, between the pope, the king of Naples, the duke of Milan, and the Florentines, for the defence of the duke of Ferrara. Sixtus, having engaged in the common caufe, was not inactive. Having firft warned the Venetians to defift from the further ·progrefs of the war, and finding his remonftrances difregarded, he folemnly excommunicated his late allies (a). The Venetians however perfifted in their purpofe, regardlefs of his denunciations, and having captured the town of Ficarola, laid fiege to the city of Ferrara itfelf.

At this important juncture a congrefs was held at Cremona, for the purpofe of confidering on the moft effectual means of reprefling the growing power of the Venetians, and of fecuring the reft of Italy from the effects of their ambition. The perfons who affembled on this occafion were Alfonzo duke of Calabria, Lodovico Sforza, Lorenzo de' Medici, Lodovico Gonzaga marquis of Mantua, the duke of Ferrara; and on the part of the pope, Girolamo Riario, and the Cardinal of Mantua, with others of inferior note. The king of France, aware of the character of Riario, advifed Lorenzo by letter not to truft himfelf to this interview (b); but the important

(a) *Fabr. in vità Laur. adnot. & monum.* ii. 234.

(b) Thus he addreffes Lorenzo in a letter dated xiii. Kal. Febr. 1482, *Fabr. adnot. & mon. v.* ii. *p.* 243. " Alla Giornata di Ferrara " dove dite avere promeffo andare, vi avrei configliato non andafte " punto, ma che guardafte bene tener ficura voftra perfona; perchà

confequences

confequences expected from it induced him to difregard the precaution. Among other arrangements it was determined that the Milanefe fhould endeavour to form a diverfion by an attack on the Venetian territory, and that the duke of Calabria fhould repair with a powerful body of troops to the relief of the duke of Ferrara. By thefe decifive meafures, a fpeedy and effectual ftop was put to the further progrefs of the Venetian arms, whilft the allied troops over-ran the territories of Bergamo, of Brefcia, and of Verona. Finding their attempt to fubjugate the city of Ferrara fruftrated, and folicitous for the fafety of their own dominions, the Venetians had recourfe to negotiation, and had fufficient influence with Lodovico Sforza to prevail upon him to defert the common caufe. His dereliction induced the allies to accede to propofitions for peace, which, though fufficiently favorable to the Venetians, fecured the duke of Ferrara from the ambition of his powerful neighbours, and reprefled that fpirit of encroachment which the Venetians had manifefted, as well on this as on former occafions.

As foon as the affairs of Italy were fo adjufted as to give the firft indications of permanent tranquillity, Sixtus died. The coincidence of thefe events gave rife to an opinion which was rendered in fome degree credible by the knowledge of his

" non conofco nè i perfonaggi nè il luogo, dove v'habbiate a trovare,
" e v'avrei mandato uno imbafciatore di quà in voftra excufatione;
" nientedimanco, poichè l'avete promeffo, me ne reporto a voi; &
" alla buona hora fia, & a Dio. Luis."

reftlefs difpofition, that his death was occafioned by vexation at the profpect of a general peace (a). Of the character of this fucceffor of St. Peter, we have already had fufficient proof. It muft indeed be acknowledged, that no age has exhibited fuch flagrant inftances of the depravity of the Roman fee, as the clofe of the fifteenth century, when the profligacy of Sixtus IV. led the way, at a fhort interval, to the ftill more outrageous and unnatural crimes of Alexander VI. The avarice of Sixtus was equal to his ambition. He was the firft Roman pontiff who openly expofed to fale the principal offices of the church; but not fatisfied with the difpofal of fuch as became vacant, he inftituted new ones, for the avowed purpofe of felling them, and thereby contrived to obtain a certain emolument from the uncertain tenure by which he held his fee. To Sixtus IV. pofterity are alfo indebted for the inftitution of inquifitors of the prefs, without whofe licence no work was fuffered to be printed. In this indeed he gave an inftance of his prudence; it being extremely confiftent, that thofe who are confcious of their own mifconduct fhould endeavour to ftifle the voice that publifhes and perpetuates it. Even Muratori acknowledges, that this pontiff had a heavy account to make up at the tribunal of God (b).

(a) He died on the 12th of Auguft 1484, being the fifth day after peace was proclaimed at Rome. *Murat. Ann. v.* ix. *p.* 546. 549. " O perchè fuffe il termine di fua vita venuto, o perchè il dolore " della pace fatta, come nemica a quella l'ammazzaffe."

(a) " Di groffi conti avrà avuto quefto pontefice nel tribunale di " Dio." *Annal. v.* ix. *p.* 538.

The death of Sixtus IV. who for the space of thirteen years had embroiled the states of Italy in constant dissensions, was a favorable omen of the continuance of tranquillity; and the choice made by the conclave of his successor seemed still further to secure so desirable an object. Giambattista Cibò, who obtained on this occasion the suffrages of the sacred college, was a Genoese by birth, though of Greek extraction. The urbanity and mildness of his manners formed a striking contrast to the inflexible character of his predecessor. From his envoys at Rome, Lorenzo became early acquainted with the disposition of the new pope, who assumed the name of Innocent VIII. At the time of his elevation to the supremacy, he was about fifty-five years of age, and had several natural children. Vespucci, the correspondent of Lorenzo, represents him as a weak but well-disposed man, rather formed to be directed himself than capable of directing others (a).

Lorenzo had perceived the disadvantages under which he labored in his political transactions, on account of his dissensions with the papal see; and he therefore learnt with great satisfaction that the pope, soon after his elevation, had expressed a very favorable opinion of him, and had even avowed an intention of consulting him on all important occurrences. The power of the other Italian potentates was bounded by the limits of their respective dominions; but Lorenzo was well aware that the Roman

(a) Many particulars respecting this pontiff may be found in the letter from Vespucci to Lorenzo, extracted from the documents of Fabroni. *App. No.* XLIV.

B 2

pontiff, independent of his temporal poffeffions, maintained an influence that extended throughout all Chriftendom, and which might be found of the utmoft importance to the promotion of his views. He therefore feduloufly improved the occafion which the favorable opinion of Innocent afforded him; and in a fhort time obtained his confidence to fuch a degree, as to be intrufted with his moft fecret tranfactions and moft important concerns (a). This fortunate event alfo firft opened to the Medici the dignities and emoluments of the church, and thereby led the way to that eminent degree of fplendor and profperity which the family afterwards experienced.

To the carrying into effect the pacific intentions of Lorenzo, feveral obftacles yet remained. During the commotions in Italy, confequent on the confpiracy of the Pazzi, the town of Sarzana, fituated near the boundaries of the Genoefe and Florentine dominions, and which the Florentines had purchafed from Lodovico Fregofo, had been forcibly wrefted from them by Agoftino, one of his fons. The important contefts in which the Florentines were engaged had for fome time prevented them from attempting the recovery of a place, to which,

---

(a) ." Affettate che faranno quefte voftre cofe co' Genovefi Lorenzo
" conofcerà che non fu mai Pontefice, che amaffi tanto la cafa fua
" quanto io. Et avendo vifto per efperienza, quanta fia la fede,
" integrità & prudentia fua, io farò tofto governarmi fecondo i ricordi
" & pareri fui." Such was the language in which Innocent addreffed himfelf to Pier Filippo Pandolfini, the Florentine ambaffador.
Fabroni in vita, v. ii. p. 263.

according to the eftablifhed cuftom of the times, they had undoubted pretenfions; but no fooner were they relieved from the anxiety and expenfe of external war, than they bent their whole attention to this object. In order to fecure himfelf againft the expected attack, Agoftino had made a formal furrender of the town to the republic of Genoa, under which he profeffed to exercife the government. Lorenzo therefore entertained hopes, that, by the mediation of the new pope, his countrymen the Genoefe might be induced to refign their pretenfions; but his interference having proved ineffectual, the Florentines prepared to eftablifh their right by arms. The approach to Sarzana neceffarily lay by the town of Pietra-Santa, the inhabitants of which were expected to remain neuter during the conteft; but a detachment of Florentine troops, efcorting a quantity of provifions and ammunition, paffing near that place, were attacked and plundered by the garrifon (a). So unequivocal a demonftration

(a) Machiavelli, pleafed in relating inftances of that crooked policy in which he is fuppofed to have been himfelf an adept, informs us, that the Florentines, wanting a pretext for a rupture with the inhabitants of Pietra-Santa, directed a part of their baggage to pafs near that place, for the purpofe of inducing the garrifon to make an attack upon it. *Hift. lib.* 8. And Fabroni, on what authority it is not eafy to difcover, exprefsly attributes this artifice to Lorenzo de' Medici, *in vità Laur. v. i. p.* 127. But Ammirato, whofe veracity is undoubted, afferts that this incident took place without any premeditated defign on the part of the Florentines, introducing his narrative with a direct cenfure of the relation of Machiavelli: " Hor " volle più tofto il cafo, che artificio alcuno, il quale và il Machi- " avelli accattando, &c." *Ift. Fior. lib.* 25.

of hoftility rendered it neceffary for the Florentines, before they proceeded to the attack of Sarzana, to poffefs themfelves of Pietra-Santa. It was accordingly invefted, and fuch artillery as was then in ufe was employed to reduce the inhabitants to fubmiffion. The Genoefe however found means to reinforce the garrifon, whilft the ficknefs of fome of the Florentine leaders, and the inactivity of others, contributed to protract the fiege. Difpirited by refiftance, the count of Pitigliano, one of the Florentine generals, ventured even to recommend to the magiftrates of Florence the relinquifhment of the enterprife as impracticable, at leaft, for that feafon. Thefe reprefentations, inftead of altering the purpofe of Lorenzo, only excited him to more vigorous exertion; by his recommendation, the command of the Florentine troops was given to Bernardo del Nero, and foon afterwards Lorenzo joined the army in perfon. His prefence and exhortations had the moft powerful effect on his countrymen. Within the fpace of a few days after his arrival, the befiegers reduced the place to fuch extremity, that propofals were made for a capitulation, which were acceded to by Lorenzo; and the town was received into the protection of the Florentine republic, without further moleftation to the inhabitants (a).

From Pietra-Santa it was the intention of Lorenzo, notwitftanding the advanced feafon of the year, to have proceeded immediately to the attack of Sarzana, but the long and unhealthy

(a) *Ammir. Ift. Fior. lib.* 25.

fervice in which the army had been engaged, rendered a temporary ceſſation of hoſtilities in-diſpenſible. Several of the principal commanders together with Antonio Pucci, one of the Florentine commiſſioners to the army, had fallen victims to the fatigues of the war; and Lorenzo, who labored under a chronic, and perhaps an hereditary com-plaint, was foon afterwards obliged to reſort to the baths of S. Filippo for relief. Before he recovered his health, his attention was called towards a dif-ferent quarter, in which all his exertions became neceſſary to preſerve his pacific fyſtem from total deſtruction.

This commotion originated in the turbulent defigns of Sixtus IV. who had fown the feeds of it in his lifetime, although they did not fpring up till after his death. The Neapolitan nobility, exaf-perated with the princes of the houfe of Aragon, who had endeavoured to abridge their power and independence, were prepared, whenever occafion offered, to attempt the recovery of their rights. In reſtraining the exorbitant power of the nobles, which was equally formidable to the king and oppreſſive to the people, Ferdinand might have been juſtified by the expediency of the meaſure, and protected by the affections of his fubjects; but, in relieving them from the exactions of others, he began to opprefs them himfelf, and thus incau-tioufly incurred that odium, which had before been exclufively beſtowed upon his nobility. The fpirit of difaffection that foon became apparent was not unobferved by Sixtus, who, in addition to the ambitious motives by which he was generally actuated, felt no small degree of resentment against Ferdinand, for having, without his concurrence, concluded a peace with the Florentines. A secret intercourse was carried on between the pope and the Neapolitan barons, whose resentment was ready to burst out in an open flame when Sixtus died. This event retarded, but did not defeat the execution of their purpose. No sooner was Innocent seated in the chair, than they began to renew with him the intercourse which they had carried on with his predecessor. They reminded him that the kingdom of Naples was itself a fief of the Roman see; they represented the exhausted state of the king's finances, and the aversion which he had incurred from his subjects, as well by his own severity, as by the cruelties exercised in his name by the duke of Calabria; and exhorted him to engage in an attempt, the success of which was evident, and would crown his pontificate with glory (a) The pacific temper of Innocent was dazzled with the splendor of such an acquisition. He encouraged the nobility to proceed in their designs, he raised a considerable army, the command of which he gave to Roberto Sanseverino; several of the principal cities of Naples openly revolted, and the standard of the pope was erected at Salerno. On the first indication of hostilities, the king had sent his son John, who had obtained the dignity of a cardinal, to Rome, for the purpose of inducing the pope to relinquish his attempt; but the death

(a) *Valor. in vitâ Laur. p.* 51.

of the cardinal blafted the hopes, and added to the diftreffes of his father (a). Attacked at the fame time by foreign and domeftic enemies, Ferdinand faw no fhelter from the ftorm, but in the authority and affiftance of Lorenzo. The attachment that fubfifted between him and the pope was indeed known to Ferdinand; but he had himfelf fome claims upon his kindnefs, and had reafon to believe that he could not regard with indifference, an attempt which, if fuccefsful, would effect a total change in the political ftate of Italy. Lorenzo did not hefitate on the part it became him to act. No fooner was he apprized of the dangerous fituation of Ferdinand, than he left the baths of S. Filippo and haftened to Florence, where, on his firft interview with the envoy of the king, he gave him the moft unequivocal affurances of active interference and fupport. Lorenzo however faw the neceffity of applying an effectual remedy to the increafing evil, and with a degree of freedom which the urgency of the occafion required, entreated the king to relax in his feverity towards his fubjects. " It grieves me to the foul," thus he writes to Albino the Neapolitan envoy, " that the " duke of Calabria fhould have acquired, even " undefervedly, the imputation of cruelty. At all " events he ought to endeavour to remove every " pretext for the accufation, by the moft cautious

(a) His death was attributed to poifon, given to him by Antonello Sanfeverino, prince of Salerno. *Aurat. Ann. v. ix. p.* 542. The frequency of thefe imputations, though perhaps not always founded on fact, ftrongly mark the character of the age.

" regard to his conduct. If the people be difpleafed
" with the late impofitions, it would be advifable
" to abolifh them, and to require only the ufual
" payments; for one *carlino* obtained with good-
" will and affection, is better than ten accom-
" panied with diffatisfaction and refentment." He
afterwards remonftrates with the king, through the
fame channel, on his harfh and imprudent conduct
to fome merchants, who it appears had been dis-
miffed from Naples, for having demanded from
him the monies which they had advanced for his
ufe." " If the king fatisfy them not," fays he,
" by paying their demands, he ought at leaft to
" appeafe them by good words; to the end that
" he may not afford them an opportunity of treating
" his name with difrefpect, and of gaining credit
" at the fame time to what is, and to what is
" not true." The reply of Ferdinand to Albino
is fufficiently expreffive of the refpect which he
paid to thefe admonitions (*a*); but unfortunately,
the precepts which he approved in theory, he
forgot to adopt in his practice; and to the neglect
of thefe counfels, rather than to the courage or
the conduct of Charles VIII. the fubfequent ex-
pulfion of his family from the kingdom of Naples
is unqueftionably to be referred.

The authority of Lorenzo de' Medici in Florence

(*a*) In reference to this letter of Lorenzo, which may be found
in the Appendix, No. XLV. The king replies to Albino, " Lo con-
" figlio de detto Mag. Lorenzo, che abbiamo li occhi ad tutto, e
" moftramo in alcuna cofa non intendere, &c. ci è ftato gratiffimo,
" per effere prudentiffimo e fapientiffimo."

was not the authority of defpotifm, but that of
reafon; and it therefore became neceffary, that the
meafures which he might adopt fhould meet with
the approbation of the citizens at large. He ac-
cordingly, without delay, called together the prin-
cipal inhabitants, but had the mortification to find
that the propofition which he laid before them,
to afford affiftance to the king, was received by his
hearers with general difapprobation; fome exclaim-
ing againft him, as being too precipitate in involving
the republic in dangerous and expenfive wars;
whilft others condemned the freedom with which
he oppofed the Roman pontiff, and fubjected him-
felf and his fellow-citizens to thofe ecclefiaftical
cenfures, the ill effects of which they had fo recently
experienced. On this occafion, Lorenzo was re-
minded, that the Venetians would probably unite
with the pope in fubjugating the kingdom of
Naples; in which cafe, the intervention of the
Florentines would only involve them in the fame
ruin that threatened the Neapolitan ftate. The
folicitations and remonftrances of his fellow-citizens
fhook not the purpofe of Lorenzo. Through the
thick mift of popular fears and prejudices, he
diftinctly faw the beacon of the public welfare;
and the arguments of his adverfaries had already
been anticipated and refuted in his own mind.
That eloquence which he poffeffed in fo eminent
a degree was never more fuccefsfully exerted; and
the reafons that had determined his own judgment
were laid before his audience in a manner fo
impreffive, as to overpower all oppofition, and

induce them unanimoufly to concur in his opinion.
" This oration," fays Valori, " as committted to
" writing by fome of his hearers, I have myfelf
" perufed; and it is not poffible to conceive any
" compofition more copious, more elegant, or
" more convincing (*a*)."

The fituation of Ferdinand became every day
more critical. A general defection of his nobility
took place. The two brothers of the family of the
Coppula, one of whom was his prime counfellor,
and the other the treafurer of the kingdom, held
a treacherous correfpondence with his enemies;
and the duke of Calabria, who had advanced to-
wards Rome to prevent a junction of the pontifical
troops with thofe of the infurgents, was totally
defeated by Sanfeverino, and obliged to fly for
protection into the territories of Florence. It was
matter of gratification to fome, and of furprife to
all, that the very man, who, by his fanguinary
and tyrannical difpofition, had a fhort time before
fpread terror through the whole extent of Tufcany,
fhould now appear as a fugitive at Montepulciano,
imploring the affiftance of the Florentines, and
waiting the arrival of Lorenzo de' Medici; who,
being prevented by ficknefs from complying with
his expectations, difpatched two of the principal
citizens to affure the duke of the attachment of the
Florentines to the houfe of Aragon, and of their
determination to exert themfelves to the utmoft in
its defence.

(*a*) *Valor. in vitâ Laur. p.* 53.

'The military force of the republic, which feldom exceeded five thoufand men, would have rendered fmall fervice in the conteft, and it therefore became neceffary to refort to other expedients. By the pecuniary affiftance of the Florentines, the duke of Calabria was again enabled to take the field, and at their inftance feveral eminent leaders of Italy engaged in the fervice of the king. The influence that Lorenzo poffeffed with Lodovico Sforza was fuccefsfully exerted to engage the ftates of Milan in the fame caufe. The powerful Roman family of the Orfini was induced not only to difcountenance the enter-prife of the pope, but to appear openly in arms againft him; and Innocent began to dread that the conflagration which he had excited, or encouraged, in the kingdom of Naples, might extend to his own dominions. At the fame time Lorenzo de' Medici, having ftill maintained an uninterrupted intercourfe with the pope, affailed him with thofe arguments which he knew were beft calculated to produce their effect. He reprefented the evils and difgrace that muft arife to all Chriftendom, from the frequent example fet by the head of the church, of appealing on all occafions to the fword. He pointed out the improbability that the northern powers of Italy would permit the Roman fee to annex to its domi-nions, either directly or indirectly, fo extenfive a territory as the kingdom of Naples; and earneftly exhorted the pope not to wafte his refources, dif-turb his tranquillity, and endanger his fafety, in a conflict which, at beft, could only terminate in fubftituting to the houfe of Aragon fome of thofe fortunate adventurers who had led the armies employed in its expulsion. Whether the appearances of hostility operated on the fears, or the reasoning of Lorenzo on the judgment of the pope, may remain in doubt; but the ardor with which he engaged in the conflict gradually abated, and Sanseverino was left to avail himself of his own courage, and that of the troops under his command, without receiving either orders to retire, or supplies to enable him to proceed. The languor that became apparent between the contending sovereigns seemed to have communicated itself to their armies; which having met on the eighth day of May 1486, an encounter took place, in which Ammirato not only acknowledges, that not a soldier was slain, but that he had found no memorial that even one of the combatants was wounded, though the contest continued for many hours, and only terminated with the day (a). In this harmless trial of muscular strength, Sanseverino and his followers were however forced off the field, and the consequences were as decisive as if the contest had been of the most sanguinary kind; for the king, availing himself of this circumstance, and apprized by Lorenzo of the favorable alteration in the temper of the pope, lost no time in laying before him such propositions for the accommodation of their dispute, as afforded him an opportunity of declining it with

(a) Ecco che nel volersi movere, si venne l'ottavo giorno di maggio al fatto d'arme; se merita di fatto d'arme haver nome una giornata, nella quale non che fosse alcun morto, ma non si fa memoria, che fosse alcun ferito. *Ammir. Ist. Fior. lib. 25. p. 174.*

credit to himſelf, and apparent ſafety to his Neapo-
litan confederates. By the conditions of this treaty,
the king acknowledged the juriſdiction of the
apoſtolic ſee, and agreed to pay to the pope a
ſtipulated ſubſidy. Beſides which, he engaged to
pardon, freely and unconditionally, the nobles
who had revolted againſt him.

The oppreſſive conduct of the Italian ſovereigns,
or the reſtleſs diſpoſition of their ſubjects, ſeldom
admitted of a long continuance of tranquillity; and
as Lorenzo had acquired a reputation for impartiality
and moderation, the diſſenſions that occaſionally
aroſe were generally ſubmitted to his deciſion.
The political contentions in which the pope was
engaged, diſplayed indeed an ample field for the
exerciſe of his talents. Important as the favor of
the Roman ſee might be to the ſucceſs of his labors,
it was not preſerved without an unremitting atten-
tion to its intereſts. In the year 1486, Buccolino
Guzzoni, a citizen of Oſimo, a part of the papal
territories, incited the inhabitants to revolt. The
cardinal Giuliano della Rovere, afterwards Julius II.
was diſpatched by the pope to reduce the place
to obedience; but threats and entreaties were alike
ineffectual, and the inhabitants avowed their re-
ſolution to ſurrender the city to the Turks, rather
than again ſubmit to the authority of the pope.
From the ſucceſs of the inſurgents, the example
began to ſpread through the adjoining diſtricts;
when Lorenzo diſpatched Gentile, biſhop of Arezzo,
with inſtructions to treat with Buccolino for a
reconciliation. What the obſtinacy of Buccolino

had refuſed to the repreſentations of the pope, was conceded to thoſe of Lorenzo, under whoſe ſanction the terms of the treaty were ſpeedily concluded, and Buccolino accompanied the ambaſſador of Lorenzo to Florence. Muratori informs us, that the artifice by which Lorenzo extricated the pope from his turbulent adverſary, was the timely application of ſome thouſands of golden ducats; and this he accompanies with an inſinuation, which, if juſtly founded, would degrade the magnanimous character of Lorenzo to a level with that of his ſanguinary and treacherous contemporaries. "Hav-"ing invited Buccolino to Florence," ſays that "author, Lorenzo, with great addreſs, prevailed "upon him, for his further ſecurity, to repair to "Milan; but the ſecurity that he there found was "a halter from the hands of Lodovico Sforza (a)." If, however, the death of Buccolino, when the contention was over, was of ſuch importance as to induce Lorenzo to the commiſſion of ſo atrocious a crime, it is ſcarcely probable that he would have afforded his victim ſo favorable an opportunity of eſcaping the blow; but without having recourſe to conjecture, a refutation of this calumny may be found in an author, who, not being conſidered as partial to the Medici, may on this occaſion be admitted as an authentic witneſs. "After the "ſurrender of Oſimo," ſays Machiavelli, "Buccolino "reſided a conſiderable time at Florence, under "the ſafeguad of Lorenzo, honored and reſpected. "He afterwards went to Milan, where he did not

(a) Murat. Ann, r, ix. p. 554. cit. Raynal. Annal. Eccles.

"experience

" experience the fame fidelity, having been
" treacheroufly put to death there by Ludovico
" Sforza (a)"

The remonftrances of the Florentines to the
Genoefe to relinquifh the dominion of Sarzana,
being yet difregarded, and the peaceable interven-
tion of the pope and the duke of Milan appearing
to be ineffectual, Lorenzo prepared for a powerful
attack; and not only engaged the lords of Piombino,
Faenza, Pitigliano, and Bologna in his caufe, but
applied to the king of Naples for fuch affiftance as
he could afford. In his anfwer to this requifition,
Ferdinand confeffes high obligations to Lorenzo,
and after lamenting his inability to repay them in
a manner adequate to their importance, promifes
to furnifh a fupply of fhips againft the Genoefe,
and to give fuch other aid as the embarraffed ftate
of his affairs would permit (b). The command of
the army, deftined to the attack of Sarzana, was given
to Jacopo Guicciardini, and Pietro Vittorio, who,
having defeated a body of the Genoefe that oppofed
their progrefs, began the fiege of the place. The
refiftance which they met with was however more
obftinate than might have been expected. Impatient
of the delay, Lorenzo refolved to join the army,
and endeavour by his prefence to promote the
exertions of the commanders, and excite the ardor
of the foldiery. His exhortations, addreffed per-
fonally to every rank and denomination, produced
an inftantaneous effect: a vigorous attack was made;

(a) *Mac. lib.* 8.
(b) *v. App. No.* XLVI.

                                          G

and the citizens, perceiving no profpect of further
fuccour from the Genoefe, furrendered at the dif-
cretion of the conquerors. It is not improbable,
that the remembrance of the difafter which took
place on the furrender of Volterra, had operated
as an additional motive with Lorenzo to be pre-
fent at the capture of Sarzana ; however this may
be, his conduct was marked with the greateft cle-
mency to the inhabitants, and the city was received
into the protection of the Florentine ftate, to which
it was only defirable, as oppofing a barrier to the
incurfions of the Genoefe. Elated with conqueft,
the Florentine commanders wifhed to carry the war
into the ftates of Genoa; but Lorenzo oppofed him-
felf to this defign; juftly conceiving it to be in-
confiftent with the interefts of his country and his
own character to deftroy that general equilibrium
of the Italian ftates, which his utmoft endeavours
were conftantly exerted to maintain. The appre-
henfions entertained by the Genoefe were pro-
ductive however of confequences as unfavorable to
their liberties, as any which they could have ex-
perienced from a hoftile invafion. To fecure them-
felves from the expected attack, they furrendered
their ftates to the duke of Milan, probably with
the intention of again afferting their independence
as foon as they had an opportunity; an artifice to
which they had frequently reforted on former oc-
cafions (a).

In the conduct of Lorenzo towards the fmaller
governments in the vicinity of Florence, he gave

(a) Murat. Annal. v. ix. p. 555.

a ſtriking inſtance of prudence and moderation. Inſtead of feeking for pretences to fubjugate them, he, upon all occaſions, afforded them the moſt effectual aid in refiſting every effort to deprive them of their independence. In his eſtimation, thefe were the true barriers of the Tufcan territory. By the conſtant intercourfe which he maintained with the fubordinate fovereigns, and the chief nobility of Italy, he was enabled to perceive the firſt indications of difagreement, and to extinguiſh the fparks before they had kindled into a flame. The city of Perugia was held by the Baglioni, Caſtello by the Vitelli, Bologna by the Bentivoli, and Faenza by the Manfredi; all of whom reforted to him as the umpire of their frequent diſſenſions, and their protector from the refentment, or the rapacity, of their more powerful neighbours. Innumerable occaſions prefented themfelves, in which the Florentines might have extended the limits of their dominions, but it was uniformly the policy of Lorenzo, rather to fecure what the ſtate already poſſeſſed, than, by aiming at more extenſive territory, to endanger the whole; and fo fully did he accompliſh his purpofe, that the acute, but profligate Lodovico Sforza, was accuſtomed to fay, " *That Lorenzo had converted into iron what he* " *found fabricated of glaſs* (*a*)." The views of Lorenzo were not however limited by the boundaries that divide Italy from the reſt of Europe. The influence of other ſtates upon the politics of that country was daily increaſing. He had therefore,

(*a*) *Fabr. in vitâ Laur. vol. i. p.* 181.

at almoſt every court, envoys and correſpondents, on whoſe talents and integrity he had the greateſt reliance; and who gave him minute and early information of every circumſtance that might affect the general tranquillity. By theſe men, he heard, he ſaw, he felt, every motion and every change of the political machine, and was often enabled to give it an impulſe where it was ſuppoſed to be far beyond the limits of his power. In conducting a negotiation, all circumſtances ſeemed to concur in rendering him ſuccefsful; but theſe were not the effects of chance, but of deep and premeditated arrangement. Knowing the route he had to take, the obſtacles that might have obſtructed his progrefs were cautiouſly removed, before his opponents were appriized of his intentions. Hence, as one of the Florentine annaliſts expreſſes it (a), he became the balance point of the Italian potentates, whoſe affairs he kept in ſuch juſt equilibrium as to prevent the preponderancy of any particular ſtate. Surrounded as he was by ambitious deſpots, who knew no reſtraint except that of compulſion, or by reſtlefs communities conſtantly ſpringing up with elaſtic

(a) " Era venuto Lorenzo in tanta riputazione e autorità appreſſo
" gli altri principi d'Italia, &c, che tutti gli Scrittori di que' tempi,
" e le memorie ancora degli uomini, che vivono, e che ſono vivuti
" a tempi noſtri unitamente s'accordano, che, mentre ch'egli viſſe
" fu ſempre l'ago della bilancia tra' principi predetti, che mantenne
" bilanciati gli ſtati loro, e di tal maniera gli tenne uniti, e ciaſcuno
" di eſſi riſtretti dentro a' termini de' loro confini, che ſi potette dipoi,
" dopo la ſua morte, vedere queſta verità detta di ſopra," &c.
Filip. de' Nerli, Comment. de' Fatti civili di Fir. lib. 3. Ed. Ven. 1728.

vigor againſt the hand that preſſed them; it was only by unwearied attention that he could curb the overbearing, relieve the oppreſſed, allay their mutual jealouſy, and preſerve them from perpetual contention. By inducing them to graſp at unſubſtantial advantages, he placed in their hands real bleſſings; and by alarming them with imaginary terrors, averted their ſteps from impending deſtruction.

We have already ſeen, that by the terms of the treaty between the pope and the king of Naples, Ferdinand was to pay an annual ſubſidy to the Roman ſee, and was alſo to grant an unconditional pardon to his refractory nobles. The latter of theſe conditions he immediately broke, and the other he only adhered to as long as he conceived that the pope was able to compel its performance. The cruelty and perfidy ſhown by Ferdinand in his treatment of the Neapolitan nobility, fixes an indelible ſtain upon his character; but the operations of the moral world are not leſs certain than thoſe of the natural, and the treachery of Ferdinand brought forth in due time its fruits of bitternꞏfs, It is true indeed, as Muratori well obſerves, "God " does not always repay in this world, nor are his " judgments laid open to us; but if we may on " any occaſion be allowed to interpret them, it is " when they ſeem to be the retribution of cruelty. " In fact, the calamities of Ferdinand were not " long poſtponed. The lapſe of a few years de" prived him of life, and his poſterity of the " kingdom of Naples. Surely, he can never be

" worthy to rule over a people, who knows not
" how to forgive (*a*)."

The refufal of Ferdinand to comply with his
engagements, again roufed the refentment of the
pope the inadequacy of whofe temporal arms to
enforce his pretenfions, was fupplied by the fpiritual
terrors of excommunication. On this occafion. the
intervention of Lorenzo de' Medici again became
neceffary. A long negotiation enfued, in the
progrefs of which he availed himfelf of every
opportunity afforded him by the circumftances of
the times, the temper of the parties, and his own
credit and authority, to prevent the difagreement
from proceeding to an open rupture. Of his letters
written in the courfe of thefe tranfactions, fome
are yet preferved, which, whilft they difplay the
refined policy and deep difcernment of their author,
demonftrate how affiduoufly he labored to avert
the calamities of war. " It appears to me, " fays
he writing to Lanfredini his confidential envoy at
Rome, who was to lay thefe reprefentations before
the pope, " that his holinefs muft propofe to himfelf
" one of thefe three things ; either to compel the
" king by force to comply with his requifition;
" or to compromife matters with him on the moft
" advantageous terms that can be obtained; or,
" laftly, to temporize till fomething better may be
" effected.' He then enters into a full difcuffion
of the difficulties and dangers that feem likely to

(*a*) " Certo non farà giammai degno di reggere popoli, chi non
" lo mai perdonare." *Murat. Ann.* t. ix. *p.* 556,

attend the making an hoftile attack on the kingdom of Naples. He lays before the pope the fituation not only of the other ftates of Italy, but of Europe; and fhows the indefpenfible neceffity of entering into treaties for affiftance, or neutrality, before he engages in fo hazardous an attempt. Having thus endeavoured to deter the pope from adopting any violent and unadvifed meafures, he adverts to the probability of terminating their differences by negotiation; the opportunity for which, however, he thinks as yet crude and immature, and as likely to be ftill further delayed by any fevere or incautious proceedings. " With refpect to temporizing," fays he, " this is undoubtedly the only courfe to be " purfued, becaufe it is better beyond comparifon " to let matters remain in their prefent ftate, with " reputation to his holinefs, than to rifk a war; " efpecially as the king has it in his power to do " him effential injury." He concludes with a a recapitulation of his former opinions. " If the " pope can accommodate matters with the king, " confiftently with his own honor, it feems to me " that a tolerable compromife is better than a " fuccefsful war. But as difficulties prefent them- " felves to an immediate agreement, I would " endeavour to protract the difcuffion as long as " it might be done with fafety and propriety; all " that I have advanced is however upon the idea " that the pope is not prepared to carry his point " by force, for if that were the cafe, the king would " foon fubmit; but I fear he is too well apprized " how far he is liable to be injured, and on this

" account will be more obſtinate (a)." By repreſen-
tations of this nature, founded on inconteſtable
facts, and inforced by unanſwerable arguments,
Lorenzo at length ſo far mitigated the anger, or
abated the confidence of the pope, as to diſpoſe
him to liſten to propoſitions of accommodation ;
whilſt, through the medium of his ambaſſador at
Naples, he prevailed on the king to aſſent to the
payment of the ſame ſubſidy which his predeceſſors
had paid to the holy ſee. It is not eaſy to ſay to
which of the contending parties the conduct of
Lorenzo was moſt acceptable; the pope omitted
no ſubſequent opportunity of conferring on him
and his family the moſt important favors; whilſt
Ferdinand unequivocally acknowledged, that to
his friendſhip and fidelity, he and his family were
indebted, not only for the rank they held, but even
for their continuance in the kingdom of Naples (b).

The external concerns of the republic being
happily adjuſted, and the tranquillity of Italy ſe-
cured, Lorenzo applied himſelf to the regulation
of the internal diſcipline of the Florentine ſtate.
The government of this city was founded on the
broadeſt baſis of democratic equality. By its

(a) For this letter, v. App. No. XLVII.

(b) Ferdinand thus addreſſed himſelf to Antonio della Valle, one
of the agents of Lorenzo at Naples: " Lorenzo ha provato, che
" veramente ho amato lui & quella città; ed io ho avuto a provare,
" che ha amato me, e i miei figliuoli, che ſenza lui, nè io nè loro
" faremmo in queſto regno, il quale beneficio noi nè i noſtri diſ-
" cendenti mai ſi hanno a ſcordare." Pet. Lutetii Ep. ad Laur.
Fab. v. ii. p. 369. Theſe obligations are alſo warmly acknowledged
by Ferdinand in a letter to Lorenzo himſelf. v. App. No. XLVIII

fundamental principles, every perſon who con-
tributed by his induſtry to the ſupport or aggran-
dizement of the ſtate, had a right to ſhare in the
direction of it; either by delegating his power to
others, or in exerciſing a portion of the ſupreme
control, under the ſuffrages of his fellow-citizens.
Inactivity was the only circumſtance that incapa-
citated him from the enjoyment of political rights.
The Florentines, as early as the year 1282, had
claſſed themſelves into diſtinct bodies, or municipal
companies, according to their various profeſſions;
and in order to place their government on a truly
popular foundation, had determined, that no perſon
ſhould be eligible to a public office, unleſs he were
either actually, or profeſſedly, a member of one
or other of theſe companies. By this regulation,
the nobility were either excluded from the offices
of the ſtate, or, in order to obtain them, were
obliged to degrade the honors of their rank, by
the humiliating appellation of artiſan (a). From
theſe aſſociated bodies, a certain number of mem-
bers were deputed to exerciſe the ſupreme govern-
ment, in conjunction with an officer, whom
we have frequently mentioned by the name of

(a) Et ſopra tutto parve, che ſi haveſſe havuto riguardo à fondar
uno ſtato aliatto popolare, non volendo che fuſſono ricevute al governo
perſone, che non fuſſero compreſe ſotto il nome, e inſegna d'alcuna
arte; eziandio che quelle arti non eſercitaſſero, perciocché ſi come non
ſtimavano coſa convniente il levar in tutto il governo di mano de'
nobili, coſi giudicavano ſſer neceſſario, che almeno col nome che
prendevano, depoſſ ſo parte dell' alterigia che porgea loro quella
borioſa voce della nobiltà. *Ammir. Iſt. lib.* iii. c. i. *p.* 160.

Gonfaloniere, whofe authority was however fubor-
dinate to that of the delegated mechanics, or *Priori
delle arti*, who continued in office only two months,
and from three in number, had increafed, at various
intervals, to fix, to eight, and laftly to ten (*a*).
This inftitution had, in the time of Lorenzo de'
Medici, fubfifted nearly two hundred years, during
which the office of Gonfaloniere had been filled
by a regular fucceffion of twelve hundred citizens,
who had preferved the dignity and independence
of the republic, and fecured to their countrymen
the exercife of their rights. With this laudable
jealoufy of their own liberties, the Florentines did
not, like the Romans, from whom they derived their
origin, exert their power to deftroy the liberties

(*a*) The jealous temper of the Florentines in providing for the
fecurity of their liberties, is exquifitely fatirized by their firft poet:

> Or ti fa lieta, che tu hai ben onde,
>> Tu ricca, tu con pace, tu con fenno;
>> S'i' dico 'l ver, l' effetto nol nafconde
> Atene, e Lacedemona, che fenno
>> L'antiche leggi, e furon sì civili,
>> Fecero al viver bene un picciol fenno
> Verfo di te, che fai tanto fottili
>> Provvedimenti, ch'a mezzo Novembre
>> Non giunge quel, che tu d'Ottobre fili.
> Quante volte del tempo, che rimembre
>> Legge, moneta, e uficio, e coftume,
>> Ha' tu mutato, e rinnovato membre?
> E fe ben ti ricorda, e vedi lume,
>> Vedrai te fimigliante a quell' infirma,
>> Che, non può trovar pofa in fulle piume
> Ma con dar volta fuo dolore fcherma.

Dante. Purg. Cant. vi.

of others. They wifely reprefled the dangerous defire of fubjecting to their dominion furrounding ftates, nor afpired to the invidious honor of fparing the fubfervient, and overturning the proud; and, though a community of freemen, were content to be the firft in thofe accomplifhments, which the flatterer of Auguftus affected to defpife (a).

There is however reafon to conjecture, that the Florentine government, although fufficiently vigorous for internal regulation, was inadequate to the exertions of external warfare. The hand that may fteer a veffel through the tranquil ocean, may be unable to direct the helm amidft the fury of the ftorm. It may indeed well be conceived, that the delegated magiftrates, being fo extremely limited, as well with refpect to their number, as to the duration of their power, would reluctantly determine on, and cautioufly engage in meafures, which involved the welfare, and perhaps the exiftence of the community. Accordingly it appears that on important occafions it was cuftomary for the magiftrates to affemble the moft refpectable citizens, from whofe advice they might derive affiftance, and by whofe countenance they might

(a) Excudent alii fpirantia mollius æra,
  Credo equidem, vivos ducent de marmore vultus,
  Orabunt cauffas melius, cœlique meatus,
  Defcribent radio & furgentia fidera dicent:
  Tu regere imperio populos, Romane, memento,
  (Hæ tibi erunt artes,) pacique imponere morem,
  Parcere fubjectis, & debellare fuperbos.
          Æn. lib. vi.

fecure themfelves from cenfure. During the late dangerous conteft, this meafure had been frequently reforted to, and with fuch manifeft advantage, that Lorenzo, after the reftoration of the public tranquillity, recommended, and obtained the eftablifhment of a body of feventy citizens, who, in the nature of a fenate, were to deliberate and to decide on all the tranfactions of government, as well in the affairs of peace, as of war. This inftitution, for which he might have pleaded the example of the Spartan legiflator, was probably intended, not only to give a greater degree of ftability and energy to the government, but to counteract the democratic fpirit, which was fuppofed to have rifen to a dangerous excefs (a), and to operate as a fafeguard againft an abufe which was the deftruction of all the free ftates of antiquity—the exercife of the powers of government by the immediate interference of the citizens at large.

At this period, the city of Florence was at its higheft degree of profperity. The vigilance of Lorenzo had fecured it from all apprehenfions of external attack; and his acknowledged difintereftednefs and moderation had almoft exftinguifhed that fpirit of diffenfion for which it had been fo long remarkable. The Florentines gloried in their

(a) " All free governments," fays Hume, very decifively, " muft " confift of two councils, a leffer and greater; or, in other words, " of a fenate and people." " The people" as Harrington obferves, " would want wifdom without the fenate; the fenate, without the " people, would want honefty." *Idea of a perfect Commonwealth.*

illuftrious citizen, and were gratified in numbering
in their body, a man who wielded in his hands
the fate of nations, and attracted the refpect and
admiration of all Europe. Though much inferior
in population, extent of dominion, and military
character, to feveral of the other ftates of Italy,
Florence ftood at this time in the firft degree of
refpectability. The active fpirit of its inhabitants,
no longer engaged in hoftile contentions, difplayed
itfelf in the purfuits of commerce, and the improve-
ment of their manufactures. Equally enterprifing
and acute, wherever there appeared a poffibility
of profit, or of fame, they were the firft to avail
themfelves of it ; and a Florentine adventurer,
though with doubtful pretenfions, has erected to
himfelf a monument which the proudeft conqueror
might envy, and impreffed his name upon a new
world in characters that are now indelible (a). The

(a) Amerigo Vefpucci, who has contended with Columbus for the
honor of the difcovery of America, was born at Florence in the
year 1451, of a refpectable family, of which feveral individuals had
enjoyed the chief offices of the republic. The name of Amerigo was
at Florence a common name of baptifm. For an account of the con-
troverfy that has taken place refpecting the pretenfions of thefe eminent
navigators, I muft refer to Dr. Robertfon's Hiftory of America, *book* ii.
note 22. without however approving the feverity of his animadver-
fions on the refpectable Canonico Bandini, who has endeavoured,
from original and almoft contemporary documents, to fupport the
claims of his countryman. *Band. vita di Amerigo Vefp. Flor.* 1745.
However this may be, it is certain, that about the year 1507,
Vefpucci refided at Seville, with the title of mafter pilot, and with
authority to examine all other pilots; for which he had a falary affigned
him; an employment, as Tirabofchi well obferves, fuitable to a fkil-
ful navigator, but far below the pretenfions of a man who had firft

filk and linen fabrics manufactured by the Floren-
tines, were in a great degree wrought from their
native productions; but their wool was imported
from England and from Spain, whofe inhabitants
indolently refigned their natural advantages, and
purchafed again at an extravagant price their own
commodities. In almoft every part to which the
Florentines extended their trade, they were favored
with peculiar privileges, which enabled them to
avail themfelves of the riches they had already
acquired; and the fuperftitious prohibitions of the
clergy againft ufury were of little avail againft a
traffic in which the rich found employment for
their wealth, and the powerful relief in their
neceffities. The confequence of thefe induftrious
exertions was, a fudden increafe of population in
Florence; infomuch that Lorenzo was under the
neceffity of applying to the pope, for his permiffion
to build in the gardens of the monafteries within
the walls of the city. By his attention, the police was
alfo effectually reformed. A contemporary author
affures us, that there was no part of Italy where
the people were more regular in their conduct, or

difcovered the new continent. This employment, however, afforded
Vefpucci an opportunity of rendering his name immortal. As he
defigned the charts for navigation, he uniformly denominated that
continent by the name of AMERICA, which being adopted by other
mariners and navigators, foon became general. *Tirab. Storia della
Let. Ital. v. 6. par. i. p.* 192. The memory of Vefpucci is therefore
now fecured by a memorial,

> Quod non imber edax nec aquilo impotens,
> Poffit diruere, aut innumerabilis
> Annorum feries, & fuga temporum.

where atrocious crimes were lefs frequent (*a*). " We have here," fays he, " no robberies, no " nocturnal commotions, no affaffinations. By night " or by day every perfon may tranfact his concerns " in perfect fafety. Spies and informers are here " unknown. The accufation of one is not fuffered " to affect the fafety of the many; for it is a maxim " with Lorenzo, *that it is better to confide ·in all than* " *in a few.*" From the fame authority we learn, that the due adminiftration of juftice engaged his conftant attention, and that he carefully avoided giving rife to an idea, that he was himfelf above the control of the law. Where compulfory regulations loft their effect, the affiduity and example of Lorenzo produced the moft falutary confequences, and banifhed that diffipation which enervates, and that indolence which palfies fociety. By forming inftitutions for the cultivation of the ancient languages, or the difcuffion of philofophical truths, by promoting the fciences, and encouraging the ufeful and ornamental arts, he ftimulated talents into action, and excited an emulation which called forth all the powers of the mind. Even the public fpectacles, intended for the gratification of the multitude, partook of the polifhed character of the inhabitants, and were conceived with ingenuity, and enlivened with wit. The profperity and happinefs which the citizens thus enjoyed were attributed to their true fource, and Lorenzo received

(*a*) *Philippus Redditus Exhort. ad Pet. Med. Laur. fil. inter opufc. Juan. Lamii. Delic. Erudit. Flor.* 1742.

the beſt reward of his labors in the gratitude of his country.

Beyond the limits of Tuſcany, the character of this illuſtrious Florentine was more eminently conſpicuous. The glory of the republic appeared at a diſtance to be concentered in himſelf. To him, individually, ambaſſadors were frequently diſpatched by the firſt monarchs of Europe; who, as their concerns required, alternately courted his aſſiſtance or ſolicited his advice (a). In the year 1489, when the emperor Frederick III. ſent an embaſſy to Rome, he directed them to paſs through Florence to obtain the patronage of Lorenzo; being, as he ſaid, convinced of his importance in directing the affairs of Italy. An interchange of kind offices ſubſiſted between this eminent citizen and John II. king of Portugal, who was deſervedly dignified with the appellation of great, and was deſirous that the tranſactions of his life ſhould be recorded by the pen of Politiano (b). From Matteo Corvino whoſe virtues had raiſed him to the throne of Hungary, many letters addreſſed to Lorenzo are yet extant, which demonſtrate not only the warm

(a) C'étoit une choſe auſſi admirable qu'éloignée de nos mœurs, de voir ce citoyen, qui faiſait toujours le commerce, vendre d'une main les denrées du Levant, & ſoutenir de l'autre le fardeau de la république; entretenir des facteurs, & recevoir des ambaſſadeurs; réſiſter au pape, faire la guerre & la paix, être l'oracle des princes, cultiver les belles-lettres, donner des ſpectacles au peuple, & accueillir tous les ſçavans Grecs de Conſtantinople. Il égala le grand *Coſme* par ſes bienfaits, & le ſurpaſſa par ſa magnificence.

Volt. Eſſai, v. ii. p. 284.

(a) *Pol. Epiſt. lib.* x. *Ep.* 1, 2.

attachment

attachment of that monarch to the caufe of fcience and the arts, but his efteem and veneration for the man whom he confidered as their moft zealous protector (*a*). As the reputation of Lorenzo increaf-ed, the affiduities of Louis XI. of France became more confpicuous; and in exchange for profeffions of efteem, which from fuch a quarter could confer no honor, we find him foliciting from Lorenzo fubftantial favors (*b*). The commercial intercourfe between Florence and Egypt, by means of which the Florentines carried on their lucrative traffic in the productions of the eaft, was extended and improved by Lorenzo; and fuch was the eftimation in which he was held by the fultan, that, in the year 1487, an ambaffador arrived at Florence, bringing with him, as a mark of his mafter's efteem, many fingular prefents of rare animals and valuable commodities; amongft the former of which, a camelopardalis principally attracted the curiofity of the populace (*c*).

This epoch forms one of thofe fcanty portions in the hiftory of mankind, on which we may dwell without weeping over the calamities, or blufhing for the crimes of our fpecies. Accordingly, the fancy of the poet, expanding in the gleam of

(*a*) Thefe letters are preferved in the *Palazzo Vecchio*, at Florence. *Filz.* xlvii.

(*b*) A letter from Louis XI. to Lorenzo, moft earneftly entreating his affiftance in promoting the interefts of the king's favorites in a propofed nomination of cardinals by Innocent VIII. is preferved in the *Palazzo Vecchio. Filz.* lix.

(*c*) Of thefe articles Pietro da Bibbiena, the fecretary of Lorenzo, gives an inventory to Clarice his wife, v. *App. No.* XLIX. *Fabr.* ii. 337.

profperity, has celebrated thefe times as realizing the beautiful fiction of the golden age (a). This feafon of tranquillity is the interval to which Guicciardini fo ftrikingly adverts, in the commencement of his hiftory, as being " profperous beyond any " other that Italy had experienced, during the " long courfe of a thoufand years. When the " whole extent of that fertile and beautiful country " was cultivated, not only throughout its wide " plains and fruitful vallies, but even amidft its " moft fterile and mountainous regions; and under " no control but that of its native nobility and " rulers, exulted, not only in the number and " riches of its inhabitants, but in the magnificence " of its princes, in the fplendor of many fuperb " and noble cities, and in the refidence and majefty " of religion itfelf. Abounding with men eminent " in the adminiftration of public affairs, fkilled in " every honorable fcience and every ufeful art, " it ftood high in the eftimation of foreign nations. " Which extraordinary felicity, acquired at many " different opportunities, feveral circumftances " contributed to preferve, but among the reft, no " fmall fhare of it was, by general confent, afcribed " to the induftry and the virtue of Lorenzo " de' Medici; a citizen, who rofe fo far beyond " the mediocrity of a private ftation, that he regu- " lated by his counfels the affairs of Florence, then

(a) From the numerous pieces which allude to this period, I shall felect the poem of Aurelius (or Lippo) Brandolini, *De laudibus Laurentii Medicis*, as it is given in the *Carmina illuft. Poet. Ital.* v. ii. p. 439. A collection now very rarely met with. v. *App. No.* L.

" more important by its fituation, by the genius
" of its inhabitants, and the promptitude of its
" refources, than by the extent of its dominions ;
" and who having obtained the implicit confidence
" of the Roman pontiff, Innocent VIII. rendered
" his name great, and his authority important in
" the affairs of Italy. Convinced of the perils
" that might arife, both to the Florentine republic
" and to himfelf, if any of the more powerful
" ftates fhould be allowed to extend their domini-
" ons, he ufed every exertion that the affairs of
" Italy might be fo balanced, that there fhould be
" no inclination in favor of any particular ftate ;
" a circumftance which could not take place
" without the permanent eftablifhment of peace,
" and the minuteft attention to every event, how-
" ever trivial it might appear." Such are the
reprefentations of this celebrated hiftorian. It is
only to be regretted that thefe profperous days
were of fuch fhort duration. Like a momentary
calm that precedes the ravages of the tempeft,
they were fcarcely enjoyed before they were paft.
The fabric of the public happinefs, erected by
the vigilance, and preferved by the conftant care
of Lorenzo, remained indeed firm and compact
during the fhort remainder of his days ; but at
his death it diffolved like the work of enchantment,
and overwhelmed for a time in its ruins even the
defcendants of its founder.

C H A P. VII.

*DIFFERENT progress of Italian and classical literature
—Latin writings of Dante, Petrarca, and Boccaccio
—Effects produced by them—Emanuel Chrysoloras—
Consequences of improvement—Progress of the Lau-
rentian Library—Introduction of printing in Florence
—Early editions of the classic authors—Politiano cor-
rects the Pandects of Justinian—Miscellanea of Poli-
tiano—His controversy with Merula—Establishment
of the Greek academy at Florence—Joannes Argyro-
pylus—Demetrius Chalcondyles—English scholars at
Florence—Political importance obtained by men of
learning — Florentine secretaries — Bartolommeo
Scala — His controversy with Politiano — Learned
statesmen in other governments of Italy — Men of
rank devote themselves to study—Pico of Mirandula
—Learned women — Alessandra Scala — Cassandra
Fidel's — Result of the attention shown to classical
learning — Translations — Italian writers of Latin
poetry — Landino — Ugolino and Michael Verini —
Other Latin poets of the fifteenth century—Character
of the Latin poetry of Politiano — General idea of
the state of literature in Florence in the latter part
of the fifteenth century.*

O F the improvement that took place in the Italian
language in the fourteenth century, of its rapid and
unexpected decline in that which succeeded, and
of its restoration under the auspices of Lorenzo de'

Medici, fome account has already been given; but
in tracing the hiflory of the revival and progrefs of
the ancient languages, we fhall find, that as they
were influenced by other caufes, they neither
flourifhed nor declined with the fludy of the na-
tional tongue. On the contrary, a daily proficiency
was made in claffical literature, at the very time
that the Italian language was again finking into
barbarifm and neglect; and the former advanced,
by a gradual but certain progrefs, towards that
perfection which the latter fuddenly and unexpect-
edly attained, from the caufes to which we have
before adverted.

In affigning the reafon for this remarkable dif-
tinction, we muft again recur to the times of Dante,
of Petrarca, and of Boccaccio; and obferve the
effects produced by the exertions of thofe great
men, whofe talents throw a luftre over a period
which would otherwife be involved in total darknefs.
In eftimating their labors, we fhall find that their
various attempts to reduce into form their native
language, and to revive the fludy of the ancient
tongues, were not only attended with different
degrees of fuccefs, but were followed by confe-
quences precifely the reverfe of thofe which might
have been expected. With whatever juftice Petrarca
and Boccaccio might, in their own days, have
boafted of their voluminous productions in the
Latin tongue, the increafing applaufe beftowed on
their Italian writings foon obfcured their fame as
Latin authors; and they are indebted for their
prefent celebrity to works which they affected to have blufhed

to own, and were afhamed to communicate to each other (*a*). The different merits of their Latin and their Italian compofitions were however foon appreciated ; and whilft the latter were daily rifing in the eftimation of the world, the former loft a great fhare of their reputation before the clofe of the fucceeding century. " It is not to be denied (*b*)," fays a very judicious critic of that period, " that " both Dante and Petrarca were warm admirers " of the ancients ; but the Latin writings of Dante, " like a picture that has loft its color, exhibit little " more than an outline. Happy indeed had it " been, had this author been enabled to convey " his fentiments in Latin, as advantageoufly as he " has done in his native tongue. The numerous " works of Petrarca, the offspring of that folitude " in which he delighted, are lafting monuments " of his induftry and his talents. Yet his ftyle is " harfh, and fcarcely bears the character of Latinity. " His writings are indeed full of thought, but de- " fective in expreffion, and difplay the marks of " labor without the polifh of elegance ; but as we " fometimes take a potion, not for the fake of

(*a*) The Decamerone of Boccaccio was not communicated to Petrarca till many years after it was written (*Manni, Illuft. del Boccaccio, p.* 629.); and Petrarca himfelf confeffes, that the reception of his Italian writings was far more favorable than he expected.

> S'io aveffi penfato che si care,
> Foffin le voci de' fofpir miei in rima,
> Fatte l'avrei dal fofpirar mio prima,
> In numero più fpeffe, in ftil più rare.

Son. 253.

(*a*) *Paulus Cortefius, De Hominibus doctis, p.* 7. *Ed. Flor.* 1734.

" gratification, but of health, fo from thefe writings
" we muft expect to derive utility rather than
" amufement. Rude as they are, they poffefs how-
" ever fome fecret charm which renders them
" engaging. The diftinguifhed talents of Boccaccio
" funk under the preffure of the general malady.
" Licentious and inaccurate in his diction, he has
" no idea of felection. All his Latin writings are
" hafty, crude, and uninformed. He labors with
" thought, and ftruggles to give it utterance; but
" his fentiments find no adequate vehicle, and the
" luftre of his native talents is obfcured by the
" depraved tafte of the times." Whilft fuch was
the fate of the Latin productions of thefe authors,
their Italian writings were the objects rather of
adoration than applaufe. No longer confined to
the perufal of the clofet, and the gratification
of an individual, the poems of Dante and of Pe-
trarca were read in public affemblies of the inhabit-
ants of Florence, and their beauties pointed out,
or their obfcurities illuftrated, by the moft eminent
fcholars of the time. No fooner was the art of
printing difcovered, than copies of them were
multiplied with an avidity which demonftrates the
high efteem in which they were held. Even the
prolix annotations with which thefe early editions
were generally accompanied, if they do not for the
moft part difplay the talents of the critic, are a proof
of the celebrity of the author. This obfervation is
not however applicable to the commentary of
Dante by Landino, who, with a laudable perfever-
ance, has preferved the remembrance of many

hiftorical facts, and related many circumftances indifpenfibly neceffary to the explanation of the *Divina Commedia.* His induftry in the execution of a tafk fo grateful to his countrymen, was rewarded by the donation of a villa, or refidence, on the hill of Cafentino, in the vicinity of Florence, which he enjoyed under the fanction of a public decree. Whilft the annotator was thus compenfated, the exiled poet was, upwards of a century after his death reftored to his family honors, with the fame formalities as if he had been ftill living; his defcendants were permitted to enjoy the poffeffions of their illuftrious anceftor, and his buft, crowned with laurels, was raifed at the public expenfe.

It might then have been expected, that the fuccefsful efforts of thefe authors to improve their native tongue, would have been more effectual than the weak, though laudable attempts made by them to revive the ftudy of the ancient languages; but it muft be remembered, that they were all of them men of genius, and genius affimilates not with the character of the age. Homer and Shakfpeare have no imitators, and are no models. The example of fuch talents is perhaps upon the whole unfavorable to the general progrefs of improvement; and the fuperlative abilities of a few, have more than once damped the ardor of a nation (*a*). But if the

(*a*) Dopo la morte di Cicerone e di Vergilio due chiariffimi fpecchi della lingua Latina, cominciò il modo dello fcrivere Romanamente, cosi in verfi come in profa, a mutarfi & variare da fe medefimo, e andò tanto di mano in mano peggiorando, che non era guafi più quel deffo. Il medefimo nè più nè meno avvenne nella

great Italian authors were inimitable in the pro-
ductions of their native language, in their Latin
writings they appeared in a subordinate character.
Of the labors of the ancients, enough had been
discovered to mark the decided difference between
their merits and those of their modern imitators;
and the applauses bestowed upon the latter, were
only in proportion to the degree in which they
approached the models of ancient eloquence.
This competition was therefore eagerly entered
into; nor had the success of the first revivers of
these studies deprived their followers of the hope
of surpassing them (a). Even the early part of the
fifteenth century produced scholars as much
superior to Petrarca, and his coadjutors, as they
were to the monkish compilers, and scholastic
disputants, who immediately preceded them; and
the labors of Leonardo Aretino, Gianozzo Manetti,
Guarino Veronese, and Poggio Bracciolini, prepared
the way for the still more correct and classical
productions of Politiano, Sannazaro, Pontano, and
Augurelli. The declining state of Italian literature,

lingua fiorentina; perchè spenti Dante, il Petrarca, e'l Boccaccio,
cominciò a variare e mutarsi il modo e la guisa del favellare, e dello
scrivere fiorentinamente, e tanto andò di male in peggio che quasi
non si riconosceva più, &c.

Varchi L'Ercolano, vol. i. *p.* 83. *Ed. Padova,* 1744.

(a) Difficilis in perfecto mora est; naturaliterque quod procedere
non potest, recedit. Et, ut primo ad consequendos, quos priores
ducimus, accendimur; ita ubi aut praeteriri aut aequari eos posse
desperavimus, studium cum spe senescit; & quod adi qui non potest,
sequi desinit: praeteritoque eo in quo eminere non possimus, aliquid
in quo nitamur conquirimus. *Velleius Paterc. lib.* i. *cap.* 17.

fo far then from being inconfiftent with, was rather a confequence of the proficiency made in other purfuits, which, whilft they were diftinguifhed by a greater degree of celebrity, demanded a more continued attention, and an almoft abfolute devotion both of talents and of time.

Whatever may have been the opinion in more modern times, the Italian fcholars of the fifteenth century did not attribute to the exertions of their own countrymen the reftoration of ancient learning. That they had fhown a decided predilection for thofe ftudies, and had excited an ardent thirft of further knowledge, is univerfally allowed; but the fource from which that thirft was allayed, was found in Emanuel Chryfoloras, who, after his return to his native country from his important embaffies, was prevailed upon by the Florentines to pay a fecond vifit to Italy, and to fix his refidence among them. The obligations due to Chryfoloras, are acknowledged in various parts of their works, by thofe who availed themfelves of his inftructions; and the gratitude of his immediate hearers was transfufed into a new race of fcholars, who by their eulogies on their literary patriarch, but much more by their own talents, contributed to honor his memory (a). On his arrival in Italy

(a) Chryfoloras died at Conftance, when the council was held there in 1415. A volume, confifting of eulogies upon him, lately exifted in the monaftery at *Camaldoli*. (*Zeno. Diff. Voff. v. i. p.* 214.) Poggio and Æneas Sylvius (Pius II.) each of them honored him with an epitaph. In the latter, the merit of having been the reviver of both Greek and Latin literature, is explicitly attributed to him.

in the character of an inftructor, he was accompanied
by Demetrius Cydonius, another learned Greek.
The ardor with which they were received by the
Italian fcholars, may be conjectured from a letter
of Coluccio Salutati to Demetrius, on his landing
at Venice (a). " I rejoice not fo much " fays he,
" in the honor I receive from your notice, as for
" the interefts of literature. At a time when the
" ftudy of the Greek language is nearly loft, and
" the minds of men are wholly engroffed by am-
" bition, voluptuoufnefs, or avarice, you appear
" as the meffengers of the Divinity, bearing the
" torch of knowledge into the midft of our darknefs.
" Happy indeed fhall I efteem myfelf, (if this life
" can afford any happinefs to a man to whom

> Ille ego, qui Latium prifcas imitarier artes,
> Explofis docui fermonum ambagibus, & qui,
> Eloquium magni Demosthenis & Ciceronis
> In lucem retuli, Chrysoloras nomine notus,
> Hic fitus emoriens, peregrina fede quiefco, &c.
>
> *Hod. de Græc. illuft. p.* 24.

Janus Pannonius, a fcholar of Guarino Veronefe, (for whofe hiftory
and unhappy fate, *v. Valerianus De infelicitate Literatorum.*) in an
elegant Latin panegyric on his preceptor, alfo pays a tribute of refpect
to the Greek fcholar:

> Vir fuit hic patrio Chrysoloras nomine dictus,
> Candida Mercurio quem Calliopæa crearat,
> Nutrierat Pallas; nec folis ille parentum
> Clarus erat ftudiis, fed rerum protinus omnem
> Naturam, magna complexus mente tenebat.
>
> *Jani Pannonii Quinq. ecclefiarfis Epifc. Paneg. ad Guar. Ver.*
> *præceptorem fuum ap. Frobenium. Bafil.* 1518. *p.* 11.

(a) *Mehus, in vitá Amb. Trav. p.* 356. This early vifitor has
efcap'd the refearches of Dr. Hody. *De Græc. Illuft.*

" to-morrow will bring the clofe of his fixty-fifth
" year,) if I fhould by your affiftance imbibe thofe
" principles, from which all the knowledge which
" this country poffeffes is wholly derived. Perhaps,
" even yet, the example of Cato may ftimulate me
" to devote to this ftudy the little that remains of
" life, and I may yet add to my other acquirements,
" a knowledge of the Grecian tongue."

If we advert to the night of thick darknefs in
which the world had been long enveloped, we
may eafily conceive the fenfa ions that took place
in the minds of men when the gloom began to
difperfe, and the fpectres of falfe fcience, by turns
fantaftic and terrific, gave way to the diftinct and
accurate forms of nature and of truth. The Greeks
who vifited Italy in the early part of the fifteenth
century, if they did not diffufe a thorough know-
ledge of their language, and of thofe fciences which
they exclufively poffeffed, at leaft prepared a fafe
afylum for the mufes and the arts, who had long
trembled at the approach, and at length fled before
the fierce afpect of Mahomet II. From that period
a new order of things took place in Italy; the
conftruction of language was inveftigated on phi-
lofophical principles; the maxims of found criticifm
began to fupplant the fcholaftic fubtilties which
had perverted for ages the powers of the human
mind; and men defcended from their fancied
eminence among the regions of fpeculation and
hypothefis, to tread the earth with a firm foot,
and to gain the temple of fame by a legitimate,
though laborious path.

The eftablifhment of public libraries in different parts of Italy, whilft it was one of the firft confequences of this ftriking predilection for the works of the ancients, became in its turn the active caufe of further improvement. To no defcription of individuals is the world more indebted, than to thofe who have been inftrumental in preferving the wifdom of paft ages, for the ufe of thofe to come, and thereby giving, as it were, a general fenforium to the human race. In this refpect great obligations are due to the venerable Cofmo (a). From the intercourfe that in his time fubfifted between Florence and Conftantinople, and the long vifits made by the Greek prelates and fcholars to Italy, he had the beft opportunity of obtaining the choiceft treafures of ancient learning; and the deftruction of Conftantinople may be faid to have transferred to Italy all that remained of eaftern fcience (b). After the death of Cofmo, his fon Piero purfued with fteady perfeverance the fame object, and made important additions to the various

(a) *Bandini, Lettera fopra i principj, &c. della Biblioteca Laurenziana. Fir.* 1773.

(b) The library of S. Marco, which, as we have before related, was founded by Cofmo, with the books collected by Niccolo Niccoli, and augmented at his own expenfe, was, in the year 1454, almoft buried in ruins by an earthquake, that continued at intervals for nearly forty days, during which feveral perfons loft their lives, Cofmo however not only reftored the building to its former ftate, but raifed the ceiling, fo as to admit of a more extenfive collection. At the fame time a new arrangement of the manufcripts took place, and the Greek and Oriental works were formed into a clafs diftinct from the Latin. *Alehus in vitá Amb. Trav. p.* 66. 73.

(62).

collections which Cofmo had begun, particularly
to that of his own family (a). But although the
anceftors of Lorenzo laid the foundation of the
immenfe collection of manufcripts, fince denomi-
nated the Laurentian Library, he may himfelf
claim the honor of having raifed the fuperftructure.
If there was any purfuit in which he engaged more
ardently, and perfevered more diligently than the
reft, it was that of enlarging his collection of books
and antiquities. " We need not wonder," fays
Niccolo Leoniceno, writing to Politiano (b), " at
" your eloquence and your acquirements, when
" we confider the advantages which you derive
" from the favor of Lorenzo de' Medici, the great
" patron of learning in this age; whofe meffengers
" are difperfed throughcut every part of the earth,

(a) The manufcripts acquired by Piero de' Medici are for the moft
part highly ornamented with miniatures, gilding, and other decorations,
and are diftinguished by the *fleurs de lys*. Thofe collected by Lorenzo
are marked not only with the Mediccan arms, but with a laurel
branch in allufion to his name, and the motto **semper**. When we
advert to the immenfe prices which were given for thefe works, and
the labor afterwords employed on them, they may be confidered as
the moft expenfive articles of luxury. A tafte for the exterior de-
coration of books has lately arifen in this country, in the gratification
of which no fmall share of ingenuity has been difplayed; but if we
are to judge of the prefent predilection for learning by the degree of
expenfe thus incurred, we muft confider it as greatly inferior either
to that of the Romans, during the times of the firft emperors, or of
the Italians in the fifteenth century. And yet it is perhaps difficult
to difcover, why a favorite book should not be as proper an object
of elegant ornament, as the head of a cane, the hilt of a fword, or
the latchet of a shoe.

(b) *Polit. Epift. lib. ii. Ep.* 7.

" for the purpofe of collecting books on every
" fcience, and who has fpared no expenfe in
" procuring for your ufe, and that of others who
" may devote themfelves to fimilar ftudies, the
" materials neceffary for your purpofe. I well
" remember the glorious expreffion, of Lorenzo,
" which you repeated to me, that he wifhed the
" diligence of Pico and yourfelf, would afford him
" fuch opportunities of purchafing books, that
" his fortune proving infufficient, he might pledge
" even his furniture to poffefs them." Acting under
the influence of fuch impreffions, we cannot wonder
at the progrefs made by Lorenzo, in which he
derived great affiftance from Hieronymo Donato,
Ermolao Barbaro, and Paolo Cortefi; but his prin-
cipal coadjutor was Politiano, to whom he com-
mitted the care and arrangement of his collection,
and who made excurfions at intervals through
Italy, to difcover and purchafe fuch remains of
antiquity, as fuited the purpofes of his patron (a).
Two journies, undertaken at the inftance of Lorenzo
into the eaft, by Giovanni Lafcar produced a great
number of rare and valuable works. On his return
from his fecond expedition, he brought with him
about two hundred copies, many of which he had
procured from a monaftery at Mount Athos; but

(b) Of the vigilance of Politiano in thefe purfuits, we have the
moft explicit evidence, in a letter from him to Lorenzo, firft publifhed
by Fabroni, which may juftify the forcible remark of that author on
the literary agents of Lorenzo. " Porro ipfos venaticos canes dixiffes,
" ita odorabantur omnia & perveftigabant, ut ubi quidque rarum
" effet, aliqua ratione invenirent atque compararent."

Fabr. in vitâ Laur. v. i. *p.* 153. *App. No.* LI.

this treasure did not arrive till after the death of Lorenzo, who in his laſt moments expreſſed to Politiano and Pico, his regret that he could not live to complete the collection which he was forming for their accommodation (*a*). Stimulated by the example of Lorenzo, other eminent patrons of learning engaged in the ſame purſuit. Thoſe who particularly diſtinguiſhed themſelves were Matteo Corvino king of Hungary, and Federigo duke of Urbino(*b*), to both of whom Lorenzo gave permiſſion to copy ſuch of his manuſcripts as they wiſhed to poſſeſs; nothing being more conſonant to his intentions than to diſſuſe the ſpirit of literature as extenſively as poſſible.

The newly diſcovered art of printing, contributed alſo in an eminent degree, to accelerate the progreſs of claſſical literature. This art was practiſed very early in Florence, and ſome of the Florentine authors have even been deſirous of conferring on one of their countrymen, the merit of its invention (*c*); but this acute people have too many well-founded claims on the gratitude of poſterity, to render it neceſſary for them to rely on doubtful commendation. It is however certain that whilſt Venice ſolicited the aſſiſtance of Nicolas Jenſen a native of France, and Rome began to practiſe the

(*a*) Non nihil etiam tunc quoque jocatus nobiſcum, quin utroſque intuens nos; Vellem ait diſtuliſſet me ſaltem mors hæc ad eum diem quo veſtram plane bibliothecam abſoluiſſem. *Pol. Ep. lib.* iv. *Ep.* 2.

(*b*) *Pol. Ep. lib.* iii. *Ep.* 6. *Fabr. in vitâ Laur. v.* i. *p.* 154.

(*c*) *Manni, della prima promulgazione de' Libri in Firenze.*
Fir. 1761.

art

art under the guidance of the two German printers, Sweynheym and Pannartz, Florence found amongft her own citizens, an artift equal to the tafk. Taking for his example the infcriptions on the ancient Roman feals (a), or more probably ftimulated by the fuccefs of his contemporaries, Bernardo Cennini, a Florentine goldfmith, formed the *matrices* of his letters in fteel; by means of which, with the affiftance of his two fons, Domenico and Piero, he began in the year 1471, to print the works of Virgil, with the commentary of Servius, which he publifhed at Florence in the following year (b).

Lorenzo de' Medici faw the importance of a difcovery, which had been wanting to the completion of the generous views of his anceftors, and availed himfelf of it with a degree of earneftnefs which fufficiently fhows the motives by which he was actuated. At his inftigation, feveral of the Italian fcholars were induced to beftow their attention, in collating and correcting the manufcripts

(a) *Manni, della prima promulgazione de' Libri in Firenze.* p. 3.

(b) At the clofe of the Bucolics in this edition, is the following infcription:

AD LECTOREM

Florentiæ vii. *Idus Novembras*

MCCCCLXXI.

Bernardus Cenninus Aurifex omnium judicio præftantiffimus & Dominicus ejus F. egregiæ indolis adolefcens: expreffis ante calibe charactaribus, ac deinde fufis literis, volumen hoc primum impreffierunt. Petrus Cenninus Bernardi ejufdem F. quanta potuit cura & diligentia emendavit, ut cernis. *Florentinis ingeniis nil ardui eft.* And at the clofe of the volume is another infcription, with the date of October 1472.

of the ancient authors, in order that they might
be ſubmitted to the preſs with the greateſt poſſible
accuracy. In the dialogues of Landino, publiſhed
by him under the name of *Diſputationes Camal-
dulenſes.* to which we have had occaſion to refer (*a*),
that author has devoted his third and fourth books
to a critical diſſertation on the works of Virgil,
particularly with a view of explaining ſuch parts
as are ſuppoſed to contain an allegorical ſenſe; but
he ſoon afterwards performed a much more grate-
ful office to the admirers of the Roman poet, by
correcting the errors with which his works abounded,
and endeavouring to reſtore them to their original
purity. In the proeme to this work, which he has
inſcribed to Piero de' Medici, the ſon of Lorenzo,
he recapitulates the favors which the anceſtors of
his patron have beſtowed on men of learning,
and particularly recommends to his imitation, in
this reſpect, the example of his father. He adverts
to the aſſaſſination of Giuliano de' Medici, and
attributes the preſervation of Lorenzo at that critical
juncture to his own courage and magnanimity (*b*).
Returning to his immediate ſubject, he thus pro-
ceeds: " In my dialogues of Camaldoli, I have given

(*a*) *Vol.* i. *p.* 103.

(*b*) Dabis, ſuaviſſime Petre, hoc in loco roganti mihi veniam, ſi
barbaricam illam, & omnium ſceleratiſſimam ac ſine exemplo con-
jurationem ſilentio præterierim: qua in templo marmoreo inter ſacra
ſolemnia & Julianus frater ſæviſſime trucidatus, & ipſe Laurentius,
inter ſtrictos, & undique eum petentes gladios jam jam caſurus, ita
elapſus eſt, ut non humano, ſed divino auxilio, & ſua animi præſ-
tantia, quæ audaciſſimum quemque terrere poterat, de manu inimi-
corum ereptus videatur. *Land. Spec. Lit. Flor. v.* i. *p.* 213.

" a philofophical comment on the works of Virgil.
" I now mean to perform the office of a gram-
" marian and critic on this author. In my former
" attempt, as the fubject is of more dignity, I
" have introduced your father as one of the dif-
" putants; but thefe obfervations, which are intend-
". ed to inculcate a knowledge of the Latin language,
" I confider as more properly addreffed to a young
" man of your promifing talents and cultivated
" underftanding (*a*)." In the year 1482, Landino
publifhed alfo an edition of the works of Horace,
with numerous corrections and remarks, which
he infcribed to Guido da Feltri, the fon of Federigo,
duke of Urbino (*b*), to whom he had dedicated, in
terms of the higheft commendation and refpect,
his *Difputationes Camaldulenfes*. Landino was one of
the firft fcholars who, after the revival of letters,
devoted himfelf to the important tafk of reftoring
and elucidating thefe favorite authors, and his
labors were received with unbounded applaufe.
Of his obfervations on Horace confiderable ufe has
been made by many fubfequent editors. On their
publication, Politiano accompanied them with the
following ode, not unworthy of the poet whofe
praifes it is intended to celebrate (*c*) :

(*a*) *Band. Spec. Lit. Flor. v. i. p. 225.*

(*b*) *Impreffum per Antonium Mifcominum, Florentiæ, anno
Sautis* mccclxxxii. *nonis Augufti.* Thefe commentaries were
republifhed at Venice, *per Joannem de Forlivio & Socios,* in the
following year, and feveral fubfequent editions have taken place.

(*c*) This ode is not printed in the works of Politiano, and is very
inaccurately given by Bandini. *Spec. Lit. Flor.* It is here republifhed
from the edition of Horace by Landino, *Ven.* mcccclxxxiii.

AD HORATIUM FLACCUM.

Vates Threicio blandior Orpheo,
    Seu malis fidibus fiftere lubricos
    Amnes, feu tremulo ducere pollice
    Ipfis cum latebris feras;
Vates Aeolii pectinis arbiter,
    Qui princeps Latiam follicitas chelyn,
    Nec fegnis titulos addere noxiis
    Nigro carmine frontibus;
Quis te a barbarica compede vindicat?
    Quis frontis nebulam difpulit, & fitu
    Deterfo, levibus reftituit choris,
    Curata juvenem cute?
O quam nuper eras nubilus, & malo
    Obductus fenio, quam nitidos ades
    Nunc vultus referens, docta fragrantibus
    Cinctus tempora floribus!
Talem purpureis reddere folibus
    Laetum pube nova poft gelidas nives
    Serpentem, pofitis exuviis, folet
    Verni temperies poli.
Talem'te choreis reddidit & Lyrae,
    LANDINUS, veterum laudibus æmulus,
    Qualis tu folitus Tibur ad uvidum
    Blandam tendere barbiton.
Nunc te deliciis, nunc decet & levi
    Lafcivire joco. nunc puerilibus
    Infertum thyafis, aut fide garrula,
    Inter ludere virgines.

Poet. than whom the bard of Thrace
Ne'er knew to touch a fweeter ftring;

O whether from their deep recefs
  The tenants of the wilds thou bring,
With all their fhades; whether thy ftrain
  Bid liftening rivers ceafe to flow;
Whether with magic verfe thou ftain
  A lafting blot on vice's brow;
Poet! who firft the Latian lyre
  To fweet Æolian numbers ftrung!
When late repreffed thy native fire,
  When late impervious glooms o'erhung
Thy front, O fay what hand divine
  Thy rude barbaric chains unbound,
And bade thee in new luftre fhine,
  Thy locks with vernal rofes crown'd?
As when in fpring's reviving gleam
  The ferpent quits his fcaly flough,
Once more beneath the funny beam,
  In renovated youth to glow;
To thy lov'd lyre, and choral throng,
  LANDINO thus their poet brings;
Such as thy TIBUR heard thy fong,
  Midft her cool fhades and gufhing fprings.
Again with tales of whifpered love,
  With fprightly wit of happieft vein,
Through bands of vine-crown'd youths to rove,
  Or fport amidft the virgin train.

It is greatly to the credit of Politiano that thefe
verfes were addreffed to the perfon who was his
moft formidable rival in thofe ftudies to which he
had particularly devoted his talents. In reftoring
to their original purity the ancient authors, he
was himfelf indefatigable; and if to the mu-

nificence of Lorenzo de' Medici we are to attribute
the prefervation of many of thefe works, Politiano
is perhaps entitled to our equal acknowledgments
for his elucidations and corrections of the text,
which, from a variety of caufes, was frequently
unintelligible, illegible, or corrupt. In the exercife
of his critical talents he did not confine himfelf
to any precife method, but adopted fuch as he
conceived beft fuited his purpofe; on fome occafions
only comparing different copies, diligently marking
the variations, rejecting fpurious readings, and
fubftituting the true. In other cafes he proceeded
further, and added Scholia and notes illuftrative
of the text, either from his own conjectures, or
the authority of other authors (*a*). Befides the
advantages which he derived from various copies
of the fame work, which enabled him to collate
them fo as to afcertain the true reading, he obtained

(*a*) In the edition of Cato, Varro, and Columella, published at
Paris, *ex off. Rob. Stephani*, 1543, with the corrections of Pet.
Victorius, that excellent critic thus adverts to the labors of Politiano:
" Non exemplar ipfum femper confului, fed habui excufos formis
" libros, quos cum antiquis illis *Angelus Politianus* ftudiofe olim
" contulerat, eofque, quantum mihi commodum fuit, pertractavi; illi
" enim quoque publici funt. Eruditiffimi igitur viri labor, magno
" me labore levavit; qui quidem, ut erat diligens, & accuratus, hac
" librorum collatione mirifice delectabatur: & ita poffe bonos auctores
" multis maculis purgari, vere exiftimabat. Quæcumque igitur in
" prifcis exemplaribus inveniebat, in impreffis fedulo adnotabat.
" Quod fi diutius ille vixiffet, & quæ mente deftinaverat perficere
" potuiff t, opera fedalitafque ipfius magnos ftudiofis litterarum fructus
" attuliffet, multofque qui poftea huic muneri corrigendorum librorum
" neceffario incubuerunt, magna prorfus moleftia liberaffet."

great affiftance from the collection of antiques form-
ed by Lorenzo and his anceftors; and amongft his
coins, infcriptions on marble, and other authentic
documents, frequently elucidated and determined
what might otherwife have remained in darknefs
or in doubt(*a*). At the clofe of his remarks on
Catullus, a memorial appears in his own hand-
writing, in which he indulges himfelf in an ex-
ultation of youthful vanity, in the idea of having
furpaffed all his contemporaries in the diligence
which he has fhown in correcting the ancient
authors. This memorial, which bears the date
of 1473, at which time he was only eighteen
years of age, is fubfcribed *Angelus Baffus Politianus*.
Before, however, we accufe our youthful critic of
an oftentatious difplay of learning, or an improper
confidence in his own abilities, we ought to advert
to another entry made two years afterwards at
the clofe of the works of Propertius in the fame
volume, by which he confeffes, that many of his
previous obfervations do not approve themfelves
to his riper judgment, and requefts the reader not
to form an opinion of his talents, his leaning, or
his induftry, from fuch a fpecimen. There being
many things

Me quoque, qui fcripfi, judice digna lini.

Which I, their author, well might wifh to blot (*b*).

(*a*) *Menck. in vitâ Pol. p.* 237.
(*b*) The reader may confult thefe memoranda in the Appendix,
No. LII,

In this fubfequent entry he denominates himfelf *Angelus Politianus*, which fufficiently marks the period when he chofe to difcontinue the appellation of *Bafus* (*a*) ; but what is of more importance, it ferves to convince us, that with the errors of his judgment Politiano corrected alfo thofe of his temper, and that his proficiency in learning was accompanied by an equal improvement in modefty and candor. Among the ancient authors which he has thus illuftrated are Ovid (*b*), Suetonius (*c*), Statius (*d*, The younger Pliny (*e*), The Scriptores Hiftoriæ Auguftæ (*f*), and Quintilian (*g*); fome of which have been publifhed with his emendations, while his valuable remarks on others are yet confined to the limits of the Italian libraries. The example of Politiano was followed by many other celebrated fcholars, who regarded Lorenzo de' Medici as the patron of their ftudies, and infcribed their labors with his name. Thus Domitio Calderino undertook to regulate the text of Martial (*h*), Bartolommeo Fontio employed his talents on

(*a*) On this point, which has been fo much contefted, I find the opinion of Bandini before cited in this work, *v. i. p.* 144, is confirmed by that of Laur. Mehus, *Vita Amb. Traverfarii, p.* 87.

(*b*) In the Bibliotheca Marciana.

(*c*) In the Laurentian Library. *Plut.* LXIV. *cod.* 1.

(*d*) In the Corfini Library at Rome.

(*e*) In the Laurentian Library. *Plut.* LXVII. *cod.* 7.

(*f*) Ib. *Plut.* XLIV. *cod.* 1.

(*g*) Ib. *Plut.* XLVI. *cod.* 5.

(*h*) Printed at Rome per Joannem Gensberg, 1474, *v. De Bure,* No. 2518.

Perfius (*a*), and Lancelotto on Columella (*b*). Nor were the Greek authors neglected. In the year 1488, Demetrius Chalcondyles and Demetrius Cretenfis publifhed at Florence the firft edition of the works of Homer, which is infcribed to Piero de' Medici, the fon of Lorenzo (*c*).

The fyftem of jurifprudence which in the fifteenth century prevailed throughout the greateft part of Europe, was that of the Roman or civil law, which was principally founded on the pandects or conftitutions of Juftinian. Hence the correction and explication of the fubfifting copies of this work became of high importance to the community. This tafk was referved for the indefatigable induftry of Politiano, whofe labors in this department entitle him to rank not only with the earlieft, but with the moft learned modern profeffors of this fcience. In his letters he has himfelf given fome account of his progrefs in this laborious work. Much additional information may be found in the narrative of his life by Menckenius; and Bandini, who has lately had the good fortune to recover the commentary of Politiano and reftore it to its former ftation in the Laurentian Library, has

(*a*) Publifhed in 1481. *Band. Cat. Bibl. Laur. v.* ii. *p.* 679.

(*b*) *Band. Cat. v.* ii. *p.* 561. In the preface to this author, the editor thus addreffes Lorenzo: " Ab ineunte et nim ætate, fplendidif- " fima nominis tui fama, ad tuam benevolentiam captandam ita me " compofuit, ut cunctis potius honoris tui ftudiofum oftendere hoc ævo " malim, quam in decorum tuum reticere."

(*c*) Florentiæ imp. *Thais Bernardi & Nerii Tonaidis Nerlii Florentinorum. Nono menfis Decembris Anno* 1488. 2 vol. fo. For an account of this magnificent work, v. *De Bure, No.* 2493.

publiſhed an hiſtorical narrative expreſsly on this ſubjeƈt (*a*). In the accompliſhment of this taſk, which he was induced to undertake at the inſtance of Lorenzo de' Medici, Politiano had ſingular advantages. An ancient and authentic copy found at Piſa, and ſuppoſed to have been depoſited there by the orders of Juſtinian himſelf, had on the capture of that place been transferred to Florence (*l*), and was afterwards intruſted by Lorenzo de' Medici to the ſole cuſtody of Politiano (*c*). By this he was enabled to correƈt the numerous errors, and to ſupply the defeƈts of the more recent manuſcripts, as well as of two editions which had before iſſued from the preſs (*d*). The

(*a*) *Raggionamento Iſtorico ſopra le collazioni delle Fiorentine Pandette, fatta da Angelo Poliziano, ſotto gli auſpicij del Mag. Lorenzo de' Medici, &c. Livorno* 1762.

(*b*) " Principio igitur ſcire te illud opinor, Imperatorem Juſtinia-
" num poſteaquam jus civile perpurgavit, in ordinemque redegit,
" caviſſe illud in primis, ut in omnibus civitatibus quæ dignitate
" aliqua præcellerant, exemplaria legum quam emendatiſſima publice
" aſſervarentur --- ſed nullum ex his clarius tamen aut celebratius,
" quam quod ad uſque urbis ejus captivitatem, Piſis, magna religione
" ſit cuſtoditum." *Pol. Ep. lib.* 10.

(*c*) " Hoc ergo mihi inſpicere per otium licuit, rimarique omnia,
" & olfacere, quæque vellem excerpere diligenter, & cum vulgatis
" exemplaribus comparare. Tribuit nam hoc mihi uni *Laurentius*
" *ille Medices*, vir optimus ac ſapientiſſimus; fore illud aliquando
" arbitratus, ut opera; labore induſtriaque noſtra, magna inde omnino
" utilitas eliceretur." *Ib.*

(*d*) Mr. Gibbon gives Politiano the appellation of an enthuſiaſt, for ſuppoſing this manuſcript to be the " authentic ſtandard of Juſtinian " himſelf." " This paradox," ſays he, " is refuted by the abbrevia-
" tions of the Florentine manuſcript, and the Latin charaƈters betray

civilians of the enfuing century have freely con-
feſſed their obligations to a commentator who firſt
with the true ſpirit of reſearch, applied himſelf to
the elucidation of a ſcience in itſelf ſufficiently
complex and obſcure, but which was rendered
ſtill more ſo, by the imperfect ſtate of thoſe
authorities to which its profeſſors were conſtantly
obliged to refer.

Of the critical talents of Politiano, and of the
variety and extent of his erudition, his *Miſcellanea*
alone afford a ſufficient teſtimony (*a*). For the
publication of this work, which conſiſts principally
of obſervations on the writings of the ancient

" the hand of a Greek ſcribe." *Hiſt. of the Decline and Fall of
the Roman Empire, lib.* 44. But Politiano had duly conſidered all
the peculiarities of the manuſcript, of which he was a complete judge,
and was fully of opinion that it was the production of a Latin ſcribe,
and not of a Greek. " Eſt autem," ſays he in an epiſtle to Lod.
Bologneſe (lib. xi.), " liber characteribus majuſculis, ſine ullis com-
" pendiariis notis, ſine ullis diſtinctionibus; nec *Græcus*, ſed *Latinus—*
" videlicet ille ipſe quem inter ceteros publicavit Juſtinianus." This
work, which conſiſts of two volumes, written on thin vellum, was
depoſited, ſays Mr. Gibbon, on the authority of Brenckman (*Hiſt.
Pandect. Florent. l.* 1. *c.* x. xi. xii. *p.* 62. 93.) as a ſacred relic in
a rich caſket, in the ancient palace of the republic, new bound in
purple, and ſhown to curious travellers by the monks and magiſtrates,
bare headed and with lighted tapers.

(*a*) Firſt printed by Antonio Miſcomini at Florence, with the
following ſingular colophon: *Impreſſit ex archetypo Antonius Miſ-
cominus. Familiares quidam Politiani recognovere. Politianus
ipſe nec Horthographian ſe ait, nec omnino alienam præſtare culpam.*
FLORENTIÆ ANNO SALUTIS M.CCCC.LXXXIX. *Decimo tertio kalendas
Octobris.* In 4°. This book, like all thoſe I have ſeen of the ſame
printer, is moſt elegantly and correctly executed, and is a proof of
the ſpeedy proficiency made in typography at Florence.

authors, we are alfo indebted to Lorenzo de' Medici, to whom Politiano was accuftomed, as they rode out on horfeback, to repeat the various remarks which had occurred to him in his morning ftudies (a). At the requeft of Lorenzo, he was at length induced to commit them to paper, and to arrange them in order for the prefs. On their publication he infcribed them to his great friend and benefactor; not, as he affures him, merely for the purpofe of teftifying his gratitude, for the affiftance and advice which he had in the courfe of his work received from him, but that it might obtain favor, and derive authority, from the celebrity of his name (b).

The publication of this work foon afterwards led Politiano into a controverfy, in which he conducted himfelf with firmnefs and moderation, and which terminated greatly to his honor. Lodovico Sforza, anxious to throw a veil over the guilt of his ufurpation by an attention to the promotion of letters, had prevailed upon Giorgio Merula among other learned men, to eftablifh his refidence at Milan, where he enjoyed an ample penfion from the duke. The character of Merula ftood high for his acquirements in Latin literature (c); but neither

(a) *Pol. in præf. ad Mifcel.*

(b) Nec erunt opinor hæc quoque noftra, quamquam levioris operis ftudia, feu ludicra verius, dedecori tibi Laurenti Medices, cui nunc adfcribuntur. Adfcribuntur autem non magis adeo ut me gratum beneficiis tuis approbent, aut reponant gratiam, quod auxiliarium te, quodque confiliarium habuerunt, quam ut aufpicato procedant, & ut in iis tui memoria frequentetur, ex quo liber auctoritatem capiens magni celebritate nominis commendetur. *Pol. in præf. ad Mifcell.*

(c) To Merula we are indebted for the firft edition of the comedies his proficiency in learning, nor his intercourfe with the great, nor even his advanced age, had foftened or improved a difpofition naturally jealous and auftere. He had however fingled out Politiano as the only perfon among the fcholars of Italy who, in his opinion, poffeffed any fhare of merit, and upon an interview which they had together at Milan, had acknowledged, that the reftoration of the language of the ancient Romans depended upon his exertions (a). No fooner, however, did

of Plautus, printed at Venice, *per Johannem de Colonia & Vinde-linum de Spira*, 1472. He alfo corrected and commented on the works of Juvenal, of Martial, of Quintilian, of Aufonius, the *Scriptores de re ruftica*, and other ancient authors; feveral of which have been publifhed with his remarks. Merula was the difciple of Filelfo, and like him was frequently engaged in thofe acrimonious contefts which perhaps promoted, whilft they difgraced, the caufe of literature. One of thefe debates was with Galeotto Marzio, who, about the year 1468, wrote his treatife *De homine*, in the firft book of which he defcribes the exterior, and in the fecond, the interior parts of man. This work Merula attacked with great bitternefs, and with a confiderable difplay of critical fagacity. The commentary of Merula was printed without date or place, and infcribed to Lorenzo and Giuliano de' Medici; but as the author in his dedication refers to the eftablifhment of the academy at Pifa as a recent tranfaction, it was probably publifhed about the year 1472. From this edition I fhall give the dedication, as a ftriking memorial of the early reputation which thefe illuftrious brothers had acquired as patrons of learning (v. *App. No.* LIII.). In the copy before me, the critique on Galeotto is followed by a comment on an epiftle of Sappho, infcribed to M. Ant. Maurocenus, and by fome obfervations on Virgil, addreffed to Lodovico Gonzago, prince of Mantua. Some account of the life and labors of Merula may be found in *Tirab. storia della Lett. Ital. v.* vi. *part.* 1. *p.* 291. *Zeno. Diff. Voff. vol.* ii. *p.* 83.

(a) Meminifti credo, quod in frequenti auditorio Venetiis, cum

the *Mifcellanea* of Politiano make their appearance,
than Merula availed himfelf of an opportunity
of demonftrating his own fuperiority by depreci-
ating the labour of his rival ; afferting that fuch
of the remarks of Politiano as were entitled to
commendation, might be found in the critical
works which he had himfelf previoufly publifhed,
or were in the memory of his pupils who had at-
tended his public inftru* lions (a). He even infi-
nuated that he had collected no inconfiderable
number of grofs errors, which he might probably
make public on fome future occafion. Politiano
was foon apprized of this injurious treatment ; and
as he was not flow at refenting an indignity, it
it is probable that Merula would have experienced
the weight of his refentment, had no other confidera-
tions interpofed. Merula ftood high in the opinion
of his patron, whilft Politiano was known to live on
terms of the clofeft intimacy with Lorenzo de' Medici.
An open attack might therefore have compromifed
the name of Lorenzo, whofe connexions with
Lodovicó were of too much importance to be
endangered in a literary conteft. Thus circumftan-
ced, Politiano adopted a more difcrete and ferious
method of bringing on a difcuffion. He addreffed
a letter to the duke, entreating that he would
exert his authority with Merula, to induce him
to publifh his criticifms; at the fame time tranf-
mitting for his perufal a letter to Merula of fimilar

nd me acceffiffes, palam dixerim, te illum effe, quem prifcæ &
Romanæ doctrinæ inftauratorem mihi pollicerer.

Mer. Ep. int. Ep. Pol. lib. xi. *Ep.* 5.

(*a*) *Ibid.*

import (*a*). Merula however refufed either to retract
the opinions which he had avowed, or to com-
municate to Politiano his remarks. In anfwer to
a farcafm, which Politiano might well have fpared,
he replies, " You reproach me with my grey
" locks—I feel not their effects. I yet poffefs vigor
" of mind and ftrength of body ; celerity of thought
" and tenacity of memory ; of thefe let Politiano
" beware (*b*)." Several letters on this fubject appear
in the epiftles of Politiano, and the conteft was
rifing to an extreme of violence, when Merula
fuddenly died. This event gave Politiano real
concern, not only on account of the lofs of a
man, of whofe talents he entertained a high opinion,
but as tending to deprive him ftill more effectually
of the opportunity of defending his work (*c*).
Anxious however that nothing might be omitted
which was neceffary to the vindication of his
character, he again addreffed himfelf to the duke,
with earneft entreaties to tranfmit to him the
criticifms of Merula; but to no purpofe. This
formidable compofition, if indeed it ever exifted,
was reduced to a few loofe and unimportant ob-
fervations. The letters of Lodovico, which are
remarkable for their kindnefs and attention to Poli-
tiano, feem however at length to have fatisfied his
reftlefs apprehenfions. " You can have no reafon,
" Angelo," fays the duke, " to fear any injury to
" your reputation from the fuppreffion of the

(*a*) *Pol. Epift. lib.* xi. *Ep.* 1, 2.

(*b*) *Merulæ Ep. inter Ep. Pol. lib.* xi. *Ep.* 5.

(*c*) *Pol. Epift. lib.* xi. *Ep.* 11.

" remarks of Merula, as this cannot be attributed
" to you, who, fo far from wifhing to conceal
" them, have ufed your utmoft endeavours with
" us to lay them before the public; of which
" the prefent letter may ferve as a teftimony (*a*)."

The inftitution of public feminaries for promoting the knowledge of the ancient languages, the refpect paid to thofe who undertook the tafk of inftruction, and the ample compenfation they derived, not only from the liberality of individuals, but from the public at large, powerfully co-operated with the caufes before mentioned in infufing a juft tafte for claffical literature. Of the eftablifhment of the academy at Pifa, by the exertions of Lorenzo de' Medici, a brief account has before been given (*b*); but his attention to the caufe of learning was by no means confined to this inftitution. The ftudies at Pifa were chiefly reftricted to the Latin language, or to thofe fciences of which it was the principal vehicle; but it was at Florence only that the Greek tongue was inculcated under the fanction of a public inftitution, either by native Greeks, or learned Italians who were their powerful competitors, whofe fervices were procured by the diligence of Lorenzo de' Medici, and repaid by his bounty (*c*).

(*a*) *Pol. Epift. lib.* xi. *Ep.* 21.

(*b*) *Vol.* 1. *p.* 156.

(*c*) Ille animadvertens jam tum litteras circa exitum laborare, Piis Scholas litterarum Latinarum, Florentiæ Græcarum inftituit; viros doctiffimos aere fuo ac magno undecumque accerfiit, ftudiofos & fovit, & juvit, nec prius in hoc elaborare deftitit, quam ita reftitueret, ut non facile iterum ad id precipitium pervenire poffent.

Caii Silvani Germanici Ep. ad Leonem X. *v. Band. Cat.* v. ii. *p.* 117.

Hence

Hence fucceeding fcholars have been profufe of their acknowledgments to their great patron, who firft formed that eftablifhment, from which (to ufe their own fcholaftic figure) as from the Trojan horfe, fo many illuftrious champions have fprung, and by means of which the knowledge of the Greek tongue was extended, not only through all Italy, but through France, Spain, Germany, and England, from all which countries numerous pupils attended at Florence, who diffufed the learning they had there acquired throughout the reft of Europe (a).

Of this inftitution the firft public profeffor was the eminent Johannes Argyropylus, who, after having enjoyed for feveral years the favor and protection of Cofmo and Piero de' Medici, and having had a principal fhare in the education of Lorenzo, was felected by him as the perfon beft qualified to give inftructions on the Greek tongue. Of the difciples of Argyropylus, Politiano, if not the moft diligent, was the moft fuccefsful. With the precepts which he imbibed, he acquired a predilection for the fource from whence they

Florentiam quoque & Latinis & Græcis litteris clariffime infignivit, exquifitis atque ingentibus etiam præmiis allectis utriufque facultatis viris omnium judicio peritiffimis.

> *Raph. Brandolini Ep. ad Leonem X. v. Band. v. ii. p. 371, Plut. xlvi. Cod. 2.*

(a) Quo fane tempore Florentiæ, veluti in celeberrimo totius orbis theatro, cruditiffimi viri, tanquam ex equo Trojano innumerabiles proceres, fefe in orbem terrarum effuderunt. Quamobrem non modo Italia, fed etiam Gallia, Hifpania, Germania, & Britannia hujufmodi beneficium Medicum familiæ acceptum referunt.

> *Petri Angelii Epift. ap. Band. Cat. ii. 397.*

flowed; and his writings difcover numerous in-flances of his affection and veneration for the man who firft opened to him the treafures of Grecian literature. To the unlimited applaufe beftowed by the fcholar on the mafter, one exception only occurs. Argyropylus had profeffed an open hoftility to the reputation of Cicero, whom he reprefented as a fciolift in the Greek tongue, and as unacquainted with the tenets of the different fects of philofophy, to which fo many of his writings relate. The acutenefs of Argyropylus, and the influence of his authority, degraded in the eftimation of his pupils the character of the Roman orator; and Politiano, in his riper years, feems to fhudder at the recollection of the time when the ignorance of Tully was a matter taken for granted by him and his fellow-ftudents (a). During the long refidence of Argyropylus in Italy he had acquired an extenfive knowledge of the Latin language—a fpecies of praife to which few of his countrymen are entitled. His tranflations into Latin of various tracts of Ariftotle, are, for the moft part, infcribed to his fucceffive patrons of the family of the Medici, in language expreffive of his refpect and gratitude (b). Among his auditors

(a) Et ut homo erat omnium (ut tum quidem videbatur) acerri-nius in difputando, atque aurem (quod ait Perfius) mordaci lotus aceto. praeterea verborum quoque noftrorum funditator maximus, facile id vel nobis vel ceteris, tum quidem fuis fectatoribus perfuaferat: ita ut, (quod pene dictu quoque nefas) pro conceffo inter nos habe-retur, nec philofophiam fciffe M. Tullium, nec litteras Graecas.

Pol. in Mifcel. cap. 1.

(b) *Band. Cat. Bibl. Laur. v.* iii. *p.* 3, 4. 234. 242. 359, &c.

we find Donato Acciajuoli, Janus Pannonius, and the German prelate Johannes Reuchlinus, who having had the fingular good fortune to obtain fome previous knowledge of the Greek tongue, difplayed, it is faid, on his firft interview with Argyropylus, fuch an acquaintance with it, as induced the Greek to exclaim with a figh, " *Alas,* " *Greece is already banifhed beyond the Alps* (a)."

To the induftry of Argyropylus, and the excellence of his precepts, his difciple Acciajuoli has borne ample teftimony; affirming, that whilft he inculcated his doctrines, the times of the ancient philofophers feemed to be again renewed (b). If however we may give credit to the teftimony of Paulus Jovius, the precepts and the practice of Argyropylus were not entirely confiftent with each other; and the obefity of his figure, which was fupported by an immoderate fupply of food and wine, feemed to mark him out as belonging to a different fect of philofophers (c). But the bifhop of Nocera had too many paffions to gratify, to permit him to perform the part of a faithful his-

(a) *Hodius de Græc. illuft. p.* 201.

(b) Cum poft interitum quorundam doctiffimorum hominum, ftudia Florentina magna ex parte remiffa viderentur, venit in hanc urbem Argyropylus Byzantius, vir ingenio præftans fummufque philofophus, ut juventutem litteris græcis ac bonis artibus erudiret: jamque plures annos doctrinam tradidit nobis tanta copia, tam multiplicibus variifque fermonibus, ut vifus fit temporibus noftris veterum philofophorum memoriam renovare. *Acciaiol. ap. Hod. de Græcis,* 202.

(c) Vini & cibi æque avidus & capax, & multo abdomine ventricofus, immodico melopeponum efu autumnalem accerfivit febrem, atque ita feptuagefimo ætatis anno ereptus eft. *Jovii Elog.* xxvii.

torian, and there are few of his characters that are not discolored or distorted by the medium through which they are seen. The same authors attributes the death of Argyropylus to the intemperate use of melons, which brought on an autumnal fever, that put a period to his life in the seventieth year of his age. This event took place at Rome, where he had fixed his residence some time previous to the year 1471 (*a*).

After an interval of a few years, during which there is reason to believe that the office of public Greek professor at Florence was filled by Theodorus Gaza, and not by Politiano, as asserted by Jovius, the loss of Argyropylus was supplied by Demetrius Chalcondyles, who was invited by Lorenzo de' Medici to take upon himself that employment about the year 1479 (*b*). It is generally understood that an enmity subsisted between Politiano and Chalcondyles, in consequence of which the latter

(*a*) *Hodius de Græc. illust. p.* 198. where the author has given a translation of the Greek epigram of Politiano, expressing his earnest wishes for the return of Argyropylus to Florence.

(*b*) Demetrius Chalcondyles, diligens grammaticus, & supra græcorum mores, cum nihil in eo fallaciarum aut fuci notaretur, vir utique lenis & probus, scholam Florentiæ instauravit, desertam ab Argyropylo, & a Politiano, deficientibus græcis occupatam. *Jov. Elog.* xxix. This information, if not refuted, is rendered highly problematical by the Greek epigram written by Politiano to Chalcondyles, on his arrival at Florence, in which he considers him as the successor of Gaza, and as supplying the maternal office of nourishing the unfledged offspring of literature, deserted by their former parent. A mode of expression not likely to be used by Politiano to a man who was to supersede him in his office of public instructor. A translation of this epigram is given by Hody, *p.* 211.

was eventually under the neceffity of quitting Florence, whence he retired to Milan; but for this opinion the only authority is that of Jovius, and of thofe who have implicitly confided in his relation (*a*). This author, always hoftile to the character of Politiano, would induce us to believe, that the Italian fcholar, actuated by his jealoufy of the Greek, and availing himfelf of his fuperior wit and eloquence, endeavoured to injure Chalcondyles by drawing off his pupils, and engaging them in his own auditory; and that Lorenzo de' Medici, as well in order to remove the caufes of their contention, as to avail himfelf of their mutual emulation, divided between them the tafk of educating his children. It may however be obferved that no traces of this diffenfion are to be found in the narrative of any contemporary author; and that although the known irafcibility of Politiano, and his acknowledged animofity to the Greeks, may feem to ftrengthen the credit of Jovius, yet thefe circumftances become, on further confideration, the moft decifive evidence of his want of authenticity. The antipathies of Politiano were never concealed; and his letters, which extend nearly to the time of his death, contain many inftances of that vehemence with which he attacked all thofe who he conceived had given him juft caufe

(*a*) Boiffard, Baillet, Varillas, &c. The diffenfions between Politiano and Chalcondyles have alfo engaged much of the attention of Menckenius, *Ann. Pol. vita, p.* 65. and of Bayle, *Dict. Hift. Art. Politien,* who have doubted of the veracity of the narrative of Jovius, without adducing that evidence of its improbability which a more minute examination would have fupplied.

of offence; but of any diffenfions with Chalcondyles no memorial is to be found. On the contrary, Chalcondyles is frequently noticed, both by the Italian fcholar and his correfpondents, as living with him in habits of intimacy (a). The reft of the information derived from Jovius is equally futile. The uninterrupted affection that fubfifted between Lorenzo and Politiano, would have prevented the former from adopting a meafure which the latter could only have confidered as an impeachment of his talents; but independent of inferences drawn from this fource, we have pofitive evidence, that however the children of Lorenzo might attend the incidental inftructions of others, Politiano had the conftant fuperintendence of their education, and was addreffed on all occafions as the fole perfon honored with that important truft (b).

From the Florentine inftitution, it is not difficult to difcover the progrefs of Grecian literature to the reft of Europe; but the traces of the channels by which it was conveyed are in no inftance more confpicuous than in thofe which communicated

(a) In the year 1491, being only the year previous to the death of Lorenzo de' Medici, Pomponius Lætus writes to Politiano, " Com- " menda me Medicibus patri & liberis litterarum patronis. Deinde " plurima falute Demetrium impertias." To which Politiano replies, " Medices noftri unice tibi favent. Demetrius autem falutem fibi à " te dictam totidem veri is remuneratur. In Fefulano fexto idus Augufti, mccccxci." *Pol. Ep. lib. i. Ep. 17, 18.*

(b) Thus Iod. Oduxius ad Pol. " Demetrium vero virum erudi- " uffimum, Petramque in primis *difcipulum tuum*, elegantiffimæ atque " ampliffimæ fpei adolefcentem, nomine meo falvos facito."

Pol. Ep. lib. iii. Ep. 3.

with this conntry. William Grocin (*a*), who was
for fome years profeffor of Greek literature in the
univerfity of Oxford, had made a journey to Italy
and had refided for the fpace of two years at Flo-
rence, where he attended the inftrudions of Chal-
condyles and of Politiano. Thomas Linacer (*b*),
whofe name defervedly holds the firft rank among
the early Englifh fcholars, availed himfelf of a
fimilar opportunity; and, during his abode at
Florence, was fo eminently diftinguifhed by the
elegance of his manners and his fingular modefty,
that he is faid to have been felected by Lorenzo
de' Medici as the affociate of his children in their
ftudies (*c*).

Such were the caufes that in the fifteenth century
concurred to promote the ftudy of the ancient
languages in Italy; but one circumftance yet remains
to be noticed, which was perhaps more efficacious
than any other in giving life and energy to thefe
purfuits. An acquaintance with the learned lan-
guages was, at this period, the moft direct path, not
only to riches and literary fame, but to political
eminence; and the moft accomplifhed fcholars
were, in almoft every government of Italy, the firft

(*a*) Nam & Grocinum memini, virum ut fcis multifaria doctrina
magno quoque & exercitato ingenio, his ipfis litteris duos continuos
annos, etiam poft prima illa rudimenta, folidam operam dediffe; idque
fub fummis doctoribus Demetrio Chalcondyla & Angelo Politiano.

    Guil. Latimer. in Ep. ad Erafm. ap. Mench. in vitâ Polit.

(*b*) Linacrum item acri ingenio virum, totidem aut etiam plures
annos fub iifdem præceptoribus impendiffe. *Ibid.*

(*c*) *Jovii Elog.* lxiii.

minifters of the time. This arofe in a great degree
from the very general ufe of the Latin tongue, in
the negotiations of different ftates, which rendered
it almoft impoffible for any perfon to undertake
the management of public affairs, without an hab-
itual acquaintance with that language ; but this
was more particularly exemplified in Florence,
where the moft permanent officers were uniformly
felected on account of their learning. During a
long courfe of years the place of fecretary, or
chancellor of the republic, (for thefe terms feem
to have been indifcriminately ufed,) was filled
by fcholars of the firft diftinction. In the beginning
of the fifteenth century, it was held by Coluccio
Salutati, who had been the intimate friend of
Petrarca and of Boccaccio, and is denominated by
Poggio, " *The common father and inftructor of all*
" *the learned* (a)." He was fucceeded by Leonardo
Aretino, whofe fervices to the republic were re-
paid by many privileges and favors conferred on
himfelf and his defcendants (b). After the death
of Leonardo, this office was given to Carlo Mar-
fuppini (c), and was afterwards fucceffively held
by Poggio Bracciolini (d), and Benedetto Accolti (e).
During a great part of the time that the affairs of
Florence were directed by Lorenzo de' Medici,
the chancellor of the Republic was Bartolomeo

(a) *v. ante, p.* 59. Salutati died about the year 1410.
(b) *v. ante, v.* I. *p.* 22.
(c) *Ibid.*
(d) *Ibid. p.* 26.
(e) *Ibid. p.* 93.

Scala, whofe life affords the beft example of the honors and emoluments which were derived from the cultivation of literature. Scala deduced his origin from parents of the loweft rank, nor did he poffefs from his birth even the privileges of a Florentine citizen (*a*). An early proficiency in letters recommended him to the notice of Cofmo de' Medici; and it was the pride of Scala to avow the meannefs of his birth, and the obligations which he owed to his earlieft patron (*b*). The lofs of Cofmo was amply compenfated to Scala by the favor of his defcendants, through whofe affiftance he gradually rofe to honors and to affluence, and in the year 1472 was intrufted with the feal of the republic. In imitation of his predeceffors in this office, Scala began a hiftory of Florence, of which he lived to complete only four books(*c*). His apologues are highly commended by

(*a*) E lo Scala, figliuol d'un mulinaro,
  Ovver d'un teffitor di panni lini,
  Che colle fue virtù fi fece chiaro,
  E fu Gonfalonier de' Fiorentini,
  Cavalier a Spron d'oro, e non avaro,
  Tanto è, voi m'intendete cittadini,
  Non s'ha quefti a chiamar nobile e degno,
  Che acquiftò roba, onor, virtute, e ingegno?
   L'Altiffimo, in Bart. Scalæ vita a Mannio. Flor. 1768.

(*b*) Veni nudus omnium rerum bonarum, egenus ad Remp. viliffimis ortus parentibus, multa cum fide, nullis omnino divitiis, aut titulis, nullis clientelis, nullis cognationibus. Cofmus tamen Pater patriæ noftræ me complexus eft, recepitque in familiæ obfequia, &c.
   Scalæ Ep. inter. Pol. Ep. lib. xii. *Ep.* 16.

(*c*) Hos edere Joannes Cinellius paraverat, fed id contigit Oligero Jacobæi, ope Cl. Magliabechii, fumptibus Nicolai Angeli Tinaffi, anno MDCLXXVII. *Manni, vita Bart. Scalæ, p.* 47.

Landino and Ficino. Of his poetry, fpecimens remain both in the Latin and Italian languages, and the former have obtained a place in the celebrated collection of the Latin poems of his illuftrious countrymen (a). Confidering the proverbial uncertainty of public favor, the life of Scala may be efteemed a life of unufual profperity. He tranfacted the concerns of the republic with acknowledged fidelity, induftry, and ability; arrived at the higheft dignities of the ftate; amaffed wealth; ranked with men of learning; and left at his death a numerous progeny to inherit his riches and his refpectability. In his controverfy with Politiano, he appears however as a fcholar to manifeft difadvantage; but the impetuofity of his adverfary hurried him into a conteft which it is evident he would willingly have avoided, and in which every effort to extricate himfelf only brought down a feverer chaftifement.

From the epiftles of Politiano it appears, that for fome time thefe angry difputants had fhared the favor of Lorenzo de' Medici without difcovering any fymptoms of jealoufy; and had even been in the habit of fubmitting to each other their literary works for mutual correction. Scala, however, having difcovered, or fufpected, that Lorenzo had employed Politiano to revife the letters which he had written in the execution of his office, as chancellor of the republic, began to entertain a fecret enmity againft his rival, and omitted no

(a) *Carm. illuft. Poet. Ital. v, viii. p. 489.*

opportunity of depreciating his writings (*a*). Politiano was no fooner aware that his literary reputation was attacked, than he gave a loofe to feelings which it is probable he had before with difficulty fuppreffed ; and notwithftanding the rank and refpectability of Scala, addreffed him in a ftyle that fhows the high opinion which he entertained of his own talents, and his contempt of thofe of his adverfary. Alluding in one of his letters to the parentage of Scala, he gives him the appellation of *monftrum furfuraceum.* In another, he honors him with a comment on this title (*b*). To the boafting of Scala, refpecting the approbation expreffed of him by Lorenzo, he returns an anfwer which in thefe days (whether more polifhed or more barbarous, the reader may determine) could only have been expiated in the blood of one of the difputants (*c*). In this tranfaction it muft be allowed that Politiano fuffered himfelf to be carried beyond all reafonable bounds, and forgot that refpect which he owed, if not to the character of his opponent, at leaft to his own dignity and

(*a*) Scis autem tu quoque litteras illum (Laurentium) fæpe tuas publice fcriptas rejeciffe, nobifque dediffe formandas, quæ prima odii livorifque in me tui caufa extitit. *Pol. Ep. lib.* xii. *Ep.* 1S.

(*b*) At ego *monftrum* te vocavi *furfuraceum;* monftrum quidem, quod ex colluvione monftrorum compofitus eft, furfuraceum vero quod in piftrini fordibus natus, & quidem piftrino digniffimus. *Ibid.*

(*c*) " Extat," thus Scala writes to Politiano, " & illa de me " Laurentii Medicis præclariffima vox, qua nufquam collocata melius " fuit honorem homini novo ædificatus eft." *Lib.* xii. *Ep.* 16. To which Politiano laconically replies, " De Cofmo quæ jactas, deque " Laurentio Medice, *faifa omnia.*" *Ibid. Ep.* 18.

reputation. It may perhaps be thought that Lorenzo de' Medici ought to have interpofed his authority to fupprefs a conteſt which contributed fo little to the credit of the parties, but it was not till after the death of Lorenzo that the difpute became fo outrageous. It muſt be obſerved that Menckenius, the hiſtorian of Politiano, has on this occaſion attributed to the expreſlions of Scala, an import which it is certain they were not intended to convey (*a*).

If the circumſtances before related were not

(*a*) In the early part of the quarrel, Scala has the following paſſage, in a letter to Politiano: " Tu certe præter ceteros, mi Politiane, " naturæ multum debes, illa tibi ingenium iſtud dedit: ut corporis " modo prætermittam dotes, quæ nonnihil & ipſæ habere a quibufdam " putantur momenti ad felicitatem & fortunæ commoda: quæ profecto " juvare nativam virtutem, niſi ipfa fefe deferat, vehementer folent. " Cæcus fit funditus qui hæc non viderit." " Si quid video (fay Menckenius) " funt & hæc per ludibrium forfan & per invidiam a " Scala dicta, ut obfcœnos Politiani mores perſtringeret, quaſi is " nempe corporis fui copiam principi juventuti fecerit, femper ita " amantes ſtudiofofque fui Medicæos habiturus. Ut adeo mirari vix " fatis poſſim, non fenfiffe hos aculeos nec his quidquam repofuiſſe " Politianum, &c." In fuppoſing he could fee fo much clearer into the concerns of Politiano than Politiano himſelf, Menckenius is miſtaken; it certainly never came into the head of either of the difputants, that this paſſage contained any infinuation of the nature alluded to by Menckenius. Giuliano de' Medici had been dead many years, nor had he in his lifetime given room for fuch an imputation; and at all events there is no probability that Scala would have hazarded the moſt remote infinuation of this kind, againſt a family on whofe favor he exiſted, to fay nothing of the inattention with which Politiano treats this paſſage, which he certainly conſidered only as a piece of ridicule on his *wry neck* and *hooked nofe*, and as fuch thought it below his attention.

fufficiently characteriftic of the fpirit of the times we might advert to the other governments of Italy ; where we fhould find, that offices of the higheft truft and confidence were often filled by men who quitted the fuperintendence of an academy, or the chair of a profeffor, to tranfact the affairs of a nation. Alfonfo, king of Naples, and Francefco Sforza, contended in liberality with each other, to fecure the fervice of Beccatelli (*a*). Pontano was the confidential advifer, and frequently the reprefentative to other powers, of Ferdinand, the fon of Alfonfo (*b*). The brothers of the family

(*a*) *Zeno, Diff. Voff. v.* i. *p.* 309. *& vide ante, v.* I. *p.* 53.

(*b*) Giovanni Pontano, or according to the academical appellation which he adopted, Jovianus Pontanus, was a native of Cerreto, in Umbria, but when young and friendlefs took up his refidence at Naples. His learning recommended him to Alfonfo, and afterwards to Ferdinando ; by whom he was intrufted with the higheft offices of the ftate. Befides his undertaking many important embaffies, Pontano was chief fecretary to the king, and on one occafion his reprefentative as viceroy of Naples. As a fcholar he was the only perfon of the age whofe productions can contend for fuperiority with thofe of Politiano. His poems were published by Aldus in two volumes, 1513. 1518. His profe works in three volumes, 1518, 1519. Among the latter, is a treatife *De ingratitudine*, in which he affumes the merit of having been inftrumental in concluding peace between Ferdinand and the pope, and gives a loofe to his exultation in having rendered his king fo important a fervice ; but alas, Pontano lived to give the fulleft comment on his treatife in his own conduct. For although he enjoyed the favor of the family of Arragon for nearly half a century, yet when Charles VIII. of France, in the year 1495, feized upon the kingdom of Naples, and affumed the emblems of royalty, Pontano, in the name of the Neapolitans, made the public oration to him, and took care not to forget the defects of his royal patrons, with which he had the beft opportunities of being acquainted. *Zeno, Diff. Voff.*

of Simoneta directed for a confiderable time the affairs of Milan (a). Bernardo Bembo, and Francefco Barbaro, maintained the literary, no lefs than the political dignity of the Venetian Republic, and left each of them a fon who eclipfed the reputation of his father (b). When eminent talents were not engaged in public fervices, they were rewarded by the moft flattering attention, and often by the pecuniary bounty of illuftrious individuals, who relaxed from the faftidioufnefs of rank, in the company of men of learning, or have left memorials of their regard by their epiftolary correfpondence.

Nor was it feldom that the characters of the fcholar, and of the man of rank, were united in the fame perfon. Of this Giovanni Pico of Mirandula, to whom we have before frequently adverted, is perhaps the moft illuftrious inftance. This accomplifhed nobleman, of whom many extriordinary circumftances are related, and who certainly exhibited a wonderful example of the powers of the human mind, was born at Mirandula in the year 1463, and was one of the younger children of Giovan-Francefco Pico, prince of Mirandula and Concordia (c). So quick was his

v. ii. p. 172. *Guicciard. Ift. d'Italia, lib.* ii. Pontano died in 1603. at the age of 77 years.

(a) *vide ante, v.* I. *p.* 178.

(b) Ermolao Barbaro, patriarch of Aquileia, and the cardinal Pietro Bembo, both of whom will again occur to our notice in the courfe of the work.

(c) Voltaire, who erroneoufly gives Pico the name of Jean-François, is alfo miftaken in relating that he refigned the fovereignty of Mirandula apprehenſion, ſo retentive his memory, that we are told a ſingle recital was ſufficient to fix in his mind whatever became the object of his attention. After having ſpent ſeven years in the moſt celebrated univerſities of Italy and France, he arrived at Rome in the twenty-firſt year of his age, with the reputation of being acquainted with twenty-two different languages (a). Eager to ſignalize himſelf as a diſputant, Pico propoſed for public debate nine hundred queſtions, on mathematical, theological, and ſcholaſtic ſubjects, including alſo inquiries into the moſt abſtruſe points of the Hebraic, Chaldaïc, and Arabic tongues (b). This

to reſide at Florence. *Eſſai, tom.* ii. *p.* 296. *Ed. Gen.* Pico neither enjoyed nor had any pretenſions to the ſovereignty, which, after the death of his father, devolved on his elder brother Galeotto, and afterwards on his nephew Giovan-Franceſco; by whom we have a voluminous life of his uncle, written in Latin, and prefixed to his works, which, whilſt it affords much information reſpecting this extraordinary man, diſplays a deplorable degree of ſuperſtition in the author. The mother of Pico was of the family of Boyardo the poet.

(a) " Cela," ſays Voltaire very juſtly, " n'eſt certainement pas " dans le cours ordinaire de la nature. Il n'y a point de langue qui " ne demande environ une année pour la bien ſavoir. Quiconque " dans une ſi grande jeuneſſe en ſait vingt deux, peut être ſoupçonné " de les ſavoir bien mal, ou plutôt il en ſait les elemens, ce qui eſt " ne rien ſavoir." *Eſſai, ut ſup.*

(b) Voltaire, not ſatisfied with theſe 900 queſtions, has increaſed their number to 1400; and informs us that they may be found at the head of the works of Pico. *Eſſai, ut ſup.* It is to be wiſhed that he had pointed out in what edition of the works of Pico he had diſcovered theſe queſtions; for the exiſtence of which he ſeems to have had the ſame authority as he had for ſuppoſing that the learning of thoſe days conſiſted merely in an acquaintance with the ſophiſms of the ſchoolmen, or that the ſciences were then held in contempt by meafure, which in its worſt light could only be confidered as an ebullition of youthful vanity, might, without any great injuſtice, have been fuffered to evaporate in neglect ; but the Romiſh prelates, inſtead of configning thefe propofitions to their fate, or debating them with the impartiality of philofophers, began to examine them with the fufpicious eyes of churchmen, and felected thirteen of them as heretical. To vindicate himfelf from this dangerous imputation, Pico compofed a Latin treatife of confiderable extent, which he is faid to have written in the fpace of twenty days, and which he infcribed to Lorenzo de' Medici, under whofe protection he had ſheltered himfelf from perfecution at Florence (a). The character and acquirements of Pico afforded to his contemporaries a fubject for the moſt unbounded panegyric. " He was a man," fays Politiano, " or rather a hero, on whom nature had laviſhed " all the endowments both of body and mind; " erect and elegant in his perfon, there was fome- " thing in his appearance almoſt divine. Of a " perfpicacious mind, a wonderful memory, in- " defatigable in ſtudy, diſtinct and eloquent in

princes and men of eminence. Affertions unworthy of an author who profeffes to write *fur les mœurs & l'efprit de nations.*

(a) *Apologia tredecim quæſtionum.* This treatife was publiſhed with the other Latin works of Pico, at Venice, *per Bernardinum Venetum,* an. MCCCCLXXXXVIII. in folio, from which edition I ſhall give the dedication of the *Apologia,* as it is ſtrongly expreffive of the eſteem and admiration of its author, for Lorenzo de' Medici.

v. App. No. LIV.

" ſpeech,

" fpeech, it feems doubtful whether he was more
" confpicuous for his talents or his virtues. In-
" timately converfant with every department of
" philofophy, improved and invigorated by the
" knowledge of various languages, and of every
" honorable fcience, it may truly be faid, that
" no commendation is equal to his praife."

The inftances before given of the critical talents of Pico, whatever may be thought of their accuracy, will at leaft juftify him from the reproof of Voltaire, who is of opinion that the works of Dante and Petrarca would have been a more fuitable ftudy for him, than the fummary of St. Thomas, or the compilations of Albert the great (a). But the literary purfuits of Pico were not confined to commentaries upon the works of others. From the fpecimens which remain of his poetical compofitions in his native language, there is reafon to form a favorable judgment of thofe which have perifhed. Crefcimbeni confeffes, that by his early death the Tufcan poetry fuftained a heavy lofs, and that his accomplifhed pen might have refcued it from its degraded ftate, without the intervention of fo many other eminent men, whofe labors had been employed to the fame purpofe (b). The few pieces which remain of his Latin poetry induce us to regret the feverity of their author. Thefe poems he had arranged in five books, which he fubmitted to the correction of Politiano, who, having performed his tafk, returned them to their author, with an elegant apology for

(a) Volt. Effai, tom. ii. p. 296.
(b) Crefcimb. Ift. della volgar poesia, v. ii. p. 336.

the freedoms which he had taken (*a*). Soon after-
wards Pico committed his five books to the flames,
to the great regret of Politiano, who has perpetuated
this incident by a Greek epigram (*b*). If the works
thus deftroyed were equal in merit to his Latin
elegy addreffed to Girolamo Benivieni, pofterity
have reafon to lament the lofs (*c*).

Among the circumftances favorable to the pro-
motion of letters in the fifteenth century, another
yet remains to be noticed, which it would be
unpardonable to omit; and which, if it did
not greatly contribute towards their progrefs,
certainly tended, not only to render the ftudy of
languages more general, but to remove the idea
that the acquifition of them was attended with
any extraordinary difficulty. This was the partiality
fhown to thefe ftudies, and the proficiency made
in them, by women, illuftrious by their birth, or
eminent for their perfonal accomplifhments. Among
thefe, Aleffandra, the daughter of Bartolomeo Scala
was peculiarly diftinguifhed. The extraordinary
beauty of her perfon was furpaffed by the en-
dowments of her mind. At an early age fhe was
a proficient, not only in the Latin, but the Greek
tongue (*d*), which fhe had ftudied under Joannes

(*a*) Neque ego judicis (ita me femper ames) fed Momi perfonam
indui, quem ferunt fandalium Veneris tandem culpaffe, cum Venerem
non poffet. Confodi igitur verficulos aliquos, non quod eos impro-
barem, fed quod tanquam equeftris ordinis, cedere reliquis, veluti
fenatoribus videbantur atque patriciis. *Pol. Ep. lib.* i. *Ep.* 4.

(*b*) *Ibid. lib.* i. *Ep.* 7.

(*c*) Opere di Benivieni, *p.* 75. *Ed. Ven.* 1524.

(*d*) Some of the Greek poems of Aleffandra appear in the works

Lafcar and Demetrius Chalcondyles. Such an union of excellence attracted the attention, and is fuppofed to have engaged the affections of Politiano; but Aleffandra gave her hand to the Greek Marullus, who enjoyed at Florence the favor of Lorenzo de' Medici, and in the elegance of his Latin compofitions, emulated the Italians themfelves (a). Hence probably arofe thofe diffen-

of Politiano. *Ed. Ald.* 1498. And Politiano is fuppofed to have addreffed to this Lady feveral of his amorous verfes.

(a) The works of Marullus were published at Florence, under the title of HYMNI ET EPIGRAMMATA. At the clofe we read, *Impreffit Florentiæ Societas Colubris* v. *kal. Decembris*, MCCCCLXXXXVII. His epigrams are infcribed to Lorenzo, the fon of Pier-Francefco de' Medici. The following lines to the father of his miftrefs poffefs no inconfiderable share of elegance:

AD BARTHOLOMEUM SCALAM.

Cum mufæ tibi debeant latinæ
Tot juncto pede fcripta, tot foluto
Tot fales latio lepore tinctos,
Tot cultis documenta fub figuris,
Tot volumina patriæ dicata,
Quæ nulli taceant diu minores,
Tot prætoria jura, tot curules,
Tot fafces proprio labore partos:
Pius multo tamen, o beate amice eft
Quod Scalam Latio pater dedifti.
Aucturam numerum novem fororum,
Cafto carmine caftiore vita.

The three books of Hymns of Marullus are addreffed, not to the objects of Chriftian worship, but to the Pagan deities, or the phœnomena of nature, whence, perhaps, the remark of Erafmus; " Marulli " pauca legi, tolerabilia, fi minus haberent paganitatis."

fions between Marullus and Politiano, the monuments of which yet remain in their writings (*a*).

Of yet greater celebrity is the name of Caffandra Fidelis. Defcended from anceftors who had changed their refidence from Milan to Venice, and had uniformly added to the refpectability of their rank by their uncommon learning, fhe began at an early age to profecute her ftudies with great diligence. and acquired fuch a knowledge of the learned languages, that fhe may with juftice be enumerated among the firft fcholars of the age (*b*). The letters which occafionally paffed between Caffandra and Politiano demonftrate their mutual efteem, if indeed fuch expreffion be fufficient to characterize the feelings of Politiano, who expreffes in language unufually florid, his high admiration of her extraordinary acquirements, and his expectation of the benefits which the caufe of letters would derive from her labors and example (*c*). In

(*a*) Among the epigrams of Politiano are feveral of the moft outrageous kind, againft fome perfon whom he attacks under the name of *Mabilius;* and in the poems of Marullus are fome pieces, little inferior in abufe, of which *Ecnomus* is the fubject. Under thefe masks it is fuppofed, and not without reafon, that thefe rival fcholars directed their fhafts at each other.

(*b*) The letters and orations of this lady were published at *Pavia* in 1636, by Jac. Ph. Tomafini, who has prefixed to them fome account of her life.

(*c*) " O decus Italiæ, virgo, quas dicere grates, quafve referre " parem, quod etiam honore me tuarum literarum non dedignaris? " mira profecto fides, tales proficifci à femina, quid autem à femina " dico, imò verò à puella & virgine potuiffe, &c." " Tibi verò tanta " incepta Deus optimus maximus fecundet: & cum recefferis à

the year 1491; the Florentine fcholar made a vifit
to Venice, where the favorable opinion which he
had formed of her writings was confirmed by a
perfonal interview. "Yefterday," fays he, writing
to his great patron, " I paid a vifit to the celebrat-
" ed Caffandra, to whom I prefented your refpects.
" She is indeed, Lorenzo, a furprifing woman, as
" well from her acquirements in her own lan-
" guage, as in the Latin; and in my opinion fhe
" may be called handfome. I left her, aftonifhed
" at her talents. She is much devoted to your
" interefts, and fpeaks of you with great efteem.
" She even avows her intention of vifiting you at
" Florence, fo that you may prepare yourfelf to
" give her a proper reception (a)." From a letter
of this lady, many years afterwards, to Leo X. we
learn, that an epiftolary correfpondence had fub-
fifted between her and Lorenzo de' Medici (b);
and it is with concern we perceive that the re-
membrance of this intercourfe is revived, in order
to induce the pontiff to beftow upon her fome
pecuniary affiftance; fhe being then a widow,
with a numerous train of dependants. She lived
however to a far more advanced period, and died
in the year 1558, having then completed a full

" parentibus, is autor contingat, & confors qui fit ifta virtute non
" indignus: ut quæ nunc propemodum fua fponte naturalis ingenii
" flamma femel emicuit, ita crebris deinceps aut audita flatibus, aut
" enutrita fomitibus effulgeat, ut a noftrorum hominum præcordiis
" animoque, nox omnis, geluque, penitus & languoris in litteris &
" infcitiæ difcutiatur." *Pol. Ep. int. Caff. Fid. Ep.* 101.

(a) *v. Pol. Ep. in App. No.* LI.
(b) *Caff. Fidelis. Ep.* 123.

century. Her literary acquirements, and the reputation of her early affociates, threw a luftre on her declining years; and as her memory remained unimpaired to the laft, fhe was reforted to from all parts of Italy, as a living monument of thofe happier days, which were never adverted to without regret (*a*).

That this attention to ferious ftudies, by which thefe celebrated women diftinguifhed themfelves, was the characteriftic of the fex in general, cannot perhaps be with truth afferted. The admiration beftowed on thofe who had fignalized themfelves, affords indeed a ftrong prefumption to the contrary. Yet the pretenfions of the fex to literary eminence were not confined to thefe inftances. The Italian hiftorians have noticed many other women of high rank who obtained by their learning no inconfiderable fhare of applaufe (*b*). Politiano celebrates as a tenth mufe a lady of Sienna, to whom he gives the name of Cecca (*c*); and from the numerous pieces in the learned languages, profeffedly addreffed to women, we may reafonably infer, that thefe ftudies were at that time more generally diffufed amongft them, than they have been at any fubfequent period.

Having thus adverted to fome of the principal caufes which accelerated the progrefs of claffical literature in the fifteenth century, and obferved

(*a*) *Tomafin. in vitâ Caffandræ, p. 42.*
(*b*) *Tirabofchi, Storia della Lett. Ital. vol.* vi. *parte* 2. *p.* 163.
   (*c*) Mnemofyne audito Senenfis carmine Ceccæ,
     Quando inquit decima eft nata puella nihi?

the active part which Lorenzo de' Medici took in every tranfaction that was favorable to its promotion, it may now be proper briefly to inquire what was the refult of exertions fo earneftly made and fo long continued ; and whether the tree, which had been tranfplanted with much difficulty, and nourifhed by fuch conftant attention, brought forth fruit fufficient to repay the labor that had been beftowed upon it.

One of the firft efforts of the Italian fcholars was the tranflation of the moft eminent Greek authors into Latin. Among the earlieft and moft affiduous of thefe tranflators is Leonardo Aretino, whofe verfions of various works of Plato, Xenophon, Plutarch, and other Greek authors, form a lift too extenfive to be recognifed in the prefent work (*a*). The labors of Ficino, though not fo numerous, are yet more voluminous. Some account of them is found in a Latin epiftle from their author to Politiano: " Why, my friend," fays Ficino, " have you fo often defired to know " what works I have publifhed? Is it that you " celebrate them in your verfes? But approbation " is not due to number fo much as to choice, " and merit is diftinguifhed by quality rather " than quantity (*b*)." If Ficino had adhered more

(*a*) A very full catalogue of the works of Leonardo is given by Laur. Mehus, and prefixed to his edition of the Letters of this celebrated fcholar. *Flor.* 1741. This catalogue comprifes no lefs than fixty-three different productions, many of which are tranflations from the Greek.

(*b*) *v. App. No.* LV. Of the works there mentioned, feveral have been publifhed, the early editions of which are yet held in efteem.

clofely to this maxim, it would certainly have di-
miniſhed nothing of his reputation. which is buried
under the immenfe mafs of his own labors. The
earlieſt produ&tion in this department of letters,
which united elegance with fidelity, is the tranf-
lation of the hiſtory of Herodian, by Politiano (*a*).
This work he infcribed to Innocent VIII. in a
manly and judicious addrefs, in which he briefly
ſtates the rules that he had prefcribed to himfelf
in the execution of his work, which are yet deferv-
ing of the notice of all who engage in fimilar
undertakings (*b*).

From his early years Politiano had clofely at-
tached himfelf to the ſtudy of the writings of
Homer; and whilſt he was very young, had begun

His tranflation of Plato was firſt printed at Florence without date, and
again at Venice, 1491. His verfion of Plotinus, printed by Mifcomini,
at the expenfe of Lorenzo de' Medici, though not publifhed till after
his death, is a fine fpecimen of typography; at the clofe we read,

*Magnifico Jumptu Laurentii Medicis patriæ fervatoris, impreſſit
ex archetypo Antonius Mifcominus Florentiæ Anno* MCCCCLXXXXII.
Nonis Maii.

(*a*) Printed three times in the year 1493, viz. at Rome, at Bologna
by *Plato de Benediclis*, and at the laſt-mentioned place by *Bazalerius
de Bazaleriis.* Of thefe editions the fecond is the moſt efteemed.

Maittaire, Ann. Typ. v. i. p. 558. *De Bure. Bibl. Inſt. No.* 4840.

(*b*) Quæ fane noſtræ fuerunt partes, tentavimus profe&to, utinamque
etiam effecerimus, uti omnia ex fide refpond rent, ne inepta peregri-
nitas, ne græculæ ufquam figuræ, nifi fi quæ jam pro receptis habentur,
latinam quafi polluerent caftitatem; ut eadem propemodum effet linguæ
utriufque perfpicuitas, eædemque munditiæ, idem utrobique fenfus
atque indoles, nulla vocum morofitas, nulla anxietas.

Pol. in præfat. Ed. Ald. 1498.

to tranflate the Iliad into Latin hexameter verfe (*a*).
Whoever is acquainted with the great extent of
his powers, and the peculiar energy of his Latin
compofitions, will regret that of this monument
of his induftry not a veftige remains. That he had
made a confiderable progrefs in this work, appears
from many authorities; and there is even reafon
to believe, that his perfeverance finally overcame
the difficulties of his undertaking. Ficino, writing
to Lorenzo de' Medici, and congratulating him on
the fuccefs of his attention to liberal ftudies, par-
ticularly adverts to the protection afforded by
him to Politiano, of whofe tranflation of the Grecian
bard he fpeaks in thofe terms of florid adulation
which too frequently characterize his letters (*b*).

(*a*) An epitome of the Iliad in Latin verfe, under the fictitious
name of Pindar the Theban, is amongft the MSS. of the Laurentian
Lib. *Plut.* xxxviii. *Cod.* xii. 2. and has alfo been published in the
Ed. of Homer by Spondanus Bafil, 1583. Another tranflation of the
Grecian bard is faid to have been executed in the fifteenth century,
by Niccolo Valla, who died at twenty-one years of age. *P. Cortef.
de Hom. doct. p.* 46. *Valerian. de Literat. Infel. lib.* ii. A tranfla-
tion of the Iliad into Latin profe, by Lorenzo Valla, was published
at Brefcia 1474, and Lorenzo was accufed of having availed himfelf
of a tranflation made a century before, by Leontius Pilatus, which
tranflation has alfo been infcribed to Petrarca. *Hod. de Grac. illuft. p.* 10.

(*b*) " Divites alii ferme omnes miniftros nutriunt voluptatum; Tu
" facerdotes mufarum nutris: perge precor mi Laurenti; nam illi
" voluptatum fervi evadent, tu vero mufarum delitiæ. Summus
" mufarum facerdos, Homerus, in Italiam, te duce, venit. Et qui
" hactenus circum vagus & mendicus fuit tandem apud te dulce
" hofpitium reperit. Nutris domi Homericum illum adolefcentem,
" Angelum Politianum, qui græcam Homeri perfonam latinis colori-
" bus exprimat. Exprimit jam, atque id quod mirum eft in tam

Another contemporary author has however plainly indicated that Politiano completed his important tafk. (a), to the progrefs of which he has occafionally adverted in his own works (b). Whether his youthful labors fell a facrifice to the feverity of his riper judgment, or perifhed in the general difperfion of the Medicean Library, of which he lived to be a witnefs, is a queftion which muft yet remain undecided.

The early part of the fifteenth century was diftinguifhed by a warm admiration of the writings of the ancients, and an extreme avidity to poffefs them. This was fucceeded, as might be expected, by an attention to the accuracy of

" tenere ætati, ita exprimit ut nifi quis græcum fuiffe Homerum
" noverit, dubitaturus fit, e duobus uter naturalis fit & uter pictus
" Homerus, &c." *Fic. Ep. lib.* i.

(a) Amongft the Latin poems of Aleffandro Braccio, the contemporary and friend of Politiano, and well known by his tranflation of the works of Appian, is the following epigram:

" AD LAURENTIUM MEDICEM.

" Tempora noftra tibi multum debentia Laurens,
" Non minus hoc debent, nobile propter opus,
" Maeonium, duce te quod nuper & aufpice, vatem,
" Convertit Latios Angelus in numeros,
" Cumque decore fuo cum majeftate legendum,
" Dat nobis qualem Græcia docta legit,
" Ut dubites *Latius* malit quam *Græcus Homerus*
" Effe, magis patrius hunc nifi vincat amor."

Band. Cat. Laur. lib. iii. 780.

(b) " Nam & ego is fum qui ab ineunte adolefcentia, ita hujus
" eminentiffimi poetæ ftudio ardoreque flagraverim, ut non modo
" cum totum legendo olfecerim, pœnequo contriverim, fed juvenili
" quodam, ac prope temerario aufu, vertere etiam in Latinum
" tentaverim." *Pol. Orat. in Exp. Homeri in op. Ald.* 1498.

the text, and an ardent defire of transfufing
their beauties into a language more generally
known. Towards the latter part of the century
a further progrefs was made; and from com-
menting, and tranflating, the Italians began to
emulate thefe remains of ancient genius. Thofe
who diftinguifhed themfelves during the time of
Cofmo, and Piero de' Medici, have already at-
tracted fome fhare of our notice; but it mufl in
general be acknowledged, that although their labors
exhibit at times a tolerable knowledge of the me-
chanical parts of learning, and have the body and
form of poetic compofition, yet the animating
fpirit that fhould communicate life and motion is
fought for in vain; or if it be any where difcover-
able, is only to be found in the licentious produc-
tions of Beccatelli (*a*). Of that kind of compofition
which may be called claffical, modern Italy had
feen no examples. The writings of Landino, of
which fpecimens have been already given, are
however entitled to fome fhare of approbation;
and if they be not marked by any powerful
efforts of imagination, nor remind us flrongly of
the ancient authors, they poffefs a flow of language,
and facility of diction and verfification, much
fuperior to his predeceffors. A further proficiency
was made by Naldo Naldio, or *Naldo de Naldis*, the
friend of Ficino and Politiano, and the frequent
panegyrifl of the Medici (*b*). The poem of Ugolino

(*a*) *v. ante, v.* I. *p.* 55.

(*b*) The poems of Naldio are printed in the *Selecta Poemata
Italorum, v.* vi. *p.* 412. of thefe the fifl is addreffed, *Ad Petrum*

Verini, " *De Illustratione Urbis Florentiæ*," is perhaps more estimable for the authenticity of the information it communicates, than for its poetical excellence, yet Verini has left other testimonies that entitle him to rank with the first Latin poets of his age (*a*). These pieces are principally devoted

Medicem in obitu magni Cosmi ejus genitoris, qui vere dum vixit optimus Parens cognominatus fuit. An extract from this piece in the Appendix, No. LVI. will sufficiently show, that Naldio was possessed of no inconsiderable talents for Latin poetry. Another of the poems of Naldio is addressed to Annalena, a nun, probably the sister-in-law of Bernardo Pulci (*v. ante, vol.* i. *p.* 250.), in which the poet laments the death of Albiera Albizzi, the wife of Sigismundo Stufa, on whose death Politiano has also left a beautiful Latin elegy. It is probable there were two successive authors of this name, whose works are inserted in the *Carmina illust.* It can scarcely be supposed that the same person who addressed himself to Piero on the death of his father in 1464, and had before written a poem to Cosmo on the death of his son John, should be the author of the pieces in this collection which are inscribed to Leo X. who did not enter on his pontificate till 1513. Politiano has left the following commendatory epigram on the writings of Naldio:

> Dum celebrat Medicem *Naldus*, dum laudat amicam,
> Et pariter gemino raptus amore canit,
> Tam lepidum unanimes illi ornavere libellum,
> Phœbus, Amor, Pallas, Gratia, Musa, Fides.

(*a*) The example of Landino in affixing to his poetical labors the name of his mistress (*v. ante, vol.* i. *p.* 91.) was followed by Verini, who gave the title of *Flametta* to his two books of Latin elegies, which he inscribed to Lorenzo de' Medici, and which yet remain in the Laurentian Library (*Plut.* xxxix. *cod.* 42.). Bandini supposes that Landino, as well as many other learned men of those times, had a real object of his passion, for which he gives a very satisfactory reason. " Neque hoc nomen fictum esse crediderim, quum revera " mihi compertum sit, illius ævi litteratos viros, *ut nunc quoque*

to the praifes of the Medici, and frequently advert
to the characters of Lorenzo and Giuliano, and to
the circumftances of the times (*a*).

In Michael Verini, the fon of Ugolino, we have
a furprifing inftance of early attainments in learning.
He was born in 1465 ; and although he died at the
age of feventeen years, yet in that fhort fpace of
time he had obtained the admiration, and con-
ciliated the efteem of his learned contemporaries.
His principal work is a collection of Latin *difticha*,
which exhibit great facility both of invention and
expreffion, and an acquaintance with human life
and manners far beyond his years. His Latin
letters, of which a large collection is preferved in
the Laurentian Library (*b*), and which are chiefly
addreffed to his father, are as honorable to the
paternal kindnefs of the one, as to the filial af-
fection of the other. His death is faid to have
been occafioned by his repugnance to obey the
prefcription of his phyficians, who recommended
an experiment which it feems his modefty did
not approve, and he fell a facrifice to his per-

" *accidit*, puellas in deliciis habuiffe plurimum, in earumque laudem
" carmina, ad inftar illa Ovidii quæ amatoria nuncupantur, exaraffe."
Band. Spec. Lit. Flor. v. i. p. 120.

(*a*) In the Laurentian Library (*Plut.* xxvi. *cod.* 21.) is preferved
a poem by Ugolino, to which he has given the name of *Paradifus.*
On his imaginary excurfion to the celeftial regions, the poet meets
with Cofmo de' Medici, who converfes with him at great length on
the affairs of Florence, and particularly on the fituation of his own
family.

(*b*) *Plut.* lxxxx. *cod.* 28. From thefe letters Bandini has in his
valuable catalogue given copious extracts, *v.* iii. *p.* 462, *& feq.*

tinacious chaſtity (*a*). From his letters it appears that both he and his father lived on terms of intimacy and friendſhip with Landino, Bartolomeo Fontio, and Politiano, and that Lorenzo de' Medici occaſionally paſſed a leiſure hour in convivial intercourſe with this learned family (*b*).

The reputation acquired by the Florentines in the cultivation of Latin poetry ſtimulated the exertions of other Italian ſcholars. On the memorable occaſion of the conſpiracy of the Pazzi, Platinus Platus, a Milaneſe, addreſſed to Lorenzo de' Medici a copy of verſes, which obtained his

(*a*) This event has been commemorated both in verſe and profe, in Latin and Italian, by many contemporary authors. (*v. App. No. LVII.*) Verini is not the only inſtance of the kind on record. If we may believe Ammirato, the death of the cardinal of Lisbon in 1459 was occaſioned by a ſimilar circumſtance. *Amm. Iſt. Flor. v. iii. p. 89.* That ſuch a remedy had been preſcribed to Verini, is apparent from the following affecting paſſage in one of his letters: "Inſuperabilis me valitudo confecit, membra ut ſint pallore macieque "deformia; nocte crucior, die non quieſco, & quod me acrius torquet, "in tanto dolore ſpes nulla ſalutis. Quamquam medici, & tota "domus, & amici, nihil pericli afferant, deprehendo tamen tacitos "in vultu timores, ſuſpiria, murmur, taciturnitatem, mæroris cuncta "ſigna proſpicio; ſed cui notior morbus quam mihi? Quidquid ac- "ciderit, utinam forti animo feramus; ſcio mihi nullum de vita factum "reſtare pænitendum, niſi quod potueram valitudini conſulere ſapien- "tius; verum mihi *pudor*, vel potius *ruſticitas* obfuit — vale."

(*b*) "Fingit Homerus Jovem ipſum, alioſque Deos, Olympo relicto, "apud Ethiopas divertiſſe, cœnaſſe, luſiſſe: Auguſtum etiam orbis "terrarum principem, apud privatos ſine ullo apparatu cœnaſſe: "ſed cur vetera? Laurentius Medices urbis noſtræ facile primus, "apud patrem meum pranſus eſt nonnumquam," &c.

Mic. Ver. Ep. 15. ad Sim. Caniſianum. ap. Band. Cat. v. iii. p. 483.

warm approbation (*a*) The exertions of Lorenzo in eſtabliſhing the academy at Piſa gave riſe to a poem of greater merit and importance, by Carolus de Maximis (*b*). To the authors before mentioned we may add the names of Cantalicio, Nicodemo Folengi, Aleſſandro Braccio, and Aurelio Augurelli, all of whom have cultivated Latin poetry with different degrees of ſucceſs, and have addreſſed ſome portion of their works to Lorenzo de' Medici to which the reader may not be diſpleaſed to refer (*c*).

(*a*) Laurentius Medices, quanta voluptate adficeretur in perlegendis poeticis ejuſdem (Plati) lucubrationibus, quantoque illum in pretio haberet, teſtatus eſt in epiſtola ad ipſum ſcripta, ob acceptum ex ejus carminibus non mediocre doloris levamen in nefarie patrata fratris ſui cæde: ait enim, " vetus eſt verbum, mi Platine, *inſuavem eſſe in* " *luctu muſicam :* ego vero tuis perlectis verſiculis, re ipſa reperi " nihil tam maxime ad ſolatium facere quam muſicam." *Sarius in Hiſt. Litteraria Typogr. Mediol. ap. Band. in Cat. Bib. Laur. v.* ii. *p.* 193. Theſe verſes are published in the *Select. Poem. Ital. v.* vii. *p.* 256.

(*b*) DE STUDIO PISANAE URBIS ET EJUS SITUS MAXIMA FELICITATE AD LAURENTIUM MEDICEM. This piece is preſerved in the Laurentian Library (*Plut.* lxxxxi. *cod.* 46. *v. Band. Cat. v.* iii. *p.* 850.), and contains ſo full, and at the ſame time ſo elegant an eulogy on the character of Lorenzo, and particularly on his attention to the promotion of letters, that I have given it a place in the Appendix, No. LVIII.

(*c*) The poems of Cantalicio are published in the *Carmina Illuſt. Poet. Ital. vol.* iii. *p.* 123. and are inſcribed to Lorenzo de' Medici. Thoſe of Folengi are inſerted in the ſame work, *vol.* iv. *p.* 419. Aleſſandro Braccio was equally eminent in politics and letters. He was for ſome time ſecretary of the Florentine republic, and died on an embaſſy to pope Alexander VI. His tranſlation of Appian into Italian is yet highly eſteemed, and forms part of the *Collana,* or

Of all thefe authors, though fome poffefs a confiderable fhare of merit, not one of them can contend in point of poetical excellence with Politiano, who in his compofition approaches nearer to the ftandard of the ancients than any man of his time; yet, whilft he emulates the· dignity of

feries of Italian hiftorical works. The Latiu poems of Braccio, though very numerous, have not yet been published, but are preferved in the Laurentian Library. *Plut.* lxxxxi. *cod.* 40, 41. Many of them are infcribed to Lorenzo de' M dici and other men of eminence, as Landino, Ficino, Bartolomeo Scala, Ugolini Verini, &c. I have before adduced fome lines of this author to Lorenzo de' Medici, and shall hereafter avail myfelf of an opportunity of producing a more extenfive fpecimen of his works. The following epigram addreffed to Politiano is not inapplicable to our prefent fubject:

v. Band. Cat. v. iii. *p.* 781.

AD ANGELUM BASSUM POLITIANENSEM.

Tanta tibi tenero quum furgat pectore virtus,
 Quanta vel annofo vix queat effe feni,
Ac tua grandifono reboent quum, *Baffe,* cothurno
 Carmina, magnanimo non nifi digna duce,
Et tibi fit locuples oris facundia docti,
 Teque fuis ditet Græcia litterulis,
Te precor ad longos ut fervet Jupiter annos,
 Incolumemque finat vivere poffe diu.
Nam tua Mæonio multum certantia vati
 Carmina quis dubitet, Virgilioque fore?
Atque decus clarum noftræ magnumque futurum
 Quis neget ætatis te, memorande puer?
Sis igitur felix, noftri fpes maxima faecli,
 Teque putes nobis charius effe nihil.

Aurelio Augurelli is more gen rally known. His poems have frequently been published. The firft edition is that of Verona, 1 91. in 4to; the moft correct and elegant, that of Aldus, 1505. Thefe poems rank in the firft clafs of modern Latin poetry.

Virgil,

Virgil, or reminds us of the elegance of Horace, he fuggefts not to our minds the idea of fervile imitation. Of the character of his writings various opinions have indeed been entertained. which have been detailed at large by Baillet, and ftill more copioufly by Menckenius (*a*). It may therefore be fufficient on this occafion to caution the reader againft an implicit acquiefcence in the opinions of two aminent living authors who have either obliquely cenfured, or too cautioufly approved his poetical works (*b*). In the attempt made by Politiano to reftore a juft tafte for the literature of the ancients, it is not to be denied that he had

(*a*) *Baillet Jugemens des Sçavans, vol.* iv. *p.* 18. *Menck. in vitâ Pol. paffim.*

(*b*) Tirabofchi, adopting the fentiments of Giraldi, acknowledges that Politiano was poffeffed of a vivid genius, of extenfive powers, and of uncommon and diverfified erudition; but cenfures his Latin poetry as deficient in elegance and choice of expreffion. *Tirab. Storia della Lett. Ital. vol.* vi. *par.* 2. *p.* 234. Fabroni, adverting to the Italian poetry of Politiano, infinuates, that the Latin mufes were referved and coy, to one who had obtained the favor of their fifter at fo early an age, by his verfes on the *Gioftra* of Giuliano de' Medici. *Fabr. in vitâ Laur. p.* 157. To oppofe to thefe opinions the authority of many other eminent men who have mentioned the Latin writings of Politiano with almoft unlimited praife, would only be to detail the compilations of Baillet or Menckenius. But the works of Politiano are yet open to the infpection of the inquifitive fcholar; and though certainly unequal in point of merit, perhaps according to the time of life at which they were produced, will be found, upon the whole, to poffefs a vigor of fentiment, a copioufnefs of imagination, and a claffical elegance of expreffion, which, if confidered with reference to the age in which he lived, entitle them to the higheft efteem.

powerful coadjutors in Pontano and Sanazaro (*a*), whofe labors have given to the delightful vicinity of Naples new pretenfions to the appellation of claffic ground. Nor will it diminifh his reputation if we admit that the empire which he had founded was in the next century extended and fecured by the exertions of Fracaftoro, Vida, Naugerio, and Flaminio (*b*), in whom the great poets of the Auguftan age feem once more to be revived.

(*a*) Giacopo Sanazaro, or, by his academical appellation, Actius Sincerus Samazarius, was a Neapolitan, born in the year 1458, and equally eminent by his Italian and Latin compofitions. In the former, his reputation is chiefly founded on his *Arcadia;* in the latter, on his poem in three books, *De partu Virginis,* which is allowed, however, to be greatly blemifhed by the introduction of the pagan deities to the myfteries of the Chriftian religion.

(*b*) I cannot mention thefe names without regretting the limits to which I am neceffarily confined. The rivals of Virgil, of Ovid, and of Catullus, ought not, in a work that touches on the rife of letters, to be commemorated at the foot of a page. The *Syphilis* of Fracaftoro, *five de Morbo Gallico,* though an unpromifing fubject, is beyond comparifon the fineft Latin poem that has appeared fince the times of the ancients. The writings of Vida are more generally known, and would be entitled to higher applaufe, if they did not frequently difcover to the claffical reader an imitation of the ancients that borders on fervility. Naugerio was a noble Venetian, who died young on an embaffy from the republic. In his laft moments he deftroyed all his writings then in his poffeffion, as not being fufficiently correct for the public eye; but the few that had been previoufly diftributed among his friends were collected and publifhed by them after his death, and breathe the true fpirit of poetry. In Flaminio we have the fimplicity and tendernefs of Catullus, without his licentioufnefs. To thofe who are acquainted with his writings, it will not be thought extravagant to affirm, that many of them, in the fpecies of compofition to which they are confined, were never excelled. The queftion addreffed by

Whilſt the ſtudy of polite literature was thus emerging from its ſtate of reptile torpor, the other ſciences felt the effects of the ſame invigorating beam; and the city of Florence, like a ſheltered garden in the opening of ſpring, re-echoed with the earlieſt ſounds of returning animation. The Platonic academy exiſted in full ſplendor, and ſerved as a common bond to unite, at ſtated intervals, thoſe who had ſignalized themſelves by ſcientific or literary purſuits. The abſurd pretenſions of judicial aſtrology were freely examined and openly expoſed; and obſervation and experiment were at length ſubſtituted in the place of conjecture and of fraud (*a*). Paolo Toſcanelli had already erected his celebrated Gnomon (*b*). Lorenzo da Volpaja conſtructed for Lorenzo de' Medici, a clock, or piece of mechaniſm, which not only

him to a friend, reſpecting the writings of Catullus, " Quando leggete— " non vi ſentite voi liquefare il cuore di dolcezza?" may with confidence be repeated to all thoſe who are converſant with his works.

(*a*) Pico of Mirandula was one of the firſt who entered the liſts againſt this formidable adverſary of real knowledge, in his treatiſe in twelve books, *adverſus Aſtrologos*, which is found in the general collection of his works. *Ven*. 1498.

(*b*) This Gnomon, which has juſtly been denominated the nobleſt aſtronomical inſtrument in the world, was erected by Toſcanelli, about the year 1460, for the purpoſe of determining the ſolſtices, and thereby aſcertaining the feaſts of the Romiſh church. It is fixed in the cupola of the church of S. Maria del fiore, at the height of 277 Pariſian feet. A ſmall orifice tranſmits from that diſtance the rays of the ſun to a marble ſlag, placed in the floor of the church. This inſtrument was, in the preſent century, corrected and improved at the inſtance of M. de la Condamine, who acknowledges it to be a ſtriking proof of the capacity and extended views of its author.

marked the hour of the day, but the motions of the fun and of the planets, the eclipfes, the figns of the zodiac, and the whole revolutions of the heavens (*a*). A laudable attempt was made by Francefco Berlinghieri to facilitate the ftudy of geography, by uniting it with poetry (*b*). In metaphyfics feveral treatifes made their appearance, fome of which are infcribed by their authors to Lorenzo de' Medici (*c*). His efforts to promote the important fcience of medecine, and to refcue it from the abfurdities in which it was enveloped are acknowledged by feveral of its moft eminent profeffors, who cultivated it on more rational principles, and have attributed their proficiency

(*a*) Politiano has left a very particular defcription of this curious piece of machinery. *Ep. lib.* iv. *Ep.* 8. A fingular fpectacle was alfo devifed by Lorenzo de' Medici for the amufement of the populace, a memorial of which is preferved in a poem by Naldio, *Carm. Illuft. v.* vi. *p.* 436. entitled *Elegia in feptem Stellas errantes fub humana fpecie per urbem Florentinam curribus a Laurentio Medice Patriæ Patre duci juffas, more triumphantium.* From this poem we learn that the planets were perfonified and diftinguished by their proper attributes, and that they performed their evolutions to the found of mufic, with verfes explanatory of their motions and fuppofed qualities.

> Nec tantum fignis quot erant ea fidera certis
> Monftrafti, Medices, qua fpecieque forent,
> Dulcibus at numeris fuavi modulatus ab ore
> Singula quid faciant præcipis arte cani.

(*b*) The *Geografia* of Berlinghieri was published with maps at Florence in the year 1450.

(*c*) Niccolo Fulginato addreffed to Lorenzo his treatife *De Ideis,* which yet remains in manufcript in the Laurentian Library. *Plut.* lxxxii. *cod.* 22. *Band. Cat.* iii. 201. and Leonardo Nogarola a work entitled *De Immortalitate animæ. Plut.* lxxxiii. *cod.* 22. *Band. Cat.* iii. 219.

to his bounty (a). In the practice and theory of muſic, Antonio Squarcialupi excelled all his pre-deceſſors; and Lorenzo is ſaid to have written a poem in his praiſe (b). His liberality was emulated by many other illuſtrious citizens. who were allied to him by affinity, or attached by the ties of friendſhip and of kindred ſtudies, and the innumerable literary works of this period, the production of Florentine authors, evince the ſucceſs that attended their exertions. Of theſe works many yet hold a high rank, not only for practical knowledge, but for purity of diction; and upon the whole they bear the ſtamp of induſtry, talents, and good ſenſe. And as they may be preferred,

(a) Bernardus de Torniis, dedicating to Giovanni de' Medici, when a cardinal, his treatiſe *de Cibis Quadrageſimalibus*, thus addreſ-fes him: " Laurentius, pater tuus, Reverendiſſime Domine, tanta erga " me utitur humanitate, ac tot beneficiis Tornium adſtringit, ut filiis " totique domui, perpetuo me debere profitear. D, guſtavi nutu ejus " medicinalem ſcientiam, neque ſui cauſſa defuit quidquam, quo ad " illius apicem potuerim pervenire." *Band. Cat. v.* i. *p.* 639. In the Laurentian Library are ſeveral medical works addreſſed to Lorenzo, as Joh. Calora. Compend. Febrium. *Band. Cat.* iii. 42. Joh. Aretini de Medicinæ & legum præſtantia, &c. *ib.* iii. 141.

(b) This I mention on the authority of Mr. Tenhove. " En fait " de muſique," ſays he, giving an account of Leo. Bat. Alberti, " il ne cédait qu'au ſeul Antoine Squarcialupo. J'ai ſous les yeux " un poême que Laurent de' Médicis fit en l'honneur de ce der- " nier; car quel eſt le genre de talents au quel Médicis ne faiſait pas " accueil?" *Mém. Généal. de la Maiſon de Médicis. lib.* x. *p.* 99. I regret that this poem of Lorenzo has eſcaped my reſearches. Valori relates, that Lorenzo being preſent when the character of this celebrat-ed muſician was the ſubject of cenſure, obſerved to his detractors, *If you knew how difficult it is to arrive at excellence in any ſcience, you would ſpeak of him with more reſpect. Val. in vitâ Laur. p.* 45, both in point of information and compofition, to the productions that immediately preceded them, fo they are perhaps more truly eftimable than many of thofe of the enfuing century; when, by an overftrained attention to the beauty of language, the importance of the fubject was frequently neglected or forgotten, and the talents of the firft men of the age being devoted rather to words than to things, were overwhelmed in a prolixity of language, that in the form of letters, orations, and critical differtations, became the opprobrium of literature, and the deftruction of true tafte.

C H A P. VIII.

DOMESTIC character of Lorenzo de' Medici—Accused of being addicted to licentious amours —Children of Lorenzo — His conduct towards them — Politiano accompanies them to Piſtoia — They remove to Caſſagiolo — Diſſenſions between Politiano and Madonna Clarice — He retires to Fieſole, and writes his poem entitled RUSTICUS *— Piero de' Medici — Giovanni de' Medici — Lorenzo diſcharges his debts, and quits commerce for agriculture — Villa of Poggio-Cajano—Careggi—Fieſole and other domains — Piero viſits the Pope—Giovanni raiſed to the dignity of a cardinal —Admonitory letter of Lorenzo—Piero marries Alfonſina Orſini — Viſits Milan — Learned eccleſiaſtics favored by Lorenzo — Mariana Gennazano — Girolamo Savonarola — Matteo Buſſo — Death of Madonna Clarice—Aſſaſſination of Girolamo Riario—Tragical death of Galeotto Manfredi prince of Faenza.*

HAVING hitherto traced the conduct of Lorenzo de' Medici in public life, we may now be allowed to follow him to his domeſtic retreat, and obſerve him in the intercourſe of his family, the education of his children, or the ſociety of his friends. The mind of man varies with his local ſituation, and before it can be juſtly eſtimated, muſt be viewed in thoſe moments when it expands in the warmth of confidence, and exhibits

its true colors in the funfhine of affection. Whether
it was from the fuggeftions of policy, or the ver-
fatility of his natural dipofition, that Lorenzo de'
Medici turned with fuch facility from concerns
of high importance to the difcuffion of fubjects
of amufement, and the levity of convivial in-
tercourfe, certain it is, that few perfons have
difplayed this faculty in fo eminent a degree.
" Think not, " fays Politiano, writing to his
friend (a), " that any of our learned aflociates,
" even they who have devoted their lives to
" ftudy, are to be efteemed fuperior to Lorenzo
" de' Medici, either for acutenefs in difputation.
" or for good fenfe in forming a juft decifion ; or
" that he yields to any of them in expreffing his
" thoughts with facility, variety, and elegance.
" The examples of hiftory are as familiar to him as
" the attendants that furround his table ; and when
" the nature of his fubject admits of it, his con-
" verfation is abundantly feafoned with the falt col-
" lected from that ocean, from which Venus herfelf
" firft fprung (b)." His talent for irony was peculiar,
and folly and abfurdity feldom efcaped his animad-

(a) *Ang. Polit. Lodovico Odaxio. Ep. lib.* iii. *Ep.* 6.

(b) ———— Lufufque Salefque,
Sed lectus pelago, quo Venus orta fales,

Says Jacques Moifant, Sieur de Bricux. *v.* Menagiana, *tom.* i. *p.*
59. where the author has traced this fentiment from Plutarch to
Politiano, and downwards to Victorius, Heinfius, and de Bricux.
" Quelque belle & fine, au refte," fays he, " que foit cette penfée,
" ufée aujourd'hui comme elle eft, on n'oferait plus la répéter."

verfion (*a*). In the collections formed by the Florentines, of the *motti e burle* of celebrated men, Lorenzo bears a diftinguifhed part ; but when expreffions adapted to the occafion of a moment are tranfplanted to the page of a book, and fubmitted to the cool confideration of the clofet, they too often remind us of a flower cropt from its ftalk, to be preferved in arid deformity. Poffibly too, thofe who have affumed the tafk of felection may not have been accurate in their choice, and perhaps the celebrity of his name may have been an inducement to others to attribute to him witticifms unworthy of his character. Yet the *bon-mots* of Lorenzo may rank with many of thofe which have been publifhed with importance, and read with avidity (*b*). Grazzini has alfo introduced this eminent man as amufing himfelf

(*a*) "Quum jocabatur, nihil hilarius; quum mordebat nihil afperius."

Valori, in vitâ, p. 14.

(*b*) Several of them are related by Valoii, and many others may be found in the *Facetie, Motti e Burle, di diverfi Signori, &c. Raccolte per Lod. Domenichi. Ven.* 1588. One of his kinfmen, remarkable for his avarice, having boafted that he had at his villa a plentiful ftream of fine water, Lorenzo replied, *If fo, you might afford to keep cleaner hands.* Bartolommeo Soccini, of Sienna, having obferved, in allufion to the defect in Lorenzo's fight, that the air of Florence was injurious to the eyes; *True,* faid Lorenzo, *and that of Sienna to the brain.* Being interrogated by Ugolino Martelli, why he rofe fo late in the morning, Lorenzo in return inquired from Martelli, why he rofe fo foon, and finding that it was to employ himfelf in trifles, *My morning dreams,* faid Lorenzo, *are better than thy morning's bufinefs.* When Soccini eloped from Florence, to evade his engagements as profeffor of civil law there, and being taken and brought back, was committed to prifon, he complained that a man of his eminence should undergo fuch a fhameful punifhment. *You should* with a piece of meditated jocularity, in order to free himfelf from the importunate vifits of a phyfician, who too frequently appeared at his table; but, for the veracity of this narrative, we have only the authority of a profeffed novelift (a). Nor is it likely that Lorenzo, though he frequently indulged in the licence allowed by the Roman fatirift would have forgotten the precaution with which it is accompanied (b), or would have mifemployed his time and his talents, in contriving and executing a ftale and infipid jeft.

Although there is reafon to believe that Clarice Orfini, the wife of Lorenzo, was not the object of his early paffion, yet that he lived with her in uninterrupted affection, and treated her on all

remember, faid Lorenzo, *that the shame is not in the punishment, but in the crime.* Val. p. 14. Dom. p. 121, &c.

(a) Anton-Francefco Grazzini, detto Il Lafca. *Novelle,* Ed. Lond. 1756. *La terza Cena, Nov.* x. The argument of this novel is as follows: " Lorenzo vecchio de' Medici da due travefiti, fa condurre " Maeftro Manente ubbriaco una fera dopo cena fegretamente nel fuo " palagio, e quivi e altrove lo tiene, fenza fapere egli dove fia, lungo " tempo al bujo, facendogli portar mangiare da due immafcherati; " dopo per via del Monaco buffone, da a credere alle perfone, lui " effer morto di pefte, perciocchè cavato di cafa fua un morto, in fuo " fcambio lo fa difotterrare. Il Magnifico poi con modo ftravagante " manda via Maeftro Manente, il quale finalmente creduto morto da " ognuno, arriva in Firenze, dove la moglie, penfando che fuffe l'anima " fua, lo caccia via come fe fuffe lo fpirito, e dalla gente avuto la " corfa, trova folo Burchiello, che lo riconofce, e piatendo prima la " moglie in Vefcovado, e poi alii Otto è rimeffa la caufa in Lorenzo, " il quale fatto venire Nepo da Galatrona, fa veder alle perfone, ogni " cofa effer intervenuta al Medico per forza d'incanti; ficchè riavuta " la donna, Maeftro Manente piglia per fuo avvocato San Cipriano."

(b) Nec lufiffe pudet—fed non incidere ludum. *Hor. Ep. lib.* i.

occafions with the refpect due to her rank and her virtues, appears from many circumftances. He has not however efcaped an imputation which has fometimes attached itfelf to names of great celebrity, and which indeed too often taints the general mafs of excellence with the leaven of human nature. "Such a combination of talents " and of virtues, " fays Machiavelli, " as appeared " in Lorenzo de' Medici, was not counterbalanced " by a fingle fault, although he was incredibly " devoted to the indulgence of an amorous paf- " fion (a)." In afferting a particular defect, it is remarkable that the hiftorian admits it not as an exception to his general approbation. Yet it is not to be denied, that if fuch an accufation were eftablifhed, it would be difficult to apologize for Lorenzo, although the manners of the age, and the vivacity of his natural difpofition, might be urged in extenuation of his mifconduct. In juftice however to his character, it muft be obferved, that the hiftory of the times furnifhes us with no information, either as to the circumftances attending his amours, or the particular objects of his paffion (b); nor indeed does there appear, from

(a) *Hift. Flor. lib.* viii.

(b) On lui a encore réproché le défaut des ames héroiques & fenfibles, trop de penchant à l'amour. Je fçai qu'il aima prodigieufement les femmes, & j'ignore comment cette fource inépuifable de faibleffes, n'en fut point une pour lui. S'il brûlait vivement, il brûlait fenfément; jamais fes galanteries ne firent ombrage aux citoyens, parcequ'elles n'influérent en rien fur fa conduite publique. Sa vie grave, & fa vie badine, étaient tellement féparées, qu'on eut dit qu'il y avait deux hommes en lui.

Tenhove, Mém. Généal. de la Maifon de Médicis, liv. xi. *p.* 143.

the teſtimony of his contemporaries, any reaſon to infer that he is juſtly charged with this deviation from the rules of virtue, and of decorum (a). Probably this imputation is founded only on a preſumption ariſing from the amorous tendency of ſome of his poetical writings ; and certain it is that if the offspring of imagination and the effuſions of poetry be allowed to decide, his conviction will be apparent in almoſt every line. It may perhaps be obſerved that theſe pieces were chiefly the productions of his youth, before the reſtrictions of the marriage vow had ſuppreſſed the breathings of paſſion ; but how ſhall we elude the inference which ariſes from the following lines?

> Teco l'aveſſi il ciel donna congiunto
> In matrimonio : ah che pria non veniſti
> Al mondo, o io non ſon più tardo giunto?

> O that the marriage bond had join'd our fate,
> Nor I been born too ſoon, nor thou too late!

Or from theſe, which are ſtill more explicit?

> Ma queſto van penſiero a che ſoggiorno?
> Se tu pur dianzi, ed io ſui un tempo avanti,
> Dal laccio conjugal legato intorno?

(a) In the poem of Brandolini, *De laudibus Laur. Med.* (*App. No. I..*) the attention of Lorenzo to the dictates of morality and decorum, as well in himſelf as others, is the particular ſubject of panegyric, and that by a comtemporary writer. Had the conduct of Lorenzo been notoriouſly licentious, ſuch praiſe would have been the ſevereſt ſatire.

> But why thefe thoughts irrelevant and vain!
> If I, long fince in Hymen's fetters tied,
> Am doom'd to hear another call thee bride?

Nor muft it be denied that this elegiac fragment, though incorrect and unfiniſhed, is diftinguiſhed by that pathos and glow of expreſſion which genuine paſſion can alone infpire (*a*). If in this piece Lorenzo be amorous, in others he is licentious; and if we admit the production of a moment of levity, as the evidence of his feelings, the only regret that he experienced was from the reflection, that he had in the courfe of his paſt time imprudently neglected fo many opportunities of collecting the fweets that were ſtrown in his way (*b*). But ſhall we venture to infer, that becaufe Lorenzo wrote amorous verfes, and amufed himfelf with *jeux d'efprit*, his life was diffolute, and his conduct immoral? " As poetry is the flower of fcience," fays Menage, " fo there is not a fingle perfon of " education who has not compofed, or at leaft " wiſhed to compofe verfes; and as love is a " natural paſſion, and poetry is the language of " love, fo there is no one who has written verfes " who has not felt the effects of love." If we judge with fuch feverity, what will become of the numerous throng of poets who have thought it fufficient to alledge in their juſtification, that if

(*a*) *v.* this piece, entitled *Elegia*, in the poems of Lorenzo, publiſhed at the clofe of this volume.

(*b*) See the piece entitled *La Confeſſione*, alfo printed amongſt his poems at the end of the prefent volume.

Their verse was wanton, yet their lives were chaste?

or what shall we say to the extensive catalogue of learned ecclesiastics, who have endeavoured to fill the void of celibacy, by composing verses on subjects of love (a) ?

Whatever may be thought of the conduct or the sentiments of Lorenzo on this head, it does not appear that he left any offspring of illicit love; but by his wife Clarice he had a numerous progeny, of which three sons and four daughters arrived at the age of maturity. Piero his eldest son was born on the fifteenth day of February 1471; Giovanni, on the eleventh day of December 1475; and Giuliano, his youngest, in 1478. Of these the first was distinguished by a series of misfortunes too justly merited, the two latter by an unusual degree of prosperity; Giovanni having obtained the dignity of the Tiara, which he wore by the name of Leo X. ; and Giuliano having allied himself by marriage to the royal house of France, and obtained the title of duke of Nemours.

In no point of view does the character of this extraordinary man appear more engaging than in his affection towards his children, in his care of their education, and in his solicitude for their welfare. In their society he relaxed from his important occupations, and accustomed himself to

(a) For this catalogue, from Heliodorus bishop of Tricca in Thessaly, to M. Du Bois doctor in Theology at Paris, the reader may consult the Anti-Baillet of M. Menage, written by him when upwards of seventy years of age, and the most singular instance of industry, wit, vanity, and learning that the annals of literature can produce.

fhare their pleafures and promote their amufe-
ments (*a*). By what more certain means can a
parent obtain that confidence fo neceffary to ena-
ble him to promote the happinefs of his children?
The office of an inftructor of youth he confidered
as of the higheft importance. " If," fays he, " we
" efteem thofe who contribute to the profperity
" of the ftate, we ought to place in the firft rank
" the tutors of our children, whofe labors are to
" influence pofterity, and on whofe precepts and
" exertions the dignity of our family, and of our
" country, in a great meafure depends (*b*)."

Soon after the confpiracy of the Pazzi, when
Lorenzo thought it expedient to remove his family
to Piftoia, they were accompanied by Politiano,
as the inftructor of his fons, who gave frequent
information to his patron of their fituation, and

(*a*) ——— " Si dilettaffe d'huomini faceti e mordaci, & di
" giuochi puerili, più che a tanto huomo non pareva fi conveniffe;
" in modo che molte volte fu vifto tra i fuoi figliuoli e figliuole, tra
" i loro traftulli mefcolarfi." *Mac. Hift. lib.* viii. On this fubject I
muft not omit the comment of the interefting and elegant Tenhove:
" Eft-il un fpectacle plus touchant, que celui de voir un tel homme
" dépofer le fardeau de la gloire au fein de la nature? A des yeux
" non viciés Laurent de' Medicis parait bien grand, & bien aimable.
" lors'quil joue à croix & pile avec le petit duc de Nemours, ou
" qu'il fe roule a terre avec Leon X." *Tenh. Mém. Généal. lib.*
xi. *p.* 142.

(*b*) Si feræ partus fuos diligunt, qua nos in liberos noftros indul-
gentia effe debemus? Et fi omnes, qui civitati confulunt, cari nobis
funt, certe in primis liberorum inftitutores, quorum induftria fempiter-
num tempus fpectat, quorumque præceptis, confiliis, & virtute,
retinebimus familiæ & reipublicæ dignitatem.

Laur. Med. ad Polit. ap. Fabr. v. i. *p.* 166.

the progrefs made in the education of his children.
Thefe confidential letters enable us to form a
more accurate idea of the difpofition of their
author, than we can collect from any of his
writings intended for publication. Reftlefs, im-
patient of control, concentering all merit in the
acquifition of learning, he could brook no oppofi-
tion to his authority. The intervention of Ma-
donna Clarice, in the direction of her children,
was in his judgment impertinent, becaufe fhe was
unlettered, and a woman. In one of his letters
he earneftly requefts that Lorenzo will delegate to
him a more extenfive power; whilft in another,
written on the fame day, he acknowledges that
this requeft was made under the impulfe of paffion,
and folicits indulgence for the infirmity of his
temper. The fubfequent eminence of his pupils
renders thefe letters interefting (a). What friend
of literature can be indifferent to the infancy of
Leo the Tenth? " Piero," fays Politiano, " attends
" to his ftudies with tolerable diligence. We
" daily make excurfions through the neighbour-
" hood, we vifit the gardens with which this city
" abounds, and fometimes look into the library
" of Maeftro Zambino, where I have found fome
" good pieces, both in Greek and Latin. Giovanni
" rides out on horfeback, and the people follow
" him in crowds." From Piftoia the family retired
in the clofe of the year to Caffagiolo, where they
paffed the winter; from whence Politiano continued

(a) They are given, from the collection of Fabroni, in the Appendix
to the prefent volume, N°. LIX.

his

his correfpondence with Lorenzo, and occafionally addreffed himfelf to his mother, Madonna Lucretia between whom and this eminent fcholar there fub- fifted a friendly and confidential intercourfe. Thefe letters afford an additional proof of the querulous- nefs of genius, and may ferve to reconcile medi- ocrity to its placid infignificance (a). " The only " news I can fend you," thus he writes to this lady, " is, that we have here fuch continual rains " that it is impoffible to quit the houfe, and the " exercifes of the country are changed for childifh " fports within doors. Here I ftand by the fire- " fide, in my great coat and flippers, that you " might take me for the very figure of melancholy. " Indeed I am the fame at all times; for I neither " fee, nor hear, nor do any thing that gives me " pleafure, fo much am I affected by the thoughts " of our calamities; fleeping and waking they ftill " continue to haunt me. Two days fince we were " all rejoicing upon hearing that the plague had " ceafed—now we are depreffed on being informed " that fome fymptoms of it yet remain. Were " we at Florence we fhould have fome confolation, " were it only that of feeing Lorenzo when he " returned to his houfe; but here we are in con- " tinual anxiety, and I, for my part, am half " dead with folitude and wearinefs. The plague " and the war are inceffantly in my mind. I " lament paft misfortunes, and anticipate future " evils; and I have no longer at my fide my dear " Madonna Lucretia, to whom I might unbofom

(a) v. App. No. LX.

" my cares." Such is the melancholy ſtrain in which Politiano addreſſes the mother of Lorenzo; but we ſeldom complain except to thoſe we eſteem, and this letter is a better evidence of the feelings of Politiano, than a volume of well-turned compliments.

In conciliating the regard of Clarice, Politiano was not equally fortunate. Her interference with him in his office, appeared to him as an unpardonable intruſion. " As for Giovanni," ſays he, " his mother employs him in reading the pſalter, " which I by no means commend. Whilſt ſhe " declined interfering with him, it is aſtoniſhing " how rapidly he improved, inſomuch that he " read without any aſſiſtance. There is nothing," he proceeds, " which I aſk more earneſtly of " Heaven, than that I may be able to convince " you of my fidelity, my diligence, and my " patience, which I would prove even by my " death. Many things however I omit, that amidſt " your numerous avocations I may not add to " your ſolicitude." When Politiano wróte thus to his patron, it is not to be ſuppoſed that his conduct at Caſſagiolo was diſtinguiſhed by moderation or complacency. The diſſenſions between him and Madonna Clarice conſequently increaſed, till at length the intemperance or the arrogance of Politiano afforded her a juſt pretext for compelling him to quit the houſe. By a letter from Clarice to her huſband on this occaſion, we are informed of the provocation which ſhe received, and muſt confeſs that ſhe had ſufficient cauſe for the meafures fhe adopted; for what woman can bear with patience the ftings of ridicule (a) ? " I " fhall be glad," fays fhe, " to efcape being made " the fubject of a tale of Franco's, as Luigi Pulci " was; nor do I like that Meffer Agnolo fhould " threaten that he would remain in the houfe in " fpite of me. You remember I told you, that " if it was your will he fhould ftay, I was per- " fectly contented; and although I have fuffered " infinite abufe from him, yet if it be with your " affent, I am fatisfied. But I do not believe it " to be fo." On this trying occafion, as on many others, Politiano experienced the indulgence and friendfhip of Lorenzo, who, feeing that a reconciliation between the contending perties was impracticable, allowed the banifhed fcholar a refidence in his houfe at Fiefole. No longer fretted by female oppofition, or wearied with the monotonous tafk of inculcating learning, his mind foon recovered its natural tone; and the fruits of the leifure which he enjoyed yet appear in a beautiful Latin poem, inferior in its kind only to the Georgics of Virgil, and to which he gave the title of *Rufticus*. In the clofe of this poem, he thus expreffes his gratitude to his conftant benefactor:

Talia FESULEO lentus meditabar in antro,
Rure fub urbano Medicum, qua mons facer urbem
Mæoniam, longique volumina defpicit ARNI.
Qua bonus hofpitium felix, placidamque quietem

(a) The letter of Clarice to her husband is given in the Appendix, *No.* LXI.

Indulget LAURENS, LAURENS haud ultima Phœbi
Gloria, ja&atis LAURENS fida anchora mufis;
Qui fi certa magis permiferit otia nobis,
Afﬂabor majore Deo. ————

Thus flow the ftrains, whilft here at eafe reclin'd
At length the fweets of calm repofe I find;
Where FESULÉ, with high impending brow,
O'erlooks Mæonian FLORENCE ftretch'd below.
Whilft ARNO, winding through the mild domain,
Leads in repeated folds his lengthen'd train;
Nor thou thy poet's grateful ftrain refufe,
LORENZO! fure refource of every mufe;
Whofe praife, fo thou his leifure hour prolong.
Shall claim the tribute of a nobler fong.

Were we to give implicit credit to the teftimony
of his tutor, Piero de' Medici united in himfelf all
the great qualities by which his progenitors had
been fucceffively diftinguifhed: " The talents of
" his father, the virtues of his grandfather, and the
" prudence of the venerable Cofmo (a)." Lorenzo
himfelf had certainly formed a favorable opinion
of his capacity; and is faid to have remarked that
his eldeft fon would be diftinguifhed for ability,
his fecond for probity, his third by an amiable
temper (b) The fondnefs of a parent was gratified

(a) Scis autem quam gratus multitudini fit & civibus, Petrus
nofter, non minus jam fua, quam familiæ gloria; fcilicet in quo Patris
ingenium, Patrui virtus, Patrui magni humanitas, Avi probitas, Proavi
prudentia, pietas Abavi revivifcit: omnium vero majorum fuorum
liberaitas, omniumque animus. *Pol. Ep. lib. xii. Ep.* 6.
(b) *Valori in vitâ Laur. p.* 64.

in obferving thofe inftances of an extraordinary
memory, which Piero difplayed in his childhood,
and in liftening to the poetical pieces which he was
accuftomed to recite to the familiar circle of friends,
who perhaps admired, and certainly applauded his
efforts. Among thefe were fome of the whimfical
productions of Matteo Franco (a). As he advanced
in years, his father was defirous that he fhould
always participate in the converfation of thofe
eminent fcholars who frequented the palace of the
Medici; and it was with pleafure that Lorenzo faw
the mutual attachment that fubfifted between his
fon and the profeffors of literature in general (b).
The celebrated epiftles of Politiano, which were

(a) Quin idem parens tuus, pené infantem adhuc te, quædam ex
his (Franci carminibus) facetiora, ridiculi gratia docebat, quæ tu
deinde inter adductus amicos balbutiebas, & eleganti quodam geftu,
qui quidem illam deceret ætatulam, commendabas. *Pol. Ep. ad
Pet. Med. lib. x. Ep. 12.*

(b) Landino, in his dedication of the works of Virgil to Piero de'
Medici, thus adverts to the attention of Lorenzo to the education of
his children, and particularly of Piero: " Plurima funt quæ in illo
" (Laurentio) admiror; fed illud præ ceteris, quod in liberis educandis
" indulgentioris quidem parentis numquam, optimi vero ac fapientiffi-
" mi femper, fumma fedulitate officium compleverit. In te vero
" informando, atque erudiendo, quid umquam omifit? Nam quamvis
" ipfe per fe quotidie admoneret, præciperet, ac juberet, tamen cum
" fciret quanti effet, ne a Præceptoris latere umquam difcederes, ex
" omni hominum doctorum copia, Angelum Politianum elegit, virum
" multa ac varia doctrina eruditum, Poetam vero egregium, egregi-
" umque Oratorem, ac denique totius antiquitatis diligentem per-
" fcrutatorem cui puerilem ætatem tuam & optimis moribus fingendam,
" & optimis artibus ac difciplinis excolendam traderet." *Band.
Spec. Lit. Flor. v. i. p. 222. in not.*

collected by their author at the inftance of Piero, and to whom they are infcribed in terms of grateful affection, bear ample teftimony to his acquirements; and the frequent mention made of his name by the learned correfpondents of Politiano, is a convincing proof of his attention to their interefts, and his attachment to the caufe of letters. Happy if the day that opened with fuch promifing appearances had not been fo fuddenly overclouded;

———— Sed zephyri fpes portavere paternas.

and Piero, by one inconfiderate ftep, which his fubfequent efforts could never retrieve, rendered ineffectual all the folicitude of his father, and all the leffons of his youth.

Giovanni, the fecond fon of Lorenzo, was deftined from his infancy to the church. Early brought forward into public view, and ftrongly impreffed with a fenfe of the neceffity of a grave deportment, he feems never to have been a child. At feven years of age he was admitted into holy orders, and received the tonfura from Gentile, bifhop of Arezzo. From thenceforth he was called Meffer Giovanni, and was foon afterwards declared capable of ecclefiaftical preferment. Before he was eight years of age he was appointed by Louis XI. of France, abbot of Fonte Dolce, which was immediately fucceeded by a prefentation from the fame patron, to the archbifhopric of Aix in Provence; but in this inftance the liberality of the king was oppofed by an invincible objection, for before the inveftiture could be obtained from the pope, information was received

at Florence that the archbiſhop was yet living. This
diſappointment was however compenſated by the
abbacy of the rich monaſtery of Paſignano (a). Of
the glaring indecorum of beſtowing ſpiritual func-
tions on a child, Lorenzo was fully ſenſible, and
he accordingly endeavoured to counteract the un-
favorable impreſſion which it might make on the
public mind, by inculcating upon his ſon the ſtricteſt
attention to his manners, his morals, and his im-
provement. He had too much ſagacity not to be
convinced, that the ſureſt method of obtaining the
rewards of merit is to deſerve them; and Meſſer
Giovanni was not more diſtinguiſhed from his
youthful aſſociates by the high promotions which
he enjoyed, than he was by his attention to his
ſtudies, his ſtrict performance of the duties enjoined
him, and his inviolable regard to truth.

In providing for the expenſes of the wars in
which the Florentines had been engaged, confi-
derable debts had been incurred; and as they
had not yet learnt the deſtructive expedient of
anticipating their future revenue, or transferring
their own burdens to their poſterity, it became
neceſſary to provide for the payment of theſe
demands. Beſides the debts contracted in the
name of the republic, Lorenzo had been obliged
to have recourſe to his agents in different countries
to borrow large ſums of money, which had been
applied to the exigencies of the ſtate; but it was

(a) Theſe particulars are circumſtantially related in the Ricordi
of Lorenzo, who ſeems to have intereſted himſelf in the early promotion
of his ſon with uncommon earneſtneſs. v. App. No. LXII.

no improbable conjecture, that the money which had been lavishly expended during the heat of the conteft would be repaid with reluctance when the ftruggle was over. Thefe confiderations occafioned him great anxiety; for whilft on the one hand he dreaded the difgrace of being wanting in the performance of his pecuniary engagements, he was not perhaps lefs apprehenfive on the other hand of diminifhing his influence in Florence, by the impofition of additional taxes. From this difficulty he faw no poffibility of extricating himfelf, but by the moft rigid attention, as well to the improvement of the public revenue, as to the ftate of his own concerns. The increafing profperity of the city of Florence feconded his efforts, and in a fhort time the creditors of the ftate were fully reimburfed, without any increafe of the public burdens. His own engagements yet remained incomplete; but whilft he was endeavouring, from his large property and extenfive concerns, to discharge the demands againft him, a decree providing for the payment of his debts out of the public treafury relieved him from his difficulties, and proved that the affection of his fellow-citizens yet remained unimpaired (a). Lorenzo did not however receive this mark of efteem, without bitterly exclaiming againft the negligence and imprudence of his factors and correfpondents, who, by their inattention to his affairs, had reduced him to the neceffity of accepting fuch a favor. From this period he determined to clofe his mercantile

(a) *Valori in vitâ Laur. p.* 38.

concerns with all poffible expedition, well confi-
dering, that befides the inherent uncertainty of
thefe tranfactions, the fuccefs of them depended
too much on the induftry and integrity of others.
He therefore refolved to turn his attention to
occupations more particularly under his own
infpection, and to relinquifh the fluctuating ad-
vantages of commerce, for the more certain revenue
derived from the cultivation of his rich farms and
extenfive poffeffions in different parts of Tufcany.

His villa of Poggio-Cajano was, in his intervals
of leifure, his favorite refidence. Here he erected
a magnificent manfion (*a*), and formed the com-
plete eftablifhment of a princely farmer. Of this
fertile domain, and of the labors of Lorenzo in
its cultivation and improvement, one of his con-
temporaries has left a very particular and authentic
defcription (*b*)· " The village of Cajano," fays he,
" is built on the eafy flope of a hill, and is at the
" diftance of about ten miles from Florence. The
" road to it from the city is very fpacious, and
" excellent even in winter, and is in every refpect
" fuitable for all kinds of carriages. The river
" Ombrone winds round it with a fmooth deep
" ftream, affording great plenty of fifh. The villa

(*a*) —————— Medicum quid tecta fuperba,
Carregî, & Trebii: Iefulana aut condita rupe
Comemorem? jures Luculli tecta fuperba:
Quæque fine exemplo *Cajana* palatia *Laurens*
Aedificat, quorum fcandet faftigia, tanquam
Per planum iret eques, partefque equitabit in omnes.
           Ug. Verini de illuft. Urb. lib. ii.
(*b*) *Mic. Verini Ep.* xvi. *ap. Band. Cat. Bib. Laur. v.* iii. *p.* 483.

" of Lorenzo is denominated *Ambra*, either from
" the name of the river, or on account of its ex-
" traordinary beauty. His fields are occafionally
" refrefhed with ftreams of fine and wholefome
" water, which Lorenzo, with that magnificence
" which characterizes all his undertakings, has
" conveyed by an aqueduct over mountains and
" precipices for many miles (*a*). The houfe is not
" yet built, but the foundations are laid. Its fitu-
" ation is midway between Florence and Piftoia.
" Towards the north, a fpacious plain extends to
" the river, and is protected from the floods,
" which fudden rains fometimes occafion, by an
" immenfe embankment. From the facility with
" which it is watered in fummer, it is fo fertile,
" that three crops of hay are cut in each year ;
" but it is manured every other year left the foil
" fhould be exhaufted. On an eminence about
" the midle of the farm are very extenfive ftables,
" the floors of which, for the fake of cleanlinefs, are
" laid with ftone. Thefe buildings are furrounded
" with high walls and a deep moat, and have four
" towers like a caftle. Here are kept a great number
" of moft fertile and productive cows, which afford

(*a*) This aqueduct is frequently celebrated in the poems of
Politiano.

In fontem Laurentii Medicis Ambram.

" Ut lafciva fuo furtim daret ofcula Lauro,
" Ipfi fibi occultas reperit Ambra vias."
And again,

In eumdem.

" Traxit amatrices hæc ufque ad limina Nymphas,
" Dum jactat Laurum fæpius Ambra fuum."

" a quantity of cheefe, equal to the fupply of the
" city and vicinity of Florence; fo that it is now
" no longer neceffary to procure it as formerly
" from Lombardy. A brood of hogs fed by the
" whey grow to a remarkable fize. The villa
" abounds with quails, and other birds, particu-
" larly water fowl, fo that the diverfion of fowling
" is enjoyed here without fatigue. Lorenzo has
" alfo furnifhed the woods with pheafants and
" with peacocks which he procured from Sicily.
" His orchards and gardens are moft luxuriant,
" extending along the banks of the river. His
" plantation of mulberry trees is of fuch extent,
" that we may hope ere long to have a diminution
" in the price of filk. But why fhould I proceed
" in my defcription? come and fee the place
" yourfelf; and you will acknowledge, like the
" queen of Sheba when fhe vifited Solomon, that
" the report is not adequate to the truth."

Like the gardens of Alcinous, the farm of Lorenzo
has frequently been celebrated in the language of
poetry. To his own poem, on the deftruction of
his labors by the violence of the river, we have
before adverted (a). Politiano thus concludes his
Sylva devoted to the praifes of Homer, to which,
on account of its having been written at this place,
he has given the name of *Ambra* (b):

(a) *Vol.* I. *p.* 287. and *v.* the poem of *Ambra* in *col.* iv.

(b) Politiano addreffed this poem to Lorenzo Tornabuoni, the
coufin of Lorenzo de' Medici, of whom a very favorable character
may be found in the letters of Politiano (*Lib.* xii. *Ep.* 6.). "Debe-

Macte opibus, macte ingenio, meo gloria LAURENS,
Gloria mufarum LAUREN! montefque propinquos
Perfodis, & longo fufpenfos excipis arcu,
Præglidas ducturus aquas, qua prata fupinum
Lata videt pedium, riguis uberrima lymphis;
Aggere tuta novo, pifcofif,ue undique fepta
Limitibus, per quæ multo fervante moloffo
Plena Tarentinis fuccrefcunt ubera vaccis;
Atque aliud nigris miffum (quis credat) ab Indis,
Ruminat ignotas armentum difcolor herbas.
At vituli tepidis claufi fœnilibus intus,
Expectant tota fugendas nocte parentes.
Interea magnis lac denfum bullit ahenis,
Brachiaque exertus fenior, tunicataque pubes
Comprimit, & longa ficcandum ponit in umbra.
Utque piæ pafcuntur oves, ita vaftus obefo
Corpore, fus calaber cavea ftat claufus olenti,
Atque aliam ex alia pofcit grunnitibus efcam.
Celtiber ecce fibi latebrofa cuniculus antra
Perforat; innumerus net ferica vellera bombyx;
At vaga floriferos errant difperfa per hortos,
Multiforumque replent operofa examina fuber;
Et genus omne avium captivis inftrepit alis.
Dumque Antenorei volucris criftata Timavi
Parturit, & cuftos capitoli gramina tondet,
Multa lacu fe merfat anas, fubitaque volantes
Nube diem fufcant Veneris tutela columbæ.

" tur hæc filva tibi, vel argumento, vel titulo, nam & Homeri ftudio-
" fus es, quafique nofter confectaneus, & propinquus Laurenti
" Medicis, fummi præcellentifque viri, qui fcilicet Ambram ipfam
" Cajanam, prædium (ut ita dixerim) omniferum, quafi pro laxamen-
" to fili delegit civilium laborum. Tibi ergo poemation hoc quale-
" cunque eft, nuncupamus, &c." Pridie nonas Nov. MCCCCLXXXV.

Go on, LORENZO, thou the mufe's pride,
Pierce the hard rock and fcoop the mountain's fide;
The diftant ftreams fhall hear thy potent call,
And the proud arch receive them as they fall.
Thence o'er thy fields the genial waters lead,
That with luxuriant verdure crown the mead.
There rife thy mounds th'oppofing flood that ward,
There thy domains thy faithful maftives guard.
Tarentum there her horned cattle fends,
Whofe fwelling teats the milky rill diftends;
There India's breed of various colors range,
Pleas'd with the novel fcene and paftures ftrange,
Whilft nightly clos'd within their fhelter'd ftall,
For the due treat their lowing offspring call.
Mean time the milk in fpacious coppers boils,
With arms upftript the elder ruftic toils,
The young affift the curdled mafs to fqueeze,
And place in cooling fhades the recent cheefe.
Wide o'er thy downs extends thy fleecy charge;
There the Calabrian hog obefe and large,
Loud from his fty demands his conftant food ;
And Spain fupplies thee with thy rabbit brood.
Where mulberry groves their length of fhadow fpread,
Secure the filk-worm fpins his luftrous thread;
And cull'd from every flower the plunderer meets,
The bee regales thee with her rified fweets.
There birds of various plume, and various note,
Flutter their captive wings; with cackling throat
The Paduan fowl betrays her future breed,
And there the geefe, once Rome's prefervers, feed,
And ducks amufive fport amidft thy floods,
And doves, the pride of Venus, throng thy woods.

When Lorenzo was prevented by his numerous avocations from enjoying his retreat at Poggio-Cajano, his other villas in the vicinity of Florence afforded him an opportunity of devoting to his own ufe, or the fociety of his friends, thofe fhorter intervals of time which he could withdraw from the fervice of the public. His refidence at Careggi was in every refpect fuitable to his rank. The houfe, which was erected by his grandfather, and enlarged by his father, was fufficiently commodious. The adjacent grounds, which poffeffed every natural advantage that wood and water could afford, were improved and planted under his own directions (*a*), and his gardens were provided with every vegetable, either for ornament or ufe, which the moft diligent refearch could fupply (*b*).   But Fiefole feems to

(*a*) Thefe particulars are adverted to in the following lines of Francefco Camerlini:

Allufio in Villam Caregium Laurentii Medices.

Caregium gratæ charites habitare feruntur,
  Gratus ager, chari gratior umbra loci,
Cofmus honos, patriæque pater conftruxerat ædes,
  Di pofuitque emptos ordine primus agros.
Degener haud tanto natus Petrus inde parenti,
  Curavit partes amplificare fuas.
Vixque tibi, Laurens, in tanta mole reliquit
  Quod peragas, nifi quod maxima femper agis,
Tu dignos Faunis lucos, fontefque Napæis
  Struxifti, & deceant quæ modo rura Deos.
Band. Cat. Bib. Laur. v. iii. *p.* 545.

(*b*) This was perhaps one of the earlieft collections of plants in Europe, which deferves the name of a Botanical Garden; the authority of Sabbati, who dates the commencement of that at Rome in have been the general refort of his literary friends, to many of whom he allotted habitations in the neighbourhood, during the amenity of the fummer months. Of thefe Politiano and Pico were the moft conftant, and perhaps the moft welcome guefts. Landino, Scala, and Ficino were alfo frequent in their vifits; and Crinitus, the pupil of Politiano, and Marullus, his rival in letters and in love, were occafionally admitted to this felect fociety (a). " Superior perhaps, " fays Voltaire (fubftituting however Lafcar and Chalcondyles, for Scala and Crinitus), " to that of the boafted " fages of Greece." Of the beauties of this place

the pontificate of Nicholas V. about the year 1450, being rejected by our eminent botanift Dr. Smith; who gives the priority to that of Padua in 1533. *v. Sabb. Hort. Rom. v. i. p. 1. Dr. Smith's Introduct. Difcourfe to the Tranfact. of the Linn. Soc. p. 8.* Of the garden of Lorenzo a very particular account is given by Aleffandro Braccio in a Latin poem addreffed to Bernardo Bembo, and preferved in the Laurentian Library, *Plut.* lxxxxi. *fup. cod.* 41. *Band. Cat. v.* iii. *p.* 787.; from which catalogue I fhall infert it in the Appendix, *No.* LXIII,

(a) Petrus Crinitus (or Piero de' Ricci) thus addreffes Marullus:

> Nuper Fæfuleis (ut foleo) jugis,
> Mentem Lesbiaco carmine molliter
> Solari libuit: mox teneram chelyn,
> Myrto fub virido depofui, & gradum,
>   Placuit ad urbem flectere,
> Qua nofter *Medices* pieridum Parens
> *Marulle*, hofpitium dulce tibi exhibet,
> Ac te perpetuis muneribus fovens,
> Phœbum non patitur tela refumere.
> *Laurens* Camœnarum decus.

Crin. op. Lugd. 1534. p. 555.

and of the friendly intercourfe that fubfifted
among thefe eminent men, Politiano, in a letter
to Ficino, gives us fome idea (*a*). " When you
" are incommoded," fays he, " with the heat of
" the feafon in your retreat at Careggi, you will
" perhaps think the fhelter of Fiefole not unde-
" ferving your notice. Seated between the floping
" fides of the mountain, we have here water in
" abundance, and being conftantly refrefhed with
" moderate winds, find little inconvenience from
" the glare of the fun. As you approach the houfe
" it feems embofomed in the wood, but when
" you reach it, you find it commands a full
" profpect of the city. Populous as the vicinity
" is, yet I can here enjoy that folitude fo grati-
" fying to my difpofition. But I fhall tempt you
" with other allurements. Wandering beyond the
" limits of his own plantation, Pico fometimes
" fteals unexpectedly on my retirement, and draws
" me from my fhades to partake of his fupper.
" What kind of fupper that is you well know;
" fparing indeed, but neat, and rendered grate-
" ful by the charms of his converfation. Be you
" however my gueft. Your fupper here fhall be
" as good, and your wine perhaps better, for in
" the quality of my wine I fhall contend for
" fuperiority even with Pico himfelf."

Befides his places of refidence before noticed,
Lorenzo had large poffeffions in different parts of
Tufcany. His houfe at Caffagiolo, near the village
of that name among the romantic fcenes of the

(*a*) *Pol. Ep. lib. x. Ep.* 14.

Appenines,

Appenines, had been the favorite refidence of his
grandfather Cofmo; who, on being afked why he
preferred this place to his more convenient habita-
tion at Fiefole, is faid to have affigned as a reafon,
that Caffagiolo feemed pleafanter, becaufe all the
country he could fee from his windows was his own.
At Agnana, in the territory of Pifa, Lorenzo had a
fertile domain, which he improved by draining and
bringing into cultivation the extenfive marfhes that
lay in its neighbourhood, the completion of which
was only prevented by his death (*a*). Another eftate
in the diftrict of Volterra was rendered extremely
fruitful by his labors, and yielded him an ample
revenue. Valori relates, that Lorenzo was highly
gratified with the amufement of horfe-racing, and
that he kept many horfes for this purpofe, amongft
which was a roan, that on every occafion bore
away the prize. The fame author profeffes to have
heard from Politiano, that as often as this horfe
happened to be fick, or was wearied with the courfe,
he refufed any nourifhment except from the hands
of Lorenzo, at whofe approach he teftified his
pleafure by neighing and by motions of his body,
even whilft lying on the ground; fo that it is not
to be wondered at, fays this author, by a kind of
commendation rather more ftriking than juft, that
Lorenzo fhould be the delight of mankind, when
even the brute creation expreffed an affection for
him (*b*).

(*a*) *Valor. in vitá Laur. p.* 39.

(*b*) Delectabatur maxime equorum curfu. Quare equos plurimos
habuit in delitiis, in quibus ille fuit, quem de colore morellum appel-

In the year 1484, at which time Piero de' Medici, the eldeſt ſon of Lorenzo, was about fourteen years of age, his father judged it expedient to ſend him to Rome on a viſit to the pope, and appointed Scala and Politiano as his companions. He did not however implicitly confide in their diſcretion, but drew up himſelf very full and explicit directions for the conduct of his ſon during his abſence. Theſe inſtructions yet remain, and may ſerve, as much as any circumſtance whatever, to give us an idea of the ſagacity and penetration of Lorenzo, and of his attention, not only to the regulation of the manners of his ſon, but to the promotion of his own views (a). He adviſes him to ſpeak naturally, without affectation, not to be anxious to diſplay his learning, to uſe expreſſions of civility, and to addreſs himſelf with ſeriouſneſs, and yet with eaſe to all. On his arrival at Rome, he cautions him not to take precedence of his countrymen who are his ſuperiors in age; " for though you are my ſon," ſays he, " you will remember that you are only a " citizen of Florence like themſelves. " He ſuggeſts

labant, tantae pernicitatis, ut ex omnibus certaminibus victoriam ſemper reportaverit. De hoc equo ipſe a Politiano audivi, quod mirum legentibus videatur, non tamen novum, eum, quoties vel ægrotaret, vel defeſſus eſſet, niſi a Laurentio oblatum cibum omnem faſtidire ſolitum, & quotieſcumque ille accederet, motu corporis, & hinnitu, quamvis humi proſtratum, animi lætitiam fuiſſe teſtatum, ut non jam mirum ſit tantopere hominibus gratum, quem etiam feræ dilexerint. *Valor. in vita, p.* 49.

(a) This curious paper of private inſtructions from Lorenzo to his ſon yet remains, and is given in the Appendix, from the collection of Fabroni (*No.* LXIV.).

to him what topics it will be proper for him to dwell upon in his interview with the pope; and directs him to exprefs, in the moft explicit manner, the devotion of his father to the holy fee. He then proceeds to the effential object of his miffion. " After having thus recommended me to his holinefs, " you will inform him, that your affection for your " brother induces you to fpeak a word in his favor. " You can here mention that I have educated him " for the priefthood, and fhall clofely attend to his " learning and his manners, fo that he may not dif- " grace his profeffion. That in this refpect I repofe " all my hopes on his holinefs; who, having already " given us proofs of his kindnefs and affection, " will add to our obligations by any promotion " which he may think proper to beftow upon him. " Endeavouring by thefe and fimilar expreffions to " recommend your brother to his favor as much as " lies in your power. "

In whatever manner Piero acquitted himfelf on his youthful embaffy, it is probable that this inter- view accomplifhed the object on which the future fortunes of his houfe were fo materially to depend, and Giovanni de' Medici, when only thirteen years of age, ranked with the prime fupporters of the Roman church. It feems, however, that although the pope had complied with the preffing inftances of Lorenzo, in beftowing on his fon the dignity of a cardinal, he was not infenfible of the indecorum of fuch a meafure, for he exprefsly prohibited him from affuming the infignia of his rank for three years, requefting that he would apply that interval to the diligent profecution of his ftudies. He accordingly went to Pifa, where the regularity of his conduct, and his attention to his improvement, juftified in fome degree the extraordinary indulgence which he had experienced; in confequence of which his father made the moft preffing inftances to the pope to fhorten the term of his probation. "Truft " the management of this bufinefs to me," faid Innocent, " I have heard of his good conduct, and " of the honors which he has obtained in his col- " lege difputes. I confider him as my own fon, " and fhall, when it is leaft expected, order his " promotion to be made public; befides which, it " is my intention to do much more for his advance- " ment than is at prefent fuppofed." The three years were, however, fuffered to elapfe, and the young cardinal was then admitted to all the honors of his rank, the inveftiture having been performed by Matteo Boffo, prior of the monaftery at Fiefole, who has left, in one of his letters, a particular narrative of the ceremony (a). After paffing a few days with his father at Florence, Giovanni haftened to Rome to pay his refpects to the pope. On his approach to that city he was met and congratulated by feveral other cardinals, who made no hefitation in receiving into their number fo young an affociate. By the ferioufnefs and propriety of his demeanor, he obviated as much as poffible the unfavorable impreffion which a promotion fo unprecedented had made on the public mind. Soon after his arrival

(a) *Recuperaciones Fefulanæ. Ep.* cx. As the work does not frequently occur, I fhall give this letter in the Appendix, No. LXV.

at Rome, his father addreſſed to him an admonitory letter, as conſpicuous for ſound ſenſe as for paternal affeĉtion; but which diſcovers the deep policy of Lorenzo, and the great extent of his views. This letter may, without any unreaſonable aſſumption, be conſidered as the guide of the future life and fortunes of a ſon, who afterwards attained the higheſt rank in Chriſtendom, and ſupported it with a dignity which gave it new luſtre (a).

Lorenzo de' Medici,

To Giovanni de' Medici, Cardinal.

" You, and all of us who are intereſted in your
" welfare, ought to eſteem ourſelves highly favored
" by providence, not only for the many honors
" and benefits beſtowed on our houſe, but more
" particularly for having conferred upon us, in
" your perſon, the greateſt dignity we have ever
" enjoyed. This favor, in itſelf ſo important, is
" rendered ſtill more ſo by the circumſtances with
" which it is accompanied, and eſpecially by the
" conſideration of your youth, and of our ſituation
" in the world. The firſt thing that I would there-
" fore ſuggeſt to you is, that you ought to be
" grateful to God, and continually to recolleĉt that
" it is not through your merits, your prudence,
" or your ſolicitude, that this event has taken

(a) The original will be found in the Appendix, No. LXVI.
" Hæc epiſtola," ſays Fabroni, " tanquam Cycnea fuit prudentiſſimi
" hominis vox & orationis; paulo enim poſt ille mortem obivit." *Fabr.*
in vitâ, ii. 313.

" place, but through his favor, which you can
" only repay by a pious, chaste, and exemplary
" life; and that your obligations to the perform-
" ance of these duties are so much the greater,
" as in your early years you have given some rea-
" sonable expectation that your riper age may
" produce such fruits. It would indeed be highly
" disgraceful, and as countrary to your duty as
" to my hopes, if at a time when others display
" a greater share of reason, and adopt a better mode
" of life, you should forget the precepts of your
" youth, and forsake the path in which you have
" hitherto trodden Endeavour therefore to al-
" leviate the burden of your early dignity, by
" the regularity of your life, and by your per-
" severance in those studies which are suitable to
" your profession. It gave me great satisfaction
" to learn, that, in the course of the past year,
" you had frequently, of your own accord, gone
" to communion and confession; nor do I con-
" ceive that there is any better way of obtaining
" the favor of heaven, than by habituating your-
" self to a performance of these and similar duties.
" This appears to me to be the most suitable and
" useful advice which, in the first instance, I can
" possibly give you.

" I well know, that as you are now to reside at
" Rome, that sink of all iniquity, the difficulty of
" conducting yourself by these admonitions will
" be increased. The influence of example is it-
" self prevalent; but you will probably meet with
" those who will particularly endeavour to corrupt

" and incite you to vice; becaufe, as you may
" yourfelf perceive, your early attainment to fo
" great a dignity is not obferved without envy,
" and thofe who could not prevent your receiving
" that honor, will fecretly endeavour to diminifh
" it, by inducing you to forfeit the good eftimation
" of the public; thereby precipitating you into
" that gulf into which they have themfelves fallen;
" in which attempt the confideration of your
" youth will give them a confidence of fuccefs.
" To thefe difficulties you ought to oppofe your-
" felf with the greater firmnefs, as there is at prefent
" lefs virtue amongft your brethren of the college.
" I acknowledge indeed that feveral of them are
" good and learned men, whofe lives are exem-
" plary, and whom I would recommend to you
" as patterns of your conduct. By emulating them
" you will be fo much the more known and
" efteemed, in proportion as your age, and the
" peculiarity of your fituation, will diftinguifh
" you from your colleagues. Avoid however, as
" you would Scylla or Charibdis, the imputation
" of hypocrify ; guard againft all oftentation, either
" in your conduct or your difcourfe; affect not
" aufterity, nor even appear too ferious. This
" advice you will, I hope, in time underftand and
" practife better than I can exprefs it.
   " You are not unacquainted with the great im-
" portance of the character which you have to
" fuftain, for you well know that all the Chriftian
" world would profper if the cardinals were what
" they ought to be; becaufe in fuch a cafe there

" would always be a good pope, upon which the
" tranquillity of Chriftendom fo materially de-
" pends. Endeavour then to render yourfelf fuch,
" that if all the reft refembled you, we might ex-
" pect this univerfal blefling. To give you par-
" ticular directions as to your behaviour and
" converfation, would be a matter of no fmall
" difficulty. I fhall therefore only recommend,
" that in your intercourfe with the cardinals, and
" other men of rank, your language be unaffuming
" and refpectful, guiding yourfelf however by your
" own reafon, and not fubmitting to be impelled
" by the paflions of others, who, actuated by
" improper motives, may pervert the ufe of their
" reafon. Let it fatisfy your confcience that your
" converfation is without intentional offence; and
" if, through impetuofity of temper, any one
" fhould be offended, as his enmity is without
" juft caufe, fo it will not be very lafting. On this
" your firft vifit to Rome, it will however be more
" advifable for you to liften to others than to fpeak
" much yourfelf.

" You are now devoted to God and the church;
" on which account you ought to aim at being a
" good ecclefiaftic, and to fhow that you prefer the
" honor and ftate of the church, and of the apoftolic
" fee, to every other confideration. Nor, while
" you keep this in view, will it be difficult for
" you to favor your family and your native place.
" On the contrary, you fhould be the link to bind
" this city clofer to the church, and our family
" with the city; and although it be impoffible to

" forefee what accidents may happen, yet I doubt
" not but this may be done with equal advantage
" to all; obferving, however, that you are always
" to prefer the interefts of the church.

" You are not only the youngeft cardinal in the
" college, but the young ft perfon that ever was
" raifed to that rank; and you ought therefore to
" be the moft vigilant and unaffuming. not giving
" others occafion to wait for you either in the chapel,
" the confiftory, or upon deputations. You will
" foon get a fufficient infight into the manners of
" your brethren. With thofe of lefs refpectable
" character, converfe not with too much intimacy;
" not merely on account of the circumftance in
" itfelf, but for the fake of public opinion. Con-
" verfe on general topics with all. On public
" occafions let your equipage and drefs be rather
" below than above mediocrity. A handfome houfe
" and a well-ordered family will be preferable to a
" great retinue and a fplendid refidence. Endeavour
" to live with regularity, and gradually to bring
" your expenfes within thofe bounds which in a
" new eftablifhment cannot perhaps be expected.
" Silk and jewels are not fuitable for perfons in
" your ftation. Your tafte will be better fhown in
" the acquifition of a few elegant remains of anti-
" quity, or in the collecting of handfome books,
" and by your attendants being learned and well-
" bred rather than numerous Invite others to your
" houfe oftener than you receive invitations. Prac-
" tife neither too frequently. Let your own food
" be plain, and take fufficient exercife, for thofe

(154)

" who wear your habit are foon liable, without
" great caution, to contract infirmities. The ftation
" of a cardinal is not lefs fecure than elevated; on
" which account thofe who arrive at it too frequently
" become negligent, conceiving that their object is
" attained and that they can preferve it with little
" trouble. This idea is often injurious to the life
" and character of thofe who entertain it. Be atten-
" tive therefore to your conduct, and confide in
" others too little rather than too much. There is
" one rule which I would recommend to your at-
" tention in preference to all others: Rife early in
" the morning. This will not only contribute to
" your health, but will enable you to arrange and
" expedite the bufinefs of the day; and as there
" are various duties incident to your ftation, fuch
" as the performance of divine fervice, ftudying,
" giving audience, &c. you will find the obfervance
" of this admonition productive of the greateft
" utility. Another very neceffary precaution, par-
" ticularly on your entrance into public life, is to
" deliberate every evening on what you have to
" perform the following day, that you may not be
" unprepared for whatever may happen. With
" refpect to your fpeaking in the confiftory, it will
" be moft becoming for you at prefent to refer
" the matters in debate to the judgment of his
" holinefs, alledging as a reafon your own youth
" and inexperience. You will probably be defired
" to intercede for the favors of the pope on par-
" ticular occafions. Be cautious however that you
" trouble him not too often; for his temper leads

" him to be moſt liberal to thoſe who weary him
" leaſt with their ſolicitations. This you muſt ob-
" ſerve, leſt you ſhould give him offence, remem-
" bering alſo at times to converſe with him on
" more agreeable topics ; and if you ſhould be
" obliged to requeſt ſome kindneſs from him let
" it be done with that modeſty and humility which
" are ſo pleaſing to his diſpoſition. Farewel."

As the policy of Lorenzo led him to ſupport a
powerful influence at Rome, and as he had fre-
quently experienced the good effects of the con-
nexion which ſubſiſted between him and the
family of the Orſini, he thought it adviſable to
ſtrengthen it ; and accordingly propoſed a marriage
between his ſon Piero, and Alfonſina, the daughter
of Roberto Orſini, count of Tagliacozzo and Albi.
This propoſal was eagerly liſtened to by Virginio
Orſini, who was then conſidered as the head of
that powerful family, the chiefs of which, though
ſubordinate to the pope, ſcarcely conſidered them-
ſelves as ſubjects, and frequently acted with the
independence of ſovereign princes. In the month
of March 1487, theſe nuptials were celebrated at
Naples. in the preſence of the king and his court
with extraordinary pomp (a). Lorenzo, on his
marriage with Clarice Orſini, had received no
portion ; but the reputation which he had now
acquired was more than an equivalent for the pride

(a) Si fece lo ſpoſalitio in Caſtello, nella Sala grande, preſente il
Re e tutta la Corte, con gran cena e feſta. Il Re non poeta fare
maggiori dimoſtrazioni verſo il Sig. Virginio. *Bern. Oricellarii Ep.
ap. Fabr. v. ii. p.* 316.

of anceftry, and Virginio agreed to pay 12,000 Nea-
politan ducats as a portion with his daughter (*a*).
On this occafion Piero was accompanied by Ber-
nardo Rucellai, who had married Nannina, one
of the fifters of Lorenzo, and who has not only
fignalized himfelf as a protector of learned men,
but was himfelf one of the moft accomplifhed
fcholars of his time (*b*).

(*b*) *Extant in Filz.* 1. I capitoli di matrimonio tra l'Alfonfina
de Urfinis figlia del quondam Roberto de Urfinis conte di Tagliacozzo
e d'Albi, e Piero de' Medici, comparente Virginio de Urfinis fratel
confobrino. Dos fuit Ducatorum Neapolitanorum 12,000 *Fabr. ut fup.*

(*c*) The talents and acquirements of Rucellai juftly entitled him
to the honor of fo near an alliance with the family of the Medici.
His public life has indeed incurred the cenfure of the Florentine
hiftorians of the fucceeding century, who wrote under the preffure
of a defpotic government; but it is not difficult to perceive that his
crime was an ardent love of liberty, which he preferred to the claims
of kindred, and the expectations of perfonal aggrandizement. *Ammir.*
Opufc. vol. ii. *Elog.* ii. 161. *Comment. di Nerli. p.* 64. His Latin
hiftorical works, " *De Bello Italico*," and " *De Bello Pifano*," have
merited the approbation of the difcriminating Erafmus. "Novi Venetiæ,"
fays he, " Bernardum Ocricularium (Oricellarium) cujus Hiftorias fi
" legiffes, dixiffes alterum *Salluftium*, aut certe Salluftii temporibus
fcriptas." *Apotheg. lib.* viii. The former of thefe works was firft
publifhed at London by Brindley in 1724, and again by William
Bowyer, with the treatife *de Bello Pifano*, in 1733. Bernardo was
alfo a poet, and appears in the *Canti Carnafcialefchi* as the author
of the *Trionfo della Calunnia. Cant. Carnas. p.* 125. But the poetical
reputation of Bernardo is eclipfed by that of his fon Giovanni Rucellai,
author of the tragedy of *Rofmunda*, and of that beautiful didactic
poem *Le Api*, which will remain a lafting monument that the Italian
language requires not the fhackles of rhime to render it harmonious.
" Homme de Goût (fays Tenhove) dans vos promenades folitaires
" prenez quelquefois fon poëme.

The marriage of Pier de' Medici was soon afterwards followed by that of his fister Maddalena with Francefco Cibò, the fon of the pope, and who then bore the title of count of Anguillara (*a*). Of the three other daughters of Lorenzo, Lucretia intermarried with Giacopo Salviati (*b*), Conteffina with Piero Ridolfi, and Louifa, his youngeft, after having been betrothed to Giovanni de' Medici, of a collateral branch of the fame family, died before the time appointed for the nuptials (*c*).

> " Ed odi quel che fopra un verde prato,
>> " Cinto d'abeti e d'onorati allori,
>> " Che bagna or un mufcofo e chiaro fonte,
>> " Canta de l'api del fuo florid' orto."

(*a*) Thefe nuptials were celebrated at Rome in the year 1488. Maddalena, who was very young, was accompanied by Matteo Franco, the facetious correfpondent of Pulci, (*vol. I. p.* 256.) the vivacity of whofe character did not prevent Lorenzo from felecting him for this important truft, in the execution of which he conciliated in a high degree the favor of the pope, and his courtiers.

Pol. Ep. lib. x. Ep. 12.

(*b*) *Vide vol.* I. *p.* 211.

(*c*) Befides his three fons and four daughters before enumerated, Lorenzo had other children, all of whom died in their infancy, as appears by a letter from him to Politiano; who having occafion to acquaint him with the indifpofition of fome part of his family, and being fearful of alarming him, addreffed his letter to Michellozzi, the fecretary of Lorenzo. In his anfwer, Lorenzo reproves, with fome degree of ferioufnefs, the ill-timed diftruft of Politiano, and with true floical dignity, declares that it gave him more uneafinefs than the intelligence that accompanied it. " Can you then conceive," fays he, " that my temper is fo infirm, as to be difturbed by fuch an event? " If my difpofition had been by nature weak, and liable to be impelled " by every guft, yet experience has taught me how to brave the " ftorm. I have not only known what it is to bear the ficknefs, but " even the death of fome of my children. The untimely lofs of my

In the year 1488, Piero de' Medici took a journey to Milan, to be prefent at the celebration of the nuptials of the young duke Galeazzo Sforza, with Ifabella, grand daughter of Ferdinand, king of Naples. The whole expenfe of this journey was defrayed by Lodovico Sforza, who paid a marked refpect to Piero, and directed that he fhould always appear in public at the fide of the duke. By a letter yet exifting, from the Florentine legate to Lorenzo de' Medici, it appears that thefe nuptials were celebrated with great magnificence (*a*); but amidft the fplendor of diamonds and the glitter of brocade, were entwined the ferpents of treachery and of guilt. Even in giving the hand of Ifabella to a nephew, whom he regarded rather as an implement of his ambition than as his lawful fovereign, Lodovico burnt with a criminal paffion for her himfelf; and the graveft of the Italian hiftorians affures us, that it was the public opinion that he had by means of magic and incantations prevented the confummation of a marriage, which while it promoted his political views, deprived him of the object of his love (*b*). The prejudices of the age, and the wickednefs of Lodovico, fuf-ficiently countenance the probability of fuch an attempt; but that the means employed were fo

" father when I was in my twenty-firft year, left me fo much expofed
" to the attacks of fortune, that life became a burden to me. You
" ought therefore to have known, that if nature denied me firmnefs,
" experience has fupplied the defect."

Laur. Ep. in. Ep. Pol. lib. x. Ep. 5.

(*a*) *v. App. No.* LXVII.
(*b*) *Guicciard. Hift. d Italia, lib.* i.

far fuccefsful, as to prevent that circumftance taking place for feveral months, is an affertion, of the veracity of which pofterity may be allowed to doubt.

Of this princefs an incident is recorded which does equal honor to her conjugal affection and her filial piety (*a*). When Charles VIII. of France, at the inftigation of Lodovico Sforza, entered Italy, a few years after her marriage, for the avowed purpofe of depriving her father of the throne of Naples, he paffed through Pavia, where the young duke then lay on his death-bed, not without giving rife to fufpicions that he had been poifoned. Touched with his misfortunes, and mindful of the relationfhip between Galeazzo and himfelf, who were fifters children, Charles refolved to fee him. The prefence of Lodovico, who did not chufe to rifque the confequences of a private and confidential interview, whilft it reftricted the converfation of the king to formal inquiries about the health of the duke, and wifhes for his recovery, excited both in him and in all prefent a deeper compaffion for the unhappy prince. Ifabella perceived the general fympathy; and throwing herfelf at the feet of the monarch, recommended to his protection her unfortunate hufband and her infant fon; at the fame time, by tears and entreaties, earneftly endeavouring to turn his refentment from her father and the houfe of Aragon. Attracted by her beauty, and moved by her folicitations, Charles appeared for a

---

(*a*) *Guisciard. Hift. d'Italia, lib.i.*

moment to relent, and the fate of Italy was fufpended in the balance; but the king recollecting the importance of his preparations, and the expectations which his enterprife had excited, foon fteeled his feelings againft this feminine attack, and refolved, in fpite of the fuggeftions of pity and the claims of humanity, to perfevere in his defign.

Having now fecured the tranquillity of Italy and the profperity of his family by every means that prudence could dictate, Lorenzo began to enjoy the fruits of his labors. Thefe he found in the affection and good-will of his fellow-citizens; in obferving the rapid progrefs of the fine arts, towards the promotion of which he had fo amply contributed; in the fociety and converfation of men of genius and learning; and in the inexhauftible ftores of knowledge with which he had enriched his own difcriminating and comprehenfive mind.

As his natural difpofition, or the effects of his education, frequently led him to meditate with great ferioufnefs on moral and religious fubjects, fo there were no perfons for whom he entertained a greater efteem than thofe who adorned their character as teachers of religion by a correfponding rectitude of life and propriety of manners. Amongft thefe he particularly diftinguifhed Mariano da Gena-zano, an Auguftin monk and fuperior of his order, for whofe ufe and that of his affociates, he erected in the fuburbs of Florence an extenfive building, which he endowed as a monaftery, and to which he was himfelf accuftomed occafionally to retire, with a few felect friends, to enjoy the converfation

of

of this learned ecclefiaftic. Politiano, in the pre-
face to his *Mifcellanea*, inveighing againft thofe who
affected to confider the ftudy of polite letters as
inconfiftent with the performance of facred func-
tions, adduces Mariano as an illuftrious inftance of
their union. " On this account," fays he to Lor-
enzo, " I cannot fufficiently admire your highly
" efteemed friend Mariano, whofe proficiency in
" theological ftudies, and whofe eloquence and
" addrefs in his public difcourfes, leave him with-
" out a rival. The leffons which he inculcates
" derive additional authority from his acknowled-
" ged difintereftednefs, and from the feverity of his
" private life; yet there is nothing morofe in his
" temper, nothing unpleafingly auftere; nor does
" he think the charms of poetry, or the amufe-
" ments and purfuits of elegant literature, below
" his attention." In one of his letters, the fame
author has left a very explicit account of the talents
of Mariano, as a preacher (*a*). " I was lately
" induced," fays he, " to attend one of his lectures,
" rather to fay the truth through curiofity, than
" with the hope of being entertained. His ap-
" pearance however interefted me in his favor.
" His addrefs was ftriking, and his eye marked
" intelligence. My expectations were raifed. He
" began—I was attentive; a clear voice—felect ex-
" preffion—elevated fentiment. He divides his
" fubject—I perceive his diftinctions. Nothing per-
" plexed; nothing infipid; nothing languid. He
" unfolds the web of his argument—I am enthralled.

(*a*) *Pol. Ep. lib.* iv. *Ep.* 6.

" He refutes the fophifm—I am freed. He intro-
" duces a pertinent narrative—I am interefted. He
" modulates his voice—I am charmed. He is
" jocular—I fmile. He preffes me with ferious
" truths—I yield to their force. He addreffes the
" paffions—the tears glide down my cheeks. He
" raifes his voice in anger—I tremble and wifh
" myfelf away."

Of the particular fubjects of difcuffion which
engaged the attention of Lorenzo and his affociates
in their interviews at the convent of San Gallo,
Valori has left fome account which he derived from
the information of Mariano himfelf. The exiftence
and attributes of the Deity, the infufficiency of
temporal enjoyments to fill the mind, and the
probability and moral neceffity of a future ftate,
were to Lorenzo the favorite objects of his dif-
courfe. His own opinion was pointedly expreffed.
" He is dead even to this life," faid Lorenzo, " who
" has no hopes of another (a)."

Although the citizens of Florence admired the
talents, and refpected the virtues of Mariano, their
attention was much more forcibly excited by a
preacher of a very different character, who poffeffed
himfelf of their confidence, and entitled himfelf to
their homage, by foretelling their deftruction. This
was the famous Girolamo Savonarola, who after-
wards acted fo confpicuous a part in the popular
commotions at Florence, and contributed fo effen-
tially to the accomplifhment of his own predictions.
Savonarola was a native of Ferrara, but the reputation

(a) *Valor. in vita. p.* 48.

which he had acquired as a preacher, induced Lorenzo de' Medici to invite him to Florence, where he took up his refidence in the year 1488 (a), and was appointed prior of the monaftery of S. Marco. By pretenfions to fuperior fanctity, and by a fervid and overpowering elocution, he foon acquired an aftonifhing afcendency over the minds of the people; and in proportion as his popularity increafed, his difregard of his patron became more apparent, and was foon converted into the moft vindictive animofity. It had been the cuftom of thofe who had preceded Savonarola in this office, to pay particular refpect to Lorenzo de' Medici, as the fupporter of the inftitution. Savonarola however not only rejected this ceremony, as founded in adulation, but as often as Lorenzo frequented the gardens of the monaftery, retired from his prefence, pretending that his intercourfe was with God and not with man. At the fame time, in his public difcourfes, he omitted no opportunity of attacking the reputation and diminifhing the credit of Lorenzo, by prognofticating the fpeedy termination of his authority, and his banifhment from his native place. The divine word, from the lips of Savonarola, defcended not amongft his audience like the dews of heaven; it was the piercing hail, the deftroying fword, the

(a) In 1489, according to Tirabofchi, *Storia della Lett. Ital.* t. vi. *par.* 2. *p.* 377.; but Savonarola himfelf, in his *Trattato delle Rivelationi della reformatione della Chiefa*, Ven. 1536, (if indeed the work be his,) affigns an earlier period. In this work the fanatic affumes the credit of having foretold the death of Innocent VIII. of Lorenzo de' Medici, the irruption of the French into Italy, &c.

herald of deftruction. The friends of Lorenzo frequently remonftrated with him, on his fuffering the monk to proceed to fuch an extreme of arrogance; but Lorenzo had either more indulgence or more difcretion than to adopt hoftile meafures againft a man, who, though morofe and infolent, he probably confidered as fincere. On the contrary, he difplayed his ufual prudence and moderation, by declaring that whilft the preacher exerted himfelf to reform the citizens of Florence, he fhould readily excufe his incivility to himfelf. This extraordinary degree of lenity, if it had no influence on the mind of the fanatic, prevented in a great degree the ill effects of his harangues; and it was not till after the death of Lorenzo, that Savonarola excited thofe difturbances in Florence, which led to his own deftruction, and terminated in the ruin of the republic.

Another ecclefiaftic, whofe worth and talents had conciliated the favor of Lorenzo, was Matteo Boffo, fuperior of the convent of regular canons at Fiefole. Not lefs converfant with the writings of the ancient philofophers, than with the theological ftudies of his own times, Boffo was a profound fcholar, a clofe reafoner, and a convincing orator; but to thefe he united much higher qualifications—a candid mind, an inflexible integrity, and an interefting fimplicity of life and manners. To his treatife *De veris animi gaudiis* is prefixed a recommendatory epiftle from Politiano to Lorenzo de' Medici, highly favorable to the temper and character of the author (*a*). On the publication

(*a*) This treatife was firft publifhed in octavo, at Florence, by Ser Francifco Bonacuifi. Anno Salutis MCCCCLXXXXI. Sexto Idus of this piece, Boffo tranfmitted a copy to Lorenzo, with a latin letter, preferved in the *Recuperationes Fefulanæ*, another work of the fame anthor, highly deferving the attention of the fcholar (*a*). In this letter Boffo bears teftimony to the virtues and to the piety of Lorenzo ; but whether this teftimony ought to be received with greater confidence, becaufe Boffo was the confeffor of Lorenzo, the reader will decide for himfelf.

Of thefe his graver affociates, as well as of the companions of his lighter hours, Lorenzo was accuftomed to ftimulate the talents by every means in his power. His own intimate acquaintance with the tenets of the ancient philofophers, and his acute and verfatile genius, enabled him to propofe to their difcuffion, fubjects of the moft interefting nature, and either to take a chief part in the converfation, or to avail himfelf of fuch obfervations as it might occafion. It appears alfo, that at fome times he amufed himfelf with offering to their confideration fuch topics as he well knew would elude

Februarii. From this edition I shall give the introductory letter of Politiano. *v. App. No.* LXVIII.

(*a*) This book is eftimable not only for its contents, but as bring one of the fineft fpecimens of typography of the fifteenth century. Inftead of a title, we read, QUÆ HOC VOLUMINE HABENTUR VARIA DIVERSAQUE ET LONCA EX DISPERSIONE COLLECTA QUO BREVI SUB TITULO SUBJICIANTUR AC NOMINE RECUPERATIONES FESULANAS LECTOR AGNOSCITO. And at the clofe, RECUPERATIONES FESULANAS *has elegantiffimas, opus quidem aureum & penitus divinum quam caftigatiffime Impreffit omni folertia* PLATO DE BENEDICTIS *Bononienfis in alma civitate Bononiæ. Anno Salutis* MCCCCLXXXIII. *decimo tertio* KALENDAS AUGUSTAS. *Folio.* The letter from Boffo to Lorenzo de' Medici is given in the Appendix, *No.* LXIX.

their refearches, although they might exercife their powers, as men try their ftrength by fhooting arrows towards the fky. Of this we have an inftance in the fonnet addreffed by him to Salviati (*a*). " When the mind," fays he, " efcapes from the " ftorms of life, to the calm haven of reflection, " doubts arife which require folution. If no one " can effectually exert himfelf to obtain eternal " happinefs without the fpecial favor of God. " and if that favor be only granted to thofe who " are well difpofed towards its reception, I wifh " to know whether the grace of God, or the good " difpofition, firft commences ?" The learned theologian to whom this captious queftion was addreffed, took it into his ferious confideration, and after dividing it into feven parts, attempted its folution in a Latin treatife of confiderable extent, which is yet preferved in the Laurentian Library (*b*).

Lorenzo was not however deftined long to enjoy

(*a*) Lo fpirito talora a fe ridutto,
    E dal mar tempeftofo e travagliato
    Fuggito in porto tranquillo e pacato,
    Penfando ha dubbio e vuolne trar coftrutto.
S'egli è ver, che da Dio proceda tutto,
    E fenza lui nulla è, cioè il peccato;
    Per fua grazia fe ci è conceffo e dato
    Seminar qui per corre eterno frutto;
Tal grazia in quel fol fa operazione
    Ch' a riceverla è volto e ben difpofto,
    Dunque che cofa è quella ne difpone?
Qual prima fia, vorrei mi foffe efpofto,
    O tal grazia, o la buona inclinazione:
    Rifpondi or tu al dubbio, ch' è propofto.

(*b*) *Georgii Benigni Salviati, in Rhythmum acutiffimum magni Laurentii Medicis Quaeftiones feptem*, &c. PLUT. lxxxiii. *Cod.* 18.

that tranquillity which he had fo affiduoufly la-
bored to fecure. His life had fcarcely reached its
meridian, when the profpect was overhung with
dark and lowering clouds. The death of his
wife Clarice, which happened in the month of
Auguft 1488, was a fevere fliock to his domeftic
happinefs. He was then abfent from Florence, and
did not arrive in time to fee her before fhe died,
which it feems gave rife to infinuations that his
conjugal affection was not very ardent (*a*); but
the infirm ftate of his own health at this time had
rendered it neceffary for him to vifit the warm
baths, where he received an account of her death
before he was apprized of the danger of her fitua-
tion. From his youth he had been afflicted with
a diforder which occafioned extreme pain in his
ftomach and limbs. This complaint was probably
of a gouty tendency, but the then defective ftate
of medicine rendered it impoffible for him to obtain
any juft information refpecting it. The moft eminent
phyficians in Italy were confulted, and numerous
remedies were prefcribed, without producing any
beneficial effect (*b*). By frequenting the tepid baths

(*a*) Piero de Bibbiena, the fecretary of Lorenzo, writes thus to
the Florentine ambaffador at Rome; *Prid. Kal. Sextil.* 1488: A
hore 14 mori la Clarice. Se voi fentifte che Lorenzo foffe biafimato
di coftà per non efferfi trovato alla morte delle moglie, fcufatelo.
Parve al Leoni neceffario, che andaffe a prender l'acque della Villa,
e poi non fi credeva che moriffe si prefto. *Fabr. v.* ii. *p.* 384.

(*b*) Some of thefe remedies are of a fingular nature. Pietro Bono
Avogradi, in a letter dated the eleventh of February 1488, advifes
Lorenzo, as a fure method of preventing a return of the *dolore di
zonture,* or arthritic pains, with which he was afflicted, to make ufe
of a ftone called an heliotrope, which being fet in gold, and worn on

of Italy, he obtained a temporary alleviation of his
fuff-rings, but, notwithftanding all the affiftance he
could procure, his complaints rather increafed than
diminifhed, and for fome time before his death, he
had reconciled his mind to an event which he knew
could not be far diftant. When his fon Giovanni
took his departure for Rome, to appear in the
character of cardinal, Lorenzo with great affection
recommended him to the care of Filippo Valori
and Andrea Cambino, who were appointed to ac-
company him on his journey; at the fame time
expreffing his apprehenfions, which the event but
too well juftified, that he fhould fee them no more (*a*).

In the year 1488, Girolamo Riario, whofe machi-
nations had deprived Lorenzo of a brother, and had
nearly involved Lorenzo himfelf in the fame de-
ftruction. fell a victim to his accumulated crimes.
By the affiftance of Sixtus IV. he had poffeffed him-
felf of a confiderable territory in the vicinity of the
papal ftate, and particularly of the cities of Imola
and Forli, at the latter of which he had fixed his
refidence, and fupported the rank of an independ-
ent prince. In order to ftrengthen his intereft in
Italy, he had connected himfelf with the powerful
family of the Sforza, by a marriage with Caterina,
fifter of Galeazzo Sforza, duke of Milan, whofe un-

the finger fo as to touch the skin, would produce the defired effect.
" This," fays he, " is a certain prefervative againft both gout and
" rheumatifm; I have tried it myfelf, and found that its properties
" are divine and miraculous." With the fame letter he tranfmits to
Lorenzo his *prognoftics* for the year 1488. *App. No.* LXX.

(*a*) *Valor. in vità Laur. p.* 65.

happy fate has already been related (a). The general
tenor of the life of Riario feems to have correfpond-
ed with the fpecimen before exhibited. By a long
courfe of oppreffion he had drawn upon himfelf
the hatred and refentment of his fubjects, whom
he had reduced to the utmoft extreme of indigence
and diftrefs. Stimulated by repeated acts of barbarity,
three of them refolved to affaffinate him, and to
truft for their fafety, after the perpetration of the
deed, to the opinion and fupport of their fellow-
citizens. Although Riario was conftantly attended
by a band of foldiers, thefe men found means to
enter his chamber in the palace at the hour when
he had juft concluded his fupper. One of them
having cut him acrofs the face with a fabre, he took
fhelter under the table, whence he was dragged
out by Lodovico Orfo, another of the confpirators,
who ftabbed him through the body. Some of his
attendants having by this time entered the room,
Riario made an effort to efcape at the door, but
there received from the third confpirator a mortal
wound. It is highly probable that he was betrayed
by the guard, for thefe three men were even per-
mitted to ftrip the dead body, and throw it through
the window, when the populace immediately rofe
and facked the palace. The infurgents, having
fecured the widow and children of Riario, were
only oppofed by the troops in the fortrefs of the
town, who refufed to furrender it either to their
entreaties or their threats. Being required, under
pain of death, to exert her influence in obtaining

(a) Vol. I. p. 177.

for the populace poffeffion of the fortrefs, the prin-
cefs requefted that they would permit her to enter
it; but no fooner was fhe fecure within the walls
than fhe exhorted the foldiers to its defence, and
raifing the ftandard of the duke of Milan, threatened
the town with deftruction. The inhabitants attempt-
ed to intimidate her by preparing to execute her
children in her fight, for which purpofe they erected
a fcaffold before the walls of the fortrefs; but this
unmanly proceeding, inftead of awakening her
affections, only excited her contempt, which fhe is
faid to have expreffed in a very emphatic and extra-
ordinary manner (*a*). By her courage the inhabitants
were however refifted, until Giovanni Bentivoglio,
with a body of two thoufand foot and eight hundred
cavalry, from Bologna, gave her effectual affiftance,
and being joined by a ftrong reinforcement from
Milan, compelled the inhabitants to acknowledge
as their fovereign Ottavio Riario, the eldeft fon of
Girolamo (*b*).

Lorenzo de' Medici has not efcaped the im-
putation of having been privy to the affaffination
of his old and implacable adverfary; but neither
the relations of contemporary hiftorians, nor the
general tenor of his life, afford a prefumption on
which to ground fuch an accufation (*c*); although

(*a*) Rifpofe loro quella forte femmina, che fe aveffero fatti perir
que' figliuoli, reftavano a lei le forme per farne degli altri; e vi ha
che dice (quella giunta forfe fu immaginata e non vera) aver' ella
anche alzata la gonna per chiarirli, che dicea la verità.

Murat. Ann. vol. ix. *p.* 556.

(*b*) *Chronica Boffiana. an.* 1488. *Ed.* 1492.

(*c*) " Indignum fane facinus fuit, quod in Hieronymum Riarium
Comitem admiffum eft; cujus participem Laurentium fuiffe *multi*

it is certain, that some years previous to this event, he had been in treaty with the pope to deprive Riario of his usurpations, and to restore the territories occupied by him to the family of Ordolaffi, their former lords, which treaty was frustrated by the pope having insisted on annexing them to the states of the church (*a*). The conspirators however, soon after the death of Riario, apprized Lorenzo of the event, and requested his assistance; in consequence of which he dispatched one of his envoys to Forli, with a view of obtaining authentic in-

"*contendunt*, & ab eo ad ulcifcendas præteritorum temporum injurias "comparatum." *Fabr. in vitâ, vol. i. p.* 175. There is however great reason to suspect that the modern biographer of Lorenzo has inadvertently given weight and credit to an accusation, which, if established, would degrade his character to that of a treacherous assassin. In vindication of him against this charge, I must therefore observe, that of the many accusers to whom Fabroni adverts, I have not met with one of the early historians who has even glanced at Lorenzo as having been associated with the conspirators, or privy to the perpetration of the deed. Neither Machiavelli nor Ammirato, although they all relate the particulars of the transaction, have implicated in it the name of Lorenzo. Muratori, whose annals are compiled from contemporary and authentic documents, and who may therefore be considered as an original writer, is equally silent on this head. The ancient chronicle of Donato Boffo, printed only four years after the event, gives a yet more particular account, but alludes not to any interpofition on the part of Lorenzo; and even Raffaello Maffei, his acknowledged adverfary, though he adverts to the death of Riario, attributes it only to the interference of his own subjects. It is indeed a strong indication of the dignity of the character of Lorenzo, that a charge fo natural, and fo confiftent with the spirit of the times, should not have been alledged against him: and having been exculpated in the eyes of his contemporaries, it is furely not for pofterity to criminate him.

(*a*) *Fabron. Adnot. & Monum. v. iii. p.* 316.

formation as to the difpofition. of the inhabitants, and the views of the infurgents (*a*), when finding that it was their intention to place themfelves under the dominion of the pope, he declined any interference on their behalf. but availed him-felf of the opportunity of their diffenfions, to reftore to the Florentines the fortrefs of Piancal-doli, which had been wrefted from them by Riario (*b*). That the affaffins of Riario were fuffered

(*a*) The letter from Lodovico and Clecco d' Orfi, two of the confpirators, to Lorenzo de' Medici, written only a few days after the event, is inferted in the Appendix, and indifputably shows, that although they fuppofed Lorenzo would be gratified by the death of his adverfary, he had no previous knowledge of fuch an attempt. To this I shall alfo fubjoin the letter to Lorenzo from his envoy, which gives a minute account of the whole tranfaction, and by which it appears, that although the pope had incited the confpirators to the enterprife, by expreffing his abhorrence of the character of Riario, yet that no other perfon was privy to their purpofe. *App. No.* LXXI.

(*b*) In the attack of this place, the Florentines loft their eminent citizen, Cecca, the engineer, whofe skill had facilitated the fuccefs of their enterprife. In the *Exhortatio* of Philippus Reditus, addreffed to Piero de' Medici, *in Magnanimi fui parentis imitationem*, the MS. of which is preferved in the Laurentian Library, this incident is particularly related; and as the paffage has not hitherto been published, having been omitted, with many others, in the edition of Lami, *Delic. Erudit. vol.* xii. printed from a copy in the Riccardi Library, I shall here infert it: " Piancaldolii arx ftrenue noftris re-
" cuperatur. Ad iv. vero Kalendas Maias, nuntiata nece Hieronymi
" Riarii, Imolæ Forliviique Tyranni, Piancaldolis oppidum noftrum,
" olim ab eo per fummum nefas nobis ereptum, admirabili quadam
" noftrorum celeritate, tuo magnanimo Genitore procurante, ftrenue
" recuperatur. In cujus arcis obfidione, Francifcus, cognomine
" Ciecha, Fabrum magifter, vir vel in expugnandis vel in defendendis
" urbibus tam noftra, quam noftrorum patrum memoria perilluftris,
" fagitta ictus capite, pio patriæ feliciter occubuit." The death of Cecca is related with fome variation by Vaffari, *Vita del Cecca.*

to efcape with impunity, is perhaps the beft juftifica-
tion of their conduct, as it affords a ftriking proof
that he had deferved his fate.

Another event foon afterwards took place at
Faenza, which occafioned great anxiety to Lorenzo,
and called for the exertion of all his conciliatory
powers. If the lift of crimes and affaffinations which
we have before had occafion to notice, may be
thought to have difgraced the age, that which we
have now to relate exhibits an inftance of female
ferocity, which renewed in the fifteenth century
the examples of Gothic barbariy (a). By the me-

" Coftui, quando i Florentini avevano l' efercito intorno a' Piancaldoli,
" con l' ingegno fuo fece sì, che i foldati vi entrarono dentro per via
" di mine fenza colpo di fpada. Dopo feguitando più oltre il medefimo
" efercito a certe altre caftella, come volle la mala forte, volendo
" egli mifurare alcune altezze in un luogo difficile, fu uccifo; per-
" ciocché, avendo meffo il capo fuor del muro per mandar un filo
" abaffo, un prete, che era fra gli avverfarii, i quali più temevano
" l' ingegno del Cecca, che le forze di tutto il campo, fcaricatogli
" una baleftra a panca, gli conficcò di forte un verettone nella tefta,
" che il poverello di fubito fe ne morì."

(a) There is a ftriking coincidence between this event, and the
narrative of Paulus Diaconus, upon which Giovanni Ruccellai has
founded his tragedy of *Rofmunda*. Alboin, king of the Huns, having
conquered and flain in battle Comundus, king of the Geppidi, compels
his daughter *Rofmunda* to accept of him in marriage, with a view
of uniting their dominions under his fole authority; but not fatisfied
with the acceffion of power, he gratifies a brutal fpirit of revenge,
by compelling her, at a public feaft, to drink from the skull of her
flaughtered father, which he had formed into a cup. This infult the
princefs avenges, by feducing to her purpofe two of the king's in-
timate friends, who, in order to entitle themfelves to her favor,
affaffinate him in the hour of intoxication. Ruccellai has however
preferved his heroine from the crimes of proftitution and affaffination,
and has introduced a difinterefted lover in the perfon of *Almachilde*,

diation of Lorenzo, who was equally the friend of the Manfredi and the Bentivoli, a marriage had taken place between Galeotto Manfredi, prince of Faenza, and Francefca, daughter of Giovanni Bentivoglio, which for fome time feemed to be productive of that happinefs to the parties, and thofe advantages to their refpective families, which Lorenzo had in view. It was not long however before Francefca difcovered, or fufpected, that her hufband was engaged in an illicit amour, the information of which fhe thought proper to communicate both to her father and to Lorenzo. Ever on the watch to obtain further proofs of his infidelity, fhe found an opportunity of liftening to a private interview between Galeotto, and fome pretender to aftrological knowledge, in whom it feems he was credulous enough to place his confidence. Inftead, however, of gaining any intelligence as to the object of her curiofity, fhe heard predictions and denunciations, which, as fhe thought, affected the fafety of her father, and being unable to conceal her indignation, fhe broke in upon their deliberations, and reproached her hufband with his treachery. Irritated by the intrufion and thé pertinacity of his wife, Galeotto retorted with great bitternefs; but finding himfelf unequal to a conteft of this nature, he had recourfe to more violent methods, and by menaces and blows reduced her to obedience. Bentivoglio was no fooner apprized of the ignomi-

who executes vengeance on the king from generous and patriotic motives. In juftice to the author, it muft alfo be obferved, that the horrid incident upon which the tragedy is founded, is narrated only, and not reprefented before the audience.

nious treatment which his daughter had received, and of the circumflances which had given rife to it, than he refolved to carry her off from her hufband by force. Taking with him a chofen body of foldiers, he approached Faenza by night, and feizing on Francefca and her infant fon, brought them in fafety to Bologna. This ftep he followed up, by preparing for an attack on the dominions of his fon-in-law; but Galeotto having reforted to Lorenzo for his mediation, a reconciliation took place, and Francefca fhortly afterwards returned to Faenza. Whether fhe ftill harboured in her bofom the lurking paffions of jealoufy and revenge, or whether fome frefh infult on the part of her hufband had roufed her fury, is not known; but fhe formed and executed a deliberate plan for his affaffination. To this end fhe feigned herfelf fick, and requefted to fee him in her chamber. Galeotto obeyed the fummons, and on entering his wife's apartments, was inftantly attacked by four hired affaffins, three of whom fhe had concealed under her bed. Though totally unarmed, he defended himfelf courageoufly; and as he had the advantages of great perfonal ftrength and activity, would probably have effected his efcape; but when Francefca faw the conteft doubtful, fhe fprung from the bed, and grafping a fword, plunged it into his body, and accomplifhed his deftruction with her own hand. Confcious of her guilt, fhe immediately took refuge with her children in the caftle, until her father once more came to her relief. On his approach to Faenza, Bentivoglio was joined by the Milanefe troops, who had been engaged in reinftating the family of Riario at Forli. The citizens of

Faenza, conceiving that it was his intention to de-
prive them of Aftorgio, the infant fon of Galeotto, or
rather perhaps under that pretext to poffefs himfelf
of the city, refufed to furrender to him his daughter
and her family. He immediately attacked the place,
which was not only fuccefsfully defended by the
citizens, but in an engagement which took place
under the walls, Borgomini, the commander of the
Milanefe troops, loft his life, and Bentivoglio was
made a prifoner. During this difpute Lorenzo de'
Medici had warmly efpoufed the caufe of the citizens,
and had encouraged them with promifes of fupport,
in cafe they fhould find it neceffary in preferving
their independence. The fuccefs of their exertions,
and the difafter of Bentivoglio, changed the object
of his folicitude, and no fooner did he receive in-
telligence of this event, than he difpatched a mef-
fenger to Faenza, to interfere on the behalf of Ben-
tivoglio, and if poffible to obtain his releafe. This
was with fome difficulty accomplifhed, and Benti-
voglio immediately reforted to Florence to return
his thanks to his benefactor Some time afterwards
Lorenzo, at the requeft of Bentivoglio, folicited the
liberation of his daughter, which was alfo complied
with; and he was at length prevailed upon to inter-
cede with the pope, to relieve her from the eccle-
fiaftical cenfures which fhe had incurred by her
crime. The reafon given by Bentivoglio to Lorenzo,
for requefting his affiftance in this laft refpect, will
perhaps be thought extraordinary.—*He had an inten-
tion of providing her with another hufband!*

CHAP.

PROGRESS of the arts — State of them in the middle ages—Revival in Italy—Guido da Sienna—Cimabue—Giotto—Character of his works—The Medici encourage the arts—Mafaccio—Paolo Uccello—Fra Filippo—Antonio Pollajuolo—Baldovinetti—Andrea da Caftagna—Filippo Lippi—Luca Signorelli—Progrefs of Sculpture—Niccolo and Andrea Pifani—Ghiberti—Donatello—Imperfect ftate of the arts—Caufes of their improvement—Numerous works of Sculpture collected by the ancient Romans—Refearches after the remains of antiquity.—Petrarca—Lorenzo de' Medici brother of Cofmo—Niccolo Niccoli—Poggio Bracciolini—Collection of antiques formed by Cofmo—Affiduity of Lorenzo in augmenting it—Lorenzo eftablifhes a fchool for the ftudy of the antique—Michelagnolo Buonarroti—Refides with Lorenzo—Forms an intimacy with Politiano—Advantages over his predeceffors—His fculptures—Rapid improvement of tafte—Raffaelle d'Urbino—Michelagnolo unjuftly cenfured.—Other artifts favored by Lorenzo—Gian-Francefco Ruftici—Francefco Granacci—Andrea Contucci—Lorenzo encourages the ftudy of Architecture—Giuliano da San Gallo—Attempts to renew the practice of Mofaic—Invention of engraving on copper—Revival of engraving on gems and ftones.

THOSE periods of time which have been moft favorable to the progrefs of letters and fcience, have generally been diftinguifhed by an equal proficiency in the arts. The productions of Roman fculpture, in its beft ages, bear nearly the fame proportion to thofe of the Greeks, as the imitative labors of the Roman authors bear to the original works of their great prototypes. During the long ages of ignorance that fucceeded the fall of the Weftern empire, letters and the fine arts underwent an equal degradation; and it would be as difficult to point out a literary work of thofe times which is entitled to approbation, as it would be to produce a ftatue or a picture. When thefe ftudies began to revive, a Guido da Sienna, a Cimabue, rivalled a Guittone d' Arezzo, or a Piero delle Vigne. The crude buds that had efcaped the feverity of fo long a winter foon began to fwell, and Giotto, Buffalmacco, and Gaddi were the contemporaries of Dante, of Boccaccio, and of Petrarca (*a*).

It is not however to be prefumed, that, even in the darkeft intervals of the middle ages, thefe arts were entirely extinguifhed. Some traces of them are found in the rudeft ftate of fociety; and the efforts of the Europeans, the South Americans, and the Chinefe, without rivalfhip and without participation, are nearly on an equality with each other. Among the manufcripts of the Laurentian Library are preferved fome fpecimens of miniature paint-

(*a*) Videmus picturas ducentorum annorum nulla prorfus arte politas; fcripta illius ætatis rudia funt, inepta, incompta: poft Petrarcham emerferunt litteræ; poft Joctum furrexere pictorum manus; utraque ad fummam jam videmus artem pervenitte. *Æn. Silvii* (*Pii* ii.) *Epift.* 119. *ap. Baldinuc. Notiz. Dec.* 1. Such was the opinion of this pontiff, who had great learning and fome tafte. He was only miftaken in fuppofing that he had feen the perfection of the art.

ings which are unqueſtionably to be referred to the tenth century, but they bear deciſive evidence of the barbariſm of the times ; and although they certainly aim at picturefque reprefentation, yet they may with juſtice be conſidered rather as perverfe diſtortions of nature, than as the commencement of an elegant art (*a*).

Antecedent, however, to Cimabue, to whom Vaſari attributes the honor of having been the reſtorer of painting, Guido da Sienna had demonſtrated to his countrymen the poſſibility of improvement. His picture of the virgin, which yet remains tolerably entire in the church of S. Domenico, in his native place, and which bears the date of 1221, is prefumed, with reafon, to be the earlieſt work now extant of any Italian painter (*b*). The Florentine made a bolder effort, and attracted more general admiration. Every new Production of his pencil was regarded as a prodigy, and riches and honors were liberally beſtowed on the fortunate artiſt. His picture of the Madonna, after having

(*a*) Thefe pieces have lately been engraved and published in the *Etruria Pittrice*, a work which appears periodically at Florence, and contains fpecimens of the manner of the Tufcan artiſts from the earlieſt times, executed fo as to give fome idea of the original pictures. To this work, which would have been much more valuable if greater attention had been paid to the engravings, I shall, in sketching the progrefs of the art, have frequent occaſion to refer.

(*b*) Engraved in the *Etruria Pittrice*, *No.* iii. Under this picture is infcribed, in Gothic characters, the following verfe:

" Me Guido de Serſs diebus depinxit amenis

" Quem Chriſtus levis nullis velit agere peris

    A. D. MCCXXI."

excited the wonder of a Monarch, and given the name of *Borgo Allegro* to that diftrict of the city whither his countrymen reforted to gratify themfelves with a fight of it, was removed to its deftined fituation in the church of *S. Maria Novella*, to the found of mufic, in a folemn proceflion of the citizens (*a*). The modern artift who obferves this picture may find it difficult to account for fuch a degree of enthufiafm (*b*): but excellence is merely relative, and it is a fufficient caufe of approbation, if the merit of the performance exceed the ftandard of the age. Thofe productions which, compared with the works of a Raffaello, or a Titian, may be of little efteem, when confidered with reference to the times that gave them birth, may juftly be entitled to no fmall fhare of applaufe.

The glory of Cimabue was obfcured by that of his difciple Giotto (*c*), who from figuring the fheep which it was his bufinefs to tend, became the beft painter that Italy had produced (*d*). It affords no

(*a*) *Vafcri, vita di Cimabue.*

(*b*) Engraved in the *Etruria Pittrice*, No. viii. The virgin is feated with the infant on her knee, in a rich chair, which is fupported by fix angels, reprefented as adults, though lefs than the child. The head of the virgin is fomewhat inclined, the countenance melancholy, not without fome pretenfions to grace; the reft of the picture is in the true ftyle of Gothic formality.

(*c*) Credette Cimabue nella pintura,

  Tener lo campo; ed ora ha Giotto il grido,

  Si che la fama di colui ofcura.

Dante, Purg. Cant. xi.

(*d*) *Manni.* in his *Illuftr. del Boccaccio, p.* 414. deduces the name of Giotto from Angiolotto, but M Tenhove with more probability derives it from Ambrogio. *Ambrogio, Ambrogiotto, Giotto;* " Quel inadequate proof of his high reputation, when we find him indulging his humor in an imitation of the celebrated artiſt of Cos, and fending to the pope, who had defired to fee one of his drawings, a circle, ſtruck with fuch freedom, as to ſhow the hand of a maſter, yet with fuch truth, as to have given rife to a proverb (*a*). Inferior artiſts hazard not fuch freedoms with the great. Giotto feems however to have delighted in the eccentricities of the art. One of his firſt eſſays when he began to ſtudy under Cimabue was to paint a fly on the nofe of one of his maſter's portraits, which the deluded artiſt attempted to bruſh off with his hand (*b*); a tale that may rank with the horfe of Apelles, the curtain of Parrhaſius, or the grapes of Zeuxis. Boccaccio has introduced this celebrated painter with great approbation in one of his novels (*c*); a fin-

" étranger," fays this lively author, " aperçoit d'abord fous les bizarres
" déguifemens de *Biſla, Betto, Bambo, Bindo, Bacci, Tani, Cece,*
" *Giomo, Nigi, Meo, Nanni, Vanni, Mazo, Lippo, Lippozzo,*
" *Pipo Guccio, Mico, Caca, Toto, &c.* les noms de batême les plus
" vulgaires & les plus communs? Les autres Italiens fe font toujours
" moqués de cet ufage Florentin, qui en effet n'eſt pas moins rifible
" que fi M. Hume, dans fa belle hiſtoire d'Angleterre, nous entretenait
" de *Billy le conquérant,* de *Tom Becket,* de *Jackey le grand terrien,*
" appellé *Sans-Terre,* des grands Rois *Ned.* **I.** & **III.** *du nom,* de
" la bigotte *Reine Molly,* de la grand *Reine Beſs,* & de fon cher
" amant *Bobby Devereux,* envoyé par elle au fupplice," &c.

Mém. Gén. &c. liv. i. *p.* 37.

(*a*) Divolgataſi poi queſta cofa, ne nacque il proverbio, che ancora è in ufo dirfi agli uomini di groſſa paſta: *Tu fei più tondo che l'O di Giotto. Vaſar. vita di Giotto.*

(*b*) *Vaſari vita di Giotto.*

(*c*) Giotto ebbe un ingegno di tanta eccellenza, che niuna cofa da la natura, madre di tutte le cofe, ed operatrice, col continuo girar de' gular converfation is faid to have occurred between him and Dante (*a*); and Petrarca held his works in fuch high efteem, that one of his pictures is the fubject of a legacy to a particular friend in his will (*b*). Upwards of a century after his death, Lorenzo de' Medici, well aware that the moft efficacious method of exciting the talents of the living is to confer due honor on departed merit, raifed a buft to his memory in the church of *S. Maria del Fiore*, the infcription for which was furnifhed by Politiano (*c*).

cieli, che egli con lo ftile, e con la penna, e col pennello non dipig-
neffe, si fimile a quella, che non fimile, anzi più tofto deffa pareffe.

Decam. Gior. vi. *Nov.* 5.

(*a*) Benvenuto da Imola, one of the commentators of Dante, relates, that whilft Giotto refided at Padua, Dante paid him a vifit, and was received by him with great attention. Obferving however that the children of Giotto bore a great refemblance to their father, whofe features and appearance were not very prepoffeffing, he inquired how it came to pafs that his pictures and his children were fo very unlike to each other, the former being fo beautiful, the latter fo coarfe, *Quia pingo de die, fed fingo de nocte,* faid the painter.

Manni, Illuft. del Bocc. p. 417.

(*b*) Tranfeo ad difpofitionem aliarum rerum ; predicto igitur domino meo Paduano, quia & ipfe per Dei gratiam non eget, & ego nihil aliud habeo dignum fe, mitto Tabulam meam five hiftoriam Beatæ virginis Mariæ, operis Jocti pictoris egregii, quæ mihi ab amico meo Michele Vannis de Florentia miffa eft, in cujus pulchritudinem ignorantes non intelligunt, magiftri autem artis ftupent.

Vafari, vita di Giotto.

(*c*) Ille ego fum per quem Pictura extincta revixit,
Cui quam recta manus tam fuit & facilis.
Naturæ derat noftræ quod defuit arti;
Plus licuit nulli pingere nec melius.

The merits of Giotto and his school are appreciated with great judgment by Vafari, who attributes to him and his predeceffor Cimabue the credit of having banifhed the infipid and fpiritlefs manner introduced by the Greek artifts, and given rife to a new and more natural ftyle of compofition. This the hiftorian denominates the *maniera di Giotto* (a). " Inftead of the harfh outline, circumfcribing the " whole figure, the glaring eyes, the pointed feet " and hands, and all the defects arifing from a total

> Miraris turrim egregiam facro ære fonantem?
> Hæc quoque de modulo crevit ad aftra meo.
> Denique fum JOTTUS, quid opus fuit illa referre?
> Hoc nomen longi carminis inftar erit.

(a) *Proemio di Giorgio Vafari* to the fecond part of his work, written, like all his other prefaces, with great judgment, candor, and hiftorical knowledge of his art. *Tractant fabrilia fabri*—The early painters are fortunate in poffeffing an hiftorian, who without envy, fpleen, or arrogance, and with as little prejudice or partiality as the imperfection of human nature will allow, has diftributed to each of his characters, his due portion of applaufe. If he has on any occafion fhown too apparent a bias in favor of an individual, it leans towards Michelagnolo Buonarroti, in whofe friendfhip he gloried, and whofe works he diligently ftudied; but an excefs of admiration for this great man will fcarcely be imputed to him as a fault. As a painter and an architect, Vafari holds a refpectable rank. In the former department, his productions are extremely numerous. One of his principal labors is his hiftorical fuite of pictures of the Medici family, with their portraits, painted for the great duke Cofmo I. in the *Palazzo Vecchio* at Florence, of which Vafari himfelf has given a particular account, published by Filippo Giunti, in 1588, and entitled *Ragionamenti del Sig. Cav. Giorgio Vafari fopra le invenzioni da lui dipinte in Firenze, &c.* Reprinted in Arezzo, 1762. In this feries of pictures are reprefented the principal incidents in the life of Lorenzo. This work has been engraved, but not in fuch a manner as to do juftice to the painter.

" want of fhadow, the figures of Giotto exhibit a
" better attitude, the heads have an air of life and
" freedom, the drapery is more natural, and there
" are even fome attempts at fore fhortening the
" limbs. " " Befides thefe improvements, " con-
tinues this author, " Giotto was the firft who repre-
" fented in his pictures, the effect of the paffions
" on the human countenance. That he did not
" proceed further muft be attributed to the difficul-
" ties which attend the progrefs of the art, and to
" the want of better examples In many of the
" effential requifites of his profeffion, he was indeed
" equalled, if not furpaffed, by fome of his con-
" temporaries. The coloring of Gaddi had more
" force and harmony, and the attitudes of his figures
" more vivacity. Simone da Sienna is to be preferred
" to him in the compofition of his fubjects, and
" other painters excelled him in other branches of
" the art; but Giotto had laid the folid foundation
" of their improvements. It is true, all that was
" effected by thefe mafters may be confidered only
" as the firft rude fketch of a fculptor towards com-
" pleting an elegant ftatue, and if no further pro-
" grefs had been made, there would not, upon the
" whole, have been much to commend; but who-
" ever confiders the difficulties under which their
" works were executed, the ignorance of the times,
" the rarity of good models, and the impoffibility
" of obtaining inftruction, will efteem them not only
" as commendable, but wonderful productions,
" and will perceive with pleafure thefe firft fparks
" of improvement which afterwards fanned into
" fo bright a flame. "

The patronage of the family of the Medici is almoſt contemporary with the commencement of the art. Giovanni de' Medici, the father of Cofmo, had employed his fellow-citizen, Lorenzo de' Bicci, to ornament with portraits a chamber in one of his houfes in Florence, which afterwards became the refidence of Lorenzo, the brother of Cofmo (*a*). The liberality of Cofmo led the way to further improvement. Under Mafaccio the fludy of nature and actual obfervation were fubflituted to cold and fervile imitation. By this mafter, his competitors, and his fcholars, every component branch of the art was carried to fome degree of perfection. Paolo Uccello was the firft who boldly furmounted the difficulty which Giotto, though fenfible of its importance, had ineffectually attempted to overcome, and gave that ideal depth to his labors, which is the effence of picturefque reprefentation (*b*). This he accomplifhed by his fuperior knowledge of perfpective, which he fludied in conjunction with the celebrated Giannozzo Manetti, and in the attainment of which the painter and the fcholar were mutually ferviceable to each other (*c*). The rules which he thence acquired he applied to practice, not only in

(*a*) *Vafar. vita di Lor. de' Bicci.*

(*b*) È da offervare che non fi trova prima di lui neffuno fcorto di figure, perciò a ragione può dirfi aver quello valent' uomo fatto un gran progreffo nell' arte. *Etruria Pittrice, No.* xiv.

(*c*) È fu il primo che poneffe fludio grande nella profpettiva, introducendo il modo di mettere le figure fu' piani, dove effe pofar devono, diminuendole a proporzione; il che, da maeftri avanti a lui, fi faceva a cafo, e fenz' alcuna confiderazione.

Baldinuc. Dec. ii. *del. par.* i. *fec.* iv.

the back-grounds of his pictures, but in his reprefentation of the human figure, of which he èxpreſſed the *Scorci*, or fore-ſhortenings, with accuracy and effect (*a*). The merit of having been the firſt to apply mathematical rules to the improvement of works of art, and the proficiency which he made in ſo neceſſary and ſo laborious a ſtudy, if it had not obtained from Vaſari a greater ſhare of praiſe, ought at leaſt to have ſecured the artiſt from that ridicule with which he ſeems inclined to treat him (*b*). The elder Filippo Lippi gave to his figures a boldneſs and grandeur before unknown. He attended alfo to the effect of his back-grounds, which were however in general too minutely finiſhed. About two years after his death, which happened in the year 1469, Lorenzo de' Medici, who was then abfent from Florence on a journey, to congratulate Sixtus IV. on his acceſſion to the pontificate, took the opportunity of paſſing through Spoletto, where he requeſted permiſſion from the magiſtrates to remove the aſhes of the artiſt to the church of *S. Maria del Fiore* at Florence. The community of that place were however unwilling to relinquiſh ſo honorable a depoſit; and Lorenzo was therefore content to

(*a*) In his picture of the inebriety of Noah, in the church of S. Maria Novella, is a figure of the patriarch ſtretched on the ground, with his feet towards the front of the picture; yet, even in this difficult attitude, the painter has ſucceeded in giving an explicit idea of his fubject. *Etrur. Pittr. No.* xiv.

(*b*) La moglie foleva dire che tutta la notte Paolo ſtava nello ſcrittoio, per trovar i termini della profpettiva, e che quando ella lo chiamava a dormire, egli le diceva, *O che dolce coſa è queſta proſpettiva!* *Vaſar Vita di Paolo.*

teftify his refpect for the memory of the painter, by engaging his fon, the younger Filippo, to erect in the church of Spoletto a monument of marble, the infcription upon which, written by Politiano, has led his hiftorian Menckenius into a miftake almoft too apparent to admit of an excufe (a).

In the anatomy of the human figure, which now began to engage the more minute attention of the painter, Antonio Pollajuolo took the lead of all his competitors. By accurate obfervation, as well on the dead as on the living, he acquired a competent knowledge of the form and action of the mufcles (*a*), which he exemplified in a ftriking manner in his picture of Hercules and Antæus,

(a) *In Philippum Fratrem Pictorem.*

 Conditus hic ego fum picturæ fama PHILIPPUS;
  Nulli ignota meæ eft gratia mira manus.
 Artifices potui digitis animare colores,
  Sperataque animos fallere voce diu.
 Ipfa incis ftupuit natura expreffa figuris,
  Meque fuis faffa eft artibus effe parem.
 Marmoreo tumulo MEDICES LAURENTIUS hic me
  Condidit: ante humili pulvere tectus eram.

From the appellation of *Frater*, given to Lippi by Politiano, Menckenius conjectures, that he was his brother. " Is enim quis fit, " cujus hic frater dicitur Philippus, fi Politianus non eft, hariolari non poffum." *Mench. in vitâ Pol. p.* 31. Filippo had entered into holy orders, whence he was called *Fra Filippo;* a circumftance which Menckenius might eafily have difcovered, though he profeffes not to have been able to obtain any information refpecting it. " Nihil enim " eâ de re fcriptores alii, etfi non defint, qui maxime excelluiffe hunc " *Philippum* nobilliffima pingendi arte fuo confirment teftimonio."

Ibid. p. 637.

(b) Egli s'intefe degli ignudi più modernamente, che fatto non avevano gli altri maeftri umanzi a lui; e fcorticò molti uomini, per vedere

painted for Lorenzo de' Medici, in which he is
faid not only to have expreffed the ftrength of the
conqueror, but the languor and inanimation of the
conquered (*a*); but his moft celebrated work is
the death of S. Sebaftian, yet preferved in the
chapel of the Pucci family at Florence, and of which
Vafari has given a particular account (*b*). In this
picture, the figure of the dying faint was painted
from nature after Gino Capponi. In the figures of
the two affaffins, who are bending their crofs-bows,
he has fhown great knowledge of mufcular action.
Baldovinetti excelled in portraits, which he frequent-
ly introduced in his hiftorical fubjects. In a picture
of the queen of Sheba on a vifit to Solomon, he
painted the likenefs of Lorenzo de' Medici, and
of the celebrated mechanic, Lorenzo da Volpaia (*c*);
and in another picture, intended as its companion,
thofe of Giuliano de' Medici, Luca Pitti, and other
Florentine citizens. The refemblance of Lorenzo

la notomia lor fotto; e fu primo a moftrare il modo di cercare i
mufcoli, che aveffero forma, ed ordine nelle figure.

Vafari vita di Pollajuolo.

(*a*) *Vafari, ut fupra.*

(*b*) *Vafari, ut fupra.* This picture is engraved and published in
the *Etruria Pittrice, No. xxiv.*

(*c*) Ritraffe coftui affai di naturale, e dove nella detta cappella fece
la ftoria della Reina Saba, che va a udire la fapienza di Salomone,
ritraffe il magnifico Lorenzo de' Medici, che fu padre di papa Leone
decimo, Lorenzo dalla Volpaja eccellentiffimo maeftro d'oriuoli, ed
ottimo aftrologo, il quale fu quello, che fece per il detto Lor. de'
Medici il belliffimo oriuolo che ha oggi il Sig. Duca Cofimo in Palazzo;
nel quale oriuolo tutte le ruote de' pianeti camminano di continuo;
il che è cofa rara, e la prima che fuffe mai fatta di quefta maniera.

Vafar. vita di Baldov. v. ante, p. 115.

was alfo introduced by Domenico Ghirlandajo, in a picture of S. Francefco taking the habit, painted by him in the chapel of the Trinity at Florence, Until this time the pictures of the Tufcan artifts had been executed in diftemper, or with colors rendered cohefive by glutinous fubftances. The practice of painting in oil, fo effentially neceffary to the duration of a picture, was now firft introduced amongft his countrymen by Andrea da Caftagna (a). The younger Filippo Lippi attempted, and not without effect, to give a greater fhare of energy and animation to his productions. His attitudes are frequently bold and diverfified; and his figures have expreffion, vivacity, and motion (b). It is deferving

(a) Era nel fuo tempo in Firenze un tal Domenico da Venezia, pittore di buon nome, col quale egli (Andrea) aveva fintamente legata grande amicizia, affine di cavargli dalla mano la maeftria di colorire a olio, che allora in Tofcana non era da alcun altro praticata, nè meno faputa, fuori che da Domenico, come gli riufci da fare. *Baldin. Dec.* iii. *fec.* v. The invention of painting in oil, though introduced fo late into Italy, is probably more ancient than has generally been fuppofed. It is commonly attributed to the Flemish artifts, Hubert and John Van Eyck, who flourished about the year 1400; but profeffor Leffing, in a fmall treatife " *fur l'ancienneté de la peinture à l'huile*," printed at Brunfwick in 1774, has endeavoured to fhow that this art is of much greater antiquity. His fuggeftions have fince been confirmed by the refearches of M. de Mechel of Basle, who, in arranging the immenfe collection of pictures of the imperial gallery of Vienna, has difcovered feveral pieces painted in oil, as early as the thirteenth and fourteenth centuries. Of thefe the earlieft is a picture by Thomas de Mutina, a Bohemian gentleman; the others are by Theodoric, of Prague, and Nic. Wurmfer, of Strasbourg; both artifts at the court of the emperor Charles IV.

v. Mechel, Catal. des Tabl. de Vienne, &c. in pref.

(b) His celebrated picture of S. Filippo and the ferpent, painted

of remark, that he prepared the way to the ſtudy
of the antique, by introducing into his pictures,
the vaſes, utenſils, arms, and dreſſes of the ancients (a).
But of all the maſters of this period, perhaps Luca
Signorelli united the moſt important excellencies;
his compoſition was good; in drawing the naked
figure he particularly excelled (b); in his picture of
the inſtitution of the euchariſt, yet exiſting in the
choir of the cathedral at Cortona (c), the figure of
Chriſt might be miſtaken for the production of one
of the Caracci. In the variety and expreſſion of
countenance, in the diſpoſition of the drapery, even
in the juſt diſtribution of light, this picture has great
merit; and if ſome remnants of the manner of the
times prevent us from giving it unlimited approba-

in the chapel of the Strozzi at Florence, and engraved in the *Etruria
Pittrice, No.* xxvii. is a ſufficient proof of the truth of this remark.
Filippo Lippi was the ſon of the former painter of the ſame name,
uſually called Fra Filippo. Lorenzo employed him to ornament his
palace at Poggio Cajano, where he painted a ſacrifice in Freſco, but
the work was left unfiniſhed.

(a) Non lavorò mai opera alcuna, nelle quale delle coſe antiche di
Roma con gran ſtudio non ſi ſerviſſe, in vaſi, calzari, trofei, bandiere,
cimieri, ornamenti di tempi, abbigliamenti di portature da capo, ſtrane
ſogge da doſſo, armature, ſcimitarre, ſpade, toghe, manti, ed altre coſe
diverſe e belle, che grandiſſimo e ſempiterno obbligo ſe gli debbe.

Vaſar. vita di Filip.

(b) Col fondamento del diſegno, e degli ignudi particolarmente, e
con la grazia della invenzione, e diſpoſizione delle hiſtorie, aperſe alla
maggior parte degli artefici la via alla ultima perfezzione dell' arte,
alla quale poi poterono dar cima quelli che ſeguirono. *Vaſar. vita di
Luca Signorelli.* It muſt however be obſerved, that Luca lived till
1521, before which time an important reformation had taken place,
in the arts.

(c) Engraved in the *Etruria Pittrice, No.* xxxii,

tion, it may certainly be confidered as the harbinger of a better tafte.

The art of fculpture, dependent on the fame principles, and fufceptible of improvement from the fame caufes as that of painting, made a proportionable progrefs. The inventive genius of the Italian artifts had very early applied it to almoft every variety of material; and figures in wood, in clay, in metals, and in marble, were fafhioned by Giovanni and Niccolo Pifano, by Agoftino and Agnolo Sanefe, which, though rude and incorrect, excited the admiration of the times in which they were produced. Their fucceffor Andrea Pifano, the contemporary of Giotto, fupported the credit of the art, which was then endangered by the fudden progrefs of its powerful rival; and in the early part of the fifteenth century the talents of Ghiberti and Donatello carried it to a degree of eminence which challenged the utmoft exertions, and perhaps even excited the jealoufy, of the firft painters of the age. It muft indeed be acknowledged, that the advantages which fculpture poffeffes are neither few nor unimportant. The fevere and fimple mode of its execution, the veracity of which it is fufceptible, and the durability of its productions, place it in a favorable point of view, when oppofed to an art whofe fuccefs is founded on illufion, which not only admits, but courts meretricious ornament, and whofe monuments are fugitive and perifhable (a).

(a) I am aware that much is to be faid on the oppofite fide of the queftion, but I mean not to difcufs a fubject upon which almoft every writer on the hiftory of the arts has either directly or incidentally exer-

Thefe arts, fo diftinct in their operations, approach each other in works in *rilievo*, which unite the fubftantial form that characterizes fculpture, with the ideal depth of picturefque compofition. In this province Donatello particularly excelled; and in Cofmo de' Medici he found a patron who had judgment to perceive, and liberality to reward his merits. But the genius of Donatello was not confined to one department. His group of Judith and Holofernes, executed in bronze for the community of Florence, his ftatue of S. George, his Annunciation, and his Zuccone, in one of the niches of the Campanile at Florence, all of which yet remain, have met with the uniform approbation of fucceeding times, and are perhaps as perfect as the narrow principles upon which the art was then conducted would allow.

Notwithftanding the exertions of thefe mafters, which were regarded with aftonifhment by their contemporaries, and are yet entitled to attention and refpect, it does not appear that they had raifed their views to the true end of the profef-fion (*a*). Their characters rarely excelled the daily

cifed his ingenuity. Among others, I may refer the reader to the *Proemi* of Vafari, the *Lezzione* of Benedetto Varchi, *della maggior-anza dell' art* , the works of Baldinucci, Richardfon, and Mengs, and to the pofthumous works of Dr. Adam Smith, lately publifhed, in which the reader will find many acute obfervations on this fubject.

(*a*) È neceffario il confeffare, che non poteva la pittura, benchè fatta viva dalle mani di que' maeftri, far gran pompa di fe ftella, perchè molto le mancava di difegno, di morbidezza, di colorito, di fcorti, di movenze, di attitudini, di rilievo, e di altre finezze e vivacità, onde ella poteffe in tutto e per tutto affomigliarfi al vero. *Baldin. Dec.* iii. *fec.* v.

prototypes

prototypes of common life; and their forms, although at times fufficiently accurate, were moftly vulgar and heavy. In the pictures which remain of this period, the limbs are not marked with that precifion which characterizes a well-informed artift. The hands and feet, in particular, appear foft, enervated, and delicate, without diftinction of fex or character. Many practices yet remained that evince the imperfect ftate of the art. Ghirlandajo and Baldovinetti continued to introduce the portraits of their employers in hiftoric compofition, forgetful of that *fimplex duntaxat & unum* with which a juft tafte can never difpenfe. Cofimo Rofelli, a painter of no inconfiderable reputation, attempted by the affiftance of gold and ultramarine, to give a factitious fplendor to his performances. To every thing great and elevated, the art was yet a ftranger; even the celebrated picture of Pollajuolo exhibits only a group of half naked and vulgar wretches, difcharging their arrows at a miferable fellow-creature, who by changing places with one of his murderers, might with equal propriety become a murderer himfelf (*a*). Nor was it till the time of

(*a*) Objects of horror and difguft, the cold detail of deliberate barbarity, can never be proper fubjects of art, becaufe they exclude the efforts of genius. Even the powers of Shakfpeare are annihilated in the butcheries of Titus Andronicus. Yet the reputation of fome of the moft celebrated Italian painters has been principally founded on this kind of reprefentation. " Ici," fays M. Tenhove, " c'eft S.
" Etienne qu'on lapide, & dont je crains que la cervelle ne rejailliffe
" fur moi; plus loin c'eft S. Barthélémi tout fanglant, tout écorché;
" je compte fes mufcles & fes nerfs. Vingt flèches ont criblé Sebaftien,
" L'horrible tête du Baptifte eft dans ce plat. Le gril de S. Laurent

Michelagnolo that painting and fculpture rofe to their true object, and inftead of exciting the wonder, began to roufe the paffions and intereft the feelings of mankind.

By what fortunate concurrence of circumftances the exquifite tafte evinced by the ancients in works of art was revived in modern times, deferves inquiry. It has generally been fuppofed that thefe arts, having left in Greece fome traces of their former fplendor, were tranfplanted into Italy by Greek artifts, who, either led by hopes of emolument, or impelled by the difaftrous ftate of their own country, fought, among the ruins of the weftern empire, a fhelter from the impending deftruction of the eaft. Of the labors of thefe mafters, fpecimens indeed remain in different parts of Italy; but, in point of merit, they exceed not thofe of the native Italians, and fome of them even bear the marks of deeper barbarifm (*a*). In fact, thefe arts were equally debafed in Greece and in Italy, and it was not

---

" fert de pendant a la chaudière de S. Jean — Je recule d'horreur." *Mém. Gén. lib.* x. May it not well be doubted, whether fpectacles of this kind, fo frequent in places devoted to religious purpofes, may not have had a tendency rather to keep alive a fpirit of ferocity and refentement, than to inculcate thofe mild and benevolent principles in which the effence of religion confifts?

(*a*) Venife, & quelques villes de la Romagne, ou de l'ancien Exarchat de Ravenne, montrent encore des traces de ces barbouillages Grecs. Le caractère d'un affez profonde barbarie s'y fait fentir. La peinture qui repréfente les obfèques de St. Ephraim, qu'on voit dans le *Mufeo Sacro*, partie de la Bibliothéque du Vatican, paffe pour le trifte chef d'œuvre de ces fils bâtards de Zeuxis.

Tenh. Mém. Gén. lib. vii.

therefore by an intercourfe of this nature that they were likely to receive improvement. Happily, however, the fame favorable circumftances which contributed to the revival of letters took place alfo with refpect to the arts; and if the writings of the ancient authors excited the admiration and called forth the exertions of the fcholar, the remains of ancient fkill in marble, gems, and other durable materials, at length caught the attention of the artift, and were converted from objects of wonder, into models of imitation. To facilitate the progrefs of thefe ftudies, other fortunate circumftances concurred. The freedom of the Italian governments, and particularly that of Florence, gave to the human faculties their full energies (a). The labors of the painter were early affociated with the myfteries of the prevailing religion, whilft the wealth and oftentation of individuals and of ftates held out rewards, fufficient to excite the endeavours even of the phlegmatic and the indolent.

From the time of the conful Mummius, who, whilft he plundered the city of Corinth of its beautiful productions of art, regarded them rather as houfehold furniture, than as pieces of exquifite fkill (b), the avidity of the Romans for the works

(a) L'uomo libero, con volontà, fa tutto quel che può, più, o meno, fecondo la fua capacità; ma lo fchiavo fa al più quello, che gli fi comanda, e guafta la fua propria volontà, colla violenza, che gli fi fa, per ubbidire. L'abito di farlo opprime finalmente la fua capacità, e la fua razza peggiora, fino, a non più defiderare quello, che difpera ottenere. *Opere di Mengs. v. i. p.* 228.

(b) Mummius tam rudis fuit, ut capta Corintho, cum maximorum

of the Greciam artifts had been progreffively in-
creafing, till at length they became the firft objects
of proconfular rapacity, and the higheft gratification
of patrician luxury. The aftonifhing number which
Verres had acquired during his government of Sicily,
forms one of the moft ftriking features of the in-
vectives of Cicero; who afferts, that throughout that
whole province, fo diftinguifhed by the riches and
tafte of its inhabitants, there was not a fingle ftatue
or figure, either of bronze, marble, or ivory, not
a picture or a piece of tapeftry, not a gem or a pre-
cious ftone, not even a gold or filver utenfil, of
the workmanfhip of Corinth or Delos, which Verres
during his prætorfhip had not fought out and ex-
amined, and if he approved of it, brought it away
with him; infomuch that Syracufe, under his go-
vernment, loft more ftatues than it had loft foldiers
in the victory of Marcellus (a). Such however was

artificum perfectas manibus tabulas ac ftatuas in Italiam portandas
locaret, juberet prædici conducentibus, fi eas perdidiffent, novas eos
reddituros. *Vel. Paterc. lib. i. c. 13.*

(a) The very minute account given by the Roman orator, in his
fourth accufation againft Verres, of the pieces of Grecian fculpture
which he obtained from Sicily, has enabled the Abbé Fraguier to draw
up a differtation which he has entitled the *Gallery of Verres. Mém. de
litt. t. ix. p. 260. Winkel. Storia delle art. del Difegno, lib. x.
c. 3. Fd. Milan,* 1779. *in not.* Amongft thofe particularly enumerat-
ed by Cicero, is a marble ftatue of Cupid by Praxiteles, a Hercules
in bronze by Myron, two Canephoræ, or female figures, reprefenting
Athenian virgins, bearing on their heads implements of facrifice, the
work of Polycletes; a celebrated ftatue of Diana, which, after having
been carried off from the citizens of Segefta by the Carthaginians, was
reftored to them by Scipio Africanus, another of Mercury, which had
been given them by the fame liberal benefactor, the ftatues of Ceres,

the defolation which took place in Italy during the middle ages, occafioned not only by natural calamities, but by the yet more deftructive operation of moral caufes, the rage of fuperftition and the ferocity of barbarian conquerors, that of the innumerable fpecimens of art, which, till the times of the later emperors, had decorated the palaces and villas of the Roman nobility, fcarcely a fpecimen or a veftige was, in the beginning of the fifteenth century, to be difcovered. Even the city of Rome could only difplay fix ftatues, five of marble and one of brafs, the remains of its former fplendor (*a*); and the complaint of Petrarca was not therefore without reafon, that Rome was in no place lefs known than in Rome itfelf (*b*).

In tracing the viciffitudes which the arts have

of Æfculapius, of Bacchus, and laftly that of Jupiter himfelf, of which the facrilegious *emateur* fcrupled not to plunder his temple at Syracufe.

Cic. in Verrem. lib. iv.

(*a*) Hoc videbitur levius fortaffe, fed me maximè movet, quod his fubjiciam; ex inumeris fermc coloffis, ftatuifque tum marmorcis, tum æneis (nam argenteas atque aureas minimè miror fuiffe conflatas) viris illuftribus ob virtutem pofitis, ut omittam varia figna, voluptatis atque artis caufa publicè ad fpectaculum collocata, marmorcas quinque tantùm, quatuor in Conftantini thermis; duas ftantes ponè equos, Phidiæ & Praxitelis opus; duas recubantes; quintam in foro martis, ftatuam quæ hodie Martis fori nomen tenet; atque æneam folam equeftrem deauratam, quæ eft ad Bafilicam Lateranenfem, Septimio S vero dicatam, tantùm videmus fupereffe. *Pog. de varietate Fortunæ, p.* 20. The equeftrian ftatue to which Poggio adverts, as that of Sep. Severus, is now recognized as the ftatue of Marcus Aurelius.

(*b*) Qui enim hodie magis ignari rerum Romanorum funt quam Romani cives? Invitus dico, nufquam minus Roma cognofcitur quam Romæ. *Epift. Fam. lib.* vi. *Ep.* 2.

experienced, we obferve with pleafure, that the fame perfons who fignalized themfelves by their attention to preferve the writings of the ancient authors, were thofe to whom pofterity is indebted for the reftoration of a better tafte in the arts Petrarca himfelf is one of the firft who difplayed a marked attention to the remains of antiquity (*a*). On his interview with the emperor Charles IV. at Mantua, he prefented to that monarch a confiderable number of coins, which he had himfelf collected; at the fame time affuring him, that he would not have beftowed them on any other perfon, and, with a degree of freedom which does him honor, recommending to the emperor, whilft he ftudied the hiftory, to imitate the virtues of the perfons there reprefented (*b*). Lorenzo de' Medici, the brother

(*a*) The famous Cola di Rienzi, who called himfelf Tribune of Rome, and attempted in the fourteenth century to eftablish the ancient republic, was, as well as his friend and panegyrift Petrarca, a great admirer of the remains of antiquity. It is not indeed improbable, as Tirabofchi conjectures, that the indulgence of this tafte firft incited him to his romantic project. The character of Rienzi is given by a contemporary author in the following terms, which may ferve as a curious fpecimen of the Italian language: " *Fo da foa joventutine* " *nutricato de latte de cloquentia, bono Grammatico, megliore Ret-* " *torico, Autorifta bravo. Deh como e quanto era veloce leitore!* " *Moito ufava Tito Livio, Seneca, e Tullio, e Balerio Maffimo:* " *moito li di ettava le magnificentie de Julio Cefare raccontare.* " *Tutto lo die fe fpeculava negl' intagli de marmo, li quali jaccio* " *intorno a Roma. Non era aitri che effe che fapeffe lejere li antichi* " *pataffij. Tutte fcritture antiche volgarizzava; quefte fiure de* " *marmo juflamente interpretava.*"

  Tirab. Storia della Let. Ital. v. v. p. 314. *Mém. pour la*   *vie de Petr. v.* ii. *p.* 335.

(*b*) Ecce (inquit) Cæfar, quibus fucceffifti; ecce quos imitari ftudeas, of Cofmo, diftinguifhed himfelf not only by his affiduity in collecting the remains of ancient authors, but alfo by a decided predilection for works of tafte, in the acquifition of which he emulated the celebrity of his brother (a). From the funeral oration pronounced by Poggio on the death of Niccolo Niccoli, to whom the caufe of literature is perhaps more indebted than to any individual who held merely a private ftation, we learn, that he was highly delighted with paintings and pieces of fculpture, of which he had collected a greater number, and of more exquifite workmanfhip, than any perfon of his time; and that vifitors thronged to fee them, not as to a private houfe, but as to a public exhibition (b). Nor was Poggio himfelf lefs attentive to the difcovery and acquifition of thefe precious remains (c). "My chamber," fays he, "is furrounded

& mirari, ad quorum formulam, atque imaginem, te componas, quos præter te unum nulli hominum daturus eram. *Epift. Fam. lib.* x.

(a) Erat enim (Laurentius) ditiffimus agri, ditiffimufque auri, atque pretiofæ veftis, & univerfæ fupellectilis, fignis, tabulis pictis, vafis cælatis, margaritis, libris, mirum in modum affluit, &c.

Ant. Tudertani Orat. in Ep. Amb. Trav.

(b) Delectabatur admodum tabulis & fignis ac variis colaturis prifcorum more. Plura enim prope folus atque exquifitiora habebat quam ceteri fere omnes. Ad quæ vifenda multi alliciebantur, ut non privato aliquo in loco, fed in Theatro quodam collocata ac expofita effe affirmares. *Poggii Op. p.* 276.

(c) "Effectus fum," fays he, in his jocular ftyle, " admodum " capitofus. Id quale fit, fcire cupis? Habeo cubiculum refertum " capitibus marmoreis, inter quæ unum eft elegans, integrum: alia " truncis naribus, fed quæ vel bonum artificem delectent. His & " nonnullis fignis que procuro, ornare volo Academiam meam Val- " darninam, quo in loco quiefcere eft animus," &c.

Poggii Epift. ad Nic. Niccl.

" with bufts in marble, one of which is whole and
" elegant.   The others are indeed mutilated, and
" fome of them are even nofelefs, yet they are fuch
" as may pleafe a good artift.   With thefe, and
" fome other pieces which I poffefs, I intend to
" ornament my country feat." In a letter from Poggio
to Francefco da Piftoia, a monk who had travelled
to Greece in fearch of antiquities, we have a much
more explicit inftance of the ardor with which
he purfued this objeĉt (a)   " By your letters from
" Chios," fays Poggio, I learn " that you have
" procured for me three bufts in marble, one of
" Minerva, another of Jupiter, a third of Bacchus.
" Thefe letters afforded me great fatisfaĉtion, for I
" am delighted beyond expreffion with pieces of
" fculpture. I am charmed with the fkill of the
" artift, when I fee marble fo wrought as to imitate
" Nature herfelf. You alfo inform me that you
" have obtained a head of Apollo, and you add
" from Virgil,

" Miros ducent de marmore vultus."

" Believe me, my friend, you cannot confer a
" greater favor on me than by returning laden
" with fuch works, by which you will abundantly
" gratify my wifhes. Different perfons labor under
" different diforders ; that which principally affeĉts
" me is an admiration of thefe produĉtions of emi-
" nent fculptors, to which I am perhaps more
" devoted than becomes a man who may pretend
" to fome fhare of learning. Nature herfelf, it is

(a) App. No. LXXII.

" true, muſt always excel theſe her copies; yet I
" muſt be allowed to admire that art, which can
" give ſuch expreſſion to inert materials, that
" nothing but breath ſeems to be wanting. Exert
" yourſelf therefore I beſeech you to collect, either
" by entreaties or rewards, whatever you can find
" that poſſeſſes any merit. If you can procure a
" complete figure, *triumphatum eſt.*" Being infor-
med by Franceſco, that a Rhodian named Suffretus
had in his poſſeſſion a conſiderable number of an-
tique ſculptures, Poggio addreſſed a letter to him,
earneſtly requeſting to be favored with ſuch ſpeci-
mens from his valuable collection as he might think
proper to ſpare, and aſſuring him, that his kindneſs
ſhould be remunerated by the earlieſt oppor-
tunity (*a*). In the ſame earneſt ſtyle, and for the
ſame purpoſe, he addreſſed himſelf to Andreolo
Giuſtiniano, a Venetian, then reſiding in Greece.
Induced by his preſſing entreaties, both Suffretus
and Giuſtiniano intruſted to the monk ſome valuable
works; but, to the great diſappointment of Poggio,
he betrayed the confidence repoſed in him, and
under the pretext that he had been robbed of them
in his voyage, defrauded Poggio of the chief part
of his treaſures, which, as it afterwards appeared,
he preſented to Coſmo de' Medici. The indignation
of Poggio on this occaſion is poured forth in a letter
to Giuſtiniano, whoſe liberality he again ſolicits and
which he profeſſes to have in ſome degree repaid,
by obtaining for him from the pope a diſpenſation

<hr>

(*a*) *App. No.* LXXIII.

to enable his daughter to marry (a). Thus facrile-
gioufly, though almoft excufably, bartering the
favors of the church, for the objects of his favor-
ite ftudy, and the gratification of his tafte.

The riches of Cofmo de' Medici, and the induftry
of Donatello (b), united to give rife to the celebrated
collection of antiquities, which, with confiderable
additions, was tranfmitted by Piero to his fon
Lorenzo, and is now denominated the *Mufeum
Florentinum*. By an eftimate or account taken by
Piero on the death of his father, it appears that
thefe pieces amounted in value to more than 28,000
florins (c). But it was referved for Lorenzo to en-
rich this collection with its moft valuable articles,
and to render it fubfervient to its true purpofe,
that of infpiring in his countrymen a correct and
genuine tafte for the arts.

Of the earneftnefs with which Lorenzo engaged
in this purfuit, fome inftances have already been
adduced (d). " Such an admirer was he," fays
Valori (e), " of all the remains of antiquity, that
" there was not any thing with which he was more
" delighted. Thofe who wifhed to oblige him were

(a) *App. No.* LXXIV.

(b) Egli (Donato) fu potiflima cagione che a Cofimo de' Medici fi
deftaffe la volontà dell' introdurre a Fiorenza le antichità, che fono
ed erano in cafa Medici, le quali tutte di fua mano acconciò.

Vafar. vita di Donato.

(c) *Fabr. in vitâ Cofm. Adnot. & Monum. p.* 231. *v. App.
No.* LXXV.

(d) *Vol.* I. *p.* 152. See alfo the letter from Politiano to Lorenzo.
App. No. LI.

(e) *Valor. in vitâ Laur. p.* 18.

" accuſtomed to collect, from every part of the
" world, medals and coins, eſtimable for their age
" or their workmanſhip, ſtatues, buſts, and whatever
" elſe bore the ſtamp of antiquity. On my return
" from Naples," adds he, " I preſented him with
" figures of Fauſtina and Africanus in marble, and
" ſeveral other ſpecimens of ancient art; nor can
" I eaſily expreſs with what pleaſure he received
" them." Having long deſired to poſſeſs the reſem-
blance of Plato, he was rejoiced beyond meaſure,
when Girolamo Roſcio of Piſtoia preſented to him
a figure in marble of his favorite philoſopher, which
was ſaid to have been found amongſt the ruins of
the academy (a). By his conſtant attention to this
purſuit, and by the expenditure of conſiderable
ſums, he collected under his roof all the remains
of antiquity that fell in his way, whether they
tended to illuſtrate the hiſtory of letters or of
arts (b). His acknowledged acquaintance with
theſe productions induced the celebrated Fra Gio-
condo, of Verona, the moſt induſtrious antiquarian
of his time, to inſcribe to him his collection of
ancient inſcriptions, of which Politiano, who was
a competent judge of the ſubject, ſpeaks with high
approbation (c).   .

(a) In the diligent reſearches made at the inſtance of Lorenzo for
the diſcovery of ancient manuſcripts, his agents frequently met with
curious ſpecimens of art. The inventory of the books purchaſed by
Giovanni Laſcar, from one Nicolo di Jacopo da Siena, concludes with
particularizing a marble ſtatue. This contract and inventory are yet
preſerved in MS. in the archives of the *Palazzo Vecchio* at Florence.
Filz. lxxxi. *No.* 26.

  (b) *Val'or. in vita Laur. p.* 18.

  (c) *Poli. Miſcell. c.* 77.

But it is not the induſtry, the liberality, or the judgment ſhown by Lorenzo in forming his magnificent collection, ſo much as the important purpoſe to which he deſtined it, that entitles him to the eſteem of the profeſſors and admirers of the arts. Converſant from his youth with the fineſt forms of antiquity, he perceived and lamented the inferiority of his contemporary artiſts and the impoſſibility of their improvement upon the principles then adopted. He determined therefore to excite among them, if poſſible, a better taſte, and by propoſing to their imitation the remains of the ancient maſters, to elevate their views beyond the forms of common life, to the contemplation of that ideal beauty which alone diſtinguiſhes works of art from mere mechanical productions. With this view he appropriated his gardens, adjacent to the monaſtery of S. Marco, to the eſtabliſhment of a ſchool or academy for the ſtudy of the antique, and furniſhed the different buildings and avenues with ſtatues, buſts, and other pieces of ancient workmanſhip. Of theſe he appointed the ſculptor Bertoldo, the favorite pupil of Donatello, but who was then far advanced in years, ſuperintendant. The attention of the higher rank of his fellow-citizens was incited to theſe purſuits by the example of Lorenzo; that of the lower claſs, by his liberality. To the latter he not only allowed competent ſtipends, whilſt they attended to their ſtudies, but appointed conſiderable premiums as the rewards of their proficiency (a).

(a) Vaſari, vita di Torrigiano, e di Michelagnolo, &c.

To this inftitution, more than to any other circum-
ftance, we may, without hefitation, afcribe the fud-
den and aftonifhing proficiency which, towards the
clofe of the fifteenth century, took place in the arts,
and which commencing at Florence, extended itfelf
in concentric circles to the reft of Europe. The
gardens of Lorenzo de' Medici are frequently cele-
brated by the hiftorian of the painters, as the nurfery
of men of genius (a); but if they had produced no
other artift than Michelagnolo Buonarroti, they
would fufficiently, have anfwered the purpofes of
their founder. 'It was here that this great man began
to imbibe that fpirit, which was deftined to effect
a reformation in the arts, and which he could perhaps
have derived from no other fource (b). Of a noble,

(a) Vafari adverts alfo to this eftablishment in his *Ragionamenti.*
" Lorenzo aveva fatto fare il Giardino, ch'è ora in fu la piazza di
" San Marco, folamente perchè lo teneva pieno di figure antiche di
" marmo, e pitture affai, e tutte eccellenti, folo per condurre una
" fcuola di giovani, i quali alla fcultura, pittura, e architettura
" attendeffino a imparare, fotto la cuftodia di Bertoldo fcultore, già
" difcepolo di Donatello, i quali giovani, tutti o la maggior parte
" furno eccellenti; fra quali fu uno il noftro Michelagnolo Buonarroti,
" che è ftato lo fplendore, la vita, e la grandezza della fcultura,
" pittura, e architettura, avendo voluto moftrare il cielo, che non
" poteva, nè doveva nafcere, fe non fotto quefto magnifico e illuftre
" uomo, per laffar la fua patria creditaria, e il mondo di tante onorate
" opere, quante fi veggono di lui oggi, e di molti altri che io ho
" vifte, di cotefta fcuola onorata." *Vafar. Ragionamenti,* p. 75.

(b) Mengs, on feveral occafions, attributes the fuperior excellence
of Michelagnolo to the fame favorable circumftance. " Michelagnolo,
" approfittandofi delle ftatue raccolte dai Medici, apri gli occhi, e
" conobbe che gli antichi avean tenuta una certa arte nell' imitare la
" verità, con cui fi faceva la imitazione più intelligibile, e più bella,
" che nello fteffo originale," and again, after giving an hiftorical

but reduced family, he had been placed by his father, when young, under the tuition of the painter Ghirlandajo, from whom Lorenzo, defirous of promoting his new eſtabliſhment, requeſted that he would permit two of his pupils to purſue their ſtudies in his gardens; at the ſame time expreſſing his hopes, that they would there obtain ſuch inſtruction, as would not only reflect honor on the inſtitution, but alſo on themſelves and on their country. The ſtudents who had the good fortune to be thus ſelected were Michelagnolo and Franceſco Granacci (a). On the firſt viſit of Michelagnolo, he found in the gardens his future adverſary, Torrigiano, who, under the directions of Bertoldo, was modelling figures in clay. Michelagnolo applied himſelf to the ſame occupation, and his work ſoon afterwards attracted the attention of Lorenzo, who, from theſe early ſpecimens, formed great expectations of his

" account of the progreſs of the arts, he adds, In quello ſtato di coſe
" ſcappò un raggio di quella ſteſſa luce, che illuminò l'antica Grecia,
" quando Michelagnolo, il quale col ſuo gran talento avea già ſuperato
" il Ghirlandajo, vide le coſe degli antichi Greci nella collezione
" del magnifico Lorenzo de' Medici."

Op. di Mengs, vol. ii. p. 99. 109.

(a) Dolendoſi adunque Lorenzo, che amor grandiſſimo portava alla pittura, e alla ſcultura, che ne' ſuoi tempi non ſi trovaſſero ſcultori celebrati, e nobili, come ſi trovavano molti pittori di grandiſſimo pregio, e fama, deliberò di fare una ſcuola; e per queſto chieſe a Domenico Ghirlandajo, che ſe in bottega ſua aveſſe de' ſuoi giovani, che inclinati foſſero a ciò, gli inviaſſe al giardino, dove egli deſiderava di eſſercitarli e creargli in una maniera, che onoraſſe ſe, e lui, e la città ſua. Laonde da Domenico gli furono per ottimi giovani dati fra gli altri Michelagnolo, e Franceſco Granacci.

Vaſar. vita di Michelagn.

talents. Encouraged by fuch approbation, be began to cut in marble the head of a faun, after an antique fculpture (*a*), which, though unaccuftomed to the chifel, he executed with fuch fkill as to aftonifh Lorenzo; who, obferving that he had made fome intentional deviations from the original, and that in particular he had reprefented the lips fmoother and had fhown the tongue and teeth, remarked to him, with his accuftomed jocularity, that he fhould have remembered that old men feldom exhibit a complete range of teeth. The docile artift, who paid no lefs refpect to the judgment, than to the rank of Lorenzo, was no fooner left to himfelf, than he ftruck out one of the teeth, giving to the part the appearance of its having been loft by age (*b*). On his next vifit, Lorenzo was equally delighted with the difpofition and the genius of his young pupil, and fending for his father, not only too.. the fon under his particular protection, but made fuch a provifion for the old man, as his age and the circumftances of his numerous family required (*c*).

(*a*) This early fpecimen of the genius of Michelagnolo is yet preferved in the Medicean gallery at Florence, in the keeper's room, and is equal, fays Bottari, to a piece of Grecian workmanship; it has been engraved and publifhed by Gori, in Condivi's life of Michelagnolo; but as Bottari obferves, " poco felicemente, e con gran pregiu- " dizio dell' originale." *v. Bottari, not. ut fup.*

(*b*) *Condivi, vita di Michelagnolo, p.* 5. &c.

(*c*) We learn from the narrative of Condivi, who relates thefe circumftances with infufferable minutenefs, that when Lodovico, the father of Michelagnolo, encouraged by the kindnefs of Lorenzo, requefted an office in the *Dogana* or cuftom houfe, *in the place of Marco Pucci,* Lorenzo, who intended to provide him with a much better eftablifhment, replied, laying his hand on his fhoulder, *Tu farai*

From this time till the death of Lorenzo, which included an interval of four years, Michelagnolo conſtantly reſided in the palace of the Medici, and ſat at the table of Lorenzo, among his moſt honored gueſts; where, by a commendable regulation, the troubleſome diſtinctions of rank were aboliſhed, and every perſon took his place in the order of his arrival. Hence the young artiſt found himſelf at once aſſociated, on terms of equality, with all that was illuſtrious and learned in Florence, and formed thoſe connexions and friendſhips which, if they do not create, are at leaſt neceſſary to promote and reward ſuperior talents (a). His leiſure hours were paſſed in contemplating the intaglios, gems, and medals, of which Lorenzo had collected an aſtoniſhing number, whence he imbibed that taſte for antiquarian reſearches, which was of eſſential ſervice to him in his more immediate ſtudies, and which he retained to the cloſe of his life (b).

Whilſt Michelagnolo was thus laying the ſure

ſempre povero. He gave him however the office for which he applied, which was worth eight ſcudi per month, _poco più o meno,_ ſays the accurate hiſtorian. _Condiv. ut ſup._

(a) Lorenzo fece dare a Michelagnolo una bonna camera in caſa, dandogli tutte quelle comodità, ch' egli deſideraua, né altrimenti trattandolo sì in altro, sì nella ſua menſa, che da figliuolo: alla quale, come d'un tal' uomo, ſedeano ogni giorno perſonaggi nobiliſſimi e di grande affare. Ed eſſendovi queſta uſanza, che qui, che da principio ſi trovavano preſenti, ciaſchedano appreſſo il magnifico ſecondo il ſuo grado ſedeſſe, non ſi movendo di luogo, per qualunque dipoi ſopraggiunto foſſe; avenne bene ſpeſſo, che Michelagnolo ſedette ſopra i figliuoli di Lorenzo, ed altre perſone pregiate, di che tal caſa di continuo fioriva ed abbondava, &c. _Cond. ut ſupr._

(b) _Condiv. ut ſupra._

foundation

foundation of his future fame, and giving daily proofs of his rapid improvement, he formed an intimacy with Politiano, who refided under the fame roof, and who foon became warmly attached to his interefts. At his recommendation, Michelagnolo executed a *baffo-rilievo* in marble, the fubject of which is the battle of the Centaurs. This piece yet ornaments the dwelling of one of his defcendants; and, although not wholly finifhed, difplays rather the hand of an experienced mafter, than that of a pupil. But its higheft commendation is, that it ftood approved even in the riper judgement of the artift himfelf; who, although not indulgent to his own productions, did not hefitate, on feeing it fome years afterwards, to exprefs his regret that he had not entirely devoted himfelf to this branch of art (a). The death of Lorenzo too foon deprived him of his protector. Piero, the fon of Lorenzo, continued indeed to fhow to him the fame marks of kindnefs which his father had uniformly done; but that prodigality, which fo fpeedily diffipated his authority, his fortune, and his fame, was extended even to his amufements; and the talents of Michelagnolo, under the patronage of Piero, inftead of impreffing on brafs or on marble the forms of immortality, were condemned to raife a ftatue of fnow (b)! Nor was this intercourfe of long

(a) Cosi la imprefa gli fuccedette, che mi rammenta udirlo dire, che quando la rivede, cognoffe quanto torto egli abbia fatto alla natura, a non feguitar prontamente l'arte della fcultura, facendo giudizio per quell' opera, quanto poteffe riufcire. *Cond. vita di M. A.*

(b) Effendo in Firenze venuta dimolta neve, Pier de' Medici, continuance, for Piero, inſtead of affording ſupport to others, was ſoon obliged to ſeek, in foreign countries, a ſhelter for himſelf.

The hiſtory of Michelagnolo forms that of all the arts which he profeſſed. In him ſculpture, painting and architecture ſeem to have been perſonified. Born with talents ſuperior to his predeceſſors, he had alſo a better fate. Ghilberti, Donatello, Verocchio, were all men of genius, but they lived during the gentile ſtate of the art (*a*). The light had now riſen, and his young and ardent mind, converſant with the fineſt forms of antiquity, imbibed, as its genuine ſource, a reliſh for their excellence. With the ſpecimens of ancient art, the depoſitaries of ancient learning were unlocked to him, and of theſe alſo he made no inconſiderable uſe. As a poet he is entitled to rank high amongſt his countrymen ; and the triple wreaths of painting, ſculpture, and architecture, with which his diſciples decorated his tomb, might, without exaggeration, have been interwoven with a fourth (*b*).

figliuol maggiore di Lorenzo, che nel medeſimo luogo del padre era reſtato, ma non nella medeſima grazia, volendo, come giovane, far fare nel mezzo della ſua corte una ſtatua di neve ſi ricordò di Michelagnolo, e fattolo cercare, gli fece far la ſtatua, &c. *Condiv.* p. 8. This ſtatue was a juſt emblem of the fortunes of its founder.

(*a*) Michelagnolo, ch'ebbe ſi grande ingegno, non traſſe dal ſuo proprio fondo la ſua arte, nè con quello ſolo avrebbe trovata la ſtrada di uſcir da' limiti di quello ſtile ſecco, e ſervile, che ſin allora regnava in Italia; e ſenza un grande ſtudio, nè ſenza l'oſſervazione delle ſtatue antiche, non ſarebbe ſtato forſe che uguale a un Donatello, e a un Ghiberti. *Opere di Mengs, v.* ii. *p.* 189.

(*b*) The poems of Michelagnolo were publiſhed by his great-nephew Michelagnolo Buonarroti il Giovane, at Florence, in 1623, and are

OF the fculptures of Michelagnolo, fome yet remain in an unfinifhed ftate, which ftrikingly difplay the comprehenfion of his ideas and the rapidity of his execution. Such are the buft of Brutus, and the ftatue of a female figure, in the gallery at Florence. In the latter the chifel has been handled with fuch boldnefs, as to induce a connoiffeur of our own country to conjecture that it would be neceffary, in the finifhing, to reftore the cavities (*a*). Perhaps a more involuntary homage was never paid to genius, than that which was extorted from the fculptor Falconet, who having prefumed upon all occafions to cenfure the ftyle of Michelagnolo, without having had an opportunity of infpecting any of his works, at length obtained a fight of two of his ftatues, which were brought into France by cardinal Richelieu. *I have feen Michelagnolo*, exclaimed the French artift, *he is terrific* (*b*).

The labors of the painter are neceffarily tranfitory for fo are the materials that compofe them. In a few years Michelagnolo will be known, like an

ranked with the *Tefti di Lingua* of Italian literature. They were again reprinted at Florence in 1726, with the *Lezzioni* of Benedetto Varchi, and Mario Guiducci, on fome of his fonnets. Tenhove has juftly appreciated their merits. " Les fonnets & les *Canzoni* de Michelange " ne font point chargés d'ornemens ambitieux; ils fe reffentent de " l'auftère fimplicité de fon génie: cependant rien ne les fait autant " valoir, que la main dont ils font partis." *Mém. Gén. liv.* xix. *p.* 317.

(*a*) *Richardfon, Defcription des Tabl. &c. vol.* iii. *p.* 67.

(*b*) " J'ai vu Michelange; *Il eft effrayant.*" *Falcon. ap. Tenh.* The pieces which occafioned this exclamation were two of the ftatues intended to compofe a part of the monument of Julius II.

ancient artist, only by his works in marble. Already it is difficult to determine, whether his reputation be enhanced or diminished by the sombre reprefentations of his pencil in the Pauline and Sixtine chapels, or by the few fpecimens of his cabinet pictures, now rarely to be met with, and exhibiting only a fhadow of their original excellence. But the chief merit of this great man is not to be fought for in the remains of his pencil, nor even in his fculptures, but in the general improvement of the public tafte which followed his aftonifhing productions. If his labors had perifhed with himfelf, the change which they effected in the opinions and the works of his contemporaries would ftill have entitled him to the firft honors of the art. Thofe who from ignorance, or from envy, have endeavoured to depreciate his productions, have reprefented them as exceeding in their forms and attitudes the limits and the poffibilities of nature, as a race of beings, the mere creatures of his own imagination ; but fuch critics would do well to confider, whether the great reform to which we have alluded could have been effected by the moft accurate reprefentations of common life, and whether any thing fhort of that ideal excellence which he only knew to embody, could have accomplifhed fo important a purpofe. The genius of Michelagnolo was a leaven which was to operate on an immenfe and heterogeneous mafs, the falt intended to give a relifh to infipidity itfelf ; it was therefore active, penetrating, energetic, fo as not only effectually to refift the contagious effects of a depraved tafte, but to communicate a portion of its fpirit to all around.

Of the contemporary artifts of Michelagnolo, fuch only are entitled to high commendation as accompanied his ftudies, or availed themfelves of his example. Among thefe appears the divine Raffaello ; fecond to his great model only in that grandeur of defign which elevates the mind, fuperior to him in that grace which interefts the heart. Endowed, if not with vigor fufficient alone to effeſt a reform, with talents the beft calculated to promote its progrefs (*a*). It is well known that the works of this exquifite mafter form two diftinſt claffes, thofe which he painted before, and thofe which he painted after he had caught from the new Prometheus a portion of the ethereal fire—thofe of the fcholar of Perugino and of the competitor of Michelagnolo. " Happy " age," exclaims, with more than common animation, the hiftorian of the painters, " and happy " artifts, for fo I may well denominate you who, " have had the opportunity of purifying your eyes " at fo clear a fountain; who have found your " difficulties removed, your crooked paths made " ftraight by fo wonderful an artift: know then, " and honor the man who has enabled you to " diftinguifh between truth and falfhood, and let " your gratitude be fhown in returning your thanks

(*a*) Raffaello fteffo ci ha lafciate nelle fue opere le tracce de' fuoi ftudj; e fenza le lezioni di Fra Bartolommeo, e la vifta delle opere di Michelagnolo, e delle cofe antiche, non goderemmo oggi le fuɔ maravigliofe pitture. *Op. di Mengs, v. ii. p.* 189.

" to heaven, and in imitating Michelagnolo in all
" things (*a*).

Genius is ever obnoxious to that criticifm which
mediocrity efcapes, nor has this teft been wanting
to the merits of Michelagnolo. The parafites of
a vicious court, and a corrupt age, have not hefi-
tated to charge him with indecency, in introducing
naked figures in his celebrated picture of the laft
judgment. This accufation was made even in his
lifetime, by one who called himfelf his friend, and

(*a*) *Vafari, vita di Michelagnolo.* Gianfrancefco Grazzini, called
Il Lafca, alfo celebrates his countryman in the true Florentine idiom:

> Giotto fu il primo, ch' alla dipintura,
> Già lungo tempo morta, deffe vita.
> E Donatello meffe la fcultura
> Nel fuo dritto fentier, ch' era fmarrita:
> Cosi l'architettura
> Storpiata, e guafta, dalle man' de' Tedefchi,
> Anzi quafi bafita,
> Da Pippo Brunellefchi,
> Solenne Architettor, fu meffa in vita;
> Onde gloria infinita
> Meritar quefti tre fpirti divini,
> Nati in Firenze e noftri cittadini.
> E di quefte tre arti, i Fiorentini
> Han fempre poi tenuto il vanto e'l pregio.
> Dopo quefto, l'egregio
> Michelagnol divin, dal cielo eletto,
> Pittor, fcultore, architettor perfetto,
> Che dove i primi tre maeftri eccellenti
> Gittaro i fondamenti,
> Alle tre nobil' arti ha pofto il tetto.
> Onde meritamente,
> Chiamato è dalla gente
> Vero maeftro, e padre del difegno, &c.

Il Lafca, fop. la dipintura della Cupola.

who faw no impropriety in reprefenting it as pro-
ceeding from the obfcene lips of Pietro Aretino (*a*).
It foon however became fo prevalent, that in the
pontificate of Paul IV. it was in contemplation to
deftroy this aftonifhing picture, which was at laft
only preferved by the expedient of covering thofe
parts which were fuppofed to be likely to excite in
the minds of the depraved fpectators ideas unfuit-
able to the folemnity of the place. The painter
who undertook this office was ever afterwards dis-
tinguifhed by the name of *Il Braghettone*. Thefe
inculpations were renewed in the fucceeding cen-
tury, by a man of talents and celebrity, who united
like Michelagnolo, the character of a painter and a
poet, without having one idea in common with
him (*b*). But what fhall we fay of an artift who

(*a*) In the dialogue of Lodovico Dolce on painting, entitled
L'Aretino — Aretino, who is fuppofed to fpeak the fentiments of the
author, obferves, " Chi ardirà di affermar, che ftia bene, che nella
" chiefa di San Pietro, prencipe degli apoftoli, in una Roma, ove
" concurre tutto il mondo, nella cappella del Pontefice, il quale,
" come ben dice il Bembo, in terra ne affembra Dio, fi veggano
" dipinti tanti ignudi, che dimoftrano difoneftamente dritti e reverfi:
" cofa nel vero, (favellando con ogni fommeffione,) di quel fantis-
" fimo luogo indegna." Fabrini, the other colloquialift, juftifies
Michelagnolo by alledging the example of Raffaello, who is faid to
have defigned the lafcivious prints engraved by Marcantonio Rai-
mondi, under which the fame Aretino wrote his infamous verfes; but
it is eafy to fee that fuch a juftification is an admiffion of the charge.
Dolce, Dialog. p. 236. Ed. Flor. 1735.

(*b*) Salvator Rofa, in his fatire entitled *La Pittura*, relating inftances
of the arrogance and pride of his predeceffors, introduces the well-
known ftory of the critic *Biagio*, who, having cenfured the famous
picture of the laft judgment, was, in return, reprefented by Michel-

could mingle with the contemplation of a fubject fo interefting to all mankind, which unites every thing terrible and fublime, and abforbs all other paffions, an idea that can only have a relation to the decorums of modern life, and to that factitious decency which, by affecting concealment, acknowledges a pruriency of imagination, to which true tafte, as well as true modefty, is a ftranger?

The favors of Lorenzo de' Medici were not however exclufively beftowed. Although he well knew how to appreciate and to reward extraordinary excellence, he was not inattentive to the juft claims

agnolo in a group of the damned. According to Salvator, Biagio thus addreffed the painter:

> Michel Agnolo mio, non parlo in gioco,
>> Quefto che dipingete è un gran giudizio,   ·
>> Ma del giudicio voi n'avete poco.
> Io non vi taffo intorno all' artifizio,
>> Ma parlo del coftume, in cui mi pare
>> Che il voftro gran faper fi cangi in vizio.
> Sapevi pur che il figlio di Noè,
>> Perchè fcoperfe le vergogne al padre,
>> Tirò l'ira di Dio fovra di fe;
> E voi, fenza temer Chrifto e la Madre
>> Fate, che moftrin le vergogne parte,
> Infin de' Santi qui l'intiere fquadre.

And that it may not be imagined that Salvator did not himfelf approve the fentiments of the critic, he adds,

> In udire il pittor quefte propofte,
>> Divenuto di rabbia roffo, e nero,
>> Non potè proferir le fue rifpofte;
> Nè potendo di lui l'orgoglio altero
>> Sfogare il fuo furor per altre bande.
> Dipinfe nell' inferno il Cavaliero.

Satir. di Salv. Rofa. Ed. Lond. 1791.

of thofe who made a proficiency in any branch of
the arts. Where the indication of talents appeared
he was folicitous to call them into action, to accele-
rate their progrefs, and to repay their fuccefs.
" It is highly deferving of notice," fays Vafari,
" that all thofe who ftudied in the gardens of the
" Medici, and were favored by Lorenzo, became
" moft excellent artifts, which can only be attributed
" to the exquifite judgment of this great patron of
" their ftudies, who could not only diftinguifh men
" of genius, but had both the will and the power
" to reward them (a)." By his kindnefs the eminent
fculptor Ruftici was placed under the care of Andrea
Verocchio (b), where he formed an intimacy with the
celebrated Lionardo da Vinci; but although he
availed himfelf of the friendfhip and the inftructions
of this wonderful man, he acknowledged Lorenzo
as the parent of his ftudies (c). Francefco Granacci,
the fellow-ftudent of Michelagnolo, partook alfo of

(a) È gran cofa ad ogni modo, che tutti coloro, i quali furono nella
fcuola del Giardino de' Medici, e favoriti dal Mag. Lorenzo vecchio,
furono tutti eccellentiffimi; la qual cofa d'altronde non può effere
avvenuta, fe non dal molto, anzi infinito giudizio di quel nobiliffimo
fignore, vero Mecenate degli uomini virtuofi; il quale come fapeva
conofcere gl' ingegni, e fpirti elevati, così poteva e fapeva riconofcergli
e premiargli. *Vafari, vita del Ruftici.*

(b) Portandofi dunque beniffimo Giovanfrancefco Ruftici, cittadin
Fiorentino, nel difegnare, e fare di terra, mentre era giovinetto, fu da
effo magnifico Lorenzo, il quale lo conobbe fpiritofo, e di bello e
buon ingegno, meffo a ftare, perchè imparaffe, con Andrea del
Verocchio, &c. *Vafari, vita del Ruftici.*

(c) Effendo poi tornata in Fiorenza la Famiglia de' Medici, Il Ruftico
fi fece conofcere al Cardinal Giovanni, per creatura di Lorenzo fuo
padre, e fu ricevuto con molte carezze. *Ibid.*

the favor of Lorenzo, and was occafionally employed
by him in preparing the fplendid pageants with
which he frequently amufed the citizens of Florence;
in the decoration of which Granacci difplayed
uncommon tafte (*a*). The reputation acquired by
the pupils of S. Marco foon extended beyond the
limits of Italy. At the requeft of the king of
Portugal, Lorenzo fent into that country Andrea
Contucci, where he left various monuments of his
talents in fculpture and architecture (*b*). The en-
couragement afforded by him to the profeffors of
every branch of the arts, may be eftimated in fome
degree by the numerous pieces executed at his ex-
penfe by the firft mafters of the time, accounts of
which are occafionally difperfed through the volumi-
nous work of Vafari. Like his anceftor Cofmo, Lo-
renzo often forgot the fuperiority of the patron in
the familiarity of the friend, and not only excufed
but delighted in the capricioufnefs which frequently
diftinguifhes men of talents. In this number was
Niccolo Groffo, a Florentine citizen, who wrought

(*a*) Francefco Granacci——fu uno di quelli, che dal Magnifico
Lorenzo de' Medici fu meffo a imparare nel fuo giardino, &c. E
perchè era molto gentile, e valeva affai in certe galanterie, che per
fefte di carnovale fi facevano nella città, fu fempre in molte cofe
fimili dal Magnifico Lorenzo de' Medici adoperato.

Vafari, vita di Fr. Granac.

(*b*) Per quefte, e per l'altre opere d'Andrea, divulgatofi il nome
fuo, fu chiefto al magnifico Lorenzo vecchio de' Medici, nel cui
giardino avea, come fi è detto, attefo agli ftudj del difegno, dal re
di Portagallo, perchè mandatogli da Lorenzo, lavorò per quel re molte
opere di fcultura, e d'architettura, e particolarmente un belliffimo
palazzo, &c. *Vafar. vita di Contucci.*

ornaments in iron with extraordinary fkill. Confci-
ous of his merits Niccolo refolved to labor only
for thofe who paid him ready money, referring his
employers to the fign fufpended at his door, which
reprefented books of account deftroyed in the flame.
Lorenzo, defirous of prefenting to fome of his pow-
erful friends abroad a fpecimen of Florentine in-
genuity, called upon Niccolo to engage him to
execute for him a piece of his workmanfhip; but
the furly artifan, who was bufy at his anvil, inftead
of acknowledging the honor intended him, bluntly
told Lorenzo that he had other cuftomers who,
having firft applied, muft be firft ferved. The in-
vincible pertinacity of Niccolo, in refufing to work
till he had received his ufual depofit, occafioned
Lorenzo to give him the name of *Il Caparra* (*a*),
by which he was ever afterwards generally known (*b*).

The ftudy of architecture, as revived by Brunel-
lefchi, received additional fupport from the encou-
ragement afforded by Lorenzo de' Medici, who,
to the munificence of his grandfather, fuperadded
a knowledge of this fcience equal to that of a
practical artift. At his inftance, and often at his
individual expenfe, the city of Florence was orna-
mented with a profufion of elegant buildings, as
well for private refidence, as public purpofes. Con-
vinced that the art was founded on fixed and
determined principles, which were only to be
difcovered in the labors of the ancients, he juftly
reprobated thofe profeffors who, neglecting the

(*a*) From *Arrha, Arrhabo*, a pledge, or earneft.
(*b*) *Vafari, vita di Simone detto il Cronaca.*

rules of Vitruvius, followed only the variable fug-
geftions of their own fancy. Nor was he lefs fevere
on thofe who, without any previous knowledge of
the art, conceived themfelves equal to the tafk of
conducting a building on an extenfive fcale, and,
in the erection of their dwellings, chofe to become
their own architects. " Such people," faid Lorenzo
" buy repentance at too dear a rate (*a*)." Of this
defcription was his relation, Francefco de' Medici,
who having erected a large houfe at Majano, and
made feveral alterations in its progrefs, complained
to Lorenzo of the great expenfe with which it had
been attended: " That is not to be wondered at,"
replied Lorenzo, " when, inftead of erecting your
" building from a model, you draw your model
" from your building (*b*)." His fuperior judgment
in works of this kind was acknowledged on many
occafions. Ferdinand, king of Naples, intending to
build a palace, conceived no one more competent
to direct him in the choice of a plan than Lorenzo.
His affiftance was alfo fought for on a fimilar occafion
by the duke of Milan; and Filippo Strozzi, in the
erection of a manfion, which in grandeur of defign
and richnefs of execution is not inferior to a royal
refidence, availed himfelf greatly of his advice and
directions (*c*). It does not however appear, that

(*a*) Illos vel maxime reprehendere folebat quicumque in diem te-
mere ædificarent, eos dicens *caro admodum emere pœnitentiam.*

Valor. in vitâ, p. 63.

(*b*) *Valor. ut fupra.*

(*c*) Multi enim, multa regia ædificia de Laurentii confilio extruxere.
In quibus Philippi Strozziæ infulares ædes, quæ amplitudine fua, &

Lorenzo on any occafion thought proper to dif-
penfe with the aid of thofe who had made this
art their more immediate ftudy. Having formed
the intention of erecting his place at Poggio-Cajano,
he obtained defigns from feveral of the beft archi-
tects of the time, and amongft the reft from Giuliano
the fon of Paolo Giamberto, whofe model was
preferred by Lorenzo, and under whofe directions
the building was carried on; but in the conftruction
of the picturefque and fingular flight of fteps, which
communicated to every part with fuch convenience,
that a perfon might afcend or defcend even on
horfeback, Lorenzo availed himfelf of a defign of
Stefano d'Ugolino, a painter of Siena, who died
about the year 1350 (a). Lorenzo was defirous that
the ceiling of the great hall fhould be formed by a
fingle arch, but was appprehenfive that it would
not be practicable, on account of its extent. Giuli-
ano was at that time erecting a refidence for himfelf
in Florence, where he took an opportunity of execu-
ting one in the manner fuggefted by Lorenzo, and
fucceeded fo effectually as to remove his doubts on
this head. The ceiling at Poggio-Cajano was accor-
dingly completed, and is acknowledged to be the

grata membrorum difpofitione, totiufque ædificii venuftate & magnifi-
centia fuperant, fine ulla controverfia, non folum privatas domos, fed
principales & regias. Magno area conftitit in urbe media: impendium ·
ad centum aureorum millia acceffurum putatur. De modulo Philippus
Laurentium confuluit, qui quidem aderat omnibus fuper hac re operam
fuam cupientibus, nec civilibus folum, fed etiam externis. *Valor. in
cita, p.* 63. For a particolar account of this fplendid refidence, *v.*
Vafari, vita di Simone detto il Cronaca.

(a) *Vafar. vita di Giuliano da San Gallo, v.* ii. *p.* 78.

largeft vaulted roof of modern workmanfhip that had then been feen (*a*). The talents of this artift induced Lorenzo to recommend him to Ferdinand king of Naples, to whom he prefented, on the part of Lorenzo, the model of an intended palace. His reception was highly honorable. On his depàrture Ferdinand fupplied him with horfes, apparel, and other valuable articles, amongft which was a filver cup containing feveral hundred ducats. Giuliano, whilft he declined accepting it, expreffed a defire that the king would gratify him with fome fpecimen of ancient art, from his extenfive collection, which might be a proof of his approbation. Ferdinand accordingly prefented him with a buft of the emperor Adrian, a ftatue of a female figure larger than life, and a fleeping Cupid ; all of which Giuliano immediately fent to Lorenzo, who was no lefs pleafed with the liberality of the artift, than with the acquifition of fo valuable a treafure (*b*). At the requeft of the celebrated Mariano Genazano, Lorenzo had promifed to erect, without the gate of San Gallo at Florence, a monaftery capable of containining one hundred monks. On the return

(*a*) Giuliano had before been employed by Lorenzo in fortifying the town of Caftellana, when that place was attacked by the duke of Calabria, in which he rendered effential fervices to his patron. The Florentines were at that time very defective in the ufe of their artillery, which they fcarcely ventured to approach, and which frequently occafioned fatal accidents to thofe who directed it; but the ingenuity of the young architect remedied this defect; in confequence of which the army of the duke was fo feverely cannonaded as to be obliged to raife the fiege. *Vafar. ut fupra.*

(*b*) *Vafar. vita di Giuliano da San Gallo.*

of Giuliano to Florence, he engaged him in this work, whence he obtained the name of *San Gallo,* by which he was always afterwards diftinguifhed (*a*). Whilft this building was carrying forwards, Giuliano was alfo employed by Lorenzo in defigning and erecting the extenfive fortifications of Poggio Imperiale, preparatory to the founding a city on that fpot, as was his intention (*b*). To this artift, who arrived at great eminence in the enfuing century, and to his brother Antonio, architecture is indebted for the completion of the Tufcan order, as now eftablifhed ; and for confiderable improvements in the Doric.

Befides the many magnificent works begun under the immediate directions of Lorenzo, he feduloufly attended to the completion of fuch buildings as had been left imperfect by his anceftors. On the church of S. Lorenzo, the building of which was begun by his great grandfather Giovanni, and continued by his Grandfather Cofmo, he expended a large fum. At the requeft of Matteo Boffo he alfo completed the monaftery begun by Brunellefchi at Fiefole (*c*),

(*b*) Giuliano remonftrated with Lorenzo on this alteration.—" By " your calling me *San Gallo,*" faid he, " I shall lofe my name, and " inftead of becoming refpectable by the antiquity of my family, I " shall have to found it anew. Surely," faid Lorenzo, " it is more " honorable to be the founder of a new family by your own talents, " than to reft your reputation on the merits of others." *Vafar. ut fupra.*
(*c*) *Vafar. ut fupra.*
(*a*) The letter of Boffo, which was addreffed to Lorenzo in the height of his profperity, and touches upon many circumftances of his life and character, is given from the *Recuperationes Fefulanæ,* in the Appendix, *No.* LXXVI.

at the fame time expreffing his regret that he fhould have rendered it neceffary to folicit him to do that which he conceived to be an indifpenfible duty (a).

Amongft the various kinds of picturefque reprefentation practifed by the Greeks and Romans, and tranfmitted by them to after-times, is that of Mofaic; a mode of execution, which, in its durability of form, and permanency of color, poffeffes diftinguifhed advantages, being unaffected by drought or moifture, heat or cold, and perifhing only with the building to which it has been originally attached. This art, during the middle ages, had experienced the fame viciffitudes as attended all thofe with which it is fo nearly connected. Some attempts had, however, been made to reftore it by Andrea Tafi, the contemporary of Giotto (b); and even Giotto himfelf had cultivated it, not without fuccefs, although the celebrated picture over the great door of St. Peter at Rome, called the *Navicella di Giotto*, is faid to be a more modern work, copied from a former one of that artift (c). Lorenzo was defirous of introducing this mode of execution into more general practice. On expreffing to Graffione, a Florentine painter, his intention of ornamenting with work of this kind the vault of a large cupola, the painter ventured to obferve to him that he had not artifts equal to the tafk: " We have money enough " to make them," replied Lorenzo; and although

(a) *Fabr. in vità, v. i. p.* 148.

(b) *Vafar. vita di Andrea.*

(c) *Tenh. Mém. Généal. liv.* vii. *p.* 131.

Graffione

Graffione ftill continued incredulous (*a*), Lorenzo foon afterwards met with a perfon who fuited his purpofe in the painter Gherardo, who had generally applied himfelf to works in miniature. The fpecimen produced by Gherardo for the infpection of Lorenzo was a head of S. Zenobio, with which he was fo well pleafed, that he refolved to enlarge the chapel of that faint at Florence, in order to give the artift an opportunity of exhibiting his talents in a wider field. With Gherardo he affociated Domenico Ghirlandajo, as a more complete mafter of defign, and the work was commenced with great fpirit. Vafari affures us, that if death had not interpofed there was reafon to believe from the part that was executed, that thefe artifts would-have performed wonderful things (*b*).

But if the attempts made by Lorenzo to reftore the practice of Mofaic were thus in a great degree fruftrated, a difcovery was made about the fame period which proved an ample fubftitute for it, and which has given to the works of the painter that

(*a*) Graffione, with that familiarity which the artifts appear to have ufed towards Lorenzo, replied, " Eh Lorenzo, i danari non fanno i " maeftri, ma i maeftri fanno i danari."

(*b*) By whofe death the further progrefs of this work was interrupted, may be doubted. The words of Vafari are, "Per lo che Gherardo, " affottigliando l'ingegno, harebbe fatto con Domenico mirabiliffime " cofe, fe la morte non vi fi fuffe interpofta; come fi può giudicare " dal principio della detta capella, che rimafe imperfetta." But, by a fubfequent paffage in the life of Ghirlandajo, it feems it was the death of Lorenzo that prevented the completion of the work, " —— " come, per la morte del predetto Magnifico Lorenzo, rimafe imperfetta " in Fiorenza la Capella di S. Zanobi, comminciata a lavorare di " Mufaico Domenico in compagnia di Gherardo miniatore."

permanency which even the durability of Mofaic might not perhaps have fnpplied. This was the art of transferring to paper impreffions from engravings on copper, or other metals; an invention which has tended more than any other circumftance to diffufe throughout Europe a juft and general tafte for the arts.

This difcovery is attributed by the Italians to Mafo, or Tomafo Finiguerra, a goldfmith of Florence, who being accuflomed to engrave on different metals for the purpofe of inlaying them, occafionally tried the effects of his work by taking off impreffions, firft on fulphur, and afterwards on paper, by means of a roller, in fuch a manner that the figures feemed to have been traced with a pen. It does not appear that Finiguerra ever applied this invention to any other purpofe than that of afcertaining the progrefs of his work; nor have the refearches of the moft diligent inquirers difcovered a fingle print that can with any degree of probability be attributed to him; but Baccio Baldini, another goldfmith, conceiving that this difcovery might be applied to more important purpofes, began to engrave on metals, folely with a view of tranfmitting impreffions to paper. Poffeffing, however, no great fkill in defign, he prevailed on Sandro Botticello to furnifh him with drawings fuitable for his purpofe. The concurrence of Antonio Pollajuoli, and Andrea Mantegna, carried the art to greater perfection. Of the works of the laft-mentioned mafter many fpecimens yet remain, which do credit to his talents. The beginning of the enfuing century produced a much fuperior artift in Marcantonio Raimondi, by whofe induftry the numerous productions of Raffaello, the tranfcripts of his rich and creative mind, were committed to paper with an accuracy which he himfelf approved, and may ferve as a ftandard to mark in future times the progrefs or the decline of the arts (a).

(a) The credit of having given rife to this elegant and ufeful art has been contended for by different countries, and their various pretenfions have been weighed and confidered by many authors. It is however general'y agreed, that it begun with the goldfmiths, and was afterwards adopted by the painters. The union of thefe two profeffions has thus produced a third, which has rifen to confiderable importance. The Germans, who have difputed with the Italians the honor of the invention with the greateft degree of plaufibility, have not in point of fact controverted the narrative given by the Italians of the rife of the art, nor brought forwards any account of their own, but have fimply endeavoured to show that it was practifed in Germany at an earlier period. Mr. Heineken afferts, that the earlieft prints engraved in Italy that bear a date, are the maps to the edition of Ptolemy, printed at Rome in 1478; the earlieft picturefque reprefentations, thofe prefixed to fome of the cantos of Dante in 1482; whilft he adduces inftances of German execution that bear the date of 1466, by comparing the manner of which with other pieces, apparently of earlier workmanship, he conjectures that the art had its rife in Germany about the year 1440. *Idée Générale, p.* 232. *Non noftrum tantas componere lite.* I fhall only obferve, that little dependance is to be placed on conjectures from prints without a date, particularly thofe of German workmanship, as the artifts of that country continued to produce them in the moft rude and Gothic ftyle, both as to defign and execution, long after the beginning of the fixteenth century, when Albert Dürer, and Luca van Leyden had fet them a better example. On the other hand, impartiality obliges me to remark, that Thirabofchi, who ftrenuoufly claims for his countrymen the merit of the difcovery, has not difcuffed this fubject with his ufual accuracy. Firft, he is miftaken in afferting that Baldinucci fixes the commencement of the art in the beginning of the fifteenth century, *Storia della Lett. Ital. v.* ii. *p.* 2. *p.* 399. Baldinucci only fays in

Whilſt the art of transferring to paper impreſſions from copper was thus firſt practiſed, that of engraving in gems and ſtones was again ſuccefsfully revived. The predilection of Lorenzo de' Medici for the beautiful ſpecimens of ſkill which the ancients have left in materials of this nature, has frequently been noticed (a). Of thoſe which once formed a part of his immenſe collection, ſome occaſionally occur that ſeem to have been the objects of his more particular

general, that the art had its beginning in the fifteenth century. " *Queſt'* " *arte ebbe ſuo principio nel ſecolo del* 1400." Secondly, on the authority of a document produced by Manni, he ſuppoſes that Tomaſo Finiguerra, the inventor of the art, died prior to the year 1424; but both Vaſari and Baldinucci inform us, that the Finiguerra in queſtion was contemporary with Pollajuolo, who was only born in 1426. It is ſingular that this judicious author did not reflect how ſlight that evidence muſt be which reſts merely on a ſimilarity of name, particularly in Florence, where, for the ſake of diſtinction, it was often neceſſary to reſort to the patronymics for ſeveral generations. *v. Vaſari, vite de' Pittori, paſſim. Baldinucci comminciamento e progreſſo dell' arte dell' intagliare in Rame. Fir.* 1686. *Heincken Idée générale d une Collection complette d Eſtampes, &c.*

(a) The collection of antiques formed by Lorenzo is thus celebrated by a contemporary author:

> Cælatum argento, vel fulvo quidquid in auro eſt
> Ædibus hoc, LAURENS, vidimus eſſe tuis.
> Praxitelis, Phœnicis, Ariſtonis, atque Myronis
> Fingere tam doctæ quod potuere manus
> Cunachus, aut Mentor, Pythias, vel uterque Polycles
> Lyſippus quidquid, Callimachuſque dedit.
> Quæ collegiſti miro virtutis amore
> Magnanimum reddunt nomen ubique tuum.
> Artificum monumenta foves, referuntur in auro
> Argento, tabulis, & lapide ora Deûm.

F. Camerlini, ap. Band. Cat. Bibl. Laur. v. iii. *p.* 545.

admiration, and bear upon fome confpicuous part the name of their former proprietor, thus exprefſed LAVR. MED. (*a*).   Nor is it improbable that Michel-

(*a*) Thefe letters appear on a cameo in onyx of different colors, reprefenting the entry of Noah and his family into the aik, of which an engraving is given by Gori in his edition of the life of Michelagnolo by Condivi.   Among the gems or cameos of this defcription, of which I have met with impreffions, or *geſſi*, are thofe of Diomed with the palladium, or a large oval cameo, in which the letters LAUR. MED. are engraved on the fide of the rock or ftone on which he fits — A centaur, with the letters engraved on the exergue — Dædalus fixing on the wings of Icarus; the infcription is on the pedeftal upon which Icarus ftands, extending his wings over the upper part of the piece; and laftly, the celebrated gem reprefenting Apollo and Marfyas, of which I fhall tranfcribe a more particular account from the excellent work of Mr. Tenhove. " La gravure antique qui fervait de cachet
" à Laurent, & qui appartient encore au Grand-Duc de Tofcane, eft
" un morceau accompli.   Les fuffrages qu'elle a mérités dans tous les
" tems, font fuffifamment atteftés par cette foule de copies qui en
" ont été faites dans les tems anciens & modernes.   Apollon dans
" une attitude noble tient fa lyre, & regarde avec dédain Marfyas,
" qui, les mains liées derrière le dos, & attaché à un arbre, attend
" la jufte punition de fa témérité.   Le jeune Scythe qui doit exécuter
" la fentence, eft à genoux aux pieds d'Apollon, & femble implorer
" fa clémence.   Le carquois & les flèches du Dieu font fufpendus
" à une des branches de l'arbre, & fur la terraffe font les flûtes qui
" ont fi mal fervi le Satyre.   Cette même pierre montée en bague avait
" autrefois décoré la main parricide de Néron; ce monftre était dans
" l'ufage d'en fceller fes fanguinaires refcrits.   On fçait qu'il eut la
" folie de s'eftimer le premier muficien de fon tems, & par le choix
" qu'il fit de ce fujet il voulut fans doute écarter les concurrens, &
" intimider ceux qui oferaient entrer en lice avec lui. Peut-être même
" regarda-t'il fa main gauche & prit-il Apollon pour modèle, loifqu'il
" fit fouetter jufqu'au fang & écorcher, pour ainfi dire, ce chanteur
" Menedème dont il était jaloux, & dont les hurlemens mêmes lui
" parurent fi mélodieux, qu'il ne pût s'empêcher d'y applaudir avec

agnolo, who paſſed among theſe treaſures a confi-
derable portion of his time, was indebted to the
liberality of Lorenzo for the beautiful Intaglio which
he is ſuppoſed to have worn as his ſeal (*a*).

The protection and encouragement afforded by Lo-
renzo to every other branch of art, was not with-held
from this his favorite department. From the early
part of the fifteenth century, ſome ſpecimens of the
aſtoniſhing proficiency of the ancients in works of
this nature had occaſionally been diſcovered; and
as the public taſte improved, they were ſought for
with avidity, and only to be purchaſed at confider-
able prices. In the pontificate of Martin V. and
again in that of Paul II. ſome attempts had been
made to rival, or at leaſt to imitate, theſe productions,
but the firſt artiſt whoſe name ſtands recorded in
modern times is Giovanni delle Corniuole, ſo called
from his having generally exerciſed his ſkill upon
the ſtone called a Cornelian. The muſeum of Lo-
renzo de' Medici was the ſchool in which he ſtudied.
The proficiency he made correſponded to the

" tranſport.——Les vûes de Laurent étaient un peu plus raiſonnables,
" ſans doute il ne choiſit cette pierre qu' à cauſe de la beauté merveil-
" leuſe du travail."

(*a*) Chiaro documento ſi ha, che uno degli eſtimatori è raccoglitori
intelligenti de' più prezioſi avanzi dell' erudita antichità, e di gioie
intagliate da eccellenti Maeſtri greci, e di medaglie, e di altre ſimili
rarità, fu il Mag. Lorenzo, per tale celebrato, e riconoſciuto dall' inſigno
Izec. Span mio nella Diſs. i. *De preſtan & uſu Numiſm. antiquor.*
Nè è maraviglia ſe Michelagnolo potè acquiſtare la ſtupendiſſima
gemma annulare, la quale paſſò poi nelle mani e nel teſoro del re
Criſtianiſſimo; e forſe ch' anch' eſſo altre ſi fatte rarità averà acquiſtate
de' più eccellenti artefici greci.

Gori. Notiz. Storic. ſopra la vita di Michelagn. di Condivi, p. 101.

advantages which he poffeffed, and anfwered the purpofes which his liberal patron had in view. The numerous pieces of his workmanfhip in various fizes, and on various materials, were the admiration of all Italy. One of his moft celebrated productions was the portrait of Savonarola, who was then in the meridian of his popularity at Florence. Giovanni immediately met with a formidable competitor in a Milanefe, who alfo loft the name of his family in that of his art, and was called Domenico de' Camei. The likenefs of Lodovico Sforza, engraved by Domenico in a large onyx, was confidered as the moft extraordinary fpecimen of modern fkill. By thefe mafters, and their fcholars, this elegant, but unobtrufive branch of the fine arts kept pace with its more oftentatious competitors; and even in the moft flourifhing period of their elevation, under the pontificate of Leo X. the eye that had contemplated the divine fculptures of Michelagnolo, or had dwelt with delight on the paintings of Raffaello, or of Titian, might have turned with pleafure to the labors of Valerio Vicentino, or of Giovanni Bolognefe, which compreffed into the narroweft bounds the accurate reprefentations of beauty, ftrength, or grace, and gave to the moft ineftimable productions of nature the higheft perfection of art.

CHAP. X.

LORENZO de' MEDICI intends to retire from public life—Is taken sick and removes to Careggi—His conduct in his last sickness—Interview with Pico and Politiano—Savonarola visits him--Death of Lorenzo—His character—Review of his conduct as a statesman—Attachment of the Florentines to him—Circumstances attending his death—Testimonies of respect to his memory—Death of Innocent VIII. and accession of Alexander VI.—Irruption of the French into Italy—Expulsion of the Medici from Florence—Death of Ermolao Barbaro—Of Pico of Mirandula—Of Agnolo Politiano—Absurd accounts respecting the death of Politiano—His monody on Lorenzo—Politiano celebrated by Cardinal Bembo—Authentic account of his death—Disturbances excited by Savonorola—Adherents of the Medici decapitated--Disgrace and execution of Savonarola—Death of Piero de' Medici—His character--Sonnet of Piero de' Medici-Cardinal Giovanni de' Medici—Restoration of the family to Florence—Elevation of Leo X.—Leo promotes his relations—Restores his dominions to peace—Rise of the reformation—Age of Leo X.—The Laurentian Library restored—Giuliano de' Medici duke of Nemours—Ippolito de' Medici—Lorenzo de' Medici duke of Urbino—Alessandro de' Medici—Descendants of Lorenzo de' Medici the brother of Cosmo—Giovanni de' Medici—Lorenzo de' Medici—Alessandro assumes the sovereignty of Florence—Is assassinated by Lorenzino—Motives and consequences of the attempt—Cosmo de' Medici first grand duke—Death of Filippo Strozzi, and final extinction of the republic—Conclusion.

THAT love of leifure which is infeparable from a mind confcious of its own refources, and the confideration of his declinining ftate of health, were probably the motives that induced Lorenzo de' Medici to aim at introducing his two elder fons into public life at fo early and almoft premature an age. The infirmities under which he labored not only difqualified him at times from attending with his accuftomed vigilance to the affairs of the republic, but rendered it alfo neceffary for him often to abfent himfelf from Florence, and to pafs fome portion of his time at the warm baths in various parts of Italy, of which thofe of Siena and Porrettana, afforded him the moft effectual relief. At thofe feafons which were not embittered by ficknefs, he appears to have flattered himfelf with the expectation of enjoying the reward of his public labors, and partaking of the general happinefs which he had fo effentially contributed to promote, in a peaceful and dignified retirement, enlivened by focial amufements, by philofophic ftudies, and literary purfuits. Thefe expectations were built upon the moft fubftantial foundation, the confcioufnefs that he had difcharged his more immediate duties and engagements; but his feelings on this occafion are beft expreffed in his own words (a): " What, " fays he, " can be more defirable to a well-regulated mind, " than the enjoyment of leifure with dignity? This

____

(a) *Ap. Fabr. in vitâ Laur. v.* I. *p.* 196.

" is what all good men wish to obtain, but which
" great men alone accomplish. In the midst of public
" affairs we may indeed be allowed to look forwards
" to a day of rest; but no rest should totally seclude
" us from an attention to the concerns of our country.
" I cannot deny that the path which it has been my
" lot to tread has been arduous and rugged, full of
" dangers, and beset with treachery; but I confole
" myfelf in having contributed to the welfare of my
" country, the profperity of which may now rival
" that of any other state, however flourishing. Nor
" have I been inattentive to the interefts and advance-
" ment of my own family, having always propofed
" to my imitation the example of my grandfather
" Cofmo, who watched over his public and private
" concerns with equal vigilance. Having now obtain-
" ed the object of my cares, I truft I may be allowed
" to enjoy the fweets of leifure, to fhare the reputa-
" tion of my fellow-citizens, and to exult in the glory
" of my native place." His intentions were more
explicitly made known to his faithful companion
Politiano, who relates, that fitting with him in his
chamber a few days before his death, converfing on
fubjects of letters and philofophy, he then told him
that he meant to withdraw himfelf as much as poffi-
ble from the tumult of the city, and to devote the
remainder of his days to the fociety of his learned
friends; at the fame time expreffing his confidence
in the abilities of his fon Piero, on whom it was his
intention that the conduct of the affairs of the republic
fhould principally devolve (a).

(a) *Polit. Ep. lib. iv. Ep. 2.* But Guicciardini informs us that

The profpect of relaxation and happinefs he was not however deftined to realize. Early in the year 1492, the complaint under which he labored attacked him with additional violence, and whilft the attention of his phyficians was employed in adminiftering relief, he contracted a flow fever which efcaped their obfervation, or eluded their fkill, until it was too late effectually to oppofe its progrefs. The laft illnefs of Lorenzo de' Medici, like that of moft other great men, is reprefented as being extraordinary in its nature. Politiano defcribes his diforder as a fever, of all others the moft infidious, proceeding by infenfible degrees, not like other fevers, by the veins or arteries, but attacking the limbs, the inteftines, the nerves, and deftroying the very principle of life. On the firft approach of this dangerous complaint he had removed from Florence to his houfe at Careggi, where his moments were enlivened by the fociety of his friends, and the refpectful attentions of his fellow-citizens. For medical advice, his chief reliance was upon the celebrated Pier Leoni of Spoleto, whom he had frequently confulted on the ftate of his health; but as the diforder increafed, further affiftance was fought for, and Lazaro da Ticino. another phyfician, arrived at Careggi. It feems to have been the opinion of Politiano that the advice of Lazaro was too late reforted to; but if we may judge from the nature of

Lorenzo was well aware of the real character of his fon, " e fi era " fpeffo lamentato, con li amici più intimi, che l'imprud nza ed " arroganza del figliuolo, partorirebbe la rovina della fua cafa."

Guic. Hift. lib. i.

the medicines employed by him, he rather con-
tributed to accelerate than to avert the fatal moment.
The mixture of amalgamated pearls and jewels, with
the moft expenfive potions, might indeed ferve to
aftonifh the attendants, and to fcreen the ignorance
of the phyfician, but were not likely to be attended
with any beneficial effect on the patient. Whether
it was in confequence of this treatment, or from the
nature of the diforder itfelf, a fudden and unexpected
alteration foon took place; and whilft his friends
relied with confidence on the exertions made in his
behalf, he funk at once into fuch a ftate of debility
as totally precluded all hopes of his recovery, and
left him only the care of preparing to meet his doom
in a manner confiftent with the eminence of his
character, and the general tenor of his life.

Notwithftanding the diverfity of occupations which
had fucceffively engaged his attention, and the levity,
not to fay licentioufnefs, of fome of his writings,
the mind of Lorenzo had always been deeply fufcep-
tible of religious impreffions. This appears not only
from his attention to the eftablifhment and reform of
monaftic houfes (*a*), but from his *laudi*, or hymns,
many of which breathe a fpirit of devotion nearly
bordering on enthufiafm. During his laft ficknefs,
this feature of his character became more prominent;
nor did he judge it expedient, or perhaps think it
excufable, to feparate the effential from the cere-
monial part of religion. Having therefore performed
the offices of the church with peculiar fervor, and
adjufted with fincerity and decorum his fpiritual

(*a*) Of this feveral inftances are given by his hiftorian Valori, *p.* 58, &c.

concerns, he requefted a private interview with his
fon Piero, with whom he held a long and interefting
converfation on the ftate of the republic, the fitua-
tion of his family, and the conduct which it would
be expedient for Piero to purfue. Of the precepts
which he thought it neceffary to inculcate on his
fucceffor, we derive fome information from Politiano,
which was probably obtained from the relation of
his pupil (a). "I doubt not," faid Lorenzo, "that you
" will hereafter poffefs the fame weight and authority
" in the ftate which I have hitherto enjoyed; but as
" the republic, although it form but one body, has
" many heads, you muft not expect that it will be
" poffible for you on all occafions fo to conduct your-
" felf as to obtain the approbation of every individu-
" al. Remember, therefore, in every fituation to pur-
" fue that courfe of conduct which ftrict integrity
" prefcribes, and confult the interefts of the whole

(b) The circumftances preceding and attending the death of Lorenzo
are minutely related by Politiano in a letter to Jacopo Antiquario,
lib. iv. *Ep.* 2. upon the authority of which I have principally relied,
as will be feen, without troubling the reader with continual references,
by adverting to the letter in the Appendix, *No.* LXXVII. Fabroni
has incorporated this letter in the body of his work, as both the narra-
tive and the evidence of the facts it relates; but as Politiano has mingled
with much authentic information many inftances of that fuperftition
which infefted the age, and has, perhaps, shown too unlimited a
partiality to the family of his patrons, I have thought it incumbent
on me to feparate, according to the beft of my judgment, the documents
of hiftory from the dreams of the nurfery, and the reprefentations of
truth from the encomiums of the friend, leaving my reader to confult
the original, and to adopt as much more of the account as he may
think fit.

" community, rather than the gratification of a part."
These admonitions, if attended to, might have pre-
ferved Piero from the ruin which the neglect of them
foon brought down, and may yet ferve as a leffon to
thofe whofe authority refts, as all authority muft final-
ly reft, on public opinion. The dutiful and patient
attendance of Piero on his father during his ficknefs
was however a pledge to Lorenzo that his laft inftruc-
tions would not be forgotten, and, by confirming the
favorable fentiments which he appears to have en-
tertained of the talents and the difpofition of his fon,
ferved at leaft to alleviate the anxiety which he muft
have felt on refigning, thus prematurely the direction
of fuch a vaft and rapid machine into young and in
experienced hands.

At this interefting period, when the mind of Lo-
renzo, relieved from the weight of its important
concerns, became more fenfibly alive to the emotions
of friendfhip, Politiano entered his chamber. Lorenzo
no fooner heard his voice than he called on him to
approach, and, raifing his languid arms, clafped the
hands of Politiano in his own, at the fame time
ftedfaftly regarding him with a placid, and even a
cheerful countenance. Deeply affected at this filent
but unequivocal proof of efteem, Politiano could
not fupprefs his feelings, but, turning his head afide,
ditempted as much as poffible to conceal his fobs and
his tears. Perceiving his agitation, Lorenzo ftill con-
tinued to grafp his hand as if intending to fpeak to
him when his paffion had fubfided, but finding him
unable to refift its impulfe, he flowly, and as it were
unintentionally relaxed his hold, and Politiano, haft-
ening into an inner apartment, flung himfelf on a

bed, and gave way to his grief. Having at length compofed himfelf, he returned into the chamber, when Lorenzo again called to him, and inquired with great kindnefs why Pico of Mirandula had not once paid him a vifit during his ficknefs. Politiano apologized for his friend, by affuring Lorenzo that he had only been deterred by the apprehenfion that his prefence might be troublefome. " On the con-" trary," replied Lorenzo, " if his journey from the " city be not troublefome to him, I fhall rejoice to " fee him before I take my final leave of you." Pico accordingly came, and feated himfelf at the fide of Lorenzo, whilft Politiano, reclining on the bed, near the knees of his revered benefactor, as if to prevent any extraordinary exertion of his declining voice, prepared for the laft time to fhare in the pleafures of his converfation. After excufing himfelf to Pico for the tafk he had impofed upon him, Lorenzo expreffed his efteem for him in the moft affectionate terms, profeffing that he fhould meet his death with more cheerfulnefs after this laft interview. He then changed the fubject to more familiar and lively topics, and it was on this occafion that he expreffed, not without fome degree of jocularity, his wifhes that he could have obtained a reprieve, until he could have completed the library deftined to the ufe of his auditors. This interview was fcarcely ter-minated when a vifitor of a very different character arrived. This was the haughty and enthufiaftic Savonarola, who probably thought, that in the laft moments of agitation and of fuffering, he might be enabled to collect materials for his factious purpofes.

With apparent charity and kindnefs, the prieft ex-
horted Lorenzo to remain firm in the catholic faith;
to which Lorenzo profeffed his ftrict adherence. He
then required an avowal of his intention, in cafe of
his recovery, to live a virtuous and well-regulated
life ; to this he alfo fignified his fincere affent. Laftly
he reminded him, that, if needful, he ought to bear
his death with fortitude. " With cheerfulnefs,"
replied Lorenzo, " if fuch be the will of God." On
his quitting the room, Lorenzo called him back, and
as an unequivocal mark that he harboured in his
bofom no refentment againft him for the injuries
which he had received, requefted the prieft would
beftow upon him his benediction; with which he
inftantly complied, Lorenzo making the ufual ref-
ponfes with a firm and collected voice (a).

(a) In the life of Savonarola, written in Latin, at confiderable length,
by Giovanfranceico Pico prince of Mirandula, nephew of the celebrated
Pico whom we have had occafion fo frequently to mention, an account
is given of this interview, which differs in its moft effential particulars
from that which is above related. If we may credit this narrative,
Lorenzo, when at the point of death, fent to requeft the attendance of
Savonarola, to whom he was defirous of making his confeffion. Savona-
rola accordingly came, but, before he would confent to receive him
as a penitent, required that he should declare his adherence to the true
faith; to which Lorenzo affented. He then infifted on a promife from Lo-
renzo, that if he had unjuftly obtained the property of others, he would
return it. Lorenzo, after a fhort hefitation, replied, "Doubtlefs, father, I
" shall do this, or, if it be not in my power, I shall enjoin it as a duty upon
" my heirs." Thirdly, Savonarola required that he should reftore the
republic to liberty, and eftablish it in its former ftate of independence;
to which Lorenzo not chufing to make any reply, the prieft left him
without giving him his abfolution. *Savonar. vita, inter vit. felect. viror.
op. Bates. Lond. 1704.* A ftory that exhibits evident fymptoms of

No

No fpecies of reputation is fo cheaply acquired as that derived from death-bed fortitude. When it is fruitlefs to contend, and impoffible to fly, little applaufe is due to that refignation which patiently awaits its doom. It is not therefore to be confidered as enhancing that dignity of character which Lorenzo had fo frequently difplayed, that he fuftained the laft conflict with equanimity. "To judge from " his conduct, and of his fervants," fays Politiano, " you would have thought that it was they who " momentarily expected that fate, from which he " alone appeared to be exempt." Even to the laft the fcintillations of his former vivacity were perceptible. Being afked, on taking a morfel of food how he relifhed it, " As a dying man always does," was his reply. Having affectionately embraced his .furrounding friends, and fubmitted to the laft ceremonies of the church, he became abforbed in meditation, occafionally repeating portions of fcripture, and accompanying his ejaculations with elevated eyes, and folemn geftures of his hands, till the energies of life gradually declining, and preffing to his lips a magnificent crucifix, he calmly expired.

In the height of his reputation, and at a premature period of life, thus died Lorenzo de' Medici; a man who may be felected from all the characters of ancient and modern hiftory, as exhibiting the moft remarkable inftance of depth of penetration, ver-

that party-fpirit which did not arife in Florence until after the death of Lorenzo, and which, being contradictory to the account left by Politiano, written before the motives for mifreprefentation exifted, is only rendered deferving of notice by the neceffity of its refutation.

fatility of talent, and comprehenfion of mind (*a*).
Whether genius be a predominating impulfe, direct-
ing the mind to fome particular object, or whether
it be an energy of intellect that arrives at excellence
in any department in which it may be employed,
it is certain that there are few inftances in which,
a fuccefsful exertion in any human purfuit has not
occafioned a dereliction of many other objects, the
attainment of which might have conferred im-
mortality. If the powers of the mind are to bear
down all obftacles that oppofe their progrefs, it
feems neceffary that they fhould fweep along in
fome certain courfe, and in one collected mafs.
What then fhall we think of that rich fountain which,
whilft it was poured out by fo many different chan-
nels, flowed through each with a full and equal
ftream? To be abforbed in one purfuit, however
important, is not the characteriftic of the higher
clafs of genius, which, piercing through the various
combinations, and relations of furrounding cir-
cumftances, fees all things in their juft dimenfions
and attributes to each its due. Of the various
occupations in which Lorenzo engaged, there is
not one in which he was not eminently fuccefsful;
but he was moft particularly diftinguifhed in thofe
which juftly hold the firft rank in human eftima-

(*a*) " Soyons avares," fays M. Tenhove, " du titre facré de grand
" homme, prodigué fi fouvent & fi ridiculement aux plus minces per-
" fonnages, mais ne le refufons point à Laurent de Medicis. Malheur
" à l'ame froide & mal organifée, qui ne fentirait pas fon extrême
" mérite! On peut en toute fûreté s'eftimer de fon admiration pour
" lui." *Mém. Gén. liv.* xi. *p.* 146.

tion. The facility with which he turned from subjects of the highest importance to those of amusement and levity, suggested to his countrymen the idea that he had two distinct souls combined in one body. Even his moral character seems to have partaken in some degree of the same diversity, and his devotional poems are as ardent as his lighter pieces are licentious. On all sides he touched the extremes of human character, and the powers of his mind were only bounded by that impenetrable circle which prescribes the limits of human nature.

As a statesman, Lorenzo de' Medici appears to peculiar advantage. Uniformly employed in securing the peace and promoting the happiness of his country by just regulations at home, and wise precautions abroad, and teaching to the surrounding governments those important lessons of political science, on which the civilization and tranquillity of nations have since been found to depend. Though possessed of undoubted talents for military exploits, and of sagacity to avail himself of the imbecility of neighbouring powers, he was superior to that avarice of dominion which, without improving what is already acquired, blindly aims at more extensive possessions. The wars in which he engaged were for security, not for territory; and the riches produced by the fertility of the soil, and the industry and ingenuity of the inhabitants of the Florentine republic, instead of being dissipated in imposing projects and ruinous expeditions, circulated in their natural channels, giving happiness to the individual, and respectability to the state. If he was not insensible to the charms

of ambition, it was the ambition to deferve rather
than to enjoy; and he was always cautious not to
exact from the public favor more than it might be
voluntarily willing to beftow. The approximating
fuppreffion of the liberties of Florence, under the
influence of his defcendants, may induce fufpicions
unfavorable to his patriotifm; but it will be difficult,
not to fay impoffible, to difcover, either in his con-
duct or his precepts, any thing that ought to ftigmatize
him as an enemy to the freedom of his country. The
authority which he exercifed was the fame as ·that
which his anceftors had enjoyed, without injury to
the republic, for nearly a century, and had def-
cended to him as infeparable from the wealth, the
refpectability, and the powerful foreign connexions
of his family. The fuperiority of his talents enabled
him to avail himfelf of thefe advantages with irre-
fiftible effect; but hiftory fuggefts not an inftance in
which they were devoted to any other purpofe than
that of promoting the honor and the independence
of the Tufcan ftate. It was not by the continuance,
but by the dereliction of the fyftem that he had
eftablifhed, and to which he adhered to the clofe of
his life, that the Florentine republic funk under the
degrading yoke of defpotic power; and to his pre-
mature death we may unqueftionably attribute, not
only the deftruction of the commonwealth, but all
the calamities that Italy foon afterwards fuftained.

The fympathies of mind, like the laws of chemical
affinity, are uniform. Great talents attract admira-
tion, the offering of the underftanding; but the
qualities of the heart can alone excite affection, the

offering of the heart. If we may judge of Lorenzo de' Medici by the ardor with which his friends and contemporaries have expreffed their attachment, we fhall form conclufions highly favorable to his fenfibility and his focial virtues. The exaction of thofe attentions ufually paid to rank and to power, he left to fuch as had no other claims to refpect; he rather chofe to be confidered as the friend and the equal, than as the dictator of his fellow-citizens. His urbanity extended to the loweft ranks of fociety; and while he enlivened the city of Florence by magnificent fpectacles and amufing reprefentations, he partook of them himfelf with a relifh that fet the example of feftivity. It was the general opinion in Florence, that whoever was favored by Lorenzo could not fail of fuccefs. Valori relates, that in the reprefentation of an engagement on horfeback, one of the combatants, who was fuppofed to contend under the patronage of Lorenzo, being overpowered and wounded, avowed his refolution to die rather than fubmit to his adverfary, and it was not without difficulty that he was refcued from the danger, to receive from the bounty of Lorenzo the reward of his well-meant though miftaken fidelity.

The death of Lorenzo, which happened on the eighth day of April 1492, was no fooner known at Florence than a general alarm and confternation fpread throughout he city, and the inhabitants gave way to the moft unbounded expreffions of grief. Even thofe who were not friendly to the Medici lamented in this misfortune the profpect of the evils to come. The agitation of the public mind was increafed by a fingular coincidence of calamitous events, which the fuperftition of the people confider-ed as portentous of approaching commotions. The phyfician, Pier Leoni, whofe prefcriptions had failed of fuccefs, being apprized of the relult, left Careggi in a ftate of diftraction, and precipitated himfelf into a well in the fuburbs of the city (*a*) Two days preceding the death of Lorenzo, the great dome of the *Reparata* was ftruck with lightning, and on the fi le which approached towards the chapel of the M dici, a part of the building fell. It was

(*a*) Whether L oni died a voluntary death has been doubted. The enemies of the M dici, who upon the death of Lorenzo began to medi-tate the ruin of his family, have accufed Pi ro his fon with the perpe-tration of the de d, and this opinion is openly avowed by Giacopo Sanazaro in an Italian po m in *terza Rima*, in which he has imitated Dante with great fuccefs, *v. App. No.* LXXVIII. But I muft obferve, that this po m bears internal evid nce of its having been written after the Medici were driven from Florence, when their enemies were la-boring by every poffible means to render them odious. On the other hand, befides the teftimony of Politiano that Leoni accelerated his own death, we have that of Petrus Crinitus (Piero Ricci), a contemporary author, who, in his treatife *De honefta Difciplina*, has a chapter *De homin bus qui fe ipfos in puteum jaciant*, in which he thus adverts to the death of Leoni: " Sed enim quod nuper accidit in Petro Leonio, " mirificum certe vifum eft; quando is, & in philofophia vir excellens, " ac prudentia prope egregia, in puteum fe Florentino fuburbano " immerfit." *Lib.* iii. *cap.* 9. This circumftance is alfo related by Valerianus. *De infel. literatorum, lib.* i. It appears, however, from an account of the death of Lorenzo, publifhed by Fabroni, from a MS. diary of an anonymous Florentine author yet preferved in the Maglia-bechi library, *Cod.* xvii. *Clafs.* 25. that Leoni entertained apprehenfions for his fafety from the attendants of Lorenzo, who, without juft caufe, fufpected that he had occafioned his death by poifon. I fhall give the extract from this diary in the Appendix, *No.* LXXIX.

alſo obſerved that one of the golden *palle* or balls, in the emblazonment of the Medicean arms, was at the ſame time ſtruck out. For three nights, gleams of light were ſaid to have been perceived proceeding from the hill of Fieſole, and hovering above the church of S. Lorenzo, where the remains of the family were depoſited. Beſides theſe incidents, founded perhaps on ſome caſual occurrence, and only rendered extraordinary by the workings of a heated imagination, many others of a ſimilar kind are related by contemporary authors, which, whilſt they exemplify that credulity which characterizes the human race in every age, may at laſt ſerve to ſhow that the event to which they were ſuppoſed to allude was conceived to be of ſuch magnitude as to occaſion a deviation from the ordinary courſe of nature (*a*). From Careggi the body of Lorenzo was conveyed to the church of his patron ſaint, amidſt the tears and lamentations of all ranks of people, who bewailed the loſs of their faithful protector, the glory of their city, the companion of their amuſements, their common father and friend. His obſequies were without oſtentation, he having a ſhort time before his death given expreſs directions to

(*a*) *Ficinus in fine Plotini. Flor.* 1492. *Ammir. lib.* xxvi. *c.* iii. *p.* 186. Even Machiavelli, an author ſeldom accuſed of ſuperſtition, ſeems on this occaſion to concede his incredulity to the general opinion. " Nè morì mai alcuno, non ſolamente in Firenze, ma in Italia, con " tanta fama di prudenza, nè che tanto alla ſua patria doleſſe. E come " dalla ſua morte ne doveſſe naſcere grandiſſime rovine, ne moſtrò il " cielo molti evidentiſſimi ſegni, &c." *Hiſt. lib.* viii. This author concludes his celebrated hiſtory, as Guicciardini begins, with the higheſt eulogium on the character of Lorenzo.

that effect. Not a tomb or an infcription marks the place that received his afhes; but the ftranger, who, fmitten with the love of letters and of arts, wanders amidft the fplendid monuments erected to the chiefs of this illuftrious family, the work of Michelagnolo and of his powerful competitors, whilft he looks in vain for that infcribed with the name of Lorenzo, will be reminded of his glory by them all.

Throughout the reft of Italy the death of Lorenzo was regarded as a public calamity of the moft alarming kind. Of the arch which fupported the political fabric of that country he had long been confidered as the centre, and his lofs feemed to threaten the whole with immediate deftruction. When Ferdinand, king of Naples, was informed of this event, he exclaimed, " this man has lived long enough for " his own glory, but too fhort a time for Italy (a)." Such of the Italian potentates as were more nearly connected with the Medici fent ambaffadors to Florence on this occafion. Letters of condolance were tranfmitted to Piero from almoft all the fovereigns of Europe. Many diftinguifhed individuals alfo paid this laft tribute to the memory of their friend and benefactor (b). Among thefe communications, dictated by flattery, by friendfhip, and by political motives, there is one of a more interefting nature.

(a) " Satis fili vir immortalitate digniffimus vixit, fed parum Italiæ. " Utinam ne quis eo fublato, moliatur, quæ vivo, tentare aufus non fuiffet." In which Ferdinand was fuppofed to allude to Lod. Sforza.

Fabr. vita Laur. v. i. p. 212.

(b) Thefe letters, forming a collection in two volumes, are yet preferved in *MS.* in the *Palazzo Vecchio* at Florence, *Filz.* xxv. *No.* xv.

This is a letter from the young cardinal Giovanni de' Medici to his elder brother, written four days after the death of their father, which evinces that the cardinal was not without apprehenfions from the temper and difpofition of Piero, and does equal honor to his prudence and to his filial piety.

The Cardinal Giovanni de' Medici, at Rome, to Piero de' Medici, at Florence.

" My deareft brother, now the only 'fupport of
" our family; what I have to communicate to thee,
" except my tears, I know not; for when I reflect
" on the lofs we have fuftained in the death of our
" father, I am more inclined to weep than to relate
" my forrow. What a father have we loft! How
" indulgent to his children! Wonder not then that
" I grieve, that I lament, that I find no reft. Yet,
" my brother, I have fome confolation in reflecting
" that I have thee, whom I fhall always regard in
" the place of a father. Do thou command — I fhall
" cheerfully obey. Thy injunctions will give me
" more pleafure than I can exprefs — order me —
" put me to the teft, there is nothing that fhall pre-
" vent my compliance. Allow me however, my
" Piero, to exprefs my hopes, that in thy conduct
" to all, and particularly to thofe around thee, I
" may find thee as I could wifh — beneficent, liberal,
" affable, humane; by which qualities there is
" nothing but may be obtained, nothing but may
" be preferved. Think not that I mention this from
" any doubt that I entertain of thee, but becaufe
" I efteem it to be my duty. Many things ftrengthen

" and confole me; the concourfe of people that
" furround our houfe with lamentations, the fad
" and forrowful appearance of the whole city, the
" public mourning, and other fimilar circum-
" ftances, thefe in a great degree alleviate my grief;
" but that which relieves me more than all the reft,
" is, that I have thee, my brother, in whom I place
" a confidence that no words can defcribe, &c. *Ex*
" *urbe, die* 12*th Ap.* 1492 (*a*)."

The common mediator of Italy being now no
more, the fame interefted and unenlightened motives
which had fo often rendered that country the feat
of treachery and of bloodfhed again began to operate,
and the ambitious views of the different fovereigns
became the more dangerous as they were the more
concealed. Such was the confidence which they
had placed in Lorenzo, that not a meafure of im-
portance was determined on by any of them without
its being previoufly communicated to him, when, if
he thought it likely to prove hoftile to the general
tranquillity, he was enabled either to prevent its ex-
ecution, or at leaft to obviate its ill effects; but upon
his death a general fufpicion of each other took place,
and laid the foundation of the unhappy confequences
that foon afterwards enfued. The impending evils of
Italy were accelerated by the death of Innocent VIII.
who furvived Lorenzo only a few months, and ftill
more by the elevation to the pontificate of Roderigo
Borgia, the fcourge of Chriftendom, and the op-
probrium of the human race (*b*).

(*a*) For the original, *v. App. No.* LXXX.
(*b*) A ftriking inftance of the influence which Lorenzo had obtained

Piero de' Medici, on whom the eyes and expectations of the public were turned, gave early indications that he was unable to fuftain the weight that had devolved upon him. Elated with the authority derived from his father, but forgetting the admonitions by which it was accompanied, he relaxed the reins that controlled all Italy, to grafp at the fupreme dominion of his native place. For this purpofe he fecretly formed a more intimate connexion with the king of Naples and the pope, which being difcovered by the penetrating eye of Lodovico Sforza, raifed in him a fpirit of jealoufy, which the profeffions and affurances of Piero could never allay. An interval of diffatisfaction, negotiation, and difiruft took place, till at length the folicitations of Lodovico and the ambition of Charles VIII. brought into Italy a more formidable and warlike race, whofe arrival fpread a general terror and alarm, and convinced, too late, the ftates and fovereigns of that country of the folly of their

over the mind of Innocent VIII. appears from one of his unpublifhed letters preferved in the *Palazzo Vecchio* at Florence (*Filz.* lix. *No.* xiv), dated the 16th day of June 1488, from which we collect, that the pope had tranfmitted to him the lift of an intended promotion of cardinals, which Lorenzo returns, informing him that he approves of the nomination of fuch of them whofe names he has marked with a pen, and exhorting him to carry his intentions with refpect to them into execution, concluding his letter with reminding the pope *chè fi può confolare ancor lui, fe ne ricordi.* In fact, the affumption of Giovanni de' Medici to the purple took place early in the following year; and as Innocent VIII. only made one promotion of cardinals during his pontificate, it appears that Lorenzo had fufficient addrefs to procure the name of his fon, who was then only thirteen years of age, to be included in the lift.

mutual diffenfions. Even Lodovico himfelf, who
in the expectation of weakening his rivals, and of
vefting in himfelf the government of Milan, had
inceffantly labored to accomplifh this object, no
fooner faw its approach than he fhrunk from it in
terror; and whilft he was obliged, for the fake of
confiftency, to perfevere in exhorting Charles to
proceed in his enterprife againft the kingdom of
Naples, he endeavoured by fecret emiffaries to ex-
cite againft him the moft formidable oppofition of
the Italian powers. Lodovico having for this pur-
pofe difpatched an envoy to Florence, Piero con-
ceived that he had obtained a favorable opportunity
of convincing the king of France of the infincerity
of his pretended ally, and thereby of deterring him
from the further profecution of his undertaking; but
however laudable his purpofe might be, the means
which he adopted for its accomplifhment reflect but
little credit on his talents. In the palace of the
Medici was an apartment which communicated
with the gardens by a fecret door, conftructed by
Lorenzo de' Medici for the purpofe of convenience
and retirement. In this room, Piero, pretending
to be fick, contrived an interview with the agent
of Lodovico, whilft the envoy of Charles VIII.
fecreted behind the door, was privy to their
converfation (a). Whether Piero had not the ad-
drefs to engage the Milanefe fufficiently to develope
the views of his mafter, or whether the French
envoy found the Italian politicians equally unde-
ferving of confidence, refts only on conjecture;

(a) Oricell. de bello Ital. p. 24.

but the communication of this incident to Charles tended not in the flighteft degree to avert the impending calamity. On the contrary, the conduct of Piero being made known to Lodovico, rendered any further communication between them impoffible, and by preventing that union of the Italian ftates, which alone could have oppofed with effect the further progrefs of the French arms, facilitated an enterprife that could owe its fuccefs only to the mifconduct of its opponents (a).

This unfortunate event led the way to another incident more immediately deftructive to the credit and authority of Piero de' Medici. Charles, at the head of his troops, had, without refiftance, reached the confines of the Florentine ftate, and had attacked the town of Sarzana, which Lorenzo, after having recovered it from the Genoefe, had ftrongly fortified. The approach of fuch a formidable body of men, the reputation they had acquired, and the atrocities they had committed in their progrefs, could not fail of exciting great confternation in Florence, where the citizens began freely to exprefs their diffatisfaction with Piero de' Medici, who they afferted had, by his rafh and intemperate meafures, provoked the refentment of a powerful fovereign, and endangered the very exiftence of the republic. This crifis fuggefted to Piero the fituation in which his father ftood, when, in order to terminate a war which threatened him with deftruction, he had haftened to Naples, and, placing himfelf in the power of an avowed enemy, had returned to Florence with the credentials

(a) *Guicciard. Hift. d'Italia, lib. i.*

of peace (*a*). The prefent feafon appeared to him favorable for a fimilar attempt; but, as Guicciardini judicioufly obferves, it is dangerous to guide ourfelves by precedent, unlefs the cafes be exactly alike; unlefs the attempt be conducted with equal prudence, and, above all, unlefs it be attended with the fame good fortune (*b*). The impetuofity of Piero prevented him from obferving thefe diftinctions — haftening to the French camp, he threw himfelf at the feet of Charles, who received his fubmiffion with coldnefs and difdain (*c*). Finding his entreaties ineffectual, he became lavifh in his offers to promote the interefts of the king, and, as a pledge of his fidelity, propofed to deliver up to him not only the important fortrefs of Sarzana, which had till then fuccefsfully refifted his attacks, but alfo the town of Pietra Santa, and the cities of Pifa and Leghorn, Charles at the fame time undertaking to reftore them, when he had accomplifhed his conqueft of the kingdom of Naples (*d*). The temerity of Piero in

(*a*) *v. ante, Vol.* I. *p.* 224.

(*b*) *Guicciard. Hift. d'Italia, lib.* i.

(*c*) *Oricell. de bello Ital. p.* 59.

(*d*) The French were themfelves aftonifhed at the prodigality of Piero, and the facility with which he delivered into their hands places of fo much importance. " Ceux qui traitoyent avec Pierre," fays P. " de Commines. m'ont compté, & à plufieurs autres l'ont dit, en fe " raillant & moquant de lui, qu'ils étoient ébahis comme fi tot accordia " fi grand chofe, & à quoi ils ne s'attendoient point." *Mem. de Commines, li.. vii. p.* 198. The day after Piero had entered into his unfortunate treaty, Lodovico Sforza arrived at the French camp, when Piero, who was not at open enmity with him, excufed himfelf for not having met him on the road, becanfo Lodovico had miffed his provoking the refentment of Charles, added to his inability to ward off, and his pufillanimity in refifting the blow, completed what his ambition and his arrogance had begun, and for ever deprived him of the refpect and confidence of his fellow-citizens. On his return to Florence, after this difgraceful compromife, he was refufed admittance into the palace of the magiftrates, and, finding that the people at large were fo highly exafperated againft him as to endanger his perfonal fafety, he haftily withdrew himfelf from his native place, and retreated to Venice (*a*).

way. " It is true enough," faid Lodovico, " that one of us has loft " his way, but perhaps it may prove to be yourfelf.' *Guic. lib.* i.

(*a*) Condivi relates an extraordinary ftory refpecting Piero de' Medici, communicated to him by Michelagnolo, who had it feems formed an intimacy with one Cardiere, an improvvifatore, that frequented the houfe of Lorenzo, and amufed his evenings with finging to the lute. Soon after the death of Lorenzo, Cardiere informed Michelagnolo, that Lorenzo had appeared to him, habited only in a black and ragged mantle thrown over his naked limbs, and had ordered him to acquaint Piero de' Medici, that he would in a short time be banished from Florence. Cardiere, who feems judiciously to have feared the refentment of the living more than that of the dead, declined the office; but foon afterwards Lorenzo entering his chamber at midnight, awoke him, and reproaching him with his inattention, gave him a violent blow on the cheek. Having communicated this fecond vifit to his friend, who advifed him no longer to delay his errand, he fet out for Carreggi, where Piero then refided, but meeting him with his attendants about midway between that place and Florence, he there delivered his meffage, to the great amufement of Piero and his followers; one of whom, Bernardo Divizio, afterwards Cardinal da Bibbiena, farcaftically asked him, *Whether, if Lorenzo had been defirous of giving information to his fon, it was likely he would have preferred fuch a meffenger to a perfonal communication?* The biographer adds, with great folemnity, " La vifion del Cardiere, o delufion diabolica, o

The diftrefs and devaftation which the inhabitants of Italy experienced for a feries of years after this event, have afforded a fubject upon which their hiftorians have dwelt with melancholy accuracy. Amidft thefe difafters, there is perhaps no circum- ftance that fo forcibly excites the regret of the friends of letters, as the plundering of the palace of the Medici, and the difperfion of that invaluable library, whofe origin and progrefs have before been traced. The French troops that had entered the city of Flo- rence without oppofition, led the way to this facrile- gious deed, in the perpetration of which they were joined by the Florentines themfelves, who openly carried off, or fecretly purloined, whatever they could difcover that was interefting, rare, or valuable. Befides the numerous manufcripts in almoft every language, the depredators feized, with contentious avidity, the many ineftimable fpecimens of the arts with which the houfe of the Medici abounded, and which had long rendered it the admiration of ftran- gers, and the chief ornament of the city. Exquifite pieces of ancient fculpture, vafes, cameos, and gems of various kinds, more eftimable for their work- manfhip than for their native value, fhared in the general ruin ; and all that the affiduity and the riches

---

" predizion divina, o forte immaginazione, ch' ella fi foffe, fi verificò."— But the awful fpectre is now before me—I fee the terrified mufician ftart from his flumbers; his left hand grafps his beloved lyre, whilft, with his right thrown over his head, he attempts to shroud himfelf from the looks of Lorenzo, who, with a countenance more in forrow than in anger, points out to him his deftined miffion. To realize this fcene fo as to give it intereft and effect, required the glowing imagi- nation and the animated pencil of a FUSELI.

of

of Lorenzo and his anceſtors had been able to ac-
cumulate in half a century, was diſſipated or de-
moliſhed in a day (*a*).

The ſame reverſe of fortune that overwhelmed the
political labors of Lorenzo, that rendered his deſcen-
dants fugitives, and diſperſed his effects, ſeemed to
extend to his friends and aſſociates, almoſt all of
whom unhappily periſhed within a ſhort interval
after his death, although in the common courſe of

(*a*) The deſtruction of this invaluable collection is pathetically relat-
ed by Bernardo Ruccellai. " Hic me ſtudium charitaſque litterarum
" antiquitatis admonet, ut non poſſim non deplorare inter ſubitas
" fundatiſſimæ familiæ ruinas, Mediceam bibliothecam, inſigneſqĥe
" theſauros, quorum pars a Gallis, pars a paucis e noſtris, rem tur-
" piſſimam honeſta ſpecie prætendentibus, furaciſſime ſubrepta ſunt.
" Nam cum jam pridem gens Medicea floreret omnibus copiis, terra,
" marique cuncta exquirere, dum ſibi Græcarum, Latinaruinque lit-
" terarum monumenta, toreumata, gemmas, margaritas, aliaque
" hujuſcemodi opera, natura ſimul & antiquo artificio conſpicua com-
" pararent," &c. " Teſtimonio ſunt litteræ gemmis ipſis inciſæ, Lau-
" rentii nomen præferentes, quas ille ſibi familiæque ſuæ proſpiciens
" ſcalpendas curavit, futurum ad poſteros regii ſplendoris monumen-
" tum," &c. " Hæc omnia magno conquiſita ſtudio, ſummiſque parta
" opibus, & ad multum ævi in deliciis habita, quibus nihil nobilius,
" nihil Florentiæ quod magis viſendum putaretur, uno puncto temporis
" in prædam ceſſere; tanta Gallorum avaritia, perfidiaque noſtrorum
" fuit." *De bello Ital. p.* 52, *&c.* This event is alſo commemorated
by P. de Commines, **who**, with true Gothic ſimplicity, relates the
number, weight, and ſaleable value of the articles of which the palace
of the Medici was plundered. The antique vaſes he denominates,
" beaux pots d'agate --- & tant de beaux camayeux, bien taillés que
" merveilles (qu' autrefois j'avois veus) & bien trois mille medales
" d'or & d'argent, bien la peſanteur de quarante livres; & croi qu'il
" n'y avoit point autant de belles medales en Italie. Ce qu'il perdit
" ce jour en la cité valoit cent mille ecus & plus."

Mém. de Com. liv. vii. *c.* 9.

 R

nature they might have expected a longer life. The firſt of theſe eminent men was Ermolao Barbaro, of whoſe friendly intercourſe with Lorenzo many teſti-monies remain, and who died of the plague in the year 1493, when only thirty-nine years of age (*a*).

(*a*) The life and learned labors of Ermolao have afforded a ſubject of much diſcuſſion to Voſſius, Bayle, and others, and have been con-ſidered with particular accuracy by Apoſtolo Zeno, *Differt. Vofs. v.* ii. *p.* 348. *& feq.* His firſt work was a treatiſe *De Cælibatu*, which he wrote at eighteen years of age. His *Caſtigationes Plinianæ* entitle him to rank with the moſt ſucceſsful reſtorers of learning. Politiano denominates him, *Hermolaus Barbarus barbariæ hoſtis acerrimus. Mifcel. cap.* xc. Being on an embaſſy to Rome in the year 1491, Innocent VIII. conferred on him the high dignity of Patriarch of Aquileja, which he accepted without regarding the decree of the Venetian government, which directed that none of their miniſters at the court of Rome ſhould receive any eccleſiaſtical preferment without the conſent of the council. His father, who held the ſecond office in the ſtate, is ſaid to have died of chagrin, becauſe he could not prevail upon his countrymen to approve the preferment of his ſon. But Ermolao availed himſelf of his diſmiſſion from public buſineſs, to return with greater earneſtneſs to this ſtudies, and in two years wrote more than he had done for twenty years preceding. In his laſt ſickneſs at Rome, Pico of Mirandula ſent him a remedy for the cure of the plague, compoſed of the oil of ſcorpions, the tongues of aſps, &c. " Ut " nihil fieri poſſet contra peſtilentem morbum commodius aut preſen-" tius." *Crin. de honeſt. diſcip. lib.* i. *c.* 7. But this grand panacea arrived too late. " Egli non è da tacerſi," ſays Apoſtolo Zeno, " un " gran fregio di queſto valente uomo, ed è, che viſſe, e morì *vergine.*" Which information is confirmed by the authority of Piero Dolfini, who, in a letter to Ugolino Verini, aſſerts, QUOD ABSQUE ULLA CARNIS CON-TAGIONE VIXERIT. *Difs. Vofs.* ii. *p.* 365. A very particular account of the manners and perſon of Ermolao is given in a letter from Piero de' Medici to his father Lorenzo, then abſent at the baths of Vignone, from which it appears, that he had paid a viſit to Florence, and was received there with great honor as the friend of Lorenzo.

App. No. LXXXI.

This event was fucceeded by the death of Pico of Mirandula, who in his thirty-fecond year fell a victim to his avidity for fcience, and has left pofterity to regret that he turned his aftonifhing acquifitions to fo little account. Nor did Politiano long furvive his great patron. He died at Florence on the twenty-fourth day of September 1494, when he had juft completed his fortieth year.

It is painful to reflect on the propenfity which has appeared in all ages to fully the moft illuftrious characters by the imputation of the moft degrading crimes. Jovius, with apparent gravity, informs us, that Politiano, having entertained a criminal paffion for one of his pupils, died in the paroxyfm of an amorous fever, whilft he was finging his praifes on the lute (a); and this prepofterous tale has been repeated, with fingular variations, by many fubfequent writers. To attempt a ferious refutation of fo abfurd a charge would be an ufelefs undertaking; but it may not be uninterefting to inquire by what circumftances it was firft fuggefted; as it may ferve to fhow on how flight a foundation detraction can erect her fuperftructure. On the death of Lorenzo de' Medici, Politiano attempted to pour forth his grief in the following monody to his memory, which,

(a) Ferunt eum ingenui adolefcentis infano amore percitum, facile in letalem morbum incidiffe. Correpta enim cithará, quum eo incendio, & rapida febre torreretur, fupremi furoris carmina decantavit; ita, ut mox delirantem, vox ipfa & digitorum nervi, & vitalis denique fpiritus, inverecunda urgente morte, defererent: quum maturando judicio integræ ftatæque ætatis anni, non fine gravi Mufarum injuria, doloreque feculi, feftinante fato eriperentur. *Jovii. Elog. cap.* xxxvii.

although left in an unfinished state, and not to be
ranked in point of compofition with many of his
other writings, is ftrongly expreffive of the anguifh
and agitation of his mind:

Monodia in Laurentium Medicem.

Quis dabit capiti meo
Aquam? quis oculis meis
Fontem lachrymarum dabit?
Ut nocte fleam,
Ut luce fleam.
Sic turtur viduus folet;
Sic cygnus moriens folet;
Sic lufcinia conqueri.
Heu mifer, mifer;
O dolor, dolor.
— LAURUS impetu fulminis
Illa illa jacet fubito;
LAURUS omnium celebris
Mufarum choris,
Nympharum choris,
Sub cujus patula coma,
Et Phœbi lyra blandius
Et vox dulcius infonat.
Nunc muta omnia,
Nunc furda omnia.
— Quis dabit capiti meo
Aquam? quis oculis meis
Fontem lachrymarum dabit?
Ut nocte fleam,
Ut luce fleam.
Sic turtur viduus folet;

Sic cygnus mor.ens folet;
Sic lufcinia conqueri.
Heu mifer, mifer;
O dolor, dolor.

———

Who from perennial ftreams fhall bring
Of gufhing floods a ceafelefs fpring?
That through the day in hopelefs woe,
That through the night my tears may flow.
As the reft turtle mourns his mate,
As fings the fwan his coming fate,
As the fad nightingale complains,
I pour my anguifh and my ftrains.
Ah wretched, wretched paft relief,
O grief, beyond all other grief.

—Through heaven the gleamy lightning flies,
And prone on earth my LAUREL lies:
That laurel, boaft of many a tongue,
Whofes praifes every mufe has fung,
Which every dryad of the grove,
And all the tuneful fifters love.
That laurel, that erewhile difplayed
Its ample honors; in whofe fhade
To louder notes was ftrung the lyre,
And fweeter fang th' Aonian quire,
Now filent, filent all around,
And deaf the ear that drank the found.

—Who from perennial ftreams fhall bring,
Of gufhing floods a ceafelefs fpring?
That through the day in hopelefs woe,
That through the night my tears may flow.

As the reft turtle mourns his mate,
As fings the fwan his coming fate,
As the fad nightingale complains,
I pour my anguifh and my ftrains.
Ah wretched, wretched paft relief,
O grief, beyond all other grief.

Such was the object of the affections of Politiano, and fuch the amorous effufion, in the midft of which he was intercepted by the hand of death; yet if we advert to the charges which have been brought againft him, we fhall find that they are chiefly, if not wholly, to be attributed to a mifreprefentation, or perverfion, of thefe lines. Of thofe who, after Jovius have repeated the accufation, one author informs us, that the verfes which Politiano addreffed to the object of his love were fo tender and impaffioned, that he expired juft as he had finifhed the fecond couplet (*a*). Another relates that in the frenzy of a fever he had eluded the vigilance of his guard, and efcaping from his bed, feized his lute, and began to play upon it under the window of a young Greek of whom he was enamoured, whence he was brought back by his friends, half dead, and expired in his

(*a*) *Varillas, Anecdotes de Florence, lib.* iv. *p.* 196. " La paffion
" criminelle qu'il avoit pour un de fes écoliers de haute qualité, ne
" pouvant être affouvie, lui donna la fièvre chaude. Dans la violence
" de l'accès, il fit une chanfon pour l'objet dont il étoit charmé, fe
" leva du lit, prit un luth, & fe mit à la chanter fur un air fi tendre,
" & fi pitoyable, qu'il expira en achevant *le fecond couplet;* le même
" jour que Charles VIII. paffa les Alpes pour aller à la conquéte de
" Naples." This author feems equally mifinformed as to the manner
and the time of the death of Politiano.

bed foon afterwards (*a*). We are next informed, that in a fit of amorous impatience, he occafioned his own death, by ftriking his head againft the wall (*b*): whilft a fourth author affures us, that he was killed by a fall from the ftairs, as he was finging to his lute an elegy which he had compofed on the death of Lorenzo de' Medici (*c*). The contrariety of thefe relations, not one of which is fupported by the flighteft pretence to ferious or authentic teftimony, is itfelf a fufficient proof of their futility. Some years after the death of Politiano, the celebrated cardinal Bembo, touched with the untimely fate of a man whom he was induced by a fimilarity of tafte and character to love and admire, paid a tribute of gratitude and refpect to his memory in a few elegiac verfes, in which, alluding to the unfinifhed monody of Politiano, he reprefents him as finking under the ftroke of fate, at the moment when, frantic with

(*a*) " Politien, ce bel efprit, qui parloit fi bien Latin, s'appeloit
" Ange; mais il s'en falloit beaucoup qu'il en eut la pureté. La
" paffion honteufe & l'abominable amour dont il brûloit pour un jeune
" garçon, qui étoit Grec de naiffance, à flétri à perpétuité fa mémoire,
" & caufa fa mort. Car étant tombé dans un fièvre chaude, il fe leva
" brufquement de fon lit, la nuit, que fa garde étoit endormie, prit le
" luth à la main, & en alla jouer fous la fenètre du petit Grec. On
" l'en retira à demi mort, & on le remporta dans fon lit, où il expira
" bientôt après," &c. *Ab. Faydit, Remarques fur Virgile & fur Homere, &c. Menck, in vità Pol. p.* 472.

(*b*) " Vulgo fertur," fays Voffius, *De Hift. Lat. lib.* iii. c. 8. " obiiffe
" Politianum fœdi amoris impatientia capite in parietem illifo."

Ap. Menck. 470.

(*c*) *Bullart, Acad. des Hommes illuftres, tom.* i. *p.* 275. " Politien --
" tomba d'un efcalier comme il chantoit fur fon luth une élégie, qu'il
" avoit compofée fur la mort de Laurent de' Medicis."

excefs of grief, he was attempting, by the power of mufic, to revoke the fatal decree which had deprived him of his friend.

Politiani Tumulus.

Duceret extincto cum mors LAURENTE triumphum,
   Lætaque pullatis inveheretur equis,
Refpicit infano ferientem pollice chordas,
   Vifcera fingultu concutiente, virum.
Mirata eft, tenuitque jugum: furit ipfe, pioque
   LAURENTEM cunctos flagitat ore Deos.
Mifcebat precibus lachrymas, lachrymifque dolorem;
   Verba miniftrabat liberiora dolor.
Rifit, & antiquæ non immemor illa querelæ,
   Orphei Tartariæ cum patuere viæ,
Hic etiam infernas tentat refcindere leges,
   Fertque fuas, dixit, in mea jura manus.
Protinus & flentem percuffit dura poetam;
   Rupit & in medio pectora docta fono.
—Heu fic tu raptus, fic te mala fata tulerunt,
   Arbiter Aufoniæ, POLITIANE, lyræ.

Whilft borne in fable ftate, LORENZO's bier
   The tyrant death, his proudeft triumph, brings,
He mark'd a bard in agony fevere,
   Smite with delirious hand the founding ftrings.
He ftop'd—he gaz'd—the ftorm of paffion raged,
   And prayers with tears were mingled, tears with grief;
For loft LORENZO, war with fate he waged,
   And every god was call'd to bring relief.
The tyrant fmil'd—and mindful of the hour
   When from the fhades his confort Orpheus led,

" Rebellious too wouldst thou ufurp my power,
  " And burst the chain that binds the captive dead?"
He fpoke—and fpeaking launch'd the fhaft of fate,
  · And clos'd the lips that glow'd with facred fire.
His timelefs doom 'twas thus POLITIAN met—
  POLITIAN, mafter of th'Aufonian lyre.

The fiction of the poet, that Politiano had incurred the refentment of death by his affection for the object of his paffion, fuggefts nothing more than that his death was occafioned by forrow for the lofs of his friend ; but the verfes of Bembo feem to have given a further pretext to the enemies of Politiano, who appear to have miftaken the friend whom he has celebrated, for the object of an amorous paffion, and to have interpreted thefe lines, fo honorable to Politiano, in a manner. not only the moft unfavorable to his character, but the moft oppofite to their real purport, and to the occafion which gave them birth (a).

(a) " Nous favons maintenant la véritable mort de Politien, que " le Cardinal Bembe a déguifée dans l'épitaphe qu'il lui a dreffée. " Comme il chantoit fur le luth au deffus d'un efcalier une chanfon " qu'il avoit faite autrefois pour une fille qu'il aimoit, lorfqu'il vint " à certains vers fort pathétiques, fon luth lui tomba des mains, & lui " tomba aufli de l'efcalier en bas, & fe rompit le col." *Pier. de S. Romuald, Abrégé du Tréfor Chronol. tom.* iii. *p.* 262. *ap. Menck. p.* 476. Thefe imputations on the moral character of Politiano have alfo been frequently adverted to by other authors: thus J. C. Scaliger,

  " Obfcœno moreris fed Politiane, furore."
And in yet groffer terms by Andrea Dati:
  " Et ne te teneam diutius, quot
  " Pædicat pueros Politianus."
        v. Menagiana. v. iv. *p.* 122.

From much more authentic documents which yet remain refpecting the death of this eminent fcholar, there is reafon to conclude, that it was occafioned by his grief for the lofs of his great patron, and by the fubfequent misfortunes of a family with which he was connected by fo many endearing ties. That he had incurred the public odium in a high degree, on account of his attachment to that family is alfo certain ; and the mortification and anxiety which he on this account experienced, might contribute to accelerate the fatal event. It may alfo be obferved, that his property was plundered during the commotions at Florence, and many of his works deftroyed or loft in the general devaftation of the Laurentian Library ; which incident made a deep impreffion on his mind (a). In fhort, fuch was the fudden tide of misfortune that burft in upon him from all quarters, that it is probable his fortitude was unable to fupport the fhock ; and, notwithftanding his induftry, his accomplifhments, and his unwearied exertions in promoting the progrefs of learning, to fuch an extreme of mifery was he reduced, that he is too juftly enumerated by Valerianus amongft the unhappy children of fcience, who have afforded examples for his fingular work, *De infelicitate Literatorum.* But whatever was the immediate occafion of his death, indifputable evidence remains, that his misfortunes were not fo much to

(a) This is fufficiently apparent from the beautiful lines addreffed to him by Tito Vefpafiano Strozzi, published in the collection of the poems of the two Strozzi, father and fon. by Aldo, 1513.

v. Appendix, No. LXXXII.

be attributed to his mifconduct or his immorality, as to his fteady adherence to the family of the Medici, at a time when the public refentment againft them was excited to the higheft pitch, and that he breathed his laft in the midft of his relatives and friends, having firft expreffed his defire to be buried in the church of S. Marco, in the habit of the Domenican order. This requeft was complied with by the piety of his pupil Roberto Ubaldini, one of the monks of the convent of S. Marco, who has left a memorial in his own hand-writing of the circumftances attending his death (a). His remains were accordingly depofited in the church of S. Marco, where his memory is preferved in an epitaph very unworthy of his character and genius (b).

The various and difcordant relations refpecting the death of Politiano are happily adverted to by one of his countrymen in the following lines:

(a) The indefatigable Abate Mehus, in his life of Ambrogio Traverfari, firft produced thefe documents, which the reader will find in the Appendix, No. LXXXIII.

(b) POLITIANUS.

IN. HOC. TUMULO. JACET.

ANGELUS. UNUM.

QUI. CAPUT. ET. LINGUAS.

RES. NOVA. TRES. HABUIT.

OBIIT. AN. MCCCCLXXXXIV.

SEP. XXIV. ÆTATIS.

XL.

Pamphili Saxi,

De morte Angeli Politiani.

Quo cecidit fato noſtri decus ANGELUS ævi,
 Gentis & Etruſcæ gloria, ſcire cupis?
Icterici non hunc labes triſtiſſima morbi.
 Febris ad Elyſias vel tulit atra domos;
Non inflans humor pectus, non horrida bilis;
 Mortiferæ peſtis denique nulla lues :
Sed, quoniam rigidas ducebat montibus ornos,
 Frangebat ſcopulos, decipiebat aves,
Mulcebat tigres, ſiſtebat flumina cantu,
 Plectra movens plectro dulcius Iſmario.
Non plus Threicium laudabunt Orphea gentes,
 Calliope dixit dixit: Apollo, Linum;
Jamque tacet noſtrum rupes Heliconia nomen —
 Et ſimul hunc gladio ſuppoſuere necis.
Mors tamen hæc illi vita eſt, nam gloria magna
 Invidiâ Phœbi Calliopeſque mori.

Aſk'ſt thou what cauſe conſign'd to early fate
POLITIAN, glory of the Tuſcan ſtate?
—Not loathſome jaundice tainting all the frame,
Not rapid fever's keen conſuming flame,
Not viſcous rheum that chokes the ſtruggling breath,
Nor any vulgar miniſter of death;
—'Twas that his ſong to life and motion charm'd
The mountain oaks, the rock's cold boſom warm'd,
Stay'd the prone flood, the tyger's rage control'd,
With ſweeter ſtrains than Orpheus knew of old.—
" Dimmed is the luſtre of my Grecian fame."
Exclaim'd Calliope—" No more my name

" Meets even in Helicon its due regard, "
Apollo cry'd, and pierc'd the tuneful bard—
—Yet lives the bard in lasting fame approv'd,
Who Phœbus and the muse to envy mov'd.

The expulsion of Piero de' Medici from Florence, neither contributed to establish the tranquillity, nor to preserve the liberty of the republic. The inhabitants exulted for a time in the notion that they were freed from the tyranny of a family which had held them so long in subjection; but they soon discovered that it was necessary to supply its absence, by increasing the executive power of the state. Twenty citizens were accordingly chosen by the appellation of *Accopiatori*, who were invested, not only with the power of raising money, but also of electing the chief magistrates. This form of government met however with an early and formidable opposition; and to the violence of political dissensions, was soon superadded the madness of religious enthusiasm. The fanatic, Savonarola, having, by pretensions to immediate inspiration from God, and by harangues well calculated to impress the minds of the credulous, formed a powerful party, began to aim at political importance. Adopting the popular side of the question, he directed the whole torrent of his eloquence against the new mode of government; affirming, that he was divinely authorized to declare, that the legislative power ought to be extended to the citizens at large, that he had himself been the ambassador of the Florentines to heaven, and that Christ had condefcended to be their peculiar monarch (a). The exertions of Savonarola were fuccefsful. The newly elected magiftrates voluntarily abdicated their offices; and an effort was made to eftablifh the government on a more popular bafis, by vefting the legiflative power of the ftate in the *Configlio Maggiore*, or Council of the Citizens, and in a felect body, called the *Configiio degli Scelti*, or Select Council (b). The firft of thefe was to be compofed of at leaft one thoufand citizens, who could derive their citizenfhip by defcent, and were upwards of thirty years of age; the latter confifted of eighty members, who were elected half-yearly from the great council, and were upwards of forty years of age (c). Thefe regulations, inftead of uniting the citizens in one common intereft, gave rife to new diftinctions. The *Fratefchi*, or adherents of Savonarola, who were in general favorable to the liberty of the lower claffes of the inhabitants, regarded the friar as the meffenger of heaven, as the guide of their temporal and eternal happinefs; whilft the *Compagnacci*, or adherents to a more ariftocratical government reprefented him as a factious impoftor; and Alexander VI. feconded their caufe by fulminating againft him the anathemas of the church. Thus impelled by the moft powerful

(a) *Nerli, Commentarj de' Fatti civili di Firenze*, lib. iv. p. 65. *Aug.* 1728.

(b) To this government Machiavelli alludes in his fecond Decennale:

    " E dopo qualche difparer trovafte,

      " Nuov' ordine al governo, e furon tante,

      " Che il voftro ftato popolar fondafte."

(c) *Nerli, Comment.* lib. iv. p. 66, 67.

motives that can actuate the human mind, the citizens of Florence were feized with a temporary infanity. In the midſt of their devotions, they frequently ruſhed in crowds from the church, to aſſemble in the public ſquares, crying *Viva Criſto*, finging hymns, and dancing in circles formed by a citizen and a friar, placed alternately (*a*). The hymns fung on thefe occafions were chiefly compofed by Girolamo Benivieni, who appears to have held a diſtinguiſhed rank amongſt thefe difciples of fanaticifm (*b*). The enemies of Savonarola were as immoderate in their oppofition as his partifans were in their attachment. Even the children of the city were trained in oppofite factions, and faluted each other with ſhowers of pebbles; in which conteſts the graveſt citizens were fometimes unable to refiſt the inclination of taking a part (*c*).

(*a*) *Nerli, Comment. lib.* iv. *p.* 75.

(*b*) Some of thefe compofitions are preferved in the general collection of his poems. The following lines, which feem peculiarly adapted for fuch an occafion, may ferve as a fpecimen:

     " Non fu mai'l più bel folazzo,

       " Più giocondo nè maggiore,

       " Che per zelo, e per amore

       " Di Jesu, diventar pazzo.

       " Ognun gridi com' io grido,

       " Sempre pazzo, pazzo, pazzo."

Op. di Beniv. p. 143.

(*c*) Era talvolta, predicando il frate, in ful bello della predica fuonato tamburi, e fatti altri rumori per impedirlo; e molte volte gli fu nel venir da S. Marco a S. Liparata giù per la via del Cocomero, da' fanciulli de' fuoi avverfarj fatto baie fanciullefche, e da' fanciulli della fua parte era voluto defendere, dimanieraché, fecondo il coſtume de' fanciulli Fiorentini, facevano a' faſſi, e cosi combattendo facevano

Such was the state of Florence in the year 1497, when Piero de' Medici, who had long waited for an opportunity of regaining his authority, entered into a negotiation with several of his adherents, who undertook, at an appointed hour, to admit him within the walls of the city, with the troops which he had obtained from the Venetian republic, and from his relations of the Orsini family. Piero did not however make his appearance till the opportunity of assisting him was past. His abettors were discovered; five of them, of the chief families of Florence, were decapitated; the rest were imprisoned or sent into banishment. The persons accused would have appealed from their judges to the *Consiglio Grande*, according to a law which had lately been obtained by the influence of the *Fratefchi*; but that party, with Savonarola at their head, were clamorous for the execution of the delinquents, and in spite of the law which they had themselves introduced, effected their purpose. Amongst the five sufferers was Lorenzo Tornabuoni, the maternal cousin of

infanciullire degli uomini gravi; perchè occorse a M. Luca Corsini, benchè Dottore allai riputato, per favorire la parte del Frate mescolarsi co' fanciulli a fare a' fassi; e Giovanbattista Ridolfi, uno de' più riputati e savj cittadini che fussero a tempj suoi, posta da canto la gravità, e quel grado che a un tale, e si onorato cittadino si conveniva, prese un giorno l'armi, e in su certa occasione, per essere impedita al frate la predica intorno a S. Liparata, usci dalla casa de' Lorini vicina a quel tempio, quasi infuriato, senza seguito alcuno, con una roncola in ispalla, gridando, *Viva Criflo*; com' anche gridavano i fanciulli del Frate; e di queste cosi fatte cose ne seguivano spesso.

Nerli, Common.. lib. iv. p. 74.

Lorenzo

Lorenzo de' Medici, of whofe accomplifhments Politiano has left a very favorable account, and to whom he has infcribed his beautiful poem entitled *Ambra* (a).

The authority of Savonarola was now at its higheft pitch. Inftead of a republic, Florence affumed the appearance of a theocracy, of which Savonarola was the prophet, the legiflator, and the judge (b). He perceived not however that he had arrived at the edge of the precipice, and that by one ftep further he might incur his deftruction. Amongft the methods reforted to by the opponents of Savonarola to weaken his authority, and to counteract his pretenfions, they had attacked him with his own weapons, and had excited two Francifcan monks to declaim againft him from the pulpit. Savonarola found it neceffary to call in the aid of an affiftant, for which purpofe he felected Fra Domenico da Pefcia, a friar of his own convent of S. Marco. The conteft was kept up by each of the contending parties with equal fury, till Domenico, tranfported with zeal for the interefts of his mafter, propofed to confirm the truth of his doctrines by walking through the flames, provided any of his adverfaries

(a) *v. ante, p.* 140.

(b) This fanatical party proceeded fo far as even to ftrike a coin on the occafion, a fpecimen of which in filver is preferved in the collection of the Earl of Orford, to whofe kind communications, fince the firft edition of this work, I have been greatly indebted. On one fide is the Florentine device, or *fleur de lys*, with the motto, SENATUS POPULUSQUE FLORENTINUS; on the other, a crofs, with the motto, JESUS CHRISTUS REX NOSTER.

would fubmit to a fimilar teft. By a fingular coin-
cidence, which is alone fufficient to demonftrate to
what a degree the paffions of the people were ex-
cited, a Francifcan friar accepted the challenge, and
profeffed himfelf ready to proceed to the proof.
The mode of trial became the fubject of ferious
deliberation among the chief officers of the republic.
Two deputies were elected on behalf of each of the
parties, to arrange and fuperintend this extraordinary
conteft. The combuftibles were prepared, and over
them was erected a fcaffold, which afforded a com-
modious paffage into the midft of the flames. On
the morning of the day appointed, being the feven-
teenth of April 1498, Savonarola and his champion
made their appearance, with a numerous proceffion
of ecclefiaftics, Savonarola himfelf intonating with
a tremendous voice, the pfalm, *Exurgat Deus &
diffipentur inimici ejus.* His opponent, Fra Giuliano
Rondinelli, attended by a few Francifcan monks, came
fedately and filently to the place of trial; the flames
were kindled, and the agitated fpectators waited with
impatience for the moment that fhould renew the
miracle of the Chaldean furnace. Savonarola finding
that the Francifcan was not to be deterred from the
enterprife either by his vociferations, or by the fight
of the flames, was obliged to have recourfe to another
expedient, and infifted that his champion Domenico,
when he entered the fire, fhould bear the hoft along
with him. This facrilegious propofal fhocked the
whole affembly. The prelates who, together with
the ftate deputies, attended the trial, exclaimed
againft an experiment which might fubject the

catholic faith to too fevere a teft, and bring a fcandal upon their holy religion. Domenico however clung faft to the twig which his patron had thrown out, and pofitively refufed to encounter the flames without this facred talifman. This expedient, whilft it faved the life of the friar, ruined the credit of Savonarola. On his return to the convent of S. Marco, he was infulted by the populace, who bitterly reproached him, that after having encouraged them to cry *Viva Crifto*, he fhould impioufly propofe to commit him to the flames. Savonarola attempted to regain his authority by addreffing them from the pulpit, but his enemies were too vigilant; feizing the opportunity of his difgrace, they firft attacked the houfe of Francefco Valori, one of his moft powerful partifans, who, together with his wife, was facrificed to their fury. They then fecured Savonarola, with his affociate Domenico, and another friar of the fame convent, and dragged them to prifon. An affembly of ecclefiaftics and feculars, directed by an emiffary of Alexander VI. fat in judgment upon them. The refolution and eloquence of Savonarola, on his firft interview, intimidated his judges, and it was not till recourfe was had to the implements of torture—the *ultima theologorum ratio*, that Savonarola betrayed his weaknefs, and acknowledged the fallacy of his pretenfions to fupernatural powers. His condemnation inftantly followed, and the unhappy prieft, with his two attendants, were led to execution in the fame place, and with the fame apparatus, as had been prepared for the conteft; where, being firft ftrangled, their bodies were committed to the flames, and lest the city should be polluted by their remains, their ashes were carefully gathered and thrown into the Arno (a).

From the time that Piero de' Medici quitted the city of Florence, he experienced a continual succession of mortifications and disappointments. Flattered, deserted, encouraged, and betrayed, by the different potentates to whom he successively applied for assistance, his prospects became daily more unfavorable, and his return to Florence more improbable. In the mean time a new war had arisen in Italy. Louis XII. the successor of Charles VIII. after having, in conjunction with Ferdinand, king of Spain, accomplished the conquest of Naples, disagreed with him in the partition of the spoil, and Italy became the theatre of their struggle. On this occasion Piero entered into the service of the French, and was present at an engagement that took place between them and the Spaniards, on the banks of the Garigliano, in which they were defeated with great loss. In effecting his escape, Piero attempted to pass the river, but the boat in which he with several other men of rank had embarked, being laden with heavy cannon, sunk in the midst of the current and Piero miserably perished, after having supported an exile of ten years. By his wife Alfonsina, he left a son named Lorenzo, and a daughter Clarice.

Few men have derived from nature greater

(a) Nerli. Comment. lib. iv. p. 78. Savonarola vita, tom. ii. seu additiones. Par. 1674, passim.

advantages, and perhaps never any one enjoyed a better opportunity of improving them, than Piero de' Medici. A robuſt form, a vigorous conſtitution, great perſonal ſtrength and activity, and a ſhare of talents beyond the common lot, were the endowments of his birth. To theſe was added a happy combination of external affairs, reſulting from the opulence and reſpectability of his family, the powerful alliances by which it was ſtrengthened, and the high reputation which his father had ſo deſervedly acquired. But theſe circumſtances, apparently ſo favorable to his ſuccefs, were preciſely the cauſes of his early ruin. Preſuming on his ſecurity, he ſuppoſed that his authority could not be ſhaken, nor his purpoſes defeated. Forgetting the advice ſo often repeated to him by his father, *to remember that he was only a citizen of Florence*, he neglected or diſdained to conciliate the affections of the people. His conduct was the exact reverſe of that which his anceſtors had ſo long and uniformly adopted, and was attended with the effects which might reaſonably be expected from a dereliction of thoſe maxims that had raiſed them to the honorable diſtinction which they had ſo long enjoyed.

A few poetical compoſitions of Piero de' Medici, preſerved in the Laurentian Library, though not hitherto printed, place his character in a more favorable point of view, and exhibit his filial affection and his attachment to his native place in a very intereſting light (a). Of this the following ſonnet may be a ſufficient proof:

(a) They conſiſt of twenty one ſonnets, which are found at the cloſe

SONETTO.

'Sendo io national, e di te nato,
   Muovati patria un poco il tuo figliuolo;
   Fingiti almen pietofa del fuo duolo,
   Effendo in te nudr'to ed allevato.
Ha ciafchedun del nafcimento il fato,
   Come l'uccello il fuo garrire e volo;
   Scufemi almen in ciò non effer folo,
   Benchè folo al mio male io pur fia ftato.
E fe può nulla in te mio antico affetto,
   Per quella pietà ch'in te pur regna
   Non mi fia que.to dono da te difdetto:
—Ch' almen in cener nella patria io vegna,
   A ripofar col padre mio diletto.
   Che già ti fe si gloriofa e degna.

SONNET.

Thy offspring, FLORENCE, nurtur'd at thy breaft,
   Ah let me yet thy kind indulgence prove;
   Or if thou own no more a parent's love,
   Thy pity fure may footh my woes to reft.
Fate marks to each his lot: the fame beheft
   That taught the bird through fields of air to rove,
   And tunes his fong, my vital tiffue wove
   Of grief and care, with darkeft hues impreft.
But if, my fondnefs fcorn'd, my prayer denied,
   Death only bring the period of my woes,

of a manufcript volume of the poems of his father Lorenzo, *Plut.* xli.
Cod. xxxviii. *No.* 3. Befides which Valerianus informs us, that he
tranflated from Plutarch, a treatife on conjugal love; *Valer. de Lit.
infcl. lib.* ii.; but this performance has probably perifhed, there being
no copy of it now to be found in the Laurentian Library.

Yet one dear hope shall mitigate my doom.
—If then my father's name was once thy pride,
  Let my cold afhes find at laft repofe,
  Safe in the fhelter of his honored tomb.

Of the many ties by which Lorenzo had endea-
voured to fecure the profperity of his family amidft
the ftorms of fortune, and the ebbs and flows of
popular opinion, one only now remained—that by
which he had connected it with the church; but this
alone proved fufficient for the purpofe, and fhows
that in this, as in every other inftance, his conduct was
directed by motives of the foundeft policy. After the
expulfion of the family from Florence, the cardinal
Giovanni de' Medici, finding that the endeavours of
himfelf and his brothers to effect their reftoration
were more likely to exafperate the Florentines than
to promote that defirable event, defifted from any
further attempts, and determined to wait with pa-
tience for a more favorable opportunity. He there-
fore quitted Italy, and, whilft that country was the
theatre of treachery and war, vifited many parts of
France and Germany. His diflike to Alexander VI.
who had entered into an alliance with the Floren-
tines, and was confequently adverfe to the views of
the exiles, was an additional motive for his abfence.
After the death of Alexander in the year 1503, he
returned to Rome, and found in Julius II. a pontiff
more juft to his talents, and more favorable to his
hopes. From this time he began to take an import-
ant part in the public affairs of Italy, and was ap-
pointed legate in the war carried on by the pope,

the Venetians, and the king of Spain, againſt Louis XII. Whilſt inveſted with this dignity, he was taken priſoner by the French, in the famous battle of Ravenna, but ſoon afterwards found an opportunity of effecting his eſcape, not however without great danger and difficulty. In the mean time new diſſenſions had ſprung up at Florence, where the inhabitants, wearied with the fluctuations of a government, whoſe maxims and conduct were changed in the ſame rapid ſucceſſion as its chief magiſtrates, were at length obliged to ſeek for a greater degree of ſtability, by electing a *Gonfaloniere* for life. This authority was intruſted to Piero Soderini, who, with more integrity than ability, exerciſed it for nearly ten years. His contracted views ſuited not with the circumſtances of the times. The principal governments of Italy, with Julius at their head, had leagued together to free that country from the depredations of the French. Fearful of exciting the reſtleſs diſpoſitions of the Florentines, and perhaps of endangering the continuance of his power, the *Gonfaloniere* kept aloof from a cauſe, on the ſucceſs of which depended the tranquillity and independence of Italy. His reluctance to take an active part in the war was conſtrued into a ſecret partiality to the intereſts of the French; and, whilſt it rendered him odious to a great part of the citizens of Florence, drew upon him the reſentment of the allied powers. The victory obtained by the French at Ravenna, dearly purchaſed with the death of the gallant Gaſton de Foix, and the loſs of near ten thouſand men, proved the deſtruction of their enterpriſe; and as the caufe of the French declined, that of the Medici gained ground, as well in Florence, as in the reft of Italy. The prudence and moderation of the cardinal enabled him to avail himfelf of thefe favorable difpofitions without prematurely anticipating the confequences. During his refidence at Rome he had paid a marked attention to the citizens of Florence who occafionally reforted there, without making any apparent diftinction between thofe who had efpoufed and thofe who had been adverfe to the caufe of his family; and by his affability and hofpitality, as well as by his attention to the interefts of thofe who ftood in need of his fervices, had acquired the good opinion of his fellow-citizens. Having thus prepared the way for his fuccefs, he took the earlieft opportunity of turning the arms of the allied powers againft Florence, for the avowed purpofe of removing Piero Soderini from his office, and reftoring the Medici to their rights as citizens. On the part of Soderini little refiftance was made. The allies having fucceeded in an attack upon the town of Prato, and the friends of the Medici having openly oppofed the authority of Soderini, the tide of popular favor once more turned; and whilft the *Gonfaloniere* with difficulty effected his efcape, the cardinal made his entrance into his native place, accompanied by his younger brother Giuliano, his nephew Lorenzo, and his coufin Giulio de' Medici, the latter of whom had been his conftant attendant during all the events of his public life [a].

(a) *Guicciar. Storia d'Italia, lib.* x. *Razzi, vita di Piero Soderini. Padova,* 1737, *p.* 70, &c.

The reſtoration of the Medici, although effected by an armed force, was not diſgraced by the blood-ſhed of any of the citizens, and a few only of their avowed enemies were ordered to abſent themſelves from Florence. Scarcely was the tranquillity of the place reſtored when intelligence was received of the death of Julius II. The cardinal loſt no time in repairing to Rome, where, on the eleventh day of March 1513, being then only thirty-ſeven years of age, he was elected ſupreme head of the church, and aſſumed the name of Leo X. The high reputation which he had acquired not only counterbalanced any objections ariſing from his youth, but rendered his election a ſubject of general ſatisfaction ; and the inhabitants of Florence, without adverting to the conſequences, exulted in an event which ſeemed likely to contribute not leſs to the ſecurity than to the honor of their country. The commencement of his pontificate was diſtinguiſhed by an act of clemency which ſeemed to realize the high expectations that had been formed of it. A general amneſty was publiſhed at Florence, and the baniſhed citizens reſtored to their country. Piero Soderini, who had taken refuge in Turkey, was invited by the pope to Rome, where he reſided many years under his protection, and enjoyed the ſociety and reſpect of the prelates and other men of eminence who frequented the court, being diſtinguiſhed during the remainder of his life by the honorable title of the *Gonfaloniere (a)*.

(a) *Razzi, vita di Piero Soderini, p.* 85.

The elevation of Leo X. to the pontificate eſtab-
liſhed the fortunes of the Medici on a permanent
foundation. Naturally munificent to all, Leo was
laviſh in beſtowing upon the different branches
of his own family the higheſt honors and moſt
lucrative preferments of the church. Giulio de'
Medici was created archbiſhop of Florence, and
was ſoon afterwards admitted into the ſacred college,
where he acquired ſuch influence, as to ſecure the
pontifical chair, in which he ſucceeded Adrian VI.
who filled it only ten months after the death of
Leo. The daughters of Lorenzo, Maddalena, the
wife of Francefco Cibo, Conteſſina, the wife of
Piero Ridolfi, and Lucrezia, the wife of Giacopo
Salviati, gave no leſs than four cardinals to the
Romiſh church; there being two of the family of
Salviati, and one of each of the others. Profiting
by the examples of his predeceſſors, Leo loſt no
opportunity of aggrandizing his relations, well know-
ing that, in order to ſecure to them any laſting
benefit, it was neceſſary that they ſhould be power-
ful enough to defend themſelves, after his death,
from the rapacious aims of ſucceeding pontiffs,
who, he was well aware, would probably pay as
little regard to his family, as he had himſelf, in
ſome inſtances, paid to the friends and families of
his predeceſſors (a).

(a) Notwithſtanding his precautions, Leo could not, on all occa-
ſions, preſerve his ſurviving relations from the inſults and injuries of
his ſucceſſors. Paul III. Aleſſandro Farnefe, had in his youth been
particularly favored by Lorenzo de' Medici, who, in a letter which
yet remains from him to Lanfredini, his envoy at Rome, thus expreſſes

The pontificate of Leo X. is celebrated as one of the moſt proſperous in the annals of the Romiſh church. At the time when he aſſumed the chair, the calamities of Italy were at their higheſt pitch ; that country being the theatre of a war, in which not only all its governments were engaged, but which was rendered yet more ſanguinary by the introduction of the French, Helvetian, and Spaniſh troops. A council, which had long eſtabliſhed itſelf at Piſa, under the influence and protection of the king of France, thwarted the meaſures, and at times overawed the authority of the holy ſee ; and, in addition to all her other diſtreſſes, Italy labored under great apprehenſions from the Turks, who conſtantly threatened a deſcent on that unhappy country. The addreſs and perſeverance of Leo ſurmounted the difficulties which he had to encounter; and during his pontificate the papal dominions enjoyed a degree of tranquillity ſuperior to any other ſtate in Italy. In his relations with foreign powers, his conduct is no leſs entitled to approbation. During the conteſts that took place between thoſe powerful monarchs Charles V. and Francis I. he diſtinguiſhed himſelf by his moderation, his

himſelf reſpecting him: " Vi lo raccommandiate quanto farei Pietro " mio figlio; e vi prego lo introduciate e lo raccommandiate caldiſſi- " mamente a N. S. (il papa) che non potreſte farmi maggior piacere," &c. Yet, when the ſame Aleſſandro had arrived at the pontificate, he ſo far forgot or diſregarded his early obligations, as forcibly to diſpoſſeſs Lucrezia, the daughter of his benefactor, then in a very advanced age, of her reſidence in Rome, to make way for one of his nephews. This incident is related by Varchi with proper indignation.

Storia Fiorentina, lib. xvi. *p.* 666,

vigilance. and his political addrefs ; on which account he is juftly celebrated by an eminent hiftorian of our own country, as " the only prince of the age " who obferved the motions of the two contending " monarchs with a prudent attention, or who dif- " covered a proper folicitude for the public " fafety (a).

Leo was not however aware, that whilft he was compofing the troubles which the ambition of his neighbours, or the mifconduct of his predeceffors, had occafioned, he was exciting a ftill more formidable adverfary, that was deftined, by a flow but certain progrefs, to fap the foundations of the papal power, and to alienate that fpiritual allegiance which the Chriftian world had kept inviolate for fo many centuries. Under the control of Leo, the riches that flowed from every part of Europe to Rome, as to the heart of the ecclefiaftical fyftem, were again poured out through a thoufand channels, till the fources became inadequate to the expenditure. To fupply this deficiency, he availed himfelf of various expedients, which, whilft they effected for a time the intended purpofe, roufed the attention of the people to the enormities and abufes of the church, and in fome meafure drew afide that facred veil, which, in fhrouding her from the prying eyes of the vulgar, has always been her fafeft prefervative. The open fale of difpenfations and indulgences for the moft enormous and difgraceful crimes was too flagrant not to attract general notice. Encouraged by the diffatisfaction which was thus excited,

(a) *Robertfon, Hift. of Cha.* V. *book* i.

a daring reformer arofe, and, equally regardlefs of the threats of fecular power, and the denunciations of the Roman fee, ventured to oppofe the opinion of an individual to the infallible determinations of the church. At this critical junĉlure, Luther found that fupport which he might in vain have fought at any other period, and an inroad was made into the fanĉluary, which has ever fince been widening, and will probably continue to widen, till the mighty fabric, the work of fo many ages, fhall be laid in ruins (a). It is not however fo much for the tenets of their religious creed, as for the principles upon which they founded their diffent, that the reformers are entitled to the thanks of pofterity. That right of private judgment which they claimed for themfelves, they could not refufe to others ; and by a mode of reafoning as fimple as it was decifive, mankind arrived at the knowledge of one of thofe great truths which form the bafis of human happinefs. It appeared that the denunciations of the church were as ineffeĉlual to condemn, as its abfolution was to exculpate; and, inftead of an intercourfe between the man and his prieft, an

---

(a) The caufes and progrefs of the reformation are traced by Dr. Robertfon, in his Hiftory of Charles the V. book ii. in a manner that would difpenfe with any further elucidation, even if it were more intimately conneĉled with my fubjeĉl. This celebrated hiftorian has taken occafion to refute an affertion made by Guicciardini, and, after him, by Fr. Paolo, that Leo X. beftowed th· profits arifing from the fale of indulgences in Saxony, upon his fifter Maddalena, the wife of Francefco Cibo. *Guicciar. lib.* iii. *Sarpi, Storia del Concil. Trident. cap.* i. *Robertfon, Hift. Cha.* V. *book* ii. *in note.*

intercourfe took place between his confcience and his God.

But turning from the advantages which the world has derived from the errors of Leo X. we may be allowed for a moment to inquire what it owes to his talents and to his virtues. No fooner was he raifed to the papal chair, than Rome affumed once more its ancient character, and became the feat of genius, magnificence, letters, and arts. One of the firfts acts of his pontificate was to invite to his court two of the moft elegant Latin fcholars that modern times have produced, Piero Bembo and Giacopo Sadoleti; on each of whom he conferred the rank of cardinal. The moft celebrated profeffors of literature from every part of Europe were induced by liberal penfions to fix their refidence at Rome, where a permanent eftablifhment was formed for the ftudy of the Greek tongue, under the direction of Giovanni Lafcar. The affability, the munificence the judgment, and the tafte of this fplendid pontiff are celebrated by a confiderable number of learned men, who witneffed his accomplifhments, or partook of his bounty. Succeeding times have been equally difpofed to do juftice to fo eminent a patron of letters and have confidered the age of Leo X. as rivalling that of Auguftus. Leo has not however efcaped the reproach of having been too lavifh of his favors to authors of inferior talents, and of having expended in pompous fpectacles and theatrical reprefentations that wealth which ought to have been devoted to better purpofes (a). But fhall we condemn his con-

(a) *Tirab. Storia della Let. Ital. v.* viii. *par.* i. *p.* 19. *Andres, orig, e progreffi d ogni Letteratura, v.* i. *p.* 350.

duct, if thofe who had no claims on his juftice, were the objects of his bounty? or may it not be doubted whether this difpofition was not more favorable to the promotion of letters, than a courfe of conduct more difcriminating and fevere? Whatever kind-nefs he might fhow to thofe who endeavoured to amufe his leifure by their levity, their fingularity, or their buffoonery, no inftances can be produced of his having rewarded them by fuch diftinguifhed favors as he conftantly beftowed on real merit; and whilft we difcover amongft thofe who fhared his friendfhip and partook of his higheft bounty, the names of Bembo, Vida, Ariofto, Sadoleti, Cafa and Flaminio, we may readily excufe the effects of that fuperabundant kindnefs which rather marked the excefs of his liberality than the imperfection of his judgment.

In the attention paid by Leo X. to the collecting and preferving ancient manufcripts, and other me-morials of literature, he emulated the example of his father, and by his perfeverance and liberality at length fucceeded in reftoring to its former fplendor the celebrated library, which, on the expulfion of Piero de' Medici, had become a prey to the fury or the cupidity of the populace. Such of thefe valuable articles as had efcaped the facrilegious hands of the plunderers had been feized upon for the ufe of the Florentine ftate; but in the year 1496, the public treafury being exhaufted, and the city reduced to great extremity, the magiftrates were under the neceffity of felling them to the monks of the frater-nity of S. Marco, for the fum of three thoufand
ducats

ducats (*a*). Whilſt theſe valuable works were de-
poſited at the convent, they experienced a leſs public,
but perhaps a more deſtructive calamity, many of
them having been diſtributed as preſents by Savo-
narola, the principal of the monaſtery, to the cardi-
nals, and other eminent men, by whoſe favor he
ſought to ſhelter himſelf from the reſentment of the
pope (*b*). When the Florentines deſtroyed their
golden calf, and the wretched prieſt expiated by his
death his folly and his crimes, apprehenſions were
entertained that the library of the Medici would
once more be expoſed to the rapacity of the people ;
but ſome of the youth of the nobleſt families of
Florence, with a laudable zeal for the preſervation
of this monument of their national glory, aſſociated
themſelves together, and undertook to guard it till
the frenzy of the populace had again ſubſided (*c*).
After the death of Savonarola, the fraternity having
fallen into diſcredit, and being in their turn obliged
to ſell the library, it was purchaſed from them by
Leo X. then cardinal de' Medici, and in the year 1508

(*a*) Eodem anno libri heredem olim Petri Medicis a conventu noſtro
trium millium Ducatorum pretio comparati, quos ſupra memoravimus
in horrendo caſu noſtro, ex juſſo dominationis Florentinæ in palatium
comportatos, & per inventarium reſignatos, menſe Octobri, in conven-
tum hunc S. Marci revecti ſunt, novis ſtipulationibus factis, &c.
Maricani annal. part. i. *ap. Mehus. Ambr. Travers. vita. p.* 72, *in præf.*

(*b*) Etiam de' libri di Piero de' Medici, i quali nella Libreria di S.
Marco in buona parte ſi riduſſono, fece parte a cardinali, per cui
mezzo delle ſcomuniche e altri proceſſi contragli ſi difendeva. Tanta
forza avevano in Firenze le ſue arti. *MS. di Piero Parenti. cit. da
Tirab. Storia della Let. Ital. v.* vi. *part.* i. *p.* 105.

(*c*) *Tirab. ut ſup.*

was removed by him to Rome, where it continued during his life, and received conftant additions of the moft rare and valuable manufcripts. From Leo it devolved to his coufin Clement VII. who, upon his elevation to the pontificate, again transferred it to Florence, and by a bull, which bears date the fifteenth day of December 1532, provided for its future fecurity. Not fatisfied however with this precaution, he meditated a more fubftantial defence, and, with a munificence which confers honor on his pontificate, engaged Michelagnolo to form the defign of the fplendid edifice in which this library is now depofited, which was afterwards finifhed under the directions of the fame artift, by his friend and fcholar Vafari.

· Giuliano de' Medici, the third fon of Lorenzo, was more diftinguifhed by his attention to the caufe of literature, and by his mild and affable difpofition, than by his talents for political affairs. On the return of the family to Florence, he had been intrufted by his brother, then the cardinal de' Medici, with the direction of the Florentine ftate; but it foon appeared that he had not fufficient energy to control the jarring difpofitions of the Florentines. He therefore refigned his authority to Lorenzo, the fon of his brother Piero de' Medici, and on the elevation of Leo X. took up his refidence at Rome; where under the title of captain general of the church, he held the chief command of the papal troops. By the favor of the pope he foon afterwards obtained extenfive poffeffions in Lombardy, and having intermarried with Filiberta, fifter of Charles duke of Savoy, and a defcendant of the houfe of Bourbon, was honored by Francis I. with the title of duke of Nemours. Of his gratitude, an inftance is recorded which it would be unjuft to his memory to omit. During his exile from Florence, he had found an hofpitable afylum with Guid' ubaldo di Montefeltro duke of Urbino, who on his death left his dominions to his adopted fon, Francefco Maria delle Rovere. Incited by the entreaties of his nephew Lorenzo, Leo X. formed the defign of depriving Rovere of his poffeffions, under the ufual pretext of their having efcheated to the church for want of legitimate heirs, and of vefting them in Lorenzo, with the title of duke of Urbino; but the reprefentations of Giuliano prevented for a time the execution of his purpofe ; and it was not till after his death that Leo difgraced his pontificate by this fignal inftance of ecclefiaftical rapacity. If we may give credit to Ammirato, Giuliano at one time entertained the ambitious hope of obtaining the crown of Naples (a) ; but if fuch a defign was in contemplation, it is probable that he was incited by his more enterprifing and ambitious brother, who perhaps fought to revive the claims of the papal fee upon a kingdom, to the government of which Giuliano could, in his own right, advance no pretenfions. As a patron of learning, he fupported the ancient dignity of his family. He is introduced to great advantage in the celebrated dialogue of Bembo on the Italian tongue (b), and in the yet more diftinguifhed work

(a) *Ammir. Ift. Fior. lib.* xxix. *vol.* iii. *p.* 315.

(b) Prose di m. pietro bembo, nelle quali si raciona della

of Caſtiglione, entitled *Il libro dell Cortegiano* (*a*). *In* the Laurentian Library ſeveral of his ſonnets are yet preſerved (*b*); and ſome ſpecimens of his compoſition are adduced by Creſcimbeni, which, if they diſplay not any extraordinary ſpirit of poetry, ſufficiently prove, that, to a correct judgment, he united an elegant taſte (*c*)

Naturally of an infirm conſtitution, Giuliano did not long enjoy his honors Finding his health on the decline, he removed to the monaſtery at Fieſole,

VOLGAR LINGUA; dedicated to the cardinal Giulio de' Medici, afterwards Clement VII. firſt printed at Venice by *Giovan Tacuino, nel meſe di Settembre del* MDXXV. *cum privilegio di Papa Clemente, &c.*

(*a*) *In Venetia nelle caſe d'Aldo Romano, e d'Andrea d'Aſola ſuo ſuocero, nell' anno* MDXXVIII. *del meſe d'Aprile, in fol.* This work has frequently been reprinted under the more conciſe title of *Il Cortegiano,* by which it is alſo cited in the *Biblioteca Italiana* of Fontanini; but Apoſtolo Zeno, pleaſed with every opportunity of reproving the author whom he has undertaken to comment upon, shrewdly obſerves, in his notes on that work, " Altro è il dire ſemplicemente, " *il Cortegiano,* come il Fontanini vorrebbe; e altro, *Il libro del Corte-* " *giano,* come il Caſtiglione ha voluto dire, e lo ha detto: la prima- " maniera indicherebbe vi voler deſcrivere *il Cortegiano* per quello " che è; e la ſeconda dinota di volergli inſegnare qual eſſer deve." *Zeno, in not. alla Bib. Ital. di. Fontan. v.* ii. *p.* 353.

(*b*) PLUT. xlvi. *Cod.* xxv. *No.* 3. Another copy of his poems remains in MS. in the Strozzi Library at Florence.

(*c*) *Creſcimb. Comment. v.* iii. *p.* 38. Where the author confounds Giuliano, the ſon of Lorenzo de' Medici, with Giuliano his brother, who loſt his life in the conſpiracy of the Pazzi: and even cites the authority of Politiano, " Che i verſi volgari di lui erano a maraviglia " gravi, e pieni di nobili ſentimenti," as referring to the writings of the younger Giuliano, although ſuch opinion was expreſſed by Politiano reſpecting the works of Giuliano the brother of Lorenzo, before Giuliano his ſon was born.

in the expectation of deriving advantage from his native air; but his hopes were fruftrated, and he died there in the month of March 1516, not having then fully completed his thirty-feventh year. His death was fincerely lamented by a great majority of the citizens of Florence, whofe favor he had conciliated in a high degree by his affability, moderation, and inviolable regard to his promifes (*a*). His tomb, in the facrifty of the church of S. Lorenzo at Florence, one of the moft fuccefsful efforts of the genius of Michelagnolo, may compenfate him for the want

(*a*) Ariofto has addreffed a beautiful canzone to Filiberta of Savoy, the widow of Giuliano, commencing, *Anima eletta, che nel mondo folle*, in which the shade of the departed husband apoftrophizes his furviving wife. The following lines, referring to Lorenzo the Magnificent, may ferve to show the high veneration in which the poet held his memory:

" Quefto fopra ogni lume in te rifplende,
   " Se ben quel tempo che sì ratto corfe,
   " Tenefti di *Nemorfe*
   " Meco fcettro ducal di là da' monti;
   " Se ben tua bella mano freno torfe,
   " Al paefe gentil che Appenin fende,
   " E l'alpe e il mar difende:
   " Nè tanto val, che a quefto pregio monti,
   " Che'l facro onor de l'erudite fronti,
   " Quel Tofco e'n terra e'n cielo amato LAURO,
   " Socer ti fu, le cui mediche fronde
   " Speffo a le piaghe, donde
   " Italia morì poi, furo riftauro:
   " Che fece all' Indo e al Mauro,
   " Sentir l'odor de' fuoi rami foavi;
   " Onde pendean le chiavi
   " Che tenean chiufo il tempio delle guerre.
   " Che poi fu aperto, E NON E PIU CHI'L SERRE."

of that higher degree of reputation which he might have acquired in a longer life. His ſtatue, ſeated, and in a Roman military habit, may be conſidered rather as characteriſtic of his office, as general of the church, than of his exploits. The figures which recline on each ſide of the ſarcophagus, and are intended to repreſent day and night, have been the admiration of ſucceeding artiſts; but their allegorical purport may admit of a latitude of interpretation. Had the conqueſts of Giuliano rivalled thoſe of Alexander the Great, we might have conjectured, with Vaſari, that the artiſt meant to expreſs the extent of his glory, limited only by the confines of the earth (a); but the hyperbole would be too extravagant; and the judicious ſpectator will perhaps rather regard them as emblematical of the conſtant change of ſublunary affairs, and the brevity of human life.

By his wife Filiberta of Savoy, Giuliano de' Medici left no children; but, before his marriage, he had a natural ſon, who became an acknowledged branch of the family of the Medici, and, like the reſt of his kindred, acquired, within the limits of a ſhort life, a conſiderable ſhare of reputation. This was the celebrated Ippolito de' Medici, who, dignified with the rank of cardinal, and poſſeſſed, by the partiality of Clement VII. of an immenſe revenue, was at once the patron, the companion, and the rival of all the poets, the muſicians, and the wits of his time. Without territories, and without ſubjects, Ippolito maintained at Bologna a court far more ſplendid

(a) *Vaſari, vita di M. A. Buonarroti.*

than that of any Italian potentate. His affociates
and attendants, all of whom could boaft of fome
peculiar merit or diftinction which had entitled
them to his notice, generally formed a body of
about three hundred perfons. Shocked at his pro-
fufion, which only the revenues of the church were
competent to fupply, Clement VII. is faid to have
engaged the *maeftro di cafa* of Ippolito to remonftrate
with him on his conduct and to requeft that he
would difmifs fome of his attendants as unneceffary
to him. " No," replied Ippolito, " I do not retain
" them in my court becaufe I have occafion for
" their fervices, but becaufe they have occafion for
" mine (*a*)." His tranflation of the fecond book of
the Æneid into Italian blank verfe is confidered as
one of the happieft efforts of the language, and has
frequently been reprinted (*b*). Amongft the collec-
tions of Italian poetry may alfo be found fome pie-
ces of his own compofition, which do credit to
his talents (*c*).

(*a*) *Tirab. Storia della Let. Ital. v.* vii. *par.* i. *p.* 23.

(*b*) The firft edition is that of Rome, *apud Antonium Bladum,* 1538,
without the name of the author, who, at the foot of his dedication to
a lady, whom he defignates only by the appellation of *Illuftriffima
Signora,* affumes the title of *Il cavaliero Errante.* The fecond edition,
now before me, is entitled, IL SECONDO DI VERGILIO *in lingua volgare
volto da* HIPPOLITO DE' MEDICI *cardinale.* At the clofe we read, *In
citta di Caftello per Antonio Mazochi Cremonefe, & Nicolo de Guc-
cii da Corna, ad inftantia di M. Giovan Gallo, Dottor de leggi da
Caftello nel giorno* 20 *de Luglio* 1539. Several fubfequent editions
have appeared, as well feparately, as united with the other books of
the Æneid, tranflated by different perfons.

(*c*) Some of them are cited by Crefcimbeni, *della volgar poesia,
lib.* ii. *vol.* ii. *p.* 368.

On the voluntary refignation of Giuliano de Medici of the direction of the Florentine ftate, that important truft had been confided by Leo X. to his nephew Lorenzo, who, with the affiftance of the cardinal Giulio de' Medici, directed the helm of government according to the will of the pope; but the honor of holding the chief rank in the republic, although it had gratified the juft ambition of his illuftrious grandfather, was inadequate to the pretenfions of Lorenzo; and the family of Rovere, after a vigorous defence, in which Lorenzo received a wound which had nearly proved mortal, was obliged to relinquifh to him the fovereignty of Urbino, of which he received from the pope the ducal inveftiture in the year 1516 (a). After the death of his uncle Giuliano, he was appointed captain general of the papal troops, but his reputation for military fkill fcarcely ftands higher than that of his predeceffor. In the year 1518, he married Magdeleine de Boulogne, of the royal houfe of France, and the fole fruit of this union was Catherine de' Medici, afterwards the queen of Henry II. (b). The birth of the daughter coft the mother her life, and Lorenzo furvived her only a few days, having, if we may credit Ammirato, fallen a victim to that loathfome diforder, the peculiar fcourge of licentioufnefs, which had then recently commenced its ravages in

(a) *Nerli, Comment. lib.* vi. *p.* 130.

(b) Si, comme les poétes l'ont dit, l'ancienne Hecube, avant de mettre Paris au monde, était troublée par des fonges effrayans; quels noirs fantômes devaient agiter les nuits de Magdeleine de la Tour, enceinte de Catherine de Medicis? *Tenh. Mém. Gén. liv.* xx. *p.* 5.

Europe (a).   His tomb, of the fculpture of Michel-
agnolo, is found amongft the fplendid monuments

(a) *Ammir. Ifl. Fior. lib.* xxix. *v.* ii. *p.* 335.   This diforder, which
was firft known in Italy about the year 1495, was not in its commence-
ment fuppofed to be the refult of fexual intercourfe, but was attribut-
ed to the impure ftate of the air, to the fimple touch or breath of a
difordered perfon, or even to the ufe of an infected knife.   Hence
for a confiderable time no difcredit attached to the patient; and the
authors of that period attribute without hefitation the death of many
eminent perfons, as well ecclefiaftical as fecular, to this complaint.   In
the Laurentian Library (*Plut.* lxxii. *cod.* 38.) is a MS. entitled *Saphati
Phyfici de morbo Gallico liber,* dedicated by the author Giuliano Tanio,
of Prato, to Leo. X. in which he thus adverts to a learned profeffor
who was probably one of the firft victims of this difeafe: " Nos anno
" mccccxcv. extrema æftate, egregium utriufque juris doctorem Domi-
" num Philippum Decium, Papienfem, in Florentino Gymnafio Prati,
" Pifis tunc rebellibus, publice legentem, hac labe affectum ipfi con-
" fpeximus."   From the fame author we learn that the difordor was
fuppofed to have originated in a long continuance of hot and moift
weather, which occurred in the fame year: " Ex magna pluvia fimilis
" labes apparuit, ex quibus argunnt hunc noftræ ætatis morbum exfimili
" caufa ortum effe, ex calida fcilicet, humidaque intemperie, quia ex
" pluvia fcilicet anni mccccLxxxxv. nonis Decembris emiffa, qua
" Roma facta eft navigabilis, ac tota fere Italia inundationes paffa eft."
&c.   Thefe authorities are greatly ftrengthened by that of the illuftrious
Fracaftoro, who was not only the beft Latin poet, but the moft emi-
nent phyfician of his age, and who, in his *Syphilis,* accounts for the
diforder from fimilar caufes.   After adverting to the opinion that it had
been brought into Europe from the weftern world, then lately difco-
vered, he adds,

> " At vero, fi rite fidem obfervata merentur
> " Non ita cenfendum: nec certe credere par eft
> " Effe peregrinam nobis, tranfque æquora vectam
> " Contagem: quoniam in primis oftendere multos
> " Poffumus, attacta qui nullius, hanc tamen ipfam
> " Sponte fua fenfere luem, primique tulere.
> " Præterea, & tantum terrarum tempore parvo,
> " Contages non una fimul potuiffet obire."

of his family in the church of S. Lorenzo at Florence. He appears feated, in the attitude of deep meditation. At his feet recline two emblematical figures, the rivals of thofe which adorn the tomb of Giuliano,

It is remarkable alfo, that throughout the whole poem he has not confidered this difeafe as the peculiar refult of licentious intercourfe, on which account it is perfectly unexceptionable in point of decorum. Even the shepherd *Syphilus*, introduced as an inftance of its effects, is reprefented as having derived it from the refentment, not of Venus, but of Phœbus, excited by the adoration paid by the shepherds to Alcithous. and the neglect of his own altars; or, in other words, to the too fervid ftate of the atmofphere. Had the diforder in its origin been accompanied by the idea of difgrace or criminality, which attends it in modern times, the author of this poem would fcarcely have denominated it,

> " Infanda lues, quam noftra videtis
> " Corpora depafci, quam nulli aut denique pauci
> " Vitamus."

The poem of Fracaftoro was firft published in the year 1530; but an Italian poem on the fame fubject, by Niccolo Campana of Siena, was printed at that place in 1519, and again at Venice in 1537, entitled *Lamento di quel Tribulato di Strafcino Campana Senefe fupra el male incognito el quale tratta de la patientia & impatientia.* The ftyle of this poem is extremely grofs and ludicrous; and the author in the fuppofed excefs of his fufferings, indulges himfelf in the moft extravagant and profane ideas, as to the nature and origin of the complaint. At one time he fuppofes it to be the fame diforder as that which God permitted Satan to inflict upon Job:

> " Allor Sathan con tal mal pien di vitio,
> " Diede a Jobbe amariffimo fupplitio."

Again he afferts it to be the complaint of Simon the leper:

> " Quando Crifto guari Simon lebbrofo,
> " Era di quefto mal peffimo iniquo."

But on no occafion does he afcribe the rife of the diforder to the caufe which, from the nature of his poem, might have been expected. I shall only obferve, that the ufe of the grand mineral fpecific is ex-prefsly pointed out, in both thefe poems, as the only certain remedy.

and which are intended to reprefent morning and evening. Ariofto has alfo celebrated his memory in fome of his moft beautiful verfes (*a*). Like the Egyptians, who embalm a putrid carcafe with the richeft odors, the artift and the poet too often lavifh their divine incenfe on the moft undeferving of mankind.

Prior to his marriage with Magdeleine of Boulogne, the duke of Urbino had an illegitimate fon, named Aleffandro, in whofe perfon was confummated the deftruction of the liberties of Florence. It was commonly fuppofed that Aleffandro was the offspring of the duke by an African flave, at the time when he, with the reft of the family, were reftored to Florence; and this opinion received confirmation from his thick lips, crifped hair, and dark complexion. But it is yet more probable that he was the fon of Clement VII. Such at leaft was the information given to the hiftorian Ammirato by the grand duke Cofmo I. at the time when he read to him the memoirs which he had prepared refpecting his family ; and the predilection of the pontiff for this equivocal defcendant of the houfe of Medici adds probability to the report (*b*). But whatever was his origin, the circumftances of the times, and the ambition of thofe who protected his infancy, equally

(*a*) Such at leaft I conjecture to be the purport of his poem, which commences,

    " Nella ftagion che'l bel tempo rimena,

    " Di mia man pofi un ramufcel di Lauro."

               Rime dell' Ariofto, p. 25. ap. Giolito. 1557.

(*b*) *Ammir. Ift. Fior. lib.* xxx. *v.* iii. *p.* 335.

difpenfed with the difadvantages of his birth, and his want of inherent merit. On failure of the legitimate branch of Cofmo de' Medici, ufually ftyled the father of his country, derived through Lorenzo the Magnificent, Aleffandro and Ippolito became neceffary implements in the hands of Clement VII. to prevent the credit and authority of the family from paffing to the collateral branch derived from Lorenzo the brother of Cofmo, which had gradually rifen to great diftinction in the ftate, and of which it will now be neceffary to give a brief account.

. Pierfrancefco de' Medici, the fon of the elder Lorenzo, to whom we have before had occafion to advert (a), died in the year 1459, having bequeathed his immenfe poffeffions, obtained from his fhare in the profits acquired by the extenfive traffic of the family, to his two fons, Lorenzo and Giovanni. Following the example of their father, and emulous rather of wealth than of honors, the fons of Pierfrancefco had for feveral years confined themfelves to the limits of a private condition, although they had occafionally filled the chief offices of the republic, in common with other refpectable citizens. On the expulfion of Piero, the fon of Lorenzo the Magnificent, from Florence, in the year 1494, they endeavoured to avail themfelves of his mifconduct, and of the importance which they had gradually acquired, to afpire to the chief direction of the republic, and divefting themfelves of the invidious name of Medici, affumed that of *Popolani*. The reftoration of the defcendants of Lorenzo the

(a) v. ante, vol. I. p. 136.

Magnificent to Florence, the elevation of his fecond
fon to the pontificate, and the feries of profperity
enjoyed by the family under his aufpices, and under
thofe of Clement VII. had repreffed their ambition
or fruftrated their hopes ; and Lorenzo and Giovanni,
the fons of Pierfrancefco, paffed through life in a
fubordinate rank, the former of them leaving at his
death a fon, named Pierfrancefco, and the latter a
fon Giovanni, to inherit their immenfe wealth, and
perpetuate the hereditary rivalfhip of the two fami-
lies (a). But whilft the defcendants of Cofmo, the
father of his country, exifted only in females, or
in a fpurious offspring, thofe of his brother Lorenzo
continued in a legitimate fucceffion of males, and
were invigorated with talents the moft formidable
to their rivals, and the moft flattering to their own
hopes. Adopting from his youth a military life,
Giovanni de' Medici became one of the moft cele-
brated commanders that Italy had ever produced.
By the appellation of captain of the *bande nere*, his
name carried terror amongft his enemies. His cour-
age was of the moft ferocious kind. Equally infenfi-
ble to pity and to danger, his opponents denominated
him *Il gran Diavolo* (a). As the fervor of youth
fubfided, the talents of the commander began to

(a) Furono i due fratelli richiffimi — di meglio che centocinquanta
mila feudi, e poffedevano di beni ftabili, fra gli altri la cafa grande
di Firenze, il palazzo di Fiefole, di Trebbio, di Caffagiolo, e di
Caftello. *Ald. Manucc. vita di Cofmo, v. i. p.* 72.

(b) *Varchi, Storia Fior. lib.* ii. *p.* 25. *Ed. Leyden.* The mother
of Giovanni was Caterina Sforza, the widow of Girolamo Riario, who,
after the death of her husband, had married the elder Giovanni de'
Medici. *v. ante, p.* 168.

be developed ; but in the midſt of his honors his career was terminated by a cannon ball, in the twenty-eighth year of his age. By his wife Maria Salviati, the offspring of Lucrezia, one of the daughders of Lorenzo the Magnificent, he left a ſon, Coſino de' Medici, who, after the death of Aleſſandro, obtained the permanent ſovereignty of Tuſcany, and was the firſt who aſſumed the title of Grand Duke.

The younger Pierfranceſco left alſo a ſon, named Lorenzo, who, as well on account of his diminutive perſon, as to diſtinguiſh him from others of his kindred of the ſame name, was uſually denominated *Lorenzino*, and who was deſtined with his own hand to terminate the conteſt between the two families. Though ſmall of ſtature, Lorenzino was active and well proportioned. His complexion was dark, his countenance ſerious: when he ſmiled it ſeemed to be by conſtraint. His mother, who was of the powerful family of Soderini, had carefully attended to his education; and as his capacity was uncommonly quick, he made an early proficiency in polite letters. His elegant comedy entitled *Aridoſio*, ſtill ranks with thoſe works which are ſelected as models of the Italian language (*a*). Enterpriſing, reſtleſs,

(*a*) Creſcimbeni informs us, that this comedy was written by Lorenzino in *verſi volgari*, and printed at Bologna in 1548; and that it is alſo found in proſe, printed at Lucca in the ſame year, and reprinted at Florence in 1595. *Della volgar Poeſia, vol.* v. *p.* 141. Creſcimbeni is however miſtaken; the edition of Bologna 1545 is now before me, and is wholly written in proſe. That of Florence, 1595, is enumerated by the academicians *Della Cruſca,* as one of the *Teſti di Lingua.*

fond of commotions, and full of the examples of antiquity, he had addicted himfelf when young to the fociety of Filippo Strozzi, who to an ardent love of liberty united an avowed contempt for all the political and religious inflitutions of his time. The talents and accomplifhments of Lorenzino recommended him to Clement VII. under whofe countenance he refided for fome time at the Roman court; but an extravagant adventure deprived him of the favor of the pope, and compelled him to quit the city. It appeared one morning, that, during the preceding night, the flatues in the arch of Conflantine, and in other parts of the city, had been broken and defaced, a circumftance which fo exafperated the pope, that he iffued pofitive orders that whoever had committed the outrage, except it fhould appear to be the cardinal Ippolito de' Medici, fhould be immediately hanged (a). This exception indeed ftrongly implies that the cardinal was not free from fufpicion; but whoever was the delinquent, Lorenzino bore the whole odium of the affair, and it required all the influence that Ippolito poffeffed with the pope to refcue his kinfman from the denunciations iffued againft the offender. Lorenzino gladly took the earlieft opportunity of quitting the city, and retreated to his native place, where, transferring his refentment from the dead to the living,

---

(a) It has been fuggefted to me by very refpectable authority that the heads of thefe flatues and bas-rilievos were more probably ftolen by Lorenzino for the fake of their beauty. They are even faid to be yet extant in the mufeum at Florence.

he foon afterwards acted a principal part in a much more important tranfaction (*a*).

To the energy and activity of Lorenzino, and the courage of Giovanni de' Medici, Clement VII. could only oppofe the diffipation and inexperience of Ippolito and Aleffandro; but the turbulent difpofi-tion of the Florentines feconded his views, and the premature death of Giovanni, whilft it expofed his dominions to the ravages of the German troops, relieved him from his apprehenfions of his moft dangerous rival (*b*).   Having prevailed on the empe-ror and the king of France to concur in his defign, he feized the opportunity afforded him by the civil diffenfions of the Florentines, and, in the year 153 2, compelled them to place at the head of the govern-ment Aleffandro de' Medici, with the title of *Doge* of the Florentine republic (*c*).   The authority of

(*a*) *Varchi, Storia Fior. lib.* xv. *p.* 618.

(*b*) The authority of the fenator Nerli leaves no room for doubt on this head.   " Non poteva quella morte feguire in tempo, ch' ella deffe " più univerfale difpiacere, nè anco in tempo, che il papa più la " ftimaffe, perchè s'ella feguiva in altri tempi, che fua Santità non " aveffe avuto fi urgente pericolo fopra il capo, non gli arrecava per " avventura difpiacere alcuno, rimanendo ficuro, e libero della gelosìa " grande, ch' egli aveva del nome folamente del Sig. Giovanni, rifpetto " agl' intereffi, e alla proprietà d'Aleffandro, e d'Ippolito, i quali de- " fiderava che fuffero quelli, che poffedeffero lo ftato, le facultà, e la " grandezza di cafa Medici."

Nerli, Comment. lib. vii. *p.* 145.

(*c*) Aleffandro is generally ftyled by the Italian authors the *firft duke of Florence*, but in this they are not ftrictly accurate.   His title of *duke* was derived from Città, or Civita di Penna, and had been affumed by him feveral years before he obtained the direction of the Florentine ftate.   It muft alfo be obferved, that Aleffandro did not,

Aleffandro

Aleffandro was foon afterwards ftrengthened by his marriage with Margaretta of Auftria, a natural daughter of the emperor Charles V. The cardinal Ippolito, jealous of his fuccefs, had attempted to pre-occupy the government; difappointed in his hopes, and difgufted with his ecclefiaftical trappings, which ill fuited the rapidity of his motions, and the vivacity of his character, he united his efforts with thofe of Filippo Strozzi, who had married Clarice, the fifter of Lorenzo duke of Urbino, to deprive Aleffandro of his new dignity; but before the arrangement could be made for the meditated attack, Ippolito fuddenly died of poifon, adminifter-ed to him by one of his domeftics (*b*), leaving his competitor in the undifturbed poffeffion of his newly acquired power.

The period however now approached which was to transfer the dominion of Florence from the

---

as Robertfon conceives, " enjoy the fame abfolute dominion as his " family have retained to the prefent times," *Hift. Cha.* V. *book* v. he being only declared chief or prince of the republic, and his authority being in f me meafure counteracted or reftrained by two councils cho-fen from the citizens, for life, one of which confifted of forty-eight, and the other of two hundred members. *Varchi, Storia Fior. p.* 497. *Nerli, Com. lib.* xi, *p.* 257. 264. Thefe diftinctions are deferving of notice, as they ferve to show the gradual progrefs by which a free country is depiived of its liberties.

(*a*) The perfon who adminiftered the poifon was faid to be Giovan-Andrea di Borgo San Sepolcro, the fteward or bailiff of Ippolito, who was fuppofed to have effected this treachery at the inftance of Aleffan-dio; and this fufpicion received confirmation by his having efcaped punifhment, although he confeffed the crime; and by his having afterwards been received at the court of Aleffandro at Florence.

Varchi, Storia Fior. p. 566.

V

defcendants of Lorenzo the Magnificent, to the kindred ftock. In the fecure poffeffion of power, Aleffandro knew no reftraint. Devoted to the indulgence of an amorous paffion, he fought its gratification among women of all defcriptions, married and unmarried, religious and fecular; infomuch that neither rank nor virtue could fecure the favorite object from his licentious rapacity (a). The fpirit

(a) Notwithftanding the diffolute character of Aleffandro, it appears that he was poffeffed of ftrong natural fagacity, and, on fome occafions, adminiftered juftice not only with impartiality, but with ability. On this head, Ammirato relates an anecdote which is worth repeating: A rich old citizen of Bergamo had lent to one of his countrymen at Florence 400 crowns, which he advanced without any perfon being prefent, and without requiring a written acknowledgment. When the ftipulated time had elapfed, the creditor required his money—but the borrower, well apprized that no proof could be brought againft him, pofitively denied that he had ever received it. After many fruitlefs attempts to recover it, the lender was advifed to refort to the duke, who would find fome method of doing him juftice. Aleffandro accordingly ordered both the parties before him, and after hearing the affertions of the one and the pofitive denial of the other, he turned to the creditor, faying, " Is it poffible then, friend, that you can have lent your money " when no one was prefent?"—" There was no one indeed," replied the creditor, " I counted out the money to him on a poft."—" Go, " bring the poft then this inftant," faid the duke, " and I will make it " confefs the truth." The creditor, though aftonished on receiving fuch an order, haftened to obey, having firft received a fecret caution from the duke not to be very fpeedy in his return. In the mean time the duke employed himfelf in tranfacting the affairs of his other fuitors, till at length turning again towards the borrower, "This man," fayshe, "ftays " a long time with his poft."—" It is fo heavy, fir," replied the other, " that he could not yet have brought it." Again Aleffandro left him, and returning fome time afterwards, carelefsly exclaimed, " What kind " of men are they that lend their money without evidence—was there " no one prefent but the poft?"—" No indeed, fir," replied the knave.

of the Florentines, though finking under the yoke
of defpotifm, began to revolt at this more oppro-
brious fpecies of tyranny, and the abfentees and
malecontents became daily more numerous and
more refpectable. But whilft the ftorm was gather-
ing in a remote quarter, a blow from a kindred
hand unexpectedly freed the Florentines from
their oppreffor, and afforded them once more
an opportunity of afferting that liberty to which
their anceftors had been fo long devoted. Lorenzino
de' Medici was the fecond Brutus who burft the
bonds of confanguinity in the expectation of being
the deliverer of his country. But the principle of
political virtue was now extinct, and it was no
longer a fubject of doubt whether the Florentines
fhould be enflaved; it only remained to be deter-
mined who fhould be the tyrant. On his return
from Rome to Florence, Lorenzino had frequented
the court of Aleffandro, and, by his unwearied
affiduity and fingular accomplifhments, had ingra-
tiated himfelf with the duke to fuch a degree, as to
become his chief confidant, and the affociate of his
licentious amours. But whilft Lorenzino accompa-
nied him amidft thefe fcenes of diffipation, he had
formed the firm refolution of accomplifhing his
deftruction, and fought only for a favorable oppor-
tunity of effecting his purpofe. This idea feems to
have occupied his whole foul, and influenced all
his conduct. Even in the warmth of familiarity

" The poft is a good witnefs then," faid the duke, " and fhall make
" thee pay the man his money."

Ammir. Stor. Fior. lib. xxxi. v. iii. p. 434.

V 2

which apparently fubfifted between them, he could
not refrain from adverting to the defign of which
his mind was full, and by jefts and infinuations
gave earneft of his intention. Cellini relates, that
on his attending the duke Aleffandro with his portrait
executed as a medal, he found him indifpofed and
reclined on his bed, with Lorenzino as his compa-
nion. After boafting, as was his cuftom, of the
wonders which he could perform in his profeffion,
the artift concluded with expreffing his hopes, that
Lorenzino would favor him with a fubject for an
appofite reverfe. ‘ That is exactly what I am think-
" ing of," replied Lorenzino, with great vivacity;
" I hope ere long to furnifh fuch a reverfe as will
" be worthy of the duke, and will aftonifh the
" world (a)." The blind confidence of Aleffandro
prevented his fufpicions, and he turned on his bed
with a contemptuous fmile at the folly or the arro-
gance of his relation. But whilft Lorenzino thus
hazarded the deftruction of his enterprife by the
levity of his difcourfe, he prepared for its execution
with the moft fcrupulous caution (b). The duke
having felected as the object of his paffion the wife
of Lionardo Ginori, then on a public embaffy at
Naples, Lorenzino, to whom fhe was nearly related,
undertook with his ufual affiduity to promote the
fuit Pretending that his reprefentations had been
fuccefsful, he prevailed upon the duke to pafs the

(a) *Vita di Benvenuto Cellini*, p. 222.

(b) The particulars of this tranfaction are related at great length by
Varchi, who had his information from Lorenzino himfelf, after the
perpetration of the deed. *Storia Fior. lib.* xv.

night with him at his own houfe, where he promifed him the completion of his wifhes. In the mean time he prepared a chamber for his reception; and having engaged as his affiftant a man of defperate fortunes and charaᶜter, called Scoroncocolo, waited with impatience for his arrival. At the appointed hour, the duke having left the palace in a mafk, according to his cuftom when he was engaged in noᶜturnal adventures, came unobferved to the houfe of Lorenzino, and was received by him in the fatal chamber. After fome familiar converfation, Lorenzino left him to repofe on the bed, with promifes of a fpeedy return. On his quitting the chamber, he ftationed his coadjutor where he might be in readinefs to affift him, in cafe he fhould fail in his firft attempt, and gently opening the door, approached the bed, and inquired from the duke if he was afleep, at the fame inftant paffing his fword through his body. On receiving the wound the duke fprang up and attempted to efcape at the door; but, on a fignal given by Lorenzino, he was attacked there by Scoroncocolo, who wounded him deeply in the face. Lorenzino then grappled with the duke, and throwing him on the bed, endeavoured to prevent his cries. In the ftruggle the duke feized the finger of Lorenzino in his mouth, and retained it with fuch violence, that Scoroncocolo, finding it impoffible to feparate them fo as to difpatch the duke without danger of wounding Lorenzino, deliberately took a knife from his pocket, and cut him acrofs the throat. The completion of their purpofe was however only the commencement of their difficulties. Scoroncocolo, who probably knew not that the perfon he had affaffinated was the duke, until the tranfaction was over, was fo terrified as to be wholly unable to judge for himfelf of the meafures to be adopted for his own fafety. To the active mind of Lorenzino various expedients prefented themfelves, and he hefitated for fome time whether he fhould openly avow the deed, and call upon his countrymen to affert their liberties, or fhould endeavour to make his efcape to the abfentees, to whom the information which he had to communicate would give new energy, and a fair opportunity of fuccefs. Of thefe meafures the laft feemed on many accounts to be the moft advifable. Having therefore locked the door of the chamber, in which he left the dead body of the duke, he proceeded fecretly to Bologna, expecting there to meet with Filippo Strozzi, but finding that he had quitted that place, he followed him to Venice, where he related to him his achievements. Filippo, well acquainted with the eccentricity of his character, refufed for fome time to credit his ftory, till Lorenzino, producing the key of the chamber, and exhibiting his hand which had been mutilated in the conteft, at length convinced him of its truth. The applaufe beftowed by Filippo and his adherents on Lorenzino, was in proportion to the incredulity which they had before expreffed. He was faluted as another Brutus, as the deliverer of his country; and Filippo immediately began to affemble his adherents, in order to avail himfelf of fo favorable an opportunity of reftoring to the citizens of Florence their ancient rights (*a*).

The Italian hiftorians have endeavoured to develope the motives that led Lorenzino to the perpetration of this deed, and have fought for them in the natural malignity of his difpofition; as a proof of which he is faid to have acknowledged, that during his refidence at Rome, notwithftanding the kindnefs fhown to him by Clement VII. he often felt a ftrong inclination to murder him. They have alfo attributed them to a defire of immortalizing his name by being confidered as the deliverer of his country; to a principle of revenge for the infult which he received from the pope, in being banifhed from Rome, which he meant to repay in the perfon of Aleffandro, his reputed fon; and, laftly, to his enmity to the collateral branch of the Medici family, by which he was excluded from the chief dignity of the ftate. How far any of thefe conjectures may be well founded, it is not eafy to determine. Human conduct is often the refult of impulfes, which, whilft they arife in various directions, determine the mind towards the fame object, and poffibly all, or moft of the caufes before ftated, might have concurred in producing fo fignal an effect. Aware of the mifconftruction to which his principles were liable, Lorenzino wrote an apologetical difcourfe, which

(*a*) On this occafion a medal was ftruck, bearing on one fide the head of Lorenzino, and on the other the cap of liberty between two daggers; being the fame device as that which had before be n adopted by, or applied to, the younger Brutus. *v. Palin. Famil. Rom. p.* 142. This medal is in the collection of the earl of Oxford.

has been preferved to the prefent times, and throws confiderable light on this fingular tranfaction. In this piece he firfl attempts to demonftrate that Alef-fandro was an execrable tyrant, who, during the fix years that he held the chief authority, had exceeded the enormities of Nero, of Caligula, and of Phalaris. He accufes him of having occafioned by poifon the death, not only of the cardinal Ippolito, but of his own mother, who refided in an humble flation at *Collevecchio*, and whofe poverty he conceived was a reproach to the dignity of his rank; and denies that the blood of any branch of the Medici family flowed in his veins. He then juflifies, with great plaufibility, the conduct adopted by him after the death of the duke, in quitting the city to join the abfentees; and after vindicating himfelf from the imputation of having been induced by any other motive than an earneft defire to liberate his country from a flate of intolerable fervitude, he concludes with lamenting, that the want of energy and virtue in his fellow-citizens prevented them from availing themfelves of the opportunity which he had afforded them of re-eftablifhing their ancient government (a). But whatever were the motives of this deed, the confequences of it were fuch as have generally been the refult of fimilar attempts —the riveting of thofe chains which it was intended to break. The natural abhorrence of treachery, and the fentiment of pity excited for the devoted object, counteract the intended purpofe, and throw an odium even on the caufe of liberty itfelf. No end

(a) For the *Apologia* of Lorenzino, *v. App. No.* LXXXIV.

can juftify the facrifice of a principle, nor was a crime ever neceffary in the courfe of human affairs. The fudden burft of vindictive paffion may fometimes operate important changes on the fate of nations, but the event is feldom within the limits of human calculation. It is only the calm energy of reafon, conftantly bearing up againft the encroachments of power, that can with certainty perpetuate the freedom, or promote the happinefs of the human race.

After the perpetration of this deed, Lorenzino, not conceiving himfelf in fafety within the limits of Italy, continued his route till he arrived at Conftantinople, from whence, after a fhort refidence, he returned again to Venice. Having paffed eleven years of exile and anxiety, he was himfelf affaffinated by two Florentine foldiers, who, under the pretext of avenging the death of Aleffandro, probably fought to ingratiate themfelves with his fucceffor, by removing a perfon who derived from his birth undoubted pretenfions to the credit and authority which had for ages been attached to the chief of the houfe of Medici.

The adherents of the ruling family, at the head of whom was the cardinal Cibò, who had been the chief minifter of Aleffandro, conducted themfelves with great prudence on the death of the duke; and before they permitted the event to be made public, not only fecured the foldiery within the city, but fummoned to their affiftance all their allies in the vicinity of the Florentine ftate. They then affembled the inhabitants, avowedly to deliberate on the ftate of the republic, but in fact rather to receive than to dictate a form of government. If Lorenzino was the Brutus of his age, an Octavius was found in his cousin, Cosmo de' Medici, the son of Giovanni, general of the *bande nere*, and then about eighteen years of age. Being informed of the unexpected disposition of the citizens in his favor, Cosmo hastened from his seat at Mugello to Florence, where, on the ninth day of January 1536, he was invested with the sovereignty by the more modest title of chief of the republic. Despotism generally proceeds with cautious steps, and Augustus and Cosmo affected the name of citizen, whilst they governed with absolute authority.

To the election of Cosmo little opposition had been made within the city. The proposition of Pallas Rucellai, to admit the party of the Strozzi to their deliberations, and that of Giovanni Canigiani, to place the supreme command in an illegitimate and infant son of Alessandro, had met with few supporters (*a*). But the numerous exiles, who by compulsion, or in disgust, had quitted their native country during the government of Alessandro, had already begun to convene together from all parts of Italy, in hopes of effecting their restoration and of establishing a form of government more consistent with their views. The cardinals Ridolfi and

(*a*) Besides an illegitimate son named Giulio, Alessandro left two illegitimate daughters, Porcia and Juliet. The son entered into the church, and became grand prior of the order of S. Stefano. Porcia took the veil, and founded the convent of S. Clement at Florence. Juliet married Francesco Cantelmo, son of the duke di Popoli, a Neapolitan nobleman. *Tenh. Mém. Gén. liv.* xxii. *p.* 92.

Salviati, both grandfons of Lorenzo the Magnificent, Bartolomeo Valori, and other citizens of high rank, uniting with Filippo Strozzi, raifed a confiderable body of troops, and approached towards the city; but more powerful parties had already interpofed, and the fate of Florence no longer depended on the virtue or the courage of its inhabitants, but on the will of the emperor, or on the precarious aid of the French. Senfible of the advantages which he had already obtained by holding at his devotion the Florentine ftate, and that fuch influence was in-confiftent with a republican government, Charles V. openly approved of the election of Cofmo, and directed his troops, then in Italy, to fupport his caufe. The exiles having poffeffed themfelves of the fortrefs of *Montemurlo*, in the vicinity of Florence, were unexpectedly attacked there by the Florentine troops under the command of Aleffandro Vitelli, in the night of the firft of Auguft 1538, and their defeat fixed the deftiny of their country. Bartolomeo Valori, with his two fons, and Filippo his nephew, were made prifoners, and conducted to Florence, where he, with one of his fons, and his nephew, was decapitated. Many other of the infurgents experienced a fimilar fate. The reft were configned to the dungeons in different parts of Tufcany. Filippo Strozzi, the magnanimous affertor of the liberties of his county, languifhed upwards of twelve months in the prifons of Caftello, and his fituation became more hopelefs in proportion as the authority of Cofmo became more eftablifh-ed. After an interval of time which ought to have obliterated the remembrance of his offence, he was cruelly fubjected to torture, under the pretext of difcovering the accomplices of his unfortunate enter- prife. Finding that the remonftrances of his friends with the emperor and the duke were not only ineffectual, but that the latter had refolved to expofe his fortitude to a fecond trial, he called to his mind the example of Cato of Utica, and fell by his own hand, a devoted victim to the caufe of freedom (a).

Thus terminated the Florentine republic, which had fubfifted amidft the agitations of civil commo- tions, and the fhock of external attacks, for upwards of three centuries, and had produced from its cir- cumfcribed territory a greater number of eminent men than any other country in Europe. This fingular pre-eminence is chiefly to be attributed to the nature of its government, which called forth the talents of every rank of citizens, and admitted them without diftinction to the chief offices of the ftate. But the fplendor which the Florentines derived from examples of public virtue, and efforts of fuperlative genius, was frequently tarnifhed by the fanguinary contefts of rival parties. The benevolent genius of Lorenzo de' Medici for a time removed this reproach, and combined a ftate of high intellectual improve- ment with the tranquillity of well-ordered govern- ment. The various purfuits in which he himfelf engaged appear indeed to have been fubfervient only

(a) The life of Filippo Strozzi was written by his brother Lorenzo, with great candor and impartiality, and is published at the clofe of the Florentine hiftory of Benedetto Varchi. *Ed. Leyd. fine an.* After the death of Filippo, a paper in his own hand-writing was found in his bofom, which is given in the Appendix, *No.* LXXXV.

to the great purpofe of humanizing and improving his countrymen. His premature death left the common wealth without a pilot, and after a long feries of agitation, the haplefs wreck became a rich unexpected prize to Cofmo de' Medici. With Cofmo, who afterwards affumed the title of grand duke, commences a dynafty of fovereigns, which continued in an uninterrupted fucceffion until the early part of the prefent century, when the fceptre of Tufcany paffed from the imbecile hands of Gafton de' Medici, into the ftronger grafp of the family of Auftria. During the government of Cofmo, the talents of the Florentines, habituated to great exertions, but fuddenly debarred from further interference with the direction of the ftate, fought out new channels, and difplayed themfelves in works of genius and of art, which threw a luftre on the fovereign, and gave additional credit to the new eftablifhment; but as thofe who were born under the republic retired in the courfe of nature, the energies of the Florentines gradually declined. Under the equalizing hand of defpotifm, whilft the diffufion of literature was promoted, the exertions of original genius were fuppreffed. The numerous and illuftrious families, whofe names had for ages been the glory of the republic, the Soderini, the Strozzi, the Ridolfi, the Ruccellai, the Valori, and the Capponi, who had negotiated with monarchs, and operated by their perfonal characters on the politics of Europe, funk at once to the uniform level of fubjects, and became the fubordinate and domeftic officers of the ruling family. From this time the hiftory of

Florence is the hiftory of the alliances, the nego-
tiations, the virtues, or the vices, of its reigning
prince; and even towards thefe the annals of the
times furnifh but fcanty documents. The Florentine
hiftorians, as if unwilling to perpetuate the records
of their fubjugation, have almoft invariably clofed
their labors with the fall of the republic, and the
defire of information fortunately terminates where
the want of it begins.

I N D E X.

N. B. *The Roman Numerals refer to the Volume, and the Figures
to the Page.*

INDEX.

Dante,

D.

E.

F.

G.

INDEX.

O.

END OF THE SECOND VOLUME.

www.ingramcontent.com/pod-product-compliance
Lightning Source LLC
Chambersburg PA
CBHW031151120726
47905CB00006B/1897